Over by Christmas
Strike a Match 4

Frank Tayell

Strike a Match 4: Over By Christmas
Published by Frank Tayell
Copyright 2021
All rights reserved
ISBN: 9798466345483

Co-operation always achieves more than conflict.

All people, places, and (most) events are fictional.

The author has asserted their moral right under the Copyright, Designs and Patents Act, 1988, to be identified as the author of this work. All rights reserved. No part of this publication may be reproduced, copied, stored in a retrieval system, or transmitted, in any form or by any means, without the prior written consent of the copyright holder, nor be otherwise circulated in any form of binding or cover other than that in which it is published and without a similar condition being imposed on the subsequent purchaser.

The copyright of The Remains of the Day *is held by Kazuo Ishiguro, who, in an alternate timeline where the Blackout occurred, also holds the copyright of his play* Remaining Days. *Tickets for performances in February 2040 are now on sale at the Twynham box office.*

Post-Apocalyptic Detective Novels
Work. Rest. Repeat.
Strike a Match 1. Serious Crimes 2. Counterfeit Conspiracy
3. Endangered Nation 4. Over By Christmas

Surviving The Evacuation / Here We Stand / Life Goes On
Book 1: London, Book 2: Wasteland
Zombies vs The Living Dead
Book 3: Family, Book 4: Unsafe Haven
Book 5: Reunion, Book 6: Harvest
Book 7: Home
Here We Stand 1: Infected & 2: Divided
Book 8: Anglesey, Book 9: Ireland
Book 10: The Last Candidate, Book 11: Search and Rescue
Book 12: Britain's End, Book 13: Future's Beginning
Book 14: Mort Vivant, Book 15: Where There's Hope
Book 16: Unwanted Visitors, Unwelcome Guests
Life Goes On 1: Outback Outbreak, 2: No More News
Life Goes On3: While the Lights Are On, 4: If Not Us
Book 17: There We Stood, Book 18: Rebuilt in a Day

For more information, visit:
http://www.FrankTayell.com
www.facebook.com/FrankTayell
http://twitter.com/FrankTayell

22nd December 2039

The Story So Far
The Dover Police Station, Park Street, Dover

Police Constable Ruth Deering watched the clock as it chimed seven. Her twelve-hour shift was mere seconds from being over. Dover had two police officers: herself and Sergeant Elspeth Kettering. Where Sergeant Kettering had been a police officer in Dover for over twenty years, Ruth had only been in Dover for two months. Before then, Ruth had spent two months with Mister Henry Mitchell's Serious Crimes Unit in Britain's new capital city on the Dorset coast, Twynham. Before that, she'd been in the police academy, though she'd grown up in a refugee camp. Since she didn't know precisely how old she was, technically, she hadn't lied about her age to join the police, but she *had* exaggerated. Since every able body was now being conscripted into the army, she'd definitely made the right career choice.

Twenty years after the Blackout, Britain's population hovered at around two million, recently boosted by the influx of refugees fleeing European atrocities. Fifteen thousand lived within Dover's walls, making it one of the more populous cities in one of the more populous countries in the world.

Billions had died because of the Blackout. Some were killed immediately when the competing digital viruses caused planes to fall from the sky, cars to crash, power stations to burn, and almost every motor to explode. Many more had died when the nuclear bombs were launched. No one knew if that had been caused by the virus, but the bombs' electromagnetic pulses had brought an end to that first horror, though the real nightmare was only beginning. Famine. Plague. Floods. Droughts. Ice-age winters followed by furnace summers. Billions had died, and theirs hadn't been a swift death.

But recently, as springs and autumns lengthened, hope returned. An expedition had arrived from the Pacific. Ships sailed across the Atlantic so frequently they almost had a schedule. The children of European refugees had returned to the continent as settlers and adventurers, mining the ruined cities for lost treasures. Locally, the newspaper had a new rival in a national radio station, inaugurated with a broadcast relayed through booster-stations to the disunited U.S.A. Admittedly, a sniper had used the ceremony to attempt the assassination of the British prime minister and the U.S. ambassador, but Ruth and the rest of the Serious Crimes Unit had stopped the assassin.

Rationing had been coming to an end. Biodiesel was going to replace coal. Cinemas were re-opening, even if they were only showing very, very old films. The city gates were no longer shut at night for fear of seaborne pirates. Until the war.

Three organised groups of barbarous killers had swept across Europe, from the north, south, and east. Refugees had fled before them, all aiming for Calais, the Channel Tunnel, and the only certain escape from the horror. But the barbarians were aiming for Calais, too. The first major assault had been halted. Ruth had found herself caught in the middle of the bloody street-battle waged in Calais. They'd held the city, but the barbarians now sniped and ambushed the patrols who ventured any distance from the coast.

But Calais wasn't her concern, even if she could often hear the artillery fire, carried by the wind across the twenty-mile strait. She was a copper, and Dover was, for the moment, relatively crime-free.

The clock chimed seven. She slid the bolt on the door, locking the police station for the night. There were only two cops in Dover, a city of fifteen thousand civilians, more refugees, army conscripts, and allowed-ashore sailors. Only two coppers, but newly conscripted squads of soldiers patrolled the city, night and day, as part of their inadequate training for the front line. Yes, she really had made the right choice to become a cop.

She walked over to the smouldering fire in the half of the lobby reserved for witnesses and victims, and raked the embers. They had electricity in the police station thanks to the coal-burning power station in the old supermarket on Bridge Street. But the Royal Navy warships burned coal, too. So did the trains linking the populous southern coast with the farms and mines in Wales and Scotland. Factor in Dover's bulging population, and there wasn't enough electricity to spare for a luxury like an electric heater.

Behind the duty desk, a small staircase led upstairs to the apartments where Ruth currently lived. They'd been offices in the olden days, used by detectives and administrators. Over the last twenty years, they'd been home to dozens of different constables who'd come and gone, while Sergeant Elspeth Kettering had remained. She'd grown up in Dover, and joined the police before the Blackout. An institution in Dover, Kettering had refused all promotions to the sprawling new coastal capital on the Dorset coast. Kettering had stayed, and raised a family in the rabbit-warren terrace further along Park Street.

With the advent of this new war, Ruth's adoptive mother, Maggie, had come to Dover. Maggie Deering had returned to her original calling, and was once again a surgeon, working in the military hospital in the castle. Sergeant Kettering's eldest daughter, Eloise, had moved into the apartments above the police station, while Maggie had moved into Eloise's old room in the terrace. The arrangement suited everyone. Ruth finally had a friend her own age to talk with.

Upstairs, Ruth found Eloise in the kitchen-living room, adding a small shovel of coal into their stove.

"Where'd the coal come from?" Ruth asked.

"I won't say while you're wearing your uniform," Eloise said.

"Then I'll go change," Ruth said, guessing the answer was the power station. Eloise's father had worked there, until he'd died. Eloise had intended to follow in his footsteps, until the war. Stealing coal was a serious crime, but neither of them had time to gather firewood from the forested wild-lands of Kent, and they'd already been through three blizzard-and-thaw cycles this winter.

"Should I ask where the Christmas tree came from?" Ruth asked.

"Elgar and Edwin brought it up this afternoon," Eloise said. "They said they saw you."

"They did? I must have been busy," Ruth said.

"They must have been scared," Eloise said. "I bet they sneaked in while you were on patrol."

"They're scared of me?" Ruth asked.

"Scared and in awe," Eloise said. "You know how boys can be."

Ruth did. She'd grown up in the Milford Immigration Centre on the ruined outskirts of Bournemouth, where her adoptive mother, Maggie, had been a teacher and occasional physician. Growing up, there had been plenty of children her own age, but they'd come and gone too quickly for any real friendships to have formed. At the police academy, she'd had one friend, Simon Longfield, but he had betrayed her.

"It *is* nice to have a tree," Ruth said. The decorations were a mix of painted paper and scrap metal cut into shape. The tree itself was also made of steel. Two seven-branch, flat silhouettes cut from an old car's bodywork, and which had arrived pre-decorated with a veneer of orange rust. This year's was far from the first freezing winter. If anyone brought a wooden tree into a house during the darkest days of the year, it was never to adorn with baubles.

"What's for dinner?" Ruth asked.

"Baked potatoes, and then baked apples," Eloise said, pointing at the two trays keeping warm atop the stove. "Both of which I got off the ration. And we've enough of the seaweed pickle for both of us."

"Flash. How was work?"

"Busy. Always busy," Eloise said. "But I spent most of it scrubbing the corridors. I swear, if I were in charge, I'd insist the sailors take off their boots before coming into the castle. Not the soldiers," she added. "They mostly arrive on stretchers. But those admirals who run the navy from the upper rooms, they really need to learn how to wipe their boots."

"You should tell them," Ruth said.

"No way, because you know what I heard?" Eloise walked over to the cupboard, and took out two plates. "They want four nurses to join a delegation to Australia."

"Australia? Ah, and you don't want to be sent?"

"No, I *do*," Eloise said. "It won't be until the war's over. Since the navy has the ships, they're organising it from here, so they'll pick the nurses from here, too. Which means, if I ever want to ride on a kangaroo, I've got to smile at the admirals, even if they are messier than my brothers. Did you see today's newspaper?"

"Only the headlines," Ruth said. "Did I miss something good?"

"They printed a summary of the treaty the prime minister will be signing with Albion. There's a map, too, showing the route the procession will take."

"There's a procession? In this weather? I bet no one turns out."

"It's free entertainment," Eloise said.

"You'd watch a pretender-king march through the streets?" Ruth asked.

"Oh, I wouldn't say he's a pretender," Eloise said. "But mostly I'd go because it's over, you know? They're the last group of separatists, and now they're laying down their guns. Or their bows, I should say. With every train returning from the front with the injured and sick, it's wonderful to have this one piece of good news. The paper says that all the soldiers who were stationed in the north will be sent to Europe."

"Let's wait and see if it happens," Ruth said. "I got a telegram from Anna."

"About the signing?" Eloise asked.

"No, just to say she's not sure if she'll make it down here before Christmas."

"Oh, that's a shame. Did she say why?"

"No."

"It's probably work," Eloise said.

"I hope so," Ruth said. "But I don't like to think of her alone, in Twynham."

"She's been living alone for years, hasn't she?" Eloise said. "She's about ten years older than you, right?"

"A bit more, I think," Ruth said. "Mister Mitchell and Isaac rescued her near the beginning of the Blackout, when she was ten. She was abducted in Ireland, brought to Britain by some horse traders. But she doesn't like talking about it."

"My point is, she's used to being alone," Eloise said.

"But not while in a wheelchair," Ruth said.

"She's back at work now," Eloise said, "so she must be recovering."

"But she's still in that chair," Ruth said. "I do worry it might be permanent. Now she's spending the holidays alone, when almost everyone she knows is away at war."

That was part of the reason for her worry. The other part was that she felt responsible. Anna Riley had been shot because she had been in the lead climbing the stairs, but the man holding the shotgun had been Simon Longfield's father. Simon had been her friend at the academy. But then Ruth had learned he'd been spying on her, and the Serious Crimes Unit's investigation, for his mother. Mrs Longfield was an industrialist who had dreams of wearing Britain's rusting crown. Simon's parents had died during the raid which had put Anna Riley in the wheelchair. Isaac had made Simon disappear. Ruth didn't know if that meant he was alive or dead, nor did she care.

"You're worried," Eloise said. "Of course you are. Anna's your second-cousin by employment."

"She's my what?"

"The twins worked it out," Eloise said. "They're trying to figure out what Isaac's place in the universe is, you see."

"Them and me both," Ruth said.

"Mister Mitchell worked for your mum back when she was a professor in America, so that makes him and Isaac your cousins by employment, and so his daughter becomes a second cousin. I thought she should be your niece, but they decided that was too weird."

"Your brothers are weird," Ruth said.

"Tell me about it. Have you heard from Isaac?"

"Not a peep since he disappeared," Ruth said. "I went down to the docks earlier, but his boat isn't back either."

"Do you think he went to the front?"

"He must have done. He's probably with Mister Mitchell, causing trouble in France."

When Isaac and his followers were in Dover, Isaac squatted in the police station apartments. The enigmatic Mrs Zhang spent most of her time on their ship, mostly to prevent the navy from commandeering it. Gregory did most of the cooking. The sniper, Kelly, was meticulous, though she treated all property as communal. Isaac acted as if he owned the place, and so had a right to sell it. Despite that, Ruth did worry what had become of him, and his team.

She retreated to her room to hang up her uniform. The trousers were covered in slush-melt, but due to the power shortage, the launderette had shut up early for Christmas. She'd have to make do with a brush-clean when the uniform was dry. Christmas? It didn't feel like it. Growing up in the refugee camp, Christmas had been a big deal. There hadn't been much food, and even fewer gifts, but they'd decorated the schoolhouse, they'd had plays and pantos, songs and stories, and a giant bonfire. They'd had fun. This year, the war had cast a long shadow over the festivities.

Was it the war? Or was it also the violence she'd witnessed since leaving the police academy?

During her two months with the Serious Crimes Unit, they'd saved the old prime minister's life, and that of the American ambassador, a man who seemed certain to win the presidency in the U.S.A.'s upcoming reunification election. They'd stopped coups and plots by politicians, by police officers, and by the leadership of the Railway Company. Counterfeiting. Kidnapping. Murder. So much pain, so much death. So many innocent lives taken, or ruined.

From her coat pocket, she took out the letter from the convent in Twynham. Postmarked a week ago, it had only arrived that morning. The letter wasn't long, and penned by the Mother Superior, but was in response to one of her own, written to the man they only knew of as Ned Ludd.

The young man, an extreme technophobe, had been encouraged to sabotage the telegraph. He'd been arrested, but his delinquent co-saboteurs had all been murdered. No one knew who he was. Even *he* didn't know who he was. The poor man could barely string a sentence together, and it was rarely coherent. The charges against Ned had been dropped, and the convent had offered him a room, and work in their gardens. Ned Ludd's misguided friends hadn't been so lucky. So much pain. So much misery. So much death. All reduced to a line on the radio's news bulletin and a pull-out section in the paper.

She propped the letter on the narrow desk as a reminder to write a reply when she was in a more cheerful mood. Pulling on her favourite moth-chewed baggy jumper, she trekked back out to the living room, where Eloise had turned on the digital projector, left behind by Isaac.

"Oh, are we watching a movie tonight?" Ruth asked.

"Absolutely," Eloise said. "I don't know when either of us will get another night off. So what do you want to watch?" She cautiously tapped the button on the side of the projector, slowly scrolling through the movies preloaded on the USB.

"There are a lot more than I thought," Ruth said.

"Hundreds," Eloise said. "It's got to be nearly all the movies ever made."

The cinema in Dover had been closed again to preserve electricity. It had only been open a few months, previously having been shuttered for twenty years due to the latent taboo surrounding old-world technology. The theatre had been shut for the winter, too. The panto had been cancelled. The city gates were closed at nightfall, and a curfew began at ten. There wasn't much to do in Dover except work, and there was plenty of that for the both of them.

"How did Isaac get so many films?" Eloise asked.

"Don't ask," Ruth said. "That's the answer to any question involving him. Ooh, *The Remains of the Day*, that's what *Remaining Days* is based on."

"I'll wait to see it on stage," Eloise said. "*Lord of the Rings?*"

"The books had a lot of walking in them," Ruth said. "I get enough of that during daylight."

"*Independence Day*? That must be a political movie."

"Veto," Ruth said. "I fancy something silly and distracting, and nothing to do with politics, or policing. Maybe something about animals?"

"How about this one, *The Silence of the Lambs*? That sounds pretty tame."

"Perfect," Ruth said.

Part 1
Behind the Lines

Henry Mitchell

France and Belgium

15th - 18th December

15th December

Chapter 1 - The Front Line
The Drummond-Dumond Farm, Pas de Calais, France

Henry Mitchell walked his bicycle north along the icy highway. He'd abandoned any attempt at riding two miles, and three falls, ago. This road was in better repair than most, twenty years after the collapse of the previous civilisation, but the winter storms had left a frosting of frozen mud camouflaging the ice-filled potholes.

The old road signs told him they were halfway between Calais and Dunkirk, and still on the A16. To the west was the coastal Green Zone. To the east lay the rest of Europe. On paper, the highway marked the front line. In reality, there were no signs of life between his shadow and the horizon. Ahead lay a ruined farmhouse. Behind was a wrecked fuel tanker, gathering rust for twenty years. At his side was his guide, Jean-Luc Roseau, a twenty-three-year-old French trader who'd grown up scavenging along the old highways of Europe.

"We could still reach Dunkirk tonight," Jean-Luc said.

"You mean if I get back on the saddle?" Mitchell asked. "Why the rush? We've got plenty of time."

"The sooner we reach Dunkirk, the sooner we will get to Belgium," he said, raising a hand to check his pride and joy, a drooping moustache which nearly reached his chin.

"But the spy won't arrive in Nieuwpoort for another week," Mitchell said.

"If he's on time," Jean-Luc said. "But if he's late, we could be waiting in Nieuwpoort for days. We could miss Christmas. There will be a table for you at Monsieur Fry's restaurant."

"Isaac will meet us in Nieuwpoort with his ship," Mitchell asked. "It's about five hours sailing to Dover."

"If his ship is in Nieuwpoort," Jean-Luc said.

"It will be," Mitchell said. "Isaac is a lot of things, not all of them good, but he is a man of his word."

"*Bien sûr*. But we still need to scout the Belgian harbour for the navy, and the bridges for the army. That will take two days."

"So we'll be done by the twenty-third," Mitchell said. "You'll still be back in Dover for Christmas lunch. I might even make it back to Twynham. Regardless, it's only another sixty kilometres. We'll camp in the ruins tonight, and still reach the Dunkirk garrison soon after first light. We'll be across the border by lunch, and in Nieuwpoort by nightfall."

"If there are no new orders awaiting us in Dunkirk," Jean-Luc said. "And whether there are or not, we won't *stop* in Dunkirk. It is a week until your spy arrives in Belgium. A week living in the ruins, cooking what we can hunt over wood fires."

"I thought you grew up living like that," Mitchell said.

"Which is why I take advantage of simple luxuries when they are available," Jean-Luc said. "The garrison in Dunkirk will have hot showers. Hot food. Maybe even clean clothes."

Mitchell glanced down at his slush-speckled trousers. Wearily, he threw his leg over the crossbar and kicked off. "Fine. Dunkirk tonight, Belgium tomorrow, but I'll want a Christmas dinner from Mr Fry, as well. Two dinners. One for me. One for my daughter."

Fifty was a milestone still on Henry Mitchell's horizon, but it loomed larger each day, casting a shadow nearly as long as the winter sun on the snow-flecked French fields. He should have been back in Dover three days ago, but he'd taken a detour to gather evidence from an enemy mortar attack on the garrison at Ardres. Frustratingly, the enemy had left little behind beyond footprints and bullet casings.

Until two months ago, the Royal Navy's intelligence unit had been entirely focused on tidal heights and harbour depths. Following the attack on Calais, a new unit had been formed, run by Commissioner Weaver out of Police House in Twynham, answering directly to the Prime Minister. Henry Mitchell wasn't the only member of that unit, but where the others sought clues on where the next attack might come, he was hunting the mastermind behind them.

He'd been given the rank of Inspector-General. No real authority came with the title. Nor did a pay-rise. But the rank rang with sufficient authority that he could ignore the naval officers running the army who didn't think politicians should be running a war.

"*Monsieur*, ahead!" Jean-Luc hissed.

"Trouble?" Mitchell asked, raising his eyes, though not his head.

"*Les rosbif*," Jean-Luc said. "They have barricaded the bridge."

"Why'd they do that?" Mitchell asked, realising the answer even as he spoke. "Because of the railway depot two miles to the south."

The A16 followed the coast but always a few kilometres inland. In the south, it led to Abbeville, where it turned inland and towards the rubble of Paris. In the north, it changed its name at the border, but continued on through Belgium, the Netherlands, and Germany, all the way to Denmark and the long-destroyed bridges to Sweden.

Twenty years after the Blackout, the limited nuclear exchange, and subsequent famines and plagues, ice-age winters and furnace summers, the European Union was little more than an idea. France was in exile, and the United Kingdom was both disunited and on a certain path towards republicanism. But the regiment of conscripts guarding the bridge stood beneath the Union Jack, the old French Tricolour, and the new European Union's starfield banner.

"Halt and be recognised!" a young private in conscript-green yelled, her voice rising to a squeak at the end.

"Inspector Henry Mitchell, Military Intelligence," he said.

"*Inspecteur-Générale!*" Jean-Luc added. "*Je suis Commandant Jean-Luc Roseau de la Grande Armée Européenne.*"

The private looked doubtfully at their uniforms, clearly uncertain what to do next.

"Call your NCO," Mitchell said. "When presented with a problem, it's always best to pass it up the chain of command."

The private nodded, and hurried away.

The barricade had been built across the road, partially with broken farm equipment, and partly with the railway ties and tracks which should have been laid over this bridge as part of the new railway's expansion. Those plans had stalled as the barbarians had swept through Europe.

"That's the canal L'Aa?" Mitchell asked, walking over to the side of the bridge. Below, the storm-swollen river lapped around and into a stone-walled fishing shelter with a car-steel roof.

"The farm on the northern bank belonging to the Drummond and Dumond families," Jean-Luc said. "They began with a trading post, opened an inn, and then a farm. They maintained this section of the road."

"Their gravel and cement repairs hold up as well as any in Twynham," Mitchell said diplomatically. "Did the families make it to Dover?"

"Most did. Four cousins went south to find a missing trade caravan. That was eight weeks ago."

Mitchell could guess what had happened to them, and to the caravan.

An officer approached from the farmhouse. Like the private, he wore the hastily produced green tunic and trousers of a recent conscript, but on his belt was a Royal Navy sword, and on his face was the befuddled suspicion of a fish out of water dumped straight into a restaurant's pick-your-own tank.

"Howdy," Henry said, leaning into his childhood American accent. "Inspector Henry Mitchell, military intelligence. We're scouting northward. You are?"

"First Lieutenant Donnie Ho, HMS— I mean *Captain* Donnie Ho, First Kent Fusiliers. Do you have identification?"

"My badge," Mitchell said, pulling the chain out from beneath his coat. Unlike the conscripts, he and Jean-Luc wore the unofficial uniform of civilian scavengers: lightweight, artificial, old-world fabrics, all of a mottled grey colour which doubled as camouflage in their semi-frozen world. "You can confirm my authority by sending a telegram to the admiral in Calais. The code word is spangled."

"They haven't laid the telegraph here yet," Ho said. "We had a radio, but—" He stopped himself, as if worried he was about to reveal a military secret.

"I bet they have a telegraph at end of the railway line, two miles back," Mitchell said.

"Our orders are that no one leaves this post," Ho said.

"Well, if you don't believe us, you should put us under arrest, and give us a meal. If you do believe us, you can just offer us that meal."

"And I must inspect the damage for Madame Dumond," Jean-Luc said.

"Who's that?" Ho asked.

"Madame Dumond, matriarch of the Drummond-Dumond trading clan," Jean-Luc said. "This is their farm. As representative of the European Union Restoration Council, I shall have to file a report."

"A report?" Ho asked, instantly enraged. "There's a bloody war on!"

Mitchell hid his smile, letting the two bicker while he took in the defences.

Ten soldiers stood on the bridge, in the centre of which, facing north, was a 120mm rifled cannon. This weapon looked to be a naval gun affixed to a recently built six-wheeled carriage. A second carriage stood dangerously close, stacked with ammunition. Mitchell turned his gaze eastwards, to the no-one's land stretching all the way to the Alps. Shells on a bridge? That would be a tempting target.

"If we're going to argue, let's do it inside," Mitchell said, and began walking, before Captain Ho could object.

The Drummond-Dumond hamlet had originally been a three-storey farmhouse with four large barns and two small outbuildings built on the northeastern edge of the bridge. Since the Blackout, a steel palisade had been erected. From the withered weeds growing in the cracked cement holding the welded car roofs in place, those defences had been built in the early years. In turn, they'd constricted how far out the farm could grow, forcing the owners to build up and between. Double-decker walkways linked the house and the barn. Between them, again facing north, was another artillery piece, and another six-wheeled caisson, still attached to the four bicycles which must have towed the ammunition here. Other equipment was being uncertainly stacked by conscripts as green as their coats.

"Have you just arrived?" Mitchell asked.

"I can't discuss our deployment," Ho said.

"Mister Mitchell, is that you?" a woman called.

Mitchell turned and saw a sergeant walking towards him. It took him a moment to put a name to the young but battle-worn face: Joanna 'Jo-Jo' Johannes, whom he'd last seen in the hospital, just after the assault on Calais six weeks before. Back then, she'd been a corporal in the Marines, and recovering from a gunshot.

"Jo-Jo! Good to see you," he said. "But shouldn't you still be on the sick-list?"

"A promotion's the best medicine in the world, sir," Jo-Jo said.

"Do you know him, Sergeant?" Ho asked.

"*Everyone* knows Mister Mitchell, sir," Jo-Jo said. "He saved the prime minister, stopped the coup, and helped *me* stop them taking Calais. How is Constable Deering, sir?"

"Keeping the peace in Dover," Mitchell said. "Why are you guarding that bridge?"

"I don't think we should—" Ho began.

"The generals want bastions along the front line," Jo-Jo said. "They sent us here to build one."

"Bastions?" Mitchell asked. "First I've heard of it."

"The general believes the bastions will create a truly safe Green Zone, behind which the French farmers can return to till the land," Ho said.

"But after a long day in the fields, where will we sleep when you are in our beds?" Jean-Luc asked.

"It's about half an hour until sunset," Mitchell said. "Did you want to send that messenger back to the train depot, Captain, or will you take your sergeant's word on my identity?"

"Of course, I trust my sergeant," Ho said.

Before Captain Ho could add a caveat, Mitchell cut in. "Capital. You're here to protect this bridge. I assume your orders warn of an attack from the north, possibly on those trains parked further south."

"The previous ambushes *did* target locomotives," Ho said.

"Yes, but you've provided our enemy with an even more tempting target," Mitchell said. "You're aware they have mortars? One round hits the ammunition caisson here, and this farm becomes a crater. If they hit the caisson on the bridge, we're going to spend the next month fishing rubble out of the canal."

"They won't attack the bridge," Ho said. "The general says they need the bridges and roads intact."

"I don't know what the enemy's plans are, so there's no way a general does," Mitchell said. "I'd advise you to move the ammunition. Jean-Luc, is there a cellar here?"

"Of course."

"Move the shells below ground," Mitchell said. "But be surreptitious. Don't make it obvious what you're doing. I'm going to scout the fields."

"Do you think the enemy are out there?" Ho asked.

"I would be," Mitchell said, striding away before Captain Ho could object.

"Mind if I tag along, sir?" Jo-Jo asked, falling into step next to Mitchell.

"I never mind company," Mitchell said. He unzipped his bag, from which he drew an M4 carbine with a collapsible stock.

"Nice gun, sir," Jo-Jo said with envy.

"Borrowed from an old friend," Mitchell said. "How did you really end up back at the front, Jo-Jo?"

"They offered me the promotion, sir," she said. "Yeah, I know that makes it sound like the army's desperate, but me saying no wasn't going to magic up some more soldiers."

"Tell me about it," Mitchell said. "Is everyone else here a conscript?"

"Not all. Some were clerks or cooks. There's even a tank driver."

"But no tank," Mitchell said.

"Not unless you know something I don't," Jo-Jo said.

"Don't hold your breath unless you can hold it until the summer." He stopped, halfway across the frozen field. "These were all cabbages. Low to the ground. No cover here. I've been roaming the battlefields south of Calais this last month, piecing together scraps of evidence from all the attacks since the big one."

"There's been three, haven't there?" Jo-Jo asked.

"Three sets of simultaneous, night-time ambushes, and far too many skirmishes," Mitchell said, scanning the terrain. "The bulk of our army is bogged down trying to secure a land route to the Mediterranean."

"Why?" Jo-Jo asked.

"Beats me, because it's no way to beat the enemy," Mitchell said. "But I'm not a general. Would they hide in that orchard? Ah, but I can see right through those trees. No, the trees don't offer much cover without the leaves. This way."

An orchard had been planted in the corner of the second field. Further along the boundary line, a massive oak had been struck by lightning, and then by the wind. It had fallen, lifting its roots deep from the soil.

Mitchell gestured beyond the lightning-blasted tree, motioning she should circle left, while he went right.

There was no one there.

"Each of these night-time ambushes follows the same pattern," Mitchell said as he peered at the loose soil behind the fallen tree. "Three sets of attacks. Four in one night, then seven, then five, all timed to take place at the same time. Eleven-twenty, one-thirty, half past midnight. Each attack consists of around ten mortar shells being lobbed at a target, while five hundred to a thousand rounds of assault rifle ammo are fired. The attacks last under five minutes before our enemy vanishes into the night. And they really do vanish. The official report says they've sustained heavy casualties, but the reality is we've collected three corpses, and a few old-world rifles."

"How many people have we lost, sir?" she asked.

"About seventy. Twice that number injured severely enough to be sent back to Dover. That's not counting the daylight skirmishes. We do better there. But these night-time attacks are really taking their toll. Our enemy knows where to aim their mortars. That takes skill, but it also requires a spotter. Someone has to lie out in the frozen ground, watching the target." He crouched down. "Here, I think."

"Someone was watching us?" Jo-Jo asked.

"Yep. Doesn't mean they'll attack you, or that they'll attack tonight. But they would have seen the artillery pieces. You've been marked as a potential target. Hmm. I wonder whether they hoped to cross the bridge. If they did, now you're here, they won't be able to. In which case, you're an even more likely target. Well, this is what the generals wanted."

"It is?" she asked.

"Yep. A bastion to hold the bridge and draw their fire," Mitchell said. "Come on. We've got some work to do before dark, and some more afterwards. Just don't look back."

"You think we're being watched still?"

"Unsure, but let's assume it." He trudged back towards the farm, counting under his breath. "Assuming someone sets up a mortar at the tree, our soldiers could run from the farm in three minutes, and straight into assault rifle fire. That's how we lost seventeen at Ardres."

"We can retrain the cannon on the tree," Jo-Jo said.

"No, I've got a different idea," Mitchell said. "Find a couple of wheelbarrows. Load them with kindling. After dark, wheel them out into the field, at least twenty metres from the farm, and ten metres apart. At about nine, light them. We don't want a bonfire, just a few small blazes which burn themselves out. We'll have no lights on in the farm, so that might confuse their aim. Your unit has a radio set?"

"Yes, sir. Hasn't worked for days. It got dumped in a puddle. Someone tried washing the mud out of its innards. Should I send a runner back to the train depot?"

"No, it's getting too late," Mitchell said. "Besides, the purpose of a bastion is to be a target. The generals shouldn't need us warning them we're in danger of attack. Secure the shells below ground. Don't fire the guns. Get everyone hidden with some bricks at their backs, and orders not to shoot."

"We're not allowed to fire back?" Jo-Jo asked.

"Our enemy isn't a cohesive unit," Mitchell said. "They're a gang of killers who rampaged through Europe in the hope of looting Britain. Someone is holding them together, arming them, supplying them, organising them. But these bandits will only follow as long as they get victories. They want blood. If we don't return fire, they might attempt to take the bastion."

"And we'll massacre them," Jo-Jo said.

"Here's hoping."

16th December

Chapter 2 - The Seasonal Search for Inspiration
The Drummond-Dumond Farm, France

To My Dear Anna, Happy Christmas, with all my love, Dad.

He looked at the words he'd written on the card. It wasn't enough, but he didn't know what else to say. Letters were easy. You began with the crime du jour, and ended by posing the question of who'd done it. He often wrote a letter or three to Anna while he was out in the wastelands, even if he was unable to post them until he returned. Cards? He hated cards, but it *was* the season.

It was also, according to his watch, a new day by a whole twenty minutes. The attack had yet to come. It still could, but with each passing second, the odds dropped. Jean-Luc snored gently in the corner. But that young man had grown up on a scavenging cart. He'd sleep through an earthquake.

The previous attacks had come within an hour of midnight, leaving the enemy plenty of time to run and hide before dawn. Mitchell would give it until one. If the attack hadn't come by then, he'd sleep. Which left him an hour to finish writing the card.

Seeking inspiration, he looked around the second-storey room, which he'd claimed because it still had thick curtains to hide the light from his electric torch. One wall was painted pink, one green, one yellow, one mauve. The colour scheme matched the bedroom across the hall, so it was a choice rather than a necessity, probably decorated by someone too young to remember pre-Blackout reality real estate shows. The ceiling was white, and the floor-rug was damp, feeding a mould halo around the room's second door. That door had been built around an old window frame, and now opened onto a walkway leading to the roof of a barn.

The double-bunk told him this had been a bedroom. The near identical locker-cupboards suggested it was a room for salaried staff rather than paying guests. The curtains were heavy, threaded with gold. Probably salvaged from some rambling chateau. The desk was a globally ubiquitous Swedish flat-pack, though with a replacement hand-lathed leg etched with an apprentice's best scrollwork.

The wasted effort that had gone into replacing the table leg was made even more depressing by the graffiti on opposite walls. Latin on the green, Arabic on the pink. He couldn't read either language, and from the hesitant strokes and splodgy mid-word corrections, neither could their authors. He knew the translations well enough. The Latin was the first few verses from the Gospel of Saint Sebastian, summarising the blood-and-pain doctrine of the knights. In Arabic were the twelve missives of the first emir, supposedly dictated by an archangel the day before the Blackout. Mitchell had seen both sets of scrawls in about a tenth of the properties the enemy had overrun. Did it represent the percentage of true believers among their foes, or just those who'd learned their source text by rote? It didn't matter, and certainly wasn't interesting enough to go in a Christmas card. No, what would be of interest to Anna was news of the investigation, but he had little new information to share.

He categorised the crimes, and their perpetrators, into two groups; the lesser, though hideously violent, butchery to the south of Calais, the synchronised night-time attacks, and the daytime ambushes by lone, and increasingly starving, renegades; and there was the big crime of the insurgency itself. Someone had organised a truce between these rival terrorist cults, and was still supplying them with equipment. Cut off those supplies, and the enemy would wither. His goal was to locate the supply depot. Isaac thought Switzerland, based on an old hunch. Mitchell thought the Black Sea, based on how some of the captured Kalashnikov assault rifles had been manufactured in Bulgaria, some in Albania, and others in Turkey.

It wasn't much to share with his police officer daughter, but if he knew more, he'd be heading there, not sitting in an abandoned farmhouse only a few miles from the coast.

Perhaps the spy he and Isaac were meeting in Belgium would have learned the location of the enemy warlord. Probably not. If the spy was even still alive. Their secondary mission, though the admiralty thought it the most important, was to survey the damage to Nieuwpoort's harbour and ascertain whether it would make a suitable naval base for the springtime offensive. Mitchell didn't know when, how, or where that offensive would be launched, but nor had he known they were building a bastion on this bridge. Despite the implied seniority of his new rank, he was still just a lowly copper in pursuit of a suspect.

After Belgium, he could sail back to Kent with Isaac. If he was in England, he might as well report in to Twynham. While there, he certainly could see Anna, at least for a few hours.

In her last letter, Anna had said she was going to spend Christmas with Ruth and Maggie in Dover. That was unlikely, the words offered merely as reassurance to an anxious and absent father. Anna was back at work, and leave had been cancelled for absolutely everyone.

Ordinarily, he wouldn't worry about her being alone, but she was still in a wheelchair after having been shot. In each of her letters, she said she was almost back to full strength, but that was more daughterly reassurance. With Ruth and Maggie in Dover, Isaac as often at sea as on land, and himself as often behind enemy lines as their own, Anna was alone in Twynham.

It was good she had work to fill her days, even if it was paperwork at Police House. Between the coup, the corruption, and the collapse of the Railway Company, a cloud of suspicion hung over most members of the police. The military now had priority for recruitment, and so the police were massively understaffed, just when they also needed a military intelligence division. She'd be busy. But still...

From outside came a gunshot, and a muted, "Hold your fire, damn you!"

He capped the pen, and closed the card, putting both back in his bag; there wasn't much else in there except food, ammo, and eight grenades; four smoke, four shrapnel, and all from the prototype batch. In another month, they'd be producing enough to issue four to each soldier. Hopefully. The ammo was new-made by Isaac, recast from the government-issue rounds. The rifle was an old-world carbine, also from Isaac, also from a cache the man had claimed didn't exist.

The soldiers outside carried the ten-round, semi-automatic, government-issue rifle modelled on the old M1 Garand in service a century ago. Why? Expedient bureaucracy. With pirate raids, separatist enclaves, and escaped zoo animals, farmers needed a hunting rifle they could also use for defence. Most of the refugees who'd fought their way to Britain had arrived armed. With such an abundance of weapons, gun control was impossible, so they'd adopted ammunition control instead. By issuing a new standard cartridge which didn't fit in old-world, fully automatic weapons, they made those old guns useless. Theoretically. Until someone dismantled the new cartridges to make their own, retooled the barrel of an old-world gun, or found some forgotten stash of Kalashnikovs and bullets as their enemy had done.

He took out the night-scope. That was his own, salvaged years ago near Paris when he'd been travelling with Jean-Luc's mother, with Isaac, and with the forlorn hope that a normal world could ever be restored. He attached the scope to the carbine, turned out the light, and went outside to check the perimeter.

"Sir, sir!"

Mitchell's eyes opened. "Jo-Jo? What is it?" he asked, reaching for his holster even as he threw off the blanket.

"I've seen a light in the east," Jo-Jo said.

"Please tell me it's a star showing the way to Bethlehem," Jean-Luc said, already on his feet, his carbine in hand.

"Wish I could," Jo-Jo said. "Nah, it was electric. There and gone in a second. But it *was* there. Near that fallen tree."

"What time is it?" Mitchell asked.

"Three o'clock, sir," Jo-Jo said.

"It's getting late for an attack," Mitchell said. "But we'll take no chances. Have you told Captain Ho?"

"I came straight to you, sir."

"Wake the captain, then wake everyone," Mitchell said. "But do it quietly. No one fires without my order. The barrage usually lasts five to ten minutes. Remember, no one returns fire. If they advance, when they're halfway across the field, we'll mow them down. Jean-Luc, support the northern flank. I'll cover the south. Go."

Carbine in hand, he left the room via the door leading onto the extension-walkway. He kept low, below the windows until, halfway across, he reached the partially broken frame between the two empty bookshelves. The wheelbarrow fires had long since burned out. Below, the encampment was dark. Above, heavy clouds lumbered across the sky, cutting visibility to virtually nil. He could discern the trees along the canal, and so their enemy would be able to make out the silhouette of the farm buildings. Yes, that would be an easy target for the enemy. So would the bridge. He rested the carbine on the broken sill and peered through the night-scope, searching for the lightning-struck tree. There was no movement; there was certainly no light.

Jo-Jo might have been mistaken. Or there could be a refugee out there, waiting for dawn when their approach wouldn't result in a bullet. What he needed was flares. Mortars of their own. Better rifles. More ammunition. Radios. More night-scopes. His own flickered and then went dark. He needed more batteries, but those were scarcer than bullets. They needed so much, but if they had a single old-world armoured regiment, they'd drive the enemy east until they crushed them against the mountains.

He lifted his rifle from the window and was two steps towards the barn when the first shell exploded. The detonation shook the walkway, causing him to drop to one knee, but the blast had erupted to the south, outside the wall. Before he'd picked himself up, a second shell landed on the far side of the compound.

He scurried on, in a low crouch. Bullets tore through the air, slamming into wood and glass, but nowhere close. As he reached the edge of the walkway, a third shell landed in the courtyard below. Shrapnel ripped through the walkway, and Mitchell was thrown forward, and onto the flat platform beyond. As he landed, he rolled, away from the walkway and across the platform, and then off it, falling down onto the gently sloping roof.

A fourth shell landed near the perimeter, but the barn was now between him and the blast. Mitchell slid along the roof. As his legs slipped over the edge, he managed to catch the gutter. He fell, dangling by one hand, but the gutter wasn't strong enough to take his weight. As the next shell landed, much further away, the bracket gave, the gutter bent. He dropped, down into the farmyard.

Swearing as an alternative to screaming, he crouched close to the barn's wall. He listened to the explosions in the south, then in the north, but now the blasts erupted beyond the walls. The mortar team couldn't see their target, but the scout *had* seen the caisson of shells. That was what they were trying to find. They wouldn't, but he didn't view that as a cause for celebration because the conscripts were now returning fire.

"Cease fire!" Captain Ho yelled, running from the farmhouse towards the outer wall.

Mitchell didn't waste time with words, and rose to a sprint which he turned into a dive, knocking Ho from his feet just before a shell exploded, though on the far side of the barn.

"Get to cover. Stay quiet!" Mitchell hissed.

But it didn't matter. The shooting from the enemy had ceased. The shooting from the conscripts continued until they'd fired all ten rounds in their magazines.

Mitchell picked himself up, and made his way to the wall. "Stay down!" he called, leaning forward, peering into the darkness. "Hold your fire."

"We should attack," Ho said, following.

"Not until we've put out the fires," Mitchell said. "They'll illuminate us too easily for any stay-behind snipers. No, hold position, wait for dawn. Check your troops, Captain. See to the injured."

Mitchell began with those on the perimeter, calming some, reassuring others, until he met Jo-Jo, coming the other way.

"Sorry, sir," Jo-Jo said.

"What for?" Mitchell asked.

"For the shooting," Jo-Jo said.

"Ah, it's understandable," Mitchell said. "There was only a slim chance the enemy would attempt a ground assault. What's the damage?"

"We lost the cannon, and Jimmy Cruise lost a finger," she said. "That's the worst of it. There's a lot of bruises, and a few cuts, but it would have been chaos if they'd hit the shells. They watched us unload, didn't they?"

"Seems so, but they didn't target the bridge," Mitchell said. "That's useful to know. They want to use that bridge."

"So they'll attack again?" she asked.

"Possibly. Go make sure everyone is ready."

Chapter 3 - Evidence of an Ambush
The Drummond-Dumond Farm, France

Dawn was slow in coming, but it arrived alone, without another attack.

Mitchell climbed up onto the wall. "Stay down," he called as a few of the sentries made to copy him. After ten seconds, he released his held breath.

Captain Ho, alone among the soldiers, didn't follow Mitchell's order, and clambered up next to him. "They're gone?" Ho asked.

"Just like in every previous attack," Mitchell said. "If I were you, Captain, I'd rest half the troops now, half from midday. Prepare for an assault at dusk. But first, send a couple of runners back to the train depot. Get a telegram sent to Calais, and request a working radio. Sergeant, with us."

"Your officer is a sailor, *n'est-ce pas*?" Jean-Luc asked Sergeant Johannes as the three of them trudged across the field.

"He's okay," Jo-Jo said.

"He's not a soldier," Jean-Luc said.

"He ran the lighthouse on Anglesey," Jo-Jo said. "Then he was promoted to command the trade-ferry from Llandudno to Dundalk."

"Ah," Jean-Luc said. "A *safe* billet. So he has connections. There is a politician called Ho. The Minister for Refugees during the previous administration."

"His mum, I think," Jo-Jo said.

"She was ambassador from South Korea to London," Mitchell said. "Joined the government as an independent back in the early days. Good sort. Reliable. I fought adjacent to her at the Battle of Buxton."

"When was that?" Jo-Jo asked.

"Second year after the Blackout," Mitchell said. "A bunch of bandits got organised, and tried to take our harvest. We'd broken our backs picking wild-grown crops, no way were we giving them up. There were about a thousand of us, and three thousand of them, with barely a bullet between us. It was medieval. Your granddad was there, Jean-Luc."

"He often reminds me," Jean-Luc said.

"I'm the last person in the world who'll condemn a parent for pulling strings for their kids," Mitchell said. "And Captain Ho seems all right. He's just a bit green. He needs time. We all do. A couple of months ago, we had a few thousand Marines, twice as many sailors, and a lot of experience eradicating pirates. Conscripted farmhands, factory-cog conscripts, and redeployed sailors don't make an army. No, we've raised a militia. The generals in Twynham might find comfort in calling this a British Expeditionary Force, but I wish they'd read a bit more history and learn what happened to that army."

He led the pair to the lightning-blasted tree.

"There are no bullet casings," Jean-Luc said. "They weren't here."

"I didn't think they would be," Mitchell said, turning around so he could scan the field and the farmhouse-bastion.

"So why did you have us walk so far?" Jean-Luc asked.

"For your health, Jean-Luc," Mitchell said. "There's never any harm in an early morning stroll. We'll try the orchard."

"The soldiers reported receiving fire up and down the line, sir," Jo-Jo said.

"They're wrong," Mitchell said.

"Would you bet your rifle on it?" Jo-Jo asked.

"And what are you going to fight with when I win?" Mitchell replied. "The spotter knew we might find their perch behind that fallen tree. Perhaps they were even watching us as we went for our walk last night. Either way, they picked a different location from which to spring the ambush."

Brass casings littered the icy ground beneath the orchard's leafless trees. But they weren't all the enemy had left behind.

"Can I have one of these rifles, sir?" Jo-Jo asked.

"AKMs," Mitchell said. "The most common assault rifle in the world before the Blackout. Soviet design, originally, and not that common this side of the Alps." He picked one up. "Magazine is empty. Check the others, Jo-Jo." He took out his phone and began taking photographs of the brass, and then of the bootprints left in the mud.

"The mag's empty, sir," Jo-Jo said.

"So is this one," Jean-Luc said, checking the magazine of a different Kalashnikov.

"Figures," Mitchell said, walking back between the trees. It had originally been a small copse planted in the corner between two fields. After the Blackout, by design or by nature, the grove had grown to nearly a hundred sturdy trunks, twenty long by around five deep. The enemy firing line had been run from the front-most trees facing the farm. The mortar team had fired their artillery piece from the rear. Like with the rifles, the mortar had been left behind.

"That's a SAMOVAR," Mitchell said, taking a photograph of the mortar tube. "We suspected this was the type of mortar they were using, but weren't sure. It's another Soviet design, but manufactured and sold by the Russians to about half the world. That's good."

"What's good about it?" Jo-Jo asked.

"The enemy aren't making new weapons of their own," Mitchell said. "Whoever is backing these people is doing it with old-world salvage, and that won't last forever."

"Blood!" Jean-Luc called out. "Over here. This tree."

"Let me see," Mitchell said. "A lot of blood," he added, taking another photograph. "There's a trail of it coming from… yes, from the frontline. The blood formed a pool here where the injured sat against the tree. These are drag marks, leading through the field, heading that way. Two people helped one injured person away. C'mon."

He began striding out across the mulch-littered field. The dragged body had left an easy-to-follow trail through the abandoned crop of unharvested cabbages. December's thaw-frost cycle had destroyed the roots of the ground-level plants, leaving the leaves withered, speckled black and orange, and spotted with frozen blood.

"Before now, they've left a few rifles behind," Mitchell said. "Never a mortar. Every magazine was empty, wasn't it?"

"Sadly, yes," Jo-Jo said.

"And there were no spare magazines on the ground," Mitchell said. "If they left the mortar and the rifles behind, they wouldn't have picked up their empty magazines. They didn't reload. Counting the spent casings will prove it. The foot-soldiers were given one rifle with one pre-loaded magazine. And no one here had spare ammo."

"So the enemy is short of ammunition?" Jo-Jo asked.

"Evidence suggests not," Mitchell said. "As they retreated, they began by dragging the body away from the orchard. But it was dark, they couldn't tell where they were going, so followed the line of the furrows, thus they travelled a straight line. This is where they realised they were heading the wrong way, and turned ninety degrees, angling to that hedgerow, over there."

"There's a body," Jean-Luc said.

Jo-Jo raised her rifle, though she lowered it as they neared. "Dead, sir."

"Check what's beyond that hedge," Mitchell said.

"Looks like an old road," Jo-Jo said.

Mitchell stopped by the body. "Let's see. A woman. About thirty. Brown hair. Pale skin, even before the blood had left her body. Lightweight boots made of a breathable plastic that would cost about the same as a horse back in Twynham."

"*Non, un vélo,*" Jean-Luc said. "A *good* bicycle, but not a horse."

"Depends on the horse," Mitchell said. "The coat's lightweight, grey, and civilian. It hangs low below the hip, and the waist is tapered. Trousers are military. They have access to both civilian and military stores somewhere that had very cold winters."

He took a photograph of the face, and then of the dead woman's boots before drawing his knife and peeling back the partially frozen bandage on the woman's thigh. "Single shot. That's about an inch below her hip. Must have nicked the artery. She was standing when she was shot. The shooters were lying down. There were eight rifles, right?"

"In the orchard? Yes, sir," Jo-Jo said.

"The bandage is hastily applied. Maybe by herself," Mitchell said. "They carried her away, but by the time they reached here, she was dead. When they realised, they left her." He cleaned his knife in the mud, resheathed it, and flicked back through the photographs he'd taken last night by the lightning-struck oak. He held up an image of a boot-print next to the soles of the dead woman's shoes. "Do you see this?"

"They don't look like a match," Jo-Jo said.

"Exactly," Mitchell said. "I took that photo yesterday, by the fallen oak. That print was left by the scout, and is at least four sizes bigger."

"So she isn't the scout?" Jo-Jo asked.

"Nope, she's the leader," Mitchell said. "She made sure her people kept firing. That's why she was standing up, and so got shot in the hip. She made it back to the rear of the orchard. Either she tied the bandage or one of the mortar team did. Those two dragged her here, which is why they left their mortar behind. With no more ammo, and no one giving orders, the foot-soldiers left their useless rifles behind and fled."

"They fled after they had fired every mortar shell and every bullet," Jean-Luc said. "If she was the leader, she could have ordered them to take her to safety the moment she was shot."

"Yep," Mitchell said. "Our enemy is underequipped and utterly evil, but that doesn't make them cowards." He put his phone away, and opened the woman's coat. Beneath was a bright blue turtleneck, again old-world and very definitely civilian. At her waist was a belt on which both knife and handgun remained. "They didn't loot her body. They were in a rush," Mitchell said. "Glock 17. Two mags. Here you go, Jo-Jo, an early Christmas present."

"Seriously? Thanks, sir," she said.

"I'd clean it before use," Mitchell said. "What else do we have? A multi-tool, a small box containing a used bar of soap. Ah, I think this might be a map." He unzipped the jacket's inside pocket. "No, not a map. It's a bundle of old leaflets. Seem to be a dozen copies of the same one-sheet pamphlet. Seventeen languages. Where's the English? Ah. It seems to be a set of rules about when you can use showers and do laundry."

"What does that mean?" Jo-Jo asked.

"Nothing. It's toilet paper," Mitchell said. "Jo-Jo, return to the farm. I want this body recovered, and collect the mortars and the rifles. We'll send them back to Twynham for a more thorough examination. Jean-Luc, with me."

"You're going to follow them alone?" Jo-Jo asked.

"He is not alone," Jean-Luc said. "He is travelling with the grandest army!"

"They're long gone," Mitchell said, and pushed his way through the hedgerow. "But I want to see whether they left any other bodies behind."

While the sprawling hedgerow had added height to the embankment, decades of storms had taken away depth, filling the single-track roadway with field run-off. Though the frost lay thick, so did the footprints, heading away from the farm.

"What soldier leaves their rifle behind?" Jean-Luc asked.

"One who knows they won't get any more ammo," Mitchell said, photographing the footprints. "The mortar team was trained. So were the scout and the leader. The rest are just barbarians. Brigands.

Expendable. Here to stop us from charging the mortar. Only one magazine each; that's an interesting tactic."

"Why interesting?" Jean-Luc asked.

"Because I think it's the clue as to how we'll stop them," Mitchell said.

Just over a kilometre from where they'd found the corpse, they found the next clue: tyre marks.

"No hoof prints," Jean-Luc said as, once again, Mitchell took photographs.

"They drove," Mitchell said. "Someone should have spotted this sooner. Ah, but I didn't, so I can't blame others. Between the rain and snow, and dealing with the injured, tracks have been easy to miss. So what, precisely, *did* I miss? Two different widths of tyres. One set is narrow, one is wide. The drivers would require training, too. Bet they didn't do that around here."

"My mother can drive," Jean-Luc said.

"Right. But after a twenty-year break, she'd need a refresher course. Maybe only for a few hours, but it wouldn't be around here. Where did the truck come from? The driver, mortar team, scout, and squad leader were brought in from there. The rest, the eight foot-soldiers, were recruited nearby. Not just for this attack on us, but we can assume they used a similar set-up for each of the simultaneous mortar attacks."

"Do you think there were other attacks last night?" Jean-Luc asked.

"Probably. We'll find out soon enough," Mitchell said. "So forget the foot-soldiers, and focus on the drivers, on the truck, and on the diesel required to power it. There's no way this came from Britain. This wasn't stolen from us, and it's not biodiesel taken from the Railway Company's stores. They must have an oil well, a refinery, and a method of transporting it here, to the front. Could be a tanker. Could be carrying it in barrels. That's good."

"How is this good? They are making something new."

"Because they have a supply line," Mitchell said. "They have a logistics network. It ties them down. We can find it. Follow it back to the refinery. And that is where we find the mastermind who's organising this bloodbath. We don't know what happened last night elsewhere along the front, but before last night, the most simultaneous attacks were seven. Seven attacks. Seven trucks. Look at these tracks. The front and rear tyres don't match. Either they didn't bring spare tyres, or had no choice but to make do. That's good news, too. Our enemy is stretched thin. Their resources are scarce. That's why we'll win."

"If we can find them," Jean-Luc said.

"Yep. The truck turned around here, at this crossroads. They drove up this road, then returned that way just after the attack."

"I didn't hear an engine," Jean-Luc said.

"The wind was coming from behind us," Mitchell said. "We're in a dip, and we're a good distance from the farm. This must be their strategy with every attack. We should have realised, but now we know."

"So now will you send the soldiers to follow these tracks?" Jean-Luc asked.

"Not the soldiers, no," Mitchell said. "It's unlikely we'll catch the truck, but that doesn't mean we won't pursue."

"And this *we*, it is you and I?"

"Yep. We'll head east for a few days, then loop back west, and head straight to Belgium."

"We are not going to Dunkirk?" Jean-Luc asked.

"Sorry. Your hot shower will have to wait," Mitchell said.

They returned up the track, and found a group of soldiers by the body, led by an officer who wasn't Captain Ho.

"Henry Mitchell, why am I not surprised?" she said, though with a smile. Grey haired, knocking seventy, and wearing a much-mended uniform from two decades ago, Major-General Alice Lewis was the second in command of the European theatre. Twenty years ago, she'd been a major who was six months into a budget-cut-retirement, failing to enjoy a Mediterranean cruise. She'd taken command of the civilian ship, and ensured the survival of most of the passengers when it ran aground in Spain. Two years later, now in a naval captain's uniform, she'd been part of the force which had liberated Gibraltar from murderous pirates.

"You know me, General, always looking for trouble," Mitchell said. "And I wouldn't be much of a detective if I didn't find it. Why are you here?"

"When the bastion didn't report in, we assumed it had been overrun," she said.

"Sorry to disappoint," Mitchell said, scanning the crowd for Captain Ho. The young sailor wasn't there. "Thanks to Captain Ho's quick thinking, we suffered no fatalities."

"Then you're the lucky ones," Lewis said.

"How many other attacks were there?" Mitchell asked.

"Three," Lewis said. "Including one on Calais itself. They hit the crematorium."

"But that's next door to the aid-station," Mitchell said.

"I know," Lewis said. "At least eighteen were killed. Seven patients, eleven medical staff."

"Do you have any names?" Mitchell asked.

"Not yet," Lewis said. "The death toll will rise. We lost a further five soldiers who attempted a counterattack. They were mown down. Four attacks last night, and so far it appears this corpse is our only small victory."

"Not that small," Mitchell said. "I think she's the squad's leader. After she was injured, the enemy fled, leaving their rifles and the mortar behind. There are tyre marks further down that road. The enemy drove here. They have a refinery, tankers, somewhere to train drivers, mechanics, and a supply route to get the fuel here to the front. They have a base, General, so we finally have somewhere we can counterattack."

"If we can locate it," the general said.

"The mortar was Russian-made," Mitchell said. "As were the rifles. They might be making fuel, but they're not making new weapons."

"Letting them bleed us until they run out of ammunition is no route to victory," she said. "The Russians had an insanely vast stockpile."

"They're not coming from Russia," Mitchell said.

"How can you be certain?" Lewis asked. "The Knights of St Sebastian formed in Poland, they obliterated the farmers in Ukraine. Why can't they have found these supplies in Russia?"

"It's a hunch," Mitchell said. "Give me twenty minutes to write up my report, and I'll go confirm it."

"You intend to follow them?" she asked. "Then take some of my entourage as escort."

"No, ma'am. The enemy didn't target the bridge. Before nightfall, we knew they were watching us. Captain Ho had the foresight to set up two decoy targets using the artillery caissons. One on the bridge, one in the farmhouse. It was only the farmhouse which was targeted. They *need* that bridge. More than that, I don't think this crew intended to attack the farm last night. They planned to cross the bridge and strike further south."

"The railway depot, perhaps?" Lewis asked.

"Possibly," Mitchell said. "The presence of this garrison stalled them, but won't have stopped the enemy's broader plans. To date, the majority of the skirmishing has been to the south of Calais. I'm certain that's a feint. They want us focusing there so they can launch a bigger attack here."

"Where and when?" Lewis asked.

"That's why I'm going to follow them," Mitchell said. "Better to leave the troops here. I'll take the sergeant, and there's an old tank driver here. He'll be useful if we can catch up with their vehicles."

"And your..." She paused, looking at her entourage. "Your other mission?"

"Is still a go," Mitchell said, "but my associate will ensure it's a success even if I'm delayed. General, with this one attack, and this one body, we've stumbled onto more solid intel than we've had since this crisis began."

"The game's afoot, eh?" Lewis said. "Go, then. Captain Ho did his duty?"

"Yes, ma'am. They all did. They're a good group, and not nearly as green as their uniforms."

Chapter 4 - Rat Hunting
Arnèke, France

"You're the tank driver?" Mitchell asked, taking in the red-faced, red-haired young man who somehow managed to look simultaneously excited and apprehensive.

"Never in my life, sir," Private Hamish MacKay said, as his hand rose to a blunt salute.

"He's lying, sir," Jo-Jo said.

"I worked at the reclamation yard," MacKay said. "We were stripping old war machines for parts."

"Can you drive?" Mitchell asked.

"Since I was a bairn," MacKay said.

"And how many weeks ago was that?" Jean-Luc asked.

The young private bristled. "And how many centuries before the Big Dark were *you* born, eh?"

"I need a driver," Mitchell said. "The enemy who attacked last night came here in a truck. Wherever they're driving to, they'll need to refuel. We want the refuelling tanker. Not just to hinder any future attacks, but for any maps or other clues as to where they're getting their diesel from. Ideally, we'll steal the vehicle. I can drive, but I need a backup in case things go the way they usually do. You up for the challenge, MacKay?"

"Oh, aye, sir. Sounds a blast."

"I hope not," Mitchell said.

An hour later, they were cycling east. Jean-Luc led the way, though he'd admitted he didn't know these particular roads. Fallen trees had been trimmed. Rusting cars had dragged into abandoned fields, with drainage trenches dug along some of the new orchards. The Drummond-Dumond clan had clearly used these roads, though not regularly enough to fill the potholes.

Overhanging branches, snapped by the enemy's truck, lay sprinkled atop the muddy run-off from the neighbouring fields. Together with the tyre tracks, this gave them an easy trail to follow. Until the road joined the river.

"Don't tell me we've got to swim," MacKay said.

"Don't tell me you don't know how," Jo-Jo said. "Or was that stuff about your parents being fishers a lie, too?"

"I never said I was a tank *driver*," MacKay said. "If you jumped to conclusions—"

"Where are we, Jean-Luc?" Mitchell cut in.

"The D300," Jean-Luc said, pointing at the slow-moving river. "The river *was* the road."

Mitchell pointed upwards, at an oak overhanging the road. "See that red rag? That cloth looks far too bright to have been here long. They marked this route."

Mitchell propped his bike on its stand before walking to the verge. He picked up a broken branch. "How long has this road been underwater?"

"Only one season. It was the water-wheel," Jean-Luc said as Mitchell prodded the river's depth.

"How would a water-wheel do this?" Jo-Jo asked.

"The Drummond-Dumonds were building a water-mill for winter electricity," Jean-Luc said. "They had partially finished the dam when they were forced to flee. Partially finished has created a partial flood."

"And the road was the easiest path for the water to travel," Mitchell said, probing the depth. "Doesn't seem deep. Just a few inches. Isn't too fast. I reckon we can cycle upstream, along the road, and might even manage to keep our feet dry. But which way, Jean-Luc?"

The Frenchman peered at the slow-moving water. "North, because of the canal leading to Dunkirk. The nearest bridge is in the north. They would have used that."

"Here's hoping," Mitchell said.

"We used to cycle the flooded roads back home," MacKay said as their bicycles wobbled northward through the murky new river. "We'd compete to see who could stay dry the longest."

"Was that in Scotland?" Mitchell asked. Finally giving in to the inevitable, he dropped his foot into the submerged roadway.

"Aye, up in Sutherland," MacKay said. "My nan moved there because she was promised they would build a spaceport. She loves aliens."

"They were really building a spaceport?" Mitchell asked.

"What *is* a spaceport?" Jo-Jo added.

"It's where space-rockets were going to be launched," MacKay said. "Nan bought the cottage so she could be there when the aliens came to visit. Obviously, the kind of facility we used for launch would be the kind they'd need to land. But the Blackout came before it was built."

"Now I've got more questions," Jo-Jo said.

"North. Treeline. Birds," Mitchell said. "Something made them take flight. Jean-Luc, how far to the turning?"

"Three minutes," he said.

Either side of the new river was new-growth forests, born from wind-scattered seeds. It was a perfect home for birds to roost, and just as ideal for ambushers to hide. While their enemy would need dry ground to park their truck, there were plenty of lone and hungry bandits in this corner of France.

"Movement," Jean-Luc said.

"It's a dog," Jo-Jo said, as the sleek, four-legged furball stalked to the edge of the treeline some fifty metres ahead.

"A pack," Mitchell said as a dozen followers joined the alpha.

"Worse," MacKay said as the pack edged towards the water's edge. "It's a pack of cats!"

"Look above them," Mitchell said. "There's a red rag tied to that branch."

The turning on the opposite side of the river-road from the rag was marked with tyre ruts and recently snapped branches.

Even with the river between them and the wild cats, they cycled another ten minutes before stopping.

"If they'd remembered to remove those rags, odds are we'd have lost the trail," Mitchell said.

"Monsieur, you wound me!" Jean-Luc said, with mock indignation.

"Fine, anyone other than Jean-Luc would have," Mitchell said. "More proof they're relying on scouts."

For longer than there'd been a place called France, farmers had played unwilling host to battles on these fields. Every few hundred metres, along roads older than movable type, they came to the renovated ruin of a converted barn, the wreck of an extended farmhouse, or rubble from an urbanite's rural retreat. One thing the buildings had in common was the scavenger's scrawl on the brickwork, a letter and number code denoting they'd been searched, and whether any salvage had been left behind.

Over that were more recent scrawls, usually in ash, sometimes in mud: the sabre-like swoosh symbol of the caliphate, the mathematical unequal sign used by the Free Peoples, or the two-barred cross of the Knights of St Sebastian. One of those knights had found some old paint. Over a road sign, they'd daubed the first lines from the Gospel of St Sebastian: *Pain is a gift to the unbeliever.*

"Does that sign say Arnèke is ahead?" Mitchell asked. "Wasn't that a trading post?"

"*Non.* The village was used as a hunter's rendezvous," Jean-Luc said. "This is a foraging paradise for wild pigs. They winter in the ruins, and rustle in the woodland."

"So we'll want to check for occupants before we find somewhere to stop for lunch," Mitchell said. He sniffed. And again. "Smoke." He slid his carbine from his back to his front. "We're a good distance from that new river. Our enemy would have been awake all night. It could be they stopped around here, especially if their dead leader was the only one who knew where to go next. But there are plenty of other renegades in this wasteland. Jean-Luc, any ideas where they might have camped?"

"If we were another ten kilometres east, or twenty south, I would tell you the names of each leaf," the French scout said.

"Then we'll walk the bikes until we see the smoke."

He spotted the grey-black plume when they came level with a house in relatively good repair. Formerly a barn, it had been converted into a house with storm shutters on the ground floor, a Juliet balcony on the second, and soot stains around them all. But the smoke lay ahead, and to the north of the road.

Leaving the bikes behind the partially burned house, they quietly gathered their weapons.

"We'll get as close as we can," Mitchell whispered. "If they're slack enough to light a fire, they probably haven't bothered with a sentry."

"Assuming it's them," Jean-Luc said. "It could be refugees."

"Yep," Mitchell said. "Or locals who refused to leave their land. Or it could be lone renegades who have nothing specific to do with the attack. The fire is coming from behind that thicket. A good way behind. Follow me. Keep low. Anyone shoots, chew the mud. Don't return fire until we're certain they're hostile. Okay?"

There wasn't much cover in this pig-prowled land, but the high grass on the boundary embankment offered a shield until they reached a thicket of roses. From there, it was a fifty-metre dash to a sprawling hedgerow, which had once shielded a cottage garden from the field. The cottage had been reduced to rubble by the rusting helicopter crashed in what had been the front room. The hedge had spread through the ruin, creating an impenetrable barrier, but following its edge, they found the track. Already narrow, it had been blocked by a fallen tree so long ago, the rotten trunk was soft to the touch.

Beyond the tree, Mitchell saw tyre marks in the mud, leading up a wide drive on the far side of the fallen oak. He gestured upwards, beyond the clump of dead roots, and through a new-growth copse. Ten metres on, he raised a hand, motioning silence before cupping his ear.

He could hear singing. It could as easily be called shouting, and was familiar from every night he'd policed closing time along the docks. He motioned north, and picked his way with exaggerated care, listening around the caterwaul-clamour for the whisper of a sentry. When he reached the edge of the copse, and saw the property, he realised his caution had been utterly unnecessary.

It was a house, not a farm: two storeys, with a detached garage, surrounded by a mole-ruined lawn. Beyond lay an ornamental screen of fir trees which had grown unchecked into a wild thicket, providing the perfect cover from which to spy on the property. The house's windows were broken. Ivy trailed up the walls, and moss dangled down the roof. A sapling had taken root in the gutter, while one of its much larger cousins had collapsed onto the roof of the detached garage. The garage roof was fractured, but unbroken, while the tree was still alive. That was more than could be said for the figure pinned to the garage doors. A rope hung around his neck, while his arms were tied to his sides.

Mitchell handed his monocular to the sergeant. "Dead refugee," he whispered.

"No truck," Jean-Luc said.

"No sentries," Jo-Jo said.

"No mercy," MacKay said, having taken the monocular and aimed it at the dead refugee.

"Probably the Free Peoples," Mitchell said. "The caliphate like to behead. The knights like to torture. Probably around ten of them. Left here by the truck-driver who went to collect a new leader. They could have stashed more guns here, so we'll assume assault rifles."

From inside came the sound of laughing. Singing. Drinking. It was too loud for any of the enemy to be asleep, and too soon after the assault for any to have passed out.

"There could be more refugees inside," Mitchell whispered. He unslung his carbine. "Happy Christmas, Sergeant. That's the selector switch. Thirty rounds in the mag. You and Hamish loop around the garage. If there's an enemy inside, deal with them quietly. Take up position by the wall of the garage. Jean-Luc and I'll cover the front." He reached into his bag. "Four spare mags, Jo-Jo." He pulled out a green-ringed cylinder. "This is a smoke grenade. New made. Should work. If the garage is occupied by more than one hostile, toss the grenade inside. If I don't see smoke, we'll drop a smoke grenade in the house, and open fire. With smoke inside, they'll run for the back door. Couple of bursts should get them all. Anyone with a weapon is a hostile. Got it?"

"Yes, sir," Jo-Jo said.

"You've got five minutes to get into position."

He crouched low, watching the farmhouse, and drew his sidearm. The modified Colt M1911 had been a gift from Isaac which he'd twice returned, partly because of the mountain of armour-piercing ammunition Isaac had stockpiled. Eight rounds in the mag, with six pre-loaded magazines in his belt. Slowly, he affixed the suppressor: another gift from Isaac, another reason he'd returned the gun. From his bag, he drew two grenades, checking each had the green stripe marking them as smoke bombs. There was still a chance of civilians being inside. A very slim chance, getting smaller by the second.

Inside, glass smashed, and the enemy cheered.

"*Barbare,*" Jean-Luc whispered.

"Two minutes," Mitchell replied. "Get level with that front door. Some might come out the front. Keep one eye on the barn, and another on the upstairs. But keep a third on me. If you shoot me by accident, your mother will kill you."

"We will meet on the other side or beyond," Jean-Luc said.

"How about out here in ten minutes," Mitchell said.

Henry Mitchell moved through the trees, his eyes on the ground, his ears on the singing, waiting for a change in tone indicating he'd been spotted. When he reached a point level with the corner of the house, he changed direction, and ran down to the thick stone slabs providing a relatively clear path between the rampant shrubbery and withered-stalk lawn. Gun raised, he edged towards the house. Walking, not running. Eyes moving from one broken window to the next. Ears attuned for a change in the discordant choir.

Reaching the house, he leaned against the wall. He took a breath. Another. He didn't look for Jean-Luc, or at his watch. He knew drunks, and drunken singing, and knew it came in waves. The chorus was reaching a crescendo. In a few words, it'd stop. The choir would disperse through the house, perhaps upstairs, perhaps outside. No smoke came from the garage. Now was the moment.

He reached to his pocket, and took out his mirror. Holding it close to the window's edge, he checked the reflection. The interior had been partially knocked through, with partition doors separating the downstairs rooms. Those doors had collapsed, possibly used as firewood in the pit burning on the floor of the kitchen at the back of the house. He counted four hostiles, each with a bottle in hand, close to the fire that had already filled the house with smoke. Two British-made rifles leaned against a trio of plastic crates, but the drinkers weren't in uniform. Two wore black coats, and all four wore unwashed and ragged trousers salvaged at least a month ago.

He slotted the mirror back into his pocket, and checked the gun's safety was off. In a crouch, he stepped away from the house and rose up, firing his pistol through the window. His first two shots hit, but he emptied all eight rounds into the house as the enemy fell or dived for cover.

He sprang back to the wall, ejecting the magazine, inserting a fresh one before an arrow whispered through the window. His gun reloaded, he pulled the grenade from his pocket and tossed it into the room. He'd been told they had a ten-second timer, but smoke began hissing from the device before it hit the rotting carpet.

Jean-Luc opened fire. Mitchell couldn't see the man's target, but rolled around the wall, angling along the moss-lined border towards the rear of the house. A gunshot came from inside the house. A fully automatic burst came from beyond. Jo-Jo, or the enemy? There was no time to tell. At the corner of the house, below a green-flecked extractor vent, was a small window. Kitchen or toilet? The glass was unbroken, smeared with soot, dust, and a civilisation of mould. But the room behind it was well lit from other windows, and there were moving shadows there. Kitchen, then. He raised his pistol and fired at the shadows. His first bullet shattered the glass. Inside the smoke-filled kitchen, the enemy turned.

Mitchell fired again, just as the enemy pulled the trigger on the crossbow. The bolt went wide, slamming into the interior wall. Mitchell's second bullet hit the man in the neck. His third hit his shoulder. The enemy fell.

With the barrel of the gun, Mitchell swept the glass from the window frame, letting the smoke out, though he didn't climb inside. Instead, he stepped sideways, standing flush against the wall, listening. The gunfire had ceased.

"Clear!" he called, before climbing inside and making sure that was the case.

Chapter 5 - The Wages of Soldiering
Arnèke, France

Eight of the enemy were dead. There were no survivors. Three had died by the fire, two just outside the front door, two outside the backdoor, and one in the kitchen. The interior staircase had collapsed, and so it took MacKay two long minutes to get to the upper floor, but there was no one there, or in the barn.

"Eight brigands," Mitchell said, picking up a crossbow. "Four armed with crossbows and four with British rifles. MacKay, can you see the road from upstairs?"

"Aye, sir," he called down through the hole in the ceiling.

"Then keep watch on the road," Mitchell said, picking his way around the corpses. "Jean-Luc, the garage. Jo-Jo, go with him."

Mitchell took out his phone, photographing the dead barbarians, and their boots, before checking the weapons. The crossbows were crude, the bolts homemade. The rifles were the most recent version of the standard British government semi-automatic rifle. Looted, obviously, during one raid or another. Of more interest was the ammunition, or lack thereof. He counted a total of seventeen rounds, split between four ten-round magazines. There were no loose rounds in the brigands' pockets, nor full magazines lying nearby. At their belts were knives and a few hatchets, but no revolvers. There were certainly no Kalashnikovs.

"The garage was empty, sir," Jo-Jo said when she returned. "We found a bag. We think it belonged to the refugee. We cut him down and put him inside."

"Can't really dig a grave in this weather," Mitchell said. "Where's Jean-Luc?"

"Checking the refugee's bag for any identification," Jo-Jo said. "He was only a kid, sir. Fourteen, if that. They hung him, and tied his arms together, but they stuck a knife in the garage door beneath his feet. As long as he stood on the knife, he wouldn't suffocate."

"I've never seen that before," Mitchell said. "I should have taken a photo for the newspaper, but I suppose they wouldn't have printed it. I'll photograph the door and knife instead. This is why we're going to win, Jo-Jo. Our enemy's only chance is for the people at home to grow so sick of rationing and the other privations that they'll demand parliament call a halt to the offensive. But after the sacrifices of the last twenty years, there's no way a crime like this can be answered with anything but revenge."

"Yeah, maybe," Jo-Jo said, clearly unconvinced. "Were they knights?"

"At least two were," Mitchell said. "It's hard to tell with the others. I've counted eight black coats. Six were still wearing them. Two of those closest to the fire had removed them."

"Not much wear on this," Jo-Jo said, picking up one of the jackets. "Old-world. Mostly plastic."

"Cheap in the olden days," Mitchell said. "Fake fur hood, not properly waterproof, but warm enough for this winter. The kind of thing you might find in a large grocery store or a cheap clothing outlet. Probably boxed up, wrapped in plastic, found in the stockroom."

"One jacket each, so it's a uniform," Jo-Jo said.

"It was payment," Mitchell said. "One coat and two bottles of vodka per person. The bottles have no labels, and it smells like paint-stripper, but we'll call it vodka. Glass bottles, too. That's interesting. Must be old-world bottles. So probably distilled at an old-world bottling factory."

"You mean they have a still as well as a refinery?" Jo-Jo asked.

"Finding and drilling the oil would have been more difficult than distilling diesel," Mitchell said. "But if they can manage that, why not build a still for something to drink? Glass bottles require a very different set of technologies. So we're looking for an old bottling plant near an old oil field."

"Do you know where that might be?" Jo-Jo asked.

"I can't even guess," he said. "But each clue gets us closer. The bottles were in the topmost crate," he added, pointing to the three plastic crates next to the fire. "The two crates beneath contain canned food."

"This is our food!" Jo-Jo said with indignation as she lifted the lid. "This is all made in Britain."

"Maybe looted from Calais, or some coastal enclave they overran," Mitchell said. "Or perhaps from a farm. The trade routes worked both ways. I've taken photographs. I doubt we can identify exactly when the food was captured, but I'll give it a go. Grab enough for dinner tonight and a couple of meals tomorrow."

"We're not going back to the bastion?" Jo-Jo asked.

"Not immediately," Mitchell said. "After the ambush, the truck left the foot-soldiers here and went off somewhere else. They took the mortar team with them. These foot-soldiers clearly weren't supposed to know where the fuel was stored. I assume because that's also where the assault rifles and ammo are kept. Our enemy, our *real* enemy, doesn't want these barbarians looting the stores for themselves. So they gave them a rifle with only one magazine and instructions to fire it. By way of payment, they got the coat, and enough booze to keep them happy here for a few days."

"And they were given crossbows and British rifles," Jo-Jo said.

"No, I think those were the weapons they had before they were recruited for this mission," Mitchell said. "The bows look like the kind the traders sell to farmers up and down the coast. They were probably looted. The rifles certainly were. They're the most recent model, so they could have been taken from Calais, or maybe captured during the skirmishing in the south."

"If they were left here without any weapons, was the truck going to come back?" Jo-Jo asked.

"Possibly, but I doubt it," Mitchell said. "If they wanted to use these people again soon, they'd have kept them close, and kept them sober. Once the booze ran out, these bandits would have moved on, and the truck-driver would never be able to find them again. No, this group of brigands is expendable. They were left here to be a nuisance to us. In two or three days, they'd be sober and hungry, and would have hunted for food until they ran into one of our patrols. They'd die, but we'd waste some ammo, and waste some time, checking they weren't part of an even bigger assault."

"How can they expect to win if they just throw away soldiers like that?" Jo-Jo asked.

"It's all part of some bigger plan, that same plan which has sent the larger, more organised groups down to the south. The mortar team wasn't here. Those two *aren't* expendable, but they're useless without a mortar to fire. Let's assume they're going to collect another, and see if we can follow the truck to where."

Ten minutes later, they were back on the road, and back on their bikes.

"I may know where they are," Jean-Luc said. "A place with space for lots of vehicles, yes? There was one, near here. For repairing old trucks which traded across Europe. We collected some axles from there, four years ago."

"It was a trading post?" Mitchell asked.

"A rendezvous and occasional rest site, a day's travel from Armentières."

"Where's that?" MacKay said.

"Not far from the ruins of Lille," Jean-Luc said. "You do not wish to enter Lille. They say the spiders glow at night."

Chapter 6 - Loyalty
Eecke, France

The truck depot was south of Eecke, and was deserted except for a colony of woodpigeons nesting among the steel rafters of the hangar-like warehouse.

"I'm calling it," Mitchell said as a heavy drop of rain fell on the acre-wide concrete vehicle-stand. "We'll stay here for the night. Hamish, you're on wood-gathering detail."

"Nae bother," MacKay said.

"*Oui*, because there will be a woodpile inside," Jean-Luc said.

"Make a fire on the other side of that flatbed crane," Mitchell said. "That'll give us cover if the enemy attack."

"You think they will, sir?" Jo-Jo asked.

"I doubt it," Mitchell said. "But we'll take it in turns to stand watch tonight."

He leaned his bike against the rusting crane. "Now, let's take a look at the delicacies our enemy took as payment. Canned apple, with added vitamins. Canned beef, with extra gravy. I've always read that to mean there's barely any meat."

"It was the best they had," Jo-Jo said.

"It'll save us hunting," Mitchell said. "I can add tea tonight and coffee for breakfast. Satz tea, I'm afraid, but it's real coffee."

"We'll need water," Jo-Jo said.

"There's a forest of wood in there," MacKay said, walking out of the adjoining offices with a stack of split logs. "It's a wee bit damp, but it's dryer than anything we could gather from outside."

"Perfect," Mitchell said, taking out his tubular water bottle. He unrolled the sheath, and refolded it into a cone that slotted atop the opening.

"That's neat," Jo-Jo said. "Did you get that in Twynham?"

"South of Calais, from a guy who ran a vineyard I almost retired to," Mitchell said. "Before the Blackout, he made camping gear. Afterwards..." He trailed into silence, lost in memories. He shook himself free. "I'll go put it outside."

By the time the fire was blazing, they'd refilled their water bottles, Jean-Luc's small saucepan, and the larger steel kettle they found in the depot's office. As the stew begin to simmer, Mitchell stirred the powdered tea into the kettle.

"Did you travel a lot through Europe before the war, sir?" MacKay asked.

"Since the Blackout, yes," Mitchell said. "I was a student before then, and about to drop out. But I got a job carrying a bag for a scientist coming to a conference in Britain. That's how I was stuck here when the lights went out."

"Ah, so you weren't one of the Americans who were on the cruise ships?" MacKay asked.

"Nope. We were in London. Joined the walk south, met the cruise ships at the coast. They came ashore near Bournemouth, and that's why we ended up making that the new capital."

"But you travelled France with my mother," Jean-Luc said. "And my grandfather."

"I did," Mitchell said. "Sometimes hunting criminals. Sometimes hunting for supplies. Molybdenum," he added, as he poured the tea into their water bottles' lid-mugs.

"Is that a toast?" MacKay asked.

"Ah, why not?" Mitchell said. "But it's also the element you need to make the machines to make the graphene filters so you can make this powdered tea. Ended up going to Essen to find it. That's in Germany, but not that far across the border. The third year after the Blackout, I think that was. Not the only reason we went there, but looking back, probably the most important. Yep, I've travelled a bit. Seen a lot of Europe. A lot of Britain. Too often I've seen the darkest side."

"Britain is where a someone can live," Jean-Luc said. "But France is where they can love."

"Love's a double-edged sword, Jean-Luc," Mitchell said. "It cuts twice as deep when it's lost."

"Did you lose someone, sir?" Jo-Jo asked.

"Yep. Or the option on someone," Mitchell said. "Ah, it's complicated, but love always is. What about you, Hamish, what's your story? How did you end up in uniform?"

"I came south for the weather, sir," he said. "No, I'm serious. You don't know how bleak the northern winters can be. Up there, the sun sets before it's risen. And I had to spend most of the winters sitting up with my nan waiting for the spaceships to return."

"What spaceships?" Jean-Luc asked. "Are these piloted by little green men?"

"She said they were blue," Hamish said. "She knew her engines, though. Taught me everything. Kept three wind turbines going. Built a fourth herself. *And* kept four electric vans on the road. She converted five more electric engines to power our fishing boats. We'd drive the fish right to the garrison in Thurso. From when I was thirteen, I drove there myself. Last winter, that's where I saw the job advertised. They wanted drivers for the reclamation yard. Da didn't want me to go. Nan said I had to see the world."

"And what do you think of it now you've seen some of it?" Jo-Jo asked.

"That, despite the dark, I'd rather be home in m'own bed," MacKay said.

"What was the job advertising?" Mitchell asked.

"Easy work, high pay," MacKay said. "My nan said every job did. The garrison commander wrote a letter saying he'd seen me drive, but I still had to do a test when I got south. They had me share a room with three others. Filthy, it was. Smoke everywhere. Sutherland might be dark, but the air is so sweet you barely need to eat. Oh, and the food they gave us? Meat boiled grey, and tatties baked black. Have you no heard of a balanced plate?"

"This was with the army?" Jean-Luc asked.

"They said we were civilians, though the boss answered to the navy," MacKay said. "In the end, there was no driving. We stripped old tanks down to the bolts. Sometimes they arrived with their guns, sometimes even with ammo. A different team tested the guns. I wouldn't have minded doing that. I wouldn't have minded taking the tanks apart, if I'd had my own room."

"You didn't get on with your co-workers?" Jo-Jo asked.

"They weren't too bad. But the boss was a real numpty called Stevens who went on about restoring the empire, and the monarchy, and how France used to be British."

"Ha! England used to be French," Jean-Luc said. "But that was before we got rid of those parasitic royals."

"By guillotining them, right?" Jo-Jo said. "And didn't you go on to chop off millions of other heads? It was called The Terror, wasn't it?"

"*Oui, oui,* but then came Napoleon, and the first impartial code of laws."

"Except he reintroduced slavery in the French colonies, then tried to conquer Europe," Jo-Jo said.

"History is complicated," Jean-Luc said.

"That's what Stevens said," MacKay said. "He used to lecture us every single night. We'd go to the pub first, but two pints only, assuming you could drink an entire two pints of that swill. Then we'd have to listen to him witter on about his new empire. He had his bruisers make sure no one left. He said we were soldiers in his new loyal brigade, and soldiers needed to know the *real* history."

"The Loyal Brigade?" Mitchell asked, his copper's brain dragging him back from what-if dreams of life in a vineyard. "And you said he was calling himself Stevens?"

"Aye."

"Stevens is dead," Mitchell said. "And so are the Loyal Brigade. Nasty gang of tub-thumping separatists who tried to intimidate their way to a ballot-box victory. They fled an arrest warrant, and died at a service station on the outskirts of London. Stevens is dead, but maybe one of his people got away and decided to use the name. That sounds like something to look into. Ah. How's that stew?"

"Hope it tastes better than it looks," Jo-Jo said.

"Can't be worse than what I got at the reclamation yard," MacKay said.

"Will we be getting tanks soon, then, sir?" Jo-Jo asked.

"Not unless you fancy towing them by bike," Mitchell said. "Fuel is the new shortage. We lost most of our biodiesel when the leadership of the Railway Company went rogue. What we've got left, we need for the ships we've already converted, and for the train running through the Channel Tunnel. With so many of our resources directed towards war, we'll need some of those crops for fodder. No, if we're going to put tanks in the field, we'll have to rely on American imports. That'll be a very limited supply until we can build a few dozen fuel-freighters. We might get a few tanks to the front this summer. But where would we send them? Our enemy doesn't have a capital to capture, or a border to defend. It doesn't have farms or grain silos, or a civilian population. But it does have an oil well, if we can figure out where that is." He reached into his pocket, and took out his pen and notepad. "Tell me more about this guy who called himself Stevens."

17th December

Chapter 7 - Zero-Hours Soldier
Kemmel, Belgium

The storm began at midnight, rattling the rafters, shaking the sheet metal walls, and making sleep nearly impossible. Just before dawn, the sky calmed, and the raucous avian exodus began. Within a minute of the first coo, every pigeon was awake and flying for the door. Feathers fell like rain, as Mitchell and his team went from asleep to alert, dashing to the doorway to look for danger.

"It's nothing," Mitchell said. "They're just early risers."

"It's stopped raining," MacKay said. "I'll stoke the fire."

"No, leave it," Mitchell said. "We're up and so is the sun. We'll leave now, and stop early for lunch. Bring some of the firewood, though."

With the tyre-marks gone, and the storm having ripped an armada of branches from the trees, the trail wasn't easy to find and was twice as easy to lose. When they reached an old road marker welcoming them to Belgium, he stopped. Not because of the border, but the rusting wreck blocking the road.

"There's no way they drove down *this* road," Mitchell said. "How far are we from the trade routes?"

"There are two, both within a half day's drive," Jean-Luc said. "One follows the coast through Belgium and the Netherlands before turning east through Germany. The other is far to the south of us. It doesn't branch until it is safely beyond Lille."

"Then we'll continue the hunt until midday before heading for Dunkirk," Mitchell said.

"Not the farm?" Jo-Jo asked.

"Not Belgium?" Jean-Luc asked.

"We've got to let Twynham know what we've found," Mitchell said. "The garrison in Dunkirk should have a working radio. The sloop certainly will. Go stand by that border-marker, Hamish, and I'll take a photo you can send it to your nan."

"Are you serious, sir?"

"Life goes on, even now," Mitchell said. "From what you said, she sounds like a woman who'd appreciate a picture proving you *have* seen some of the world. Not sure how we'll print it, mind you. But we'll worry about that when we get back to our lines."

An hour later, they picked up a new trail. The tracks didn't match those left near the farm, though they'd been left by a large-tyred vehicle, without any hoof prints or bicycle treads indicating they belonged to a towed cart.

They followed the tracks for two kilometres, until the trail took an abrupt turn into a derelict campsite. Mitchell hurriedly waved his team towards a row of stunted trees, though they offered little cover.

Originally, the campground had been clipped from farmland and ringed by tall trees. Beyond that sylvan screen, near the road, was a broad parking lot, a smattering of service buildings, and the rotting roofs of a chalet-village.

"Leave the bikes," Mitchell whispered, looking up and down a road that was barely wider than a tractor. "Something very big, with double-tyres, carved a canyon in the grass opposite the narrow entrance. Very big. Must be their tanker. Was it arriving? Was it leaving? We'll steal it if we can, blow it up if we can't. Okay? On me."

He jogged inside, sheltering behind the rainbow of recycling bins taking up a house-sized plot just inside the gate. By the entrance was a tree stump, felled within an inch of the ground. The tree itself had been dragged into the car park. While there was barely any sawdust, the stump still had a dull yellow glow. Chopped down within the last month, but not within the last few days.

"Car park's empty, sir," MacKay said.

"Yep, seen that," Mitchell whispered. "Do you see the bollards blocking the footpaths? The tanker couldn't have driven further into the campsite. It was here, but it's gone. Doesn't mean all the enemy are. There are crows circling overhead. We'll head towards them. Jo-Jo and Hamish, take that path between the chalets to the east. We'll take that main path."

"What's the signal, sir?"

"For trouble? Scream, shout, or shoot," Mitchell said.

As they neared, the crows took flight, leaving their breakfast unfinished. Two bodies lay on the wooden deck outside a chalet. Their tongues and eyes had become the birds' breakfast.

"Dead a day or so," Mitchell said, using his boot to nudge a hand from which two fingers had been pecked to the bone. He gave a whistle, then beckoned Jo-Jo and Hamish over. "See anything?"

"Appears empty, sir," Jo-Jo said.

"Double-check," he said. "Jean-Luc, go with them."

Mitchell bent over the bodies, and used his knife to probe the clothing. The cause of death was obvious: a gunshot wound to the skull. Both victims were dressed in looted rags, scavenged well over a month ago and not washed since. Each had a crescent-moon brand on their left hand, indelibly marking them as being unwilling recruits to the caliphate. They hadn't been given black jackets, or even looted rifles, but broad-bladed knives still hung from their belts.

He checked the photographs he'd taken in the orchard after the ambush, but the mortar-team's boots were in far better repair than the split-seam, string-laced trainers these two wore. He took photographs of the bodies, but only with a pro-forma interest, before heading to the nearest of the cabins.

Someone had slept in there. Perhaps for a week. Perhaps longer. Certainly long enough to have built a box-stove from a car exhaust and drainpipe. Rags were wedged in the gaps around the window frame, while the broken pane had been covered with neatly sawn plyboard. The saw still lay in the corner, next to a broom and pan.

For bedding, the squatter had removed the old mattress, sleeping on a nest of folded clothes, beneath equally old sheets. Probably salvaged nearby rather than brought with them. Whatever they'd eaten, there were no signs of the food. He made his way outside, and next door, where he found the rifle crates inside a mushroom-clad cabin. The crates were empty. He took more photographs, but returned outside when he heard his team approach.

"There's no one here, sir," Jo-Jo said.

"But there was," Mitchell said. "Someone was sleeping in that cabin. One person. Here between a week and a month. In that cabin are empty rifle crates. I want to check the other cabins nearby and confirm this guard was here alone."

Thirty minutes later, Mitchell walked his team back to the car park. "One guard," he said. "One guard was left behind."

"The empty crates contained one hundred rifles," Jean-Luc said. "If there were four simultaneous attacks the night before yesterday, and if each employed around eight assault rifles, where are the other sixty?"

"Do you think there's been another attack?" Jo-Jo asked.

"Could be, or there will be another soon," Mitchell said. He paused to take a photograph of a deep wheel rut at the car park's edge. "This was a staging ground. A rendezvous. Someone lived here for at least a week and maybe a month, so it might have been used for more than one attack. One person. No bedding. They had to make their own stove with what salvage they could find nearby."

"Is that important?" MacKay asked.

"At some point, somewhere, they had time to find those black coats, the trucks, the tyres, and the rifles. They could have found a few sleeping bags or blankets. That they didn't bring any with them means they were either short of space, or worried about weight when they came west. Probably," he added. "It could just be that the guard lost their pack in some landslide, or storm, or when chased by a pack of cats."

"People are heavy," Jo-Jo said. "This is why they left the foot-soldiers behind. They didn't want to waste fuel driving those people around."

"Or feeding them," Mitchell said. "Food is heavy, too. Our enemy has invented zero-hours soldiering, hiring cannon fodder for one battle at a time."

"Where did the truck driver sleep?" MacKay asked.

"Could be in a cabin we've not found, but probably in their vehicle," Mitchell said. "Good point, though. The guard was here for between a week and a month. The trucks were only here for a day or two. All of which tells us this plan was put in place at least a month ago."

"But that would be just after the attack on Calais failed," Jo-Jo said. "They'd have needed ages to plan it."

"Months," Mitchell said. "It's another reason we'll win. Our enemy, our real enemy, devises a way to make our lives a whole lot more miserable, but then comes up with a contingency in case it fails. Superficially, that sounds like a recipe for success, except it divides their limited resources, all but ensuring eventual failure. And with each failure, they have fewer people, fewer weapons, fewer supplies."

"That's why they're nicking it from us," MacKay said.

"Why'd they kill those two, then?" Jo-Jo asked. "They were killed by their own people, weren't they?"

"Executed. Shot between the eyes," Mitchell said. "They weren't the mortar team. Maybe they were stray renegades who heard the engines and followed the trucks here. Or it could be they were too sick to be useful. Both had scurvy, and a distinct lack of teeth." He picked up his bike.

"Are we going west?" Jean-Luc asked.

"Not just yet," Mitchell said, pointing to tyre ruts left in the sodden field on far side of the campground. "The big truck went north. Let's assume it's a fuel tanker. A diesel tanker can carry about twenty-five thousand litres. A truck should manage a quarter of a litre per kilometre. The map says we're near Kemmel and about eighty kilometres east-southeast of Calais. Assume the trucks each take a winding route to their target zones and call it a hundred and fifty kilometres. Same again coming back, and it's three hundred. That's seventy-five litres per truck per attack. Seven is the greatest number of simultaneous attacks so far."

"Basically, it's a lot of fuel still left to be used," Jo-Jo said. "What are they going to do with it?"

"Let's see if we can follow it and find out," Mitchell said. "A vehicle like that would prefer wider roads, but it'll need strong bridges. So that's where we'll head next."

They lost the trail two kilometres to the north. Instead of stopping, Jean-Luc accelerated. "Ypres," he said.

"What about it?" MacKay asked.

"The Essex Farm Cemetery Bridge over the Ieperlee canal," Jean-Luc replied. "The canal often floods, so there are only three crossings we maintain. The nearest is by the old military cemetery."

Mitchell dropped back to the rear, no longer looking at the trees for broken branches, but looking above them for departing birds.

The N38 was wide enough for a fuel tanker. It would have been wide enough for four, except that the easternmost lane was stacked with a wall of rust, bracken, and the occasional nest. But the bridge over the Ieperlee canal was gone.

"It was here last year," Jean-Luc said, gingerly walking to the very edge of the cracked asphalt, and peering down at the muddy river below. "The bridge was here."

"It's not now," MacKay said, leaning over even further than Jean-Luc.

"Get back from the edge," Mitchell said. "Do you see those cracks on the roadway? The entire structure is unstable."

"Did the enemy blow the bridge?" Jo-Jo asked.

"No, this was the weather," Mitchell said, walking his bike to the side, and looking down. "The canal's burst its banks a few times. You can tell from the pattern of undergrowth down there. The bridge-supports weren't built to be submerged, which is why they were built back here, on dry ground. Flood, freeze, and thaw did the damage. But was that enough to collapse the bridge? Can you see a truck down in the canal?"

"You say step back, you say go forward," Jean-Luc muttered. "*Non.* Nothing recent."

Mitchell leaned his bike against the rusting guardrail and took out his monocular. Here, the highway ran east-west across the canal which ran almost north-south. Across the bridge sprawled a low-rise industrial zone. The ancient city lay on the other side of the canal, and to the south, but was hidden from view. "It could be that vibrations from very heavy traffic were the last straw," he said. "I can't see anything of interest over there. Jean-Luc?"

"There is something of interest to someone everywhere," he said. "But the canal is of most interest to our people. The canal links to the Yser, which links to Nieuwpoort."

"Is that important?" MacKay asked.

"It would have been," Mitchell said.

"And it will be again," Jean-Luc said. "Nieuwpoort was famous for its many marinas, built inland, along an estuary shielded from the worst of the Atlantic weather. A farming village had been re-established last spring. Before the bandits swept in."

"It's the next viable harbour north of Dunkirk," Mitchell said, putting away his monocular. "In Belgium, there was a coastal tram. The plan was to lay rail along the coastal road in France, and so link up with that old tram. We'd have a train running along the coast, and boats running along the canals. But that was before. If the tanker came over this bridge, it didn't return. Where are the next bridges?"

"For people, there are three within an hour's walk across the canal," Jean-Luc said. "But they are covered in wrecks abandoned during the Great Flight. A cart would have to go north or south at least five kilometres. A larger vehicle? It would have to travel much further."

Mitchell walked back along the bridge. "The storm's washed away any tracks. Assuming they were ever here. I'm calling it. We're heading for Dunkirk. We'll stop for lunch along the way."

Chapter 8 - Know Thy Enemy
Ypres, Belgium

An hour later, they'd lit a cooking fire inside an old barn, where the roof would disperse the smoke and the rafters were high enough they wouldn't catch fire. While the water boiled, Mitchell watched the puddles grow and merge in the yard outside.

"How far is Dunkirk?" he asked.

"Sixty kilometres," Jean-Luc said.

"We'll wait until the storm ends," Mitchell said. "What's that you're reading, Hamish?"

"A book I found in that campsite," MacKay said. "It's called *Absolute Worth in the Post-Productive Society*."

"By Andre Lidnitz," Mitchell said. "That's the Free Peoples' foundational doctrine."

MacKay dropped the book as if it might be infectious.

"You should give it a glance," Jo-Jo said. "Know your enemy and all that."

"The Free Peoples are butchers," MacKay said. "They're no better than the knights or the emir's killers."

"First time I tried to read that was on the flight to Britain," Mitchell said. "I gave up after the first chapter. That was just a few days before the Blackout."

"This?" MacKay asked, picking the book up again.

"The original was a much, much longer volume," Mitchell said. "It was the bestseller at the time. Everyone was talking about it."

"I didn't know the Free Peoples were around before the Blackout," MacKay said.

"They weren't," Mitchell said. "Lidnitz was an economist from Austria, who worked in America, and was writing about the Great Recession's impact on Greece. His theory was that those with the greatest intrinsic worth to society, like teachers, nurses, soldiers, and so on, didn't possess any of the wealth because they didn't directly create it. Without them, it would be impossible for the rich to get richer. Bankers, tech-gurus, and the landlords. He suggested a complete overhaul of the tax system to better redistribute wealth. Higher wages for some, higher taxes for the rest."

"What's the catch?" MacKay asked. "Because that sounds reasonable. How did that turn them into stone-cold murderers?"

"Some people only need the thinnest excuse," Mitchell said. "Lidnitz was just one of the many post-Keynesian economists who cropped up in the years between the collapse of the Soviet Union and the Blackout. What eventually became the Free Peoples was a loose political network in Southern Europe, with a few elected office holders in Italy, Greece, and the Balkans. After the Blackout, as best we can tell, the ideas got twisted, and used as a way to identify whom to blame for the famines and chaos. That led to piracy and theft hiding behind revolutionary rhetoric. What language is it printed in?"

"English," MacKay said.

"Were there many other copies?" Mitchell asked.

"A few dozen," MacKay said.

"All in English?"

"Aye, sir."

"Interesting. The enemy must have hoped they could distribute them in Britain after they broke through the Channel Tunnel."

"The water's boiling," Jo-Jo said. "Did you say there was coffee?"

Mitchell took the tin from his bag. "Here you go, the last of my supply." He walked over to a cracked, mud-smeared window, but all he could see were raindrops pattering against the pane. He went to the door, but the visibility was barely any better. "We might be staying here a while," he said.

"The stay-behind foot-soldiers we killed in that farm weren't Free Peoples, were they, sir?" Jo-Jo asked.

"Hard to say," Mitchell said. "At this stage, I'm not sure it matters which group they were originally with. There are a few larger, organised bands in the south, but most of their cohesion has gone. The brigands are scattered across France and beyond. They're desperate and starving. It's no wonder they'd volunteer to join a night-time assault against a bastion in exchange for a couple of meals and something to wash away their regrets."

"Who's recruiting the foot-soldiers?" Jo-Jo asked.

"I want to know how they got our rifles," MacKay said. "Have they captured much of our equipment?"

"If you ask the navy, they'll say no, but they'd be lying," Mitchell said. "A few weeks ago, I found some rifles which had come out of the armoury at Chetaïbi. That's on the North African coast in what was once Algeria. The emir's people burned it to the ground five years ago."

"Was that a big city?" MacKay asked.

"It was just a harbour-village and trading hub for fishing fleets and scavengers," Mitchell said. "But a ferry ran from there up to Sardinia, and then to Montpellier on the French coast. From Montpellier, you could travel the trade road up through France, and so to Britain."

"Not if you were in a hurry," Jean-Luc said. "It was a slow journey, and an even slower ferry. They used these magnificent sailing ships, three-masted xebecs, that had been built for a movie. Three ships. Ah, they were glorious."

"You travelled on one?" MacKay asked.

"Once, when I was much younger," Jean-Luc said. "The journey took all summer. It was so hot, the sea boiled, but those ships flew across the waves."

"So how come it was a slow journey?" MacKay asked.

"The ferries would only travel when full," Jean-Luc said. "Even with the waiting, it was still quicker than travelling across the Pyrenees, and far safer than trying to find passage through the mountains further east."

"That's why the emir targeted the harbour in Chetaïbi," Mitchell said.

"We should have done more to protect it," Jean-Luc said.

"A sentiment that's true for absolutely everywhere," Mitchell said.

"Did we recapture the harbour?" MacKay asked.

"Those terrorists didn't stay," Mitchell said. "They destroyed the village and the piers, murdered every living soul, and burned the ships. That's what they do. What they've always done. The emir's caliphate is little more than a roaming band of killers that moved up and down the African coast of the Mediterranean destroying everything they couldn't loot."

"I thought that was the Free Peoples," MacKay said.

"*Non*, the Free Peoples were wrecking the *European* coast of the inland sea," Jean-Luc said.

"And the coast of Britain," Mitchell said. "When they still had ships, they attacked us, so we chased them to France, Portugal, and back into the Med. When we found farmers and fishers working a small harbour, we'd reinforce them, supply them, trade with them. We sent doctors and medicine, food and farming equipment."

"But only so your ships didn't have to carry such great quantities of supplies," Jean-Luc said.

"I'm not saying we were entirely altruistic," Mitchell said. "But right from the beginning, some of us understood that, to ensure our long-term recovery, we had to look beyond the horizon. The plan, until last year, had been to drive a railroad from Calais down to the Mediterranean garrison at Montpellier. Some of it would run on old tracks, some on new railways built atop the old roads. The route came down to which bridges were standing."

"It is always the bridges," Jean-Luc said. "Old bridges and new craters."

"But if we can run supplies to the Med by train," Mitchell said, "we can keep a fleet there indefinitely. We can free up some transport ships for use as troop carriers, and others can be converted into warships. I won't say that a rail-link would have stopped the terrorists, but it would have pushed the problem further east."

"So that's why there is all this fighting in the south?" MacKay asked. "We're trying to build a railroad, and the terrorists want to stop us."

"Nah," Jo-Jo said. "They're fighting there because that's where the two armies slammed into each other."

"Why-ever they're there now, that is not where the future will be made," Jean-Luc said. "The European Union will reclaim the Atlantic coast, and then move east. Germany, Poland, Ukraine. There is good farming land there. Very good. We have twenty thousand settlers ready to sail tomorrow, and can have another hundred thousand at the docks within a month. But those new communities need a market to sell their surplus, and access to merchants selling what a farmer can't make. The Mediterranean? It is a dream."

"It's cause and effect," Mitchell said. "It's inertia. It's the same path of least resistance we've been forced along since the Blackout. Take the Free Peoples. The military wing of their original line-up was a group of human traffickers who worked the Africa-Europe route."

"I thought you said it was this economist," MacKay said, waving the book.

"That's how the butchers gained political legitimacy when they merged with groups in the Aegean," Mitchell said. "But before then, these criminals took over Gibraltar, and used the Rock to capture or sink any ships travelling through the strait. We didn't know about this until we sent an expedition to traverse the Med in search of oil fields in the Mid-East. Our fleet was made up of sailing boats. All but one was blown out of the water. For the enemy it was a great victory. It spurred them into switching to piracy, raiding up and down the coast. But they, too, were using sailing ships and outboard motors."

"Didn't we have any warships?" MacKay asked.

"Not back then," Mitchell said. "They'd been destroyed in the Blackout. We did have cruise ships. We picked one with the best engines, squeezed every last drop of diesel we could find into her. But a warship needs armour and weapons."

"Britain used to make a lot of those," MacKay said.

"Yep, but most of the factories were smouldering craters," Mitchell said. "The exception was a shell manufactory for Britain's Challenger tanks. There were seven MBTs at the harbour. We stripped two guns from the tanks, rebuilding the turrets on the cruise-ship's deck. The tank's armour was bolted onto the ship's super-structure. The cabins were filled with shells, and the ship was sent to war. You'll win no prizes for guessing that it wasn't a success."

"I thought we had a garrison in Gibraltar now," MacKay said.

"We do. We chased the enemy away, but we didn't defeat them," Mitchell said. "We lost the cruise ship, too. So we needed another. Fuel was running scarce, and we were already mining coal for electricity, so it seemed a sensible stop-gap to convert the next cruise-warship to burn coal. And then the next. We stripped more guns from more tanks, and put together a fleet armed with 120mm rifled cannons. That became the new standard size."

"It still is," Jo-Jo said. "That's the calibre of the artillery we had at the farmhouse."

"Right. Inertia," Mitchell said. "Because now we had a fleet, we needed a second shell factory, so we made more 120mm shells. When we started making new guns, we made them to match that calibre. It's a vicious circle which leads us to here. Semi-automatic rifles and 120mm artillery aren't the best weapons to fight skirmishers in frozen fields, but it's what we have, so it's what we give our conscript army. All because the Free Peoples destroyed that fleet of sailing ships which went looking for oil."

"But if it hadn't been them, it would have been someone else," Jo-Jo said.

"That sounds like the kind of comment they'd print in the letters page of the newspaper," MacKay said.

"I mean that even if things had gone differently in the Med, we'd still be fighting the knights," Jo-Jo said. "They came out of Poland, right?"

"Probably. Originally," Mitchell said. "The Knights of Saint Sebastian claim to be a secret society of warriors who've been defending Christendom for a thousand years. They're big on crusades and crucifixions. They claim they use blades because it purifies the soul, but that's only because they ran out of bullets a decade ago. The knights coalesced in Poland, and recruited as they went east, which is why their mythology blends Orthodox and Catholic, to which they've added a dash of Norse."

"And the emir's people are from Libya?" Jo-Jo asked.

"Not really. Back in the long ago gone-before, a terrorist group managed to seize control of Iraq for a bloody minute. Politics kicked in before they were properly wiped out. The survivors spread through Africa and the Mid-East. This lot are formed out of some of those offshoots. They're about as Islamic as the knights are Christian, but they've stolen a similar pseudo-theological veneer."

"Isn't there oil around there?" MacKay said. "Maybe that's where our enemy is getting it from."

"Maybe, but the old wells all caught fire during the Blackout, which truly was misnamed in that corner of the world," Mitchell said. "What makes the emir's caliphate so dangerous are the coups. They're averaging about one a year as an internal battle goes on over which archangel visited the first emir, but the coups don't distract them from their wider mission to convert or kill every last person on the planet."

"Numpties," MacKay said. "That's what my nan calls them. If she doesn't think anyone's listening, she calls them something a lot worse."

"Sounds about right," Mitchell said. "But they're not our problem."

"My feet would beg to differ," Jo-Jo said.

"You saw those two crow-pecked bodies today," Mitchell said. "The other bandits will be in no better health. They've chased off or killed the few farmers who worked these lands. There's not much forage in winter, so those who can't hunt will starve."

"Still seems like they'll be a problem until then," Jo-Jo said.

"The knights were a real nuisance up in the Baltic," Mitchell said. "The emir controlled the land crossings between Africa and Europe, while the Free Peoples harassed the Mediterranean. But they were still just bandits until a few years ago. Someone has equipped them, organised them, and sent them to Calais. That's who we're after. The criminal with the refinery and oil wells, who trained the drivers and mechanics, and who controls the arsenal with the mortars and rifles. The crook who encouraged these killers to wipe out all the communities between here and the steppe, and who then persuaded those same killers to leave their lands, and come here. Find them, stop them, and peace can resume. Sounds easy, right?" He took his coffee, and went to watch the rain.

"Yes," Jo-Jo said, coming to stand next to him.

"Yes what?" Mitchell said.

"Yes, it sounds easy. How are we going to do it? How are we going to find their big boss?"

"Same way you stop all criminals," Mitchell said. "By following the evidence."

18th December

Chapter 9 - Fire and Beer
Woesten, Belgium

Belgium twinkled with frost when dawn arrived. The previous day's tempest had finally ceased, though it had brought dusk early, and kept them trapped in the barn. Above, clouds slowly gathered, speaking of another coming storm. Mitchell sipped his cold tea; there was no coffee left, and no point wasting time with a fire.

"We should have nabbed more food from that farmhouse," MacKay said.

"It would be extra weight," Jean-Luc said. "It is only sixty kilometres. We'll reach Dunkirk before lunch."

"Dinner," Mitchell said. "If last night's frost was any heavier, I'd call it snow. We'll take our time. Don't want to break a leg."

"After forty kilometres, we'll reach the trade road," Jean-Luc said. "I know it so well, we could cycle backwards."

"Is that even possible?" Jo-Jo asked, looking at her bike.

"*Bien sûr*," Jean-Luc said. "I shall prove it."

"Not until we're close enough to the garrison we can carry you the rest of the way," Mitchell said.

"Is it a big place?" MacKay asked.

"Dunkirk? It was," Jean-Luc said. "It will be again. For now, it is just a military garrison. But we shall return and rebuild, like we did with the Drummond-Dumond farm, like we will with Nieuwpoort. We will rebuild along the trade routes close to the Atlantic. If the navy build their railway, we will rebuild south, too. We will begin with the vineyards and orchards close to the roads. A few days repair work will provide a small harvest which can be sold in Twynham for a living until the fields can be re-ploughed. It is what we did. What we shall do again. Each new farm is built that little bit further from Calais. Each older farm becomes that little bit further from the frontier, a little bit safer, a little bit more attractive to a settler, and so Europe was rebuilt, until the barbarians came. And so it shall be rebuilt again."

"It's a bonny dream," MacKay said, "but my nan still dreams they'll build spaceships."

Mitchell finished his tea, stowed his mug, and picked up his bike. Lost in thought, he fell in at the rear as they slowly cycled north and west. Despite the chill rising from the ground, the talk of farms and vineyards reminded him of an almost perfect summer's day at a vineyard not so far away. Almost perfect because he'd had a runaway murderer tied up in the cellar. The killer had run to France, thinking he'd not be pursued. No such luck.

That was Henry Mitchell's first time at the vineyard near Rouen, and it was almost perfect. Almost. It had given him a glimpse of a potential future where he didn't wear a gun at his hip. But he had a daughter at home, and a criminal to take to court.

In the years since, he'd returned to the vineyard on the rare occasions when time allowed, but it was that near-perfect day he allowed himself to recall. The nearly stultifying heat. The cool stream. The humming bees. The sweet vines, sweeter wine, and sweetest lips.

Jacques was dead. Murdered. Butchered. The vineyard had been destroyed. Only a shadow of his dreams remained, leaving him uncertain whether that potential future was simply a mirage. He'd not had many dreams growing up. Since the Blackout, he'd mostly had nightmares. Since he'd rescued her, he'd kept his hopes for Anna. Too busy pumping life into the justice system, he'd had little time to pursue personal happiness. But with Jacques, in that vineyard, in that moment, he'd caught a glimpse of an alternate future. Now, even that sweet summer memory was turned as bitter as the grave, as cold as death, as hollow as the revenge he had sworn to take.

"Sir?" Jo-Jo called, raising a hand to point up at the dark flecks circling beneath an increasingly dense cloud.

"Crows," Mitchell said. "I see 'em. Where are we, Jean-Luc?"

"Approaching Hoogstade," Jean-Luc said. "We are still in Belgium, and halfway to the trade route."

The buildings grew closer together. Collapsed barns became ruined cottages. Ahead, a church spire rose above the young forest. Overgrown fields changed into wild gardens in which an occasional stone sundial or plastic sunshade emerged from the encroaching wilderness. Saplings grew in the driveways of the escape-the-city mansions, while sporadic mud-patch lawns indicated only pigs lived here now. Pigs and crows.

The birds flocked above, atop, and inside a cement-slab warehouse, stained black with soot. The inferno had been contained by the concrete walls, though the gate to the old loading dock had warped into a prison-bar barrier.

They stopped on the road by the cracked driveway leading into the factory.

"Wait here," Mitchell said, and took out his phone. "Clear off," he said to the well-fed crows. Only the nearest listened, and they were too full to flap more than a few paces. The rest, inside, continued their feast. Mitchell took a photograph, and another, stopping when he had the answer to the most pressing question.

"How many, sir?" Jo-Jo asked.

"Forty to fifty," Mitchell said. "Refugees, not barbarians."

"Are you sure?" she asked.

"There are small bones near the gate," Mitchell said. "The fire began further back. The children were pushed to the gate in the hope, somehow, they might survive." He put the phone away.

"Could this be the work of the tanker crew?" MacKay asked.

"I can't see any tyre tracks on the road," Jo-Jo said.

Mitchell looked down at the storm-rinsed road. "Could be them, or some other stray group. The civilians must have been refugees, making their slow way towards the coast."

"So why were they killed?" MacKay asked.

"They kill those they can't convert," Jean-Luc said. "But converts require feeding. *C'est la guerre.*"

"It's murder," Mitchell said. "That's all. Let's move on."

Except it wasn't *just* murder. There was strategy behind it. Today's refugees were tomorrow's farmers. Without them, there'd be no harvest next year. No new school next decade, no new nation in the decade after. No new army to oppose their advance. This was the enemy's plan, the reason behind the murder and mayhem, and that there was method behind it only made the crime worse.

Dark days made for dark thoughts, and they kept him company as they cycled towards the coast, finally picking up the coastal trade route just across the old border. Yes, it was a dark day, but his heart lightened when he saw the signs for Dunkirk, and brightened when he smelled the sea.

"Where are the patrols?" MacKay asked.

"You've been listening to too much navy propaganda," Jo-Jo said.

"Your navy keep a small garrison at Port du Grand Large," Jean-Luc said. "A very small garrison. Twenty Marines so your government can say the city has not been abandoned. A sloop brings supplies once a week."

"Only twenty?" MacKay said.

"One day it will be as busy as Calais," Jean-Luc said. "It is a day's easy travel from Calais, another day's cycling to Nieuwpoort. We will repair Belgium's coastal tram, extend the line south. In a few years, we will link to Boulogne-Sur-Mer, then Paris, and Montpellier. The Pyrenees and the Alps, Spain and Denmark, Germany and Poland, and beyond. Now, let me tell you how…"

As Jean-Luc waxed poetic on his vision for the future, Mitchell tuned him out. He'd heard the tale before, from Jean-Luc's mother, and from his grandfather. One day, maybe. For now, it was as much science fiction as fantasy. Instead, he watched the ruins.

Dunkirk was on the trade route, yes, but the *road* ran two kilometres inland. For millennia, it had been a coastal conurbation. Before the Blackout, it had been an industrial harbour, a ferry port, and a marina for weekend sailors. Since the Blackout, it had become a fishing hub and urban mine. The number of professional fisherfolk had actually increased since the Blackout, though that spoke more to the productivity of lost technology than to a post-apocalyptic population boom.

It was too close to Calais, and to Dover, to compete for settlers. When the barbarians came, the fisherfolk, like in Nieuwpoort and elsewhere, had got in their boats and sailed to safety. Before the Blackout, the population had stood close to a hundred thousand, while at its modern peak, two years ago, a hundred families had occupied the better-built apartments close to the sea. But each spring, the population of fisherfolk was boosted by younger scavengers who'd grown up in the crowded refugee-quarters of cities like Dover.

For them, Dunkirk was a crumbling city with relatively few dangers where they could practice the art of searching for hidden treasures. It was where they learned how to tell copper from steel. Where they learned to find preserved clothing and shoes, rubber and rope, tools and trinkets which could be sold in the markets of Britain, or to the walled enclaves of Europe.

A new warning had been added to the old road signs: *Chien Sauvage*! Over that had been scrawled the first line from the Gospel of St Sebastian. Not in Latin, but what Mitchell thought was German. He took a photograph, mulling over the implications. The Free Peoples translated their message of equality through pain, while the knights stuck to the almost incomprehensible dead language of Latin. Were they evolving? He could hope for a schism and civil war, but a more accessible version of their mythology risked it spreading on the other side of the sea.

And because he was worrying about that, he almost didn't see the tyre marks.

Chapter 10 - White Circles
Dunkirk, France

The road dipped low, while another passed overhead. The local scavengers had abandoned any attempt to clear the mud accumulated in the underpass's dip, and instead had laid planks to be used as a walkway, but those hadn't been wide enough for the truck whose tyres had dug deep into the drift-dirt.

"One set," Mitchell said. "One vehicle, but two sets of tyres. One smaller than the other."

"Like that truck they used to attack us at the bastion," MacKay said.

"Could be," Mitchell said, taking a photograph before swiping back to the evidence he'd gathered near the Drummond-Dumond farm. "Ah, yes it— Oh. The battery's gone. Never mind. Yes, I think this is the same truck."

"Do you think they attacked the garrison here last night?" Jo-Jo asked.

"Could be," Mitchell said. "Could be they plan to do it tonight. There's one set of tracks heading into the city. If they've left, they used a different route. How far are we from the garrison?"

"A kilometre," Jean-Luc said. He pointed up to the bridge above their heads. "But to go north, we have to go west, because the bridge at the end of that road is at the bottom of the canal."

"The enemy knew that, so used this road," Mitchell said. "We'll follow."

They cycled on, until the road crossed an old railway line. Either side, on the tracks, were empty freight wagons.

"We're continuing on foot," Mitchell said. "Hide the bikes behind the freight wagons. They won't have driven the truck right to the garrison, and a mortar won't need line of sight. We'll find the truck first, and then we'll find them."

A garrison of twenty Marines sounded like a promising target, except it was a token force, dug in, and well armed. One mortar-team wouldn't dig them out. No, the only viable target was the sloop which brought supplies. The enemy would have to wait until it was at anchor before launching the shells. There was no fixed schedule, since the captain was at the whim of the general in Calais and the admiral in

Dover. If the sloop was the target, the mortar team would have to wait, and so their mode of attack had changed.

He'd been promised radio. He'd been promised flares. He'd been promised motorbikes, thermal imaging, and more troops. In fairness, so had the army, and he, at least, had been given first pick of the grenades, and second choice from Isaac's personal armoury. Anything with a circuit was viewed with suspicion, and implicitly forbidden for so long that it had been broken, scrapped, or lost to damp. Back in Britain, old technology was being sought, stockpiled, rebuilt, and re-invented. One day soon, some of it would find its way to the army. One day. Until then, and here and now, it was impossible to communicate with the garrison at the marina until they were within earshot.

Jean-Luc led them away from the main roads, and through an identikit suburb of mews houses where the window and door frames had been removed. On the front walls were painted a Franglais list of salvage to be found inside. Most of the lists on most of the houses were crossed through. Beyond that development, they came to a dismantled suburb of brick pyramids, then a supermarket parking lot filled with car parts. Like stacking bricks, dismantling old cars was a pre-graduation chore for every new class of teenage scavengers, but there was simply too much surplus steel to feed the scrapyard furnaces.

A forest grew beyond that, overtaking the rubble of a suburb ravaged by fire. Jean-Luc led them through, and back to a road which, until recently, had been kept clear of debris. There, they found the tyre tracks again. And on Avenue de Stade, just beyond the bridge over the canal, they found the truck: a high-clearance dump-bed onto which a crude cabin had been affixed. The cab was boxy, while the paintwork was recent and flaking. Mostly red, except for a white circle on the cabin walls.

It was parked outside a 1960s building with a 1990s extension, millennial cladding, and 2020s damage. Vertical signage now read *Cl-ique*, but the missing letters were easy to guess, indicating this five-storey building must have once been a medical centre.

"I hear no one," Jean-Luc whispered, as they took cover in the undergrowth.

"It's a tall building," Jo-Jo said. "Good place for a sentry."

"Maybe," Mitchell said, looking around until he spied a long-ago fire-charred ruin. "No, there to the southwest. That old fast-food barn is where I'd watch. Easier to escape from than a rooftop. The rubble provides cover, and that entire stretch of parking lot provides a perfect kill-zone between a sentry and the van."

"Do you want me to check?" Jo-Jo asked.

"No. Cover me," Mitchell said. He stood and ran.

They'd been promised flares. They'd been promised radios. They'd been promised an army. Instead they had conscripts a month away from being civilians. They weren't an army. They were a militia. The enemy weren't soldiers; they were murderers. This wasn't war; it was survival, just like every day of the last twenty years.

When he reached the edge of the car park without being shot he slowed his run to a walk, and then changed direction, angling back towards the parked truck. When he reached it, he waved over his team.

Gun raised, he checked the cabin at the back, then the cab, but the vehicle had been left unguarded.

"There's no sentry," Mitchell said. "Hamish, can you disable the truck?"

"Slashing the tyres should do it," the Scotsman said.

"I'd like the option of driving away from here," Mitchell said. "Can you do something a little less permanent? Jean-Luc, Jo-Jo, keep watch while I look around."

The rear cabin was made out of durable plastic moulded to look like slatted wood. The walls had come from a garden shed, or perhaps a summerhouse, but held in place with aluminium brackets bolted to the dump-bed's frame. Each wall had been painted red, but with a rough white circle. On the driver's side, the circle had been filled with the knights' two-bar cross. On the passenger side was the caliphate's Arabic scrawl, while the Free Peoples' unequal sign was painted on the cab. At the rear, there was no sign, and no door, just broken hinges and a ragged curtain. He pulled it down.

Inside was a bric-a-brac of litter: empty cans of British-made food, a few stray bullets, and a lot of discarded clothing. But among the litter were four long crates. Made of durable polymer, their like hadn't been made in two decades. The writing was unfamiliar. Not English, French, or German. He pulled himself up, and into the cabin, hauling open the nearest crate. It was empty, but the foam padding inside gave the shape of what had once been stored there.

He checked the other three crates before jumping back down.

"You finished, Hamish?"

"Aye, sir," he said, holding up a fistful of wires.

"I hope you know how to put those back," he said. "Jean-Luc, lead us towards the garrison. Take it slow. They'll have sentries, but wherever they are, they're sticking together."

"Is it mortars, sir?" Jo-Jo asked.

"Worse," Mitchell said. "Four shoulder-mounted missiles. I'd guess one operator per missile. At least four more hostiles to stand guard. Maybe six, but if there were too many more, they'd have left someone on guard here. MANPADS they used to call these kinds of missiles. They could take out a plane. They could take out a building. They could take out a sloop. That ship has to be their target. They'll need line-of-sight, so we've got to find a rooftop, overlooking the garrison."

Chapter 11 - I Can See Your Ship From Up Here
Dunkirk, France

Dashing from the cover of one building to the next, lurking among the rubble until they were certain a rooftop shadow wasn't a sniper, they navigated the partially cleared ruins. Around a crater, down an alley, over a bridge. North and west they ran, between stacks of bricks, piles of rusting steel, and towers of perished tyres, until they reached open ground.

An acre of close-to-sea scrubland had been marked for development, according to the storm-battered signage covering the high fence. The Dunkirk fisherfolk had turned it into grazing land, with a new stable built from salvaged brick.

"I can hear the sea," Mitchell said. "Where's the garrison?"

"The other side of the apartment-towers," Jean-Luc whispered.

"So you could see it from the apartment roofs?" Mitchell asked, scanning those rooftops with his monocular. The buildings were clustered together in L's and U's. Some three-storey, some seven, separated by car parks and access roads. He counted ten roofs on which the enemy might lurk, but hundreds of windows from which a sentry could stand watch. "Does the garrison sleep in any of those apartments?"

"No one does," Jean-Luc said. "They were stripped long ago. Now they are just used for paint-sword tournaments."

"What's that?" MacKay asked.

"You don't play it in Scotland? You wrap a rag around a stick, dip the rag in paint, and attempt to mark your opponent."

"They'll be inside one of those buildings," Mitchell said. "They've got to wait for the sloop, but it doesn't keep an exact schedule. They could expect to wait for two or three days, so they'll wait inside. One on guard watching the garrison. The rest will be close by, but lurking out of sight. That's our edge. They'll need to move from their den to a sea-facing window to fire their missiles. If we can catch them unawares, we can save the garrison, and the sloop. It'll be the topmost floor, but which building?" He raised the monocular again, scanning the dark windows.

"I'll sneak through to the garrison, sir," Jo-Jo said. "Go warn them."

"Nope," Mitchell said. "If the enemy think they've been discovered, they'll fire the missiles at the compound. If the garrison leave their compound, they'll be an even easier target. I bet the terrorists haven't had much practice with those missiles, but we've got to reduce the risk. Hamish, how long would it take to get that truck working again?"

"Just a few minutes, sir," he said.

"Are you sure?"

"Aye. Nae bother, sir."

"You and Jean-Luc go fetch the truck. Drive it here. Honk the horn. Get their attention. I'll be inside by then. When I hear the truck, I'll throw in a few smoke grenades, and skew their aim. They'll come running out. You three can shoot. Oh, and get clear of the truck once you think they've seen it. You don't want to become a consolation prize for the missiles."

"Which building are they in?" Jo-Jo asked.

"The five-storey U-shaped building, dead ahead," Mitchell said. "It's the biggest, with the most options for alternate exit points."

"So if they aren't all together, they could come out behind us and catch us in a crossfire?" Jo-Jo asked.

"Yep," Mitchell said. "Anyone got a better idea?"

"What if you're wrong about what building they're in?" MacKay asked.

"Improvise," Mitchell said. "When we start shooting, the garrison will come out. So find cover and sing the national anthem at anyone with a gun. Good luck, now go."

As Jean-Luc and Hamish disappeared back into the ruins, Mitchell unslung his carbine and handed it to the sergeant.

"Do you want my rifle, sir?" she asked.

"Nope, you'll need it when you've burned through the spare magazines," he said, handing those over as well. He drew his M1911, and then the suppressor, affixing it to the barrel.

"How long do we wait?" Jo-Jo asked.

"We don't," he said. "Stick on my heels."

He took the long route around the fenced grazing land, using the stables as partial cover, but trusting that, by now, the enemy was only interested in watching the sea. An exhaustingly tense five minutes later, he'd reached the wall of a five-storey building, originally a massive hostel, on Rue des Goulettes. Built in a U around a central car park, its main entrance was in the parking lot, but a ramp led up to the first floor.

"Main entrance is where they'd have the elevator," Mitchell said. "But a building this big will have a fire door at the other side. I'll go in there. The enemy will probably come out over there, at the main doors. I don't know what direction the Marines will come from." He frowned, and checked his watch, but he didn't know how long it would take Hamish to repair the engine, or how long it would take to drive the truck here, assuming the road was clear. "We can't wait. Good luck."

Halfway across the car park, he remembered the garrison would have artillery, and their most logical response to being shot at would be to shell the apartment building. He didn't slow. When he reached the ramp, he turned the jog into a sprint, pausing for breath at the top, his back flush against the hostel's wall.

The old signs were smeared with paint, but the ramp was part of a fire escape. He followed the signs backwards until he found the vacant doorway. Again, smeared with paint, and so was the stairwell beyond. Paint and mud, and stinking of fresh urine.

Gun raised before him, he moved slowly up the stairs. On the lower levels, the windows had been removed. Above, they remained, and were coated in the house paint used by the scavengers in their war-like game. An irate spider scampered across the stairs, abandoning its attempt to repair a floor-to-ceiling web; further proof someone had been here recently.

Slowly, he climbed, uncertain if he was listening to phantoms, or to people above. The breeze on his face was real. The top floor still had a door, though it was wedged open with a strip of bent aluminium. He aimed his gun along the corridor beyond, listening for a count of five racing heartbeats.

As he was about to step through the door, he heard a rustle of clothing from inside the first doorway beyond the corridor. He leaned close to the wall, gun aimed at head height, taking a cautious step forward, another.

From behind the door, he heard a cough.

"*Sheisse. Was zur holle!*" a woman muttered. German? Probably.

He heard more muted muttering. Another cough. Another rustle of clothing, and he stepped closer to the door.

When the woman stepped out of the door, she froze, halfway through adjusting her cheap black ski-jacket. Mitchell fired, from less than a metre distance, two shots, face and neck.

It was instinct which had caused him to fire, and instinct which had him catch her as she fell. As blood bubbled from her throat, he lifted her back into the room. Instinct which had registered the sewer-stench from the room, how the coat was identical to those worn in the farmhouse, and how the short-stocked rifle was a modified Kalashnikov. Instincts weren't always correct, but this time, they were. After laying her down, he checked the rest of the apartment now being used as a toilet. In the bathroom was an old chair, the seat cut out, with a paint-bucket beneath. The rest of the room was empty.

The woman's pockets weren't. In the left coat pocket were two magazines for the rifle. In the right was a bulbous old-world grenade. He pocketed that, unlooped her assault rifle, and slung it before leaning by the partially closed door. Once again, he listened. She wasn't poorly armed cannon-fodder. He doubted the rest were, either. Yes, his instincts had been correct, but as the truck had not yet arrived, the plan was already going awry.

A laugh came from along the corridor, echoed by someone else, who then shushed them both. The conversation continued, though it was now muted. German? Maybe not. Coming from about three doors down, and near the end of the corridor. He was debating whether to advance or wait for the truck, when he heard a faint horn outside. So faint, he wondered if the two men had. Their conversation had already ceased. But he heard footsteps. Wood clunked against damp plaster. The footsteps got louder. They got nearer. They were outside, in the corridor.

Crouching low, he swung through the doorway. Two hostiles, wearing black jackets from which they'd cut the arms. Both with Kalashnikovs, and scraggly chest-length beards knotted into braids. Mitchell's finger curled around the trigger. Head. Shoulder. Chest. Head. The two knights fell, but the second had his finger in the trigger-guard of his assault rifle. A short burst tattooed the ceiling. From outside came another faint horn, barely a whisper compared to the gunfire.

Mitchell ejected his spent mag, and loaded a full one as he walked to, then over, the corpses, keeping his pistol aimed at the doorway at the very end of the hall. It didn't have a door, but an improvised curtain, held in place with a pair of bone-handled hunting knives. A curtain which shimmied as a gun barrel was pushed through. He dived into the room the two knights had exited. Bullets stitched the corridor as an entire magazine was emptied along its length.

Mitchell picked himself up. The room he was in had chairs. Six of them. Plastic and cheap. A door was balanced on stacks of bricks as a table. On it were unopened cans of food. There was no fire or stove. But there were two missile launchers, a small row of grenades, and a larger row of rifle magazines.

He pulled a cylindrical grenade from his pocket. Sparing half a second to confirm it had green stripes, he pulled the pin and rolled the grenade outside, towards the curtain. He slotted the pistol into his belt, and had reached for the slung assault rifle when the floor shook, and the apartment rocked.

His first thought was *artillery*, his second was *missile*, his third was *damn*. There was smoke in the corridor, but there was blood and shrapnel, too. It hadn't been a smoke grenade, but an explosive, and it had ripped through the curtain, and the brigand beyond. The man's legs were gone, but so was his jaw, leaving his trunk a bloody mess, spurting blood from both ends.

Mitchell ran the length of the corridor, stepped over the bloody carcass, and entered the room. More crude curtains covered the windows, the cloth held in place with more knives. He saw binoculars. A chair. No missile launchers. But there was a radio handset. Low range. Perhaps a kilometre.

He pulled down a curtain, looking out the window and down. The garrison was obvious from its concrete abutments, wire and wood gates, and the two large cranes by the old docks.

A plume of smoke rocketed from immediately below him towards the compound. The apartment shook as the missile detonated on the pier. It had come from below. From a different floor.

Radios. They had radios!

Cursing the terrorists, government bureaucrats, and technophobic politicians, Mitchell sprinted back along the corridor, and towards the main set of stairs by the old elevator. The doors there had been removed, so he heard the footsteps. At least two pairs, and one was getting louder.

Black coat. Mitchell opened fire as soon as he saw it. The terrorist fell, but someone below returned fire. The bullets thudded into the stairwell a flight beneath.

Mitchell slowed his pace as he came in sight of the doorway to the next floor down. Search or chase? He heard gunfire coming from outside. That was where his people were.

He ran down, keeping his back to the wall, barely checking the exits to each new floor until he came out in the lobby, and a bullet spanged into the wall next to him.

"Woah! Sorry, sir!" Jo-Jo called. "Clear."

He picked himself up, and moved cautiously into the open, lowering his gun when he saw the sergeant, then the dead terrorist, bleeding from a chest wound, a loaded portable missile by his hand.

"Hamish and Jean-Luc?" he asked.

"Just outside, sir."

"Get them in here," Mitchell said. "We haven't won yet."

Chapter 12 - Messages From Afar
Dunkirk, France

Barely had Jean-Luc and Private MacKay entered the lobby before Jo-Jo raised a shout. "Incoming, sir. Could be friendly, except they don't look it."

"Hold fire!" Mitchell called, crossing to the entrance. A bullet slammed into the paint-smeared cladding a metre to the right. He ducked back inside. "We're friendly. From Twynham. Henry Mitchell, military intelligence."

"Prove it!" came the reply. "What's the best way to cheat at poker?"

"Rig the table," Mitchell called back. "Is that you, Carlton?"

"A question I ask every time I look in the mirror," came the reply. Male, with a Southern U.S. accent whose corners had been rounded by twenty years in Britain.

Mitchell edged back around the door. A green-clad soldier waved from the underpass leading through the apartment and so to the docks, then sprinted for the entrance, three soldiers on his heels.

"Carlton Greeves!" Mitchell said as the soldier ran into the lobby. "I thought you'd retired."

"I didn't read the small print," Greeves said. Thin, lanky, with a criss-cross burn on his cheek, and a patch over his left eye. "They kept me on the reserve list. I'm a major now. They say it's a promotion. Looks like you didn't retire, either."

"I guess no one did," Mitchell said. "We've been chasing this group since they attacked a bastion halfway to Calais a few nights ago."

"That's an IGLA man-portable missile," Greeves said, pointing to the missile by the corpse. "Glad to say I haven't seen one of these in a while. That's what they fired at us? I did wonder."

"There were cases for four missiles in that truck," Mitchell said. "I counted two more on the top floor, but I need to go secure them. I don't know if there are more of these people here, or in the harbour."

"You start at the top, we'll hold this position," Greeves said, picking up the missile. "Shah, take this back to bastion. Like I always say, better safe than bleeding."

"Aye-aye, sir," the private said, and sprinted for the door.

"You can take a sailor from a ship, but not the ship from a sailor," Greeves said.

"They've got grenades, too," Mitchell said as he crossed to the doorless stairway. "So we'll do this quick. Top floor. Jean-Luc, take the lead."

"*Bien sûr*. I held the record for four years."

"What record?" Hamish asked.

"Later," Mitchell said.

Doors and corners, up they went. On the top floor, Mitchell ignored the bodies, making straight for the room in which he'd seen the two missiles. They were still there.

"Jean-Luc, bag up the ammo and those grenades. Food as well, I guess. Hamish, you're in charge of those missiles. Keep your finger away from anything that might be a trigger."

"Nae kidding," he said.

Mitchell gave the two bodies in the hall a peremptory search.

"That's a lot of knives," Jo-Jo said, as Mitchell opened the coat. "They're knights?"

"Once," Mitchell said. "Two spare magazines here. Full. These people are far better equipped than the foot-soldiers who attacked the Drummond-Dumond farm. A few of the dead skirmishers in the south were found with a bandolier of grenades, or a pocket full of bullets, but rarely more than twenty rounds. These killers here knew, after their attack, they'd have to fight their way out of Dunkirk."

"Was that why they parked so far away?" Jo-Jo asked.

"Could be," Mitchell said. "But more important is that their boss wanted them to survive."

At the end of the hall, he pulled a bone-handled knife from the ragged remains of the improvised curtain.

"Is that a human bone?" Jo-Jo asked.

"It's plastic. It's imitation. Which explains why they valued it so little they were willing to leave it behind. Good."

"Why is it good?"

"Because it's not a clue," Mitchell said. "I've got far too many of those to wade through here. Speaking of wading..." He stepped over the bloody hunk of meat that had been a brigand. "Radio, chair, binoculars, and a rifle. No book, no distractions. These people were good."

"As in trained?" Jo-Jo asked.

"As in disciplined. That guy I blew to pieces there was older, too. Mid-thirties, I guess. Same is true for the woman near the bathroom. The two in the hallway were younger, but old enough to have experience. They were knights. That guy? Impossible to tell. Doubt the woman was a knight."

"This guy was in the caliphate," Jo-Jo said. "I found his missing hand. Most of it. There's a crescent-moon brand between finger and thumb."

"Interesting, but I don't think these people still owed any allegiance to the emir, the knights or the Free Peoples. They were trusted with ammunition, with missiles, and with a radio." Mitchell picked up the handset. "They were trusted with the plan. Trusted to carry it out." He tore the improvised curtain from the window, letting in daylight.

"What do you want me to do with this gear?" Jo-Jo asked.

"We'll take the bodies back to the garrison," Mitchell said. "We'll catalogue every item of clothing. Everything in their pockets. Something might give us a clue where they came from." He turned back to the window, looking down at the garrison. Smoke still rose from the compound, but as he followed the plume, rising to the horizon, he saw the enemy's real target. "Come take a look at this," he said.

"What is— oh. Ships," she said. "Three. All with funnels."

"Old ships," Mitchell said. "Old passenger ferries we converted back in the early days. They're used as freighters now. Three ships, heading right for us."

"They're the target?" Jo-Jo asked. "Not the sloop. How did the enemy know they were coming here?"

"Good question, because I didn't know," Mitchell said. "Gather the gear. Secure the weapons first. I'll speak to Greeves."

He found Major Greeves outside, by the truck.

"Looks like you've got reinforcements inbound," Mitchell said. "Three steam ships are approaching."

"*Three* ships?" Greeves asked.

"Yep. You weren't expecting them?" Mitchell asked.

"The sloop arrived yesterday with the news we'd be getting reinforcements. They didn't say when. They didn't say it would be that many."

"If you've got a working radio, you should give them a warning," Mitchell said.

As Greeves hurried back to the compound, Mitchell walked around the truck, giving it a closer inspection than before, looking for a licence plate or some other indication of which country it had come from. It was a Mercedes, with the steering wheel on the left, but that didn't narrow it down. The front tyres appeared far, far too narrow and with too small a radius for such a large vehicle.

He opened the driver's door. A webbing pouch contained maps of France, but with an information page written in German. That tallied with the language in which the dead woman had sworn. But the German border was only three hundred kilometres away. The odometer had seven figures on the clock, but how much of that was done before the Blackout? The vehicle was at least forty years old, with barely any electronics in the cab. There *were* wires. Too many wires.

He picked up the end of a wire that was clearly for drawing power from the truck's battery. A minute later, he'd found another, bolted to the back of the cab, running down through the roof. Behind the driver's seat, in a waterproof bag, he found a radio set. Not a short-range walkie-talkie, but a bulky CB. Following the wire, he climbed up to the roof and found the antenna. It was folded flat, but ran the length of cab and cabin. It would unfold to at least three times the length of the vehicle, with an extendable brace to support it when in use.

"Sir! Sir!" a private called, sprinting from the shore.

"What's up?"

"Message, sir. From Major Greeves."

Mitchell jumped down, taking the slip of paper.

"Any reply, sir?" the private asked.

"Nope," Mitchell said. "I'll wait here." He leaned against the cab, and reread the brief message. *Five hundred conscripts coming ashore. Captains have been warned of the danger. Ships will stagger their arrival.*

Five hundred conscripts? That wasn't reinforcements; it was an army. Clearly something big was going on. He'd not known about it, but the enemy must have, for them to have deployed this missile team here. Or had they got lucky? Had there been other attacks up and down the coast today?

The enemy had radio: a long-range CB, and short-range walkies that could cover a kilometre. The leader, back at the attack on the Drummond-Dumond farm, hadn't carried a walkie. Since the mortar was left behind after that attack, it was unlikely a radio had been carried away. Was that because the enemy had a limited number?

He'd have to extend the antenna on the roof, measure its height, then find someone who could remind him of the formula which would give its range. But the set in the cab was civilian. There was no encryption, so there'd have to be a code, which meant there'd be a codebook. If he could set up a listening station, maybe he could intercept a message. But who from? Who to? Or was this truck the group sending the message? He doubted they'd get so lucky.

There was no way he'd get to Nieuwpoort in time to meet the spy. He would have to wait until the conscripts had come ashore before he knew whether there were more missile-carrying ambushers in Dunkirk. He'd have to strip the truck, and the bodies, and find their codebook. The bodies at the farm would have to be collected. He might have to return to the campsite. No, he wouldn't reach Belgium in time for the rendezvous. Scouting the harbour for the navy would have to wait, and Isaac would have to meet with the spy alone. No matter, because he had the solution to this crisis before him, assuming he asked the right questions.

Part 2
The Home Front

Dover, Twynham & Belgium
Ruth, Anna, & Isaac

23rd December

23rd December 2039

Chapter 13 - Never Kiss a Telephone Pole
Priory Hill, Dover

Her breath held, Constable Ruth Deering bounded up the external metal staircase, through the apartment's open door, and only slowed when she saw the man sprawled across the upstairs living room floor. He was definitely dead. Doing her best not to disturb the scene, she jumped over the body, threw open the window, and leaned out, gasping in a lungful of the acrid garlic-scented air.

The poisonous odour lingered in her nose as she dashed back through the house, opened the door to a musty kitchen, and pushed the window up before retreating outside. On the metal landing, she took a cautious breath, then a deeper one, before slowly descending to the garden below.

It was early. Though the sun wasn't up, most of the street was. They'd been woken by the victim's downstairs neighbour yelling for the military patrol after she'd discovered the body. Anyone who'd slept through that ruckus was now being woken by those soldiers going door-to-door with instructions for everyone to check their woodpile.

Outside, in front of the house by the snow-covered vegetable patch, three women stood. Two shivered in overcoats, while the third, wearing police-blue, made notes.

"All okay, Constable?" Sergeant Elspeth Kettering asked.

Ruth nodded, still trying to rid her nostrils of that horrid fragrance of death. "He died last night," Ruth said. "Looks like arsenic poisoning to me."

"We'll let the doctor decide that," Kettering said. She'd been born in Dover a little over five decades ago, and had become an institution in the city. A police sergeant before the Blackout, she'd remained a sergeant ever since, despite many offers of promotion to the sprawling new capital of Twynham further west.

Kettering turned to the witnesses. "Let me recap, and you two can tell me if I've missed anything. Yasmin Tembe and Suzi McClaine. You both work at Mr Fry's restaurant on Biggin Street. You rent the downstairs of this house, and he has the upstairs. You usually wake him on your way to work at about ten, but this morning, you went up to his flat at five, is that right, Ms Tembe?"

"Maybe closer to five-thirty," Yasmin Tembe said. "I go for a run every morning. Always at five-thirty."

"Even in this weather?" Kettering asked. "That's very admirable."

The two women were in their early twenties. Yasmin Tembe was dressed for running, though she now wore a heavy overcoat atop her baggy sweats. Suzi McClaine wore her overcoat over an equally baggy set of almost identical tubular top and trousers. On her, since she'd been asleep, they'd be called pyjamas.

"And why did you go upstairs to wake him today?" Kettering asked.

"The back door was open," Yasmin said, pointing up the steps. "Sometimes he leaves it open. I went up to close it. I smelled... you know. I went inside, and he was dead."

"We read the news about the logs covered in arsenic," Suzi added.

"He had no pulse," Yasmin said. "He was cold. I knew he was dead. I came back outside. I was going to wake Suzi when I saw the military patrol."

"And they came to get us," Kettering said. "So you two were aware of the warning about burning utility poles?"

"And how those other two people died, and how the children got sick," Suzi said. "Mr Fry told us. He said he knew the people who died."

"He *did* know them," Kettering said. "He was born Tomash Fresnick. Changed his name when he went to secondary school. Same school as me. Just down the road from here."

"You knew Mr Fry?" Yasmin asked.

"And his mum before she passed," Kettering said. "I knew his wife, too, before she disappeared. You say Mr Fry often left his door open?"

"Not often. Some nights. When he came home... late," Yasmin said.

Ruth caught the pause. "He owned a restaurant where you work the early shift, and you wake him up," Ruth said. "Do you have keys to his flat?"

"No. We just ring the doorbell until he answers," Yasmin said.

"Or until he yells at us to say he's awake," Suzi said.

"You *always* opened his restaurant?" Ruth asked.

"He always closed up," Yasmin said.

"He'd drink with the other restaurant owners," Suzi said. "He often came home drunk."

"Not that often," Yasmin said.

"Often enough," Suzi said. "Last night, I heard him clumping around upstairs at around three."

"Three? Curfew runs from midnight to four," Kettering said.

"He has a new girlfriend," Yasmin said. "Sofia."

"Does he?" Kettering said. "That's new. Do you know her surname?"

"No, sorry," Yasmin said. "She's about his age. Maybe a little younger. I think she's from Austria. But I only met her once. She came in for lunch about a month ago."

"And some nights he *does* come home drunk," Suzi said. "He really does *climb* those stairs, and he often forgets to lock the door."

"What kind of landlord was he?" Ruth asked.

"A *good* one," Yasmin said. "He has this French guy who fixes things when they break, Jean-Luc. I think he's a scavenger, although he's gone to war now. But before, if something was broken, we'd tell Mr Fry in the morning, and Jean-Luc would have it fixed before we got home. We get meals and rent, minimum wage, *and* tips, and we don't have to work the late crowd. That's a *good* job."

"It sounds it," Kettering said. "But what about the man himself, Ms McClaine? Did you *like* him?"

"He wasn't a creep, if that's what you mean," Suzi said. "He was sad, sometimes. Quiet except when he was at the restaurant. He said no one ever ordered a side dish of tears so you couldn't be sad at work. Sometimes, on my day off, I'd see him sitting at the top of the stairs, staring at nothing. But he's been happier this last month. A lot happier."

"Since he started dating Sofia?" Kettering asked. "Ah, looks like the doc has arrived."

The horse-drawn hearse pulled to a stop outside. It wasn't just soldiers and guns which had been sent to the front. Dover had been stripped of anything which might end the war a minute sooner, and that included the ambulances. Two already-exhausted nurses climbed down from the hearse.

"Morning, Berta," Kettering said, addressing the elder of the two, Berta Lopez, a stern forty-year-old who was the picture-dictionary definition of matronly-severe. "No doc today?"

"A train just arrived from Calais," the older nurse said. "It's all hands, and we're already short-staffed. We've brought the trainees onto the ward." She nodded towards the young nurse next to her.

"These girls get up at half five to go for a run, Ellie," Kettering said, addressing the younger of the two nurses.

"And good morning to you, Mum," the nurse said. Eloise Kettering had been working in the coal power station and been about to join the navy when the war began. With a slight push from her mother, and with another from Ruth's own mother, Eloise had volunteered for the nurses instead. Eloise yawned.

"That's why you don't stay up half the night watching old films," Berta said.

"It was only a quarter of the night," Ruth said, coming to her flatmate's defence.

Growing up in a refugee resettlement centre, Ruth hadn't been short of playmates, but the children came and went too quickly to form any real friendships. She'd not clicked with any of the other cadets in the police academy, partly because she'd lied about her age when applying. No, she'd had no friends in the academy except for Simon Longfield, but he'd betrayed her on instructions from his mother, a self-obsessed dairy magnate who'd wanted to claim the defunct British crown. Simon's father had shot Anna Riley, leaving her wheelchair-bound. After exposing the plot, Isaac had dealt with Simon. Ruth wasn't sure whether Simon was alive or dead, and though she'd *thought* he was her friend, he was now someone she tried to forget.

Eloise, though, *was* a friend, who now shared the flat above the Dover Police Station, having relinquished her own bedroom to Ruth's mother. The arrangement suited everyone, and provided Ruth and Eloise with likeminded company in the few minutes of free time they had each day.

"What do you have for us?" Nurse Berta Lopez asked. "We were told it's an accidental death."

"It's another possible case of arsenic poisoning," Kettering said. "One fatality upstairs, those two were downstairs. They need to be checked. Constable, go see what Mr Fry left in his woodpile."

Ruth gave a conspiratorial grimace to Eloise, and walked back through the garden to the corrugated shed built beneath the external staircase. The woodpile was only a quarter-full, but that was better stocked than three-quarters of the homes in Dover this winter.

Many houses had electric lights now, and some had a refurbished electric oven, but most people still got their heat, and hot water, from open fires. After the Blackout, after the offshore rigs blew up, the nuclear power stations melted down, and the wind-turbines spun so fast their blades had cracked, Britain reverted to coal as a temporary measure to get through the initial crisis. Twenty years later, coal was still king. Since the new navy ships also burned coal, they were the first priority for the shipments coming from Wales. The city's power station was second, leaving virtually none for domestic heating. People had no choice but to burn whatever they could to stay warm: furniture, rags, rubbish, and old utility poles coated with an antifungal treatment of chromated copper arsenate.

"There are no sawn utility poles here," Ruth said as Kettering joined her. "It's all split logs. Well-seasoned pine. All dry and fresh."

"Tommy sells a wood-cooked pizza," Kettering said. "To me, that's the taste of summer. Fresh tomatoes, fresh mushrooms, and a three-month-old cheese. I bet he gets his logs from the restaurant. What's your initial assessment?"

"I'd like to take another look at the body," Ruth said. "But it does look like arsenic poisoning. Smells like it, too. Vomit, diarrhoea, and garlic. But that's not the same as an actual confirmation."

"No, we'll get that from the autopsy," Kettering said, "and from the lab in Twynham when they send us their results."

"Can we trust the witnesses?" Ruth asked.

"You tell me," Kettering said.

"Well, they have to wake him every morning, so I think that means he came home drunk each night," she said. "But Ms Tembe was used to closing his front door, so he can't have been a problem-boss."

"This house belonged to Tommy's mum," Kettering said. "Tommy got married just before the Blackout. His mum died a month later. A cut got infected. Couldn't find any antibiotics. His wife disappeared during the plague-years."

"Disappeared? Was Mr Fry suspected?" Ruth asked.

"No, I think Alicia caught the plague and was cremated before she could be properly identified. Tommy and Alicia used to organise catering in the refugee camp. She ran the kitchens. He'd bring up the supplies. They used to get refugees to help with the cooking, the serving, that kind of thing. Tommy went on a supply-run. We were still piecing the railway network back together, so he was travelling by bicycle-drawn cart. Took him a week to return, by which time, Alicia was gone. So were a few hundred others. It hit Tommy hard. Took him six months to recover."

"Did they have any children?" Ruth asked.

"None. Alicia was the love of his life. Don't think he dated after she died. Before the Blackout, he had a little fish and chip place close to the cliffs. He's opened a few places in the years since, but this last venture was the first that really seemed to stick."

"Was he a friend of yours?" Ruth asked.

"Not really," Kettering said. "He was a fair bit older than me. But there aren't that many of us who stayed here since the Blackout. When Eloise finished school, we went to his place for a grown-up meal. It's not really a kid's restaurant, so wasn't somewhere to take the fam. For me, socially, that meant we travelled in different circles. Professionally, he was never a bother."

"He wasn't a violent man?" Ruth asked.

"He had his troubles, but I never knew him to raise his hand in anger. Why do you ask?"

"It would be the obvious reason someone would want revenge," Ruth said.

"Revenge for what?" Kettering asked.

"Exactly," Ruth said. "But if it wasn't revenge, then the next obvious question is whether he was murdered by his downstairs neighbours."

"Is it?" Kettering asked. "That's Isaac's influence if you're jumping from an accident to murder."

"Because this would be the third death through inhalation of arsenic fumes in a month," Ruth said. "That's too many to be an accidental coincidence."

"The third in a month, yes," Kettering said. "The third since winter properly set in. The third since we've been locked in our city with no domestic coal, and little other fuel arriving. People get cold. They burn what's to hand. Utility poles are more common than trees."

"But everyone knows that they're coated in CCA," Ruth said.

"Did you know before last month?" Kettering asked. "I didn't know until the winter after the Blackout. Why should we? We had central heating. We had mobile phones, too. Landlines were already a bit of a relic. But after the Blackout, people got cold. Those winters were bitter. Utility poles were an obvious source of wood. A lot were chopped down, dragged inside, sawn up, and burned. There were a load of accidental poisonings before word spread they'd been coated in an arsenic compound."

"Exactly," Ruth said. "I didn't know before last month because there've been no accidents like this for ages. The poles that weren't chopped down are used for the telegraph, and everyone does know that tampering with that gets you a long stretch in a small cell. I think someone saw the news stories about the other victims, and staged Mr Fry's murder to look like an accident."

"Why?" Kettering asked. "What's the motive? I'm going to have another word with those two girls, see if they can provide a more solid I.D. on Tommy's girlfriend. The air upstairs should be clear by now, so take another look at the scene. Remember, if you start to feel ill, come back outside."

"Aye, Sarge." Ruth, once again, climbed the metal staircase.

CCA, chromated copper arsenate, was an olden-days chemical used to treat utility poles, garden furniture, and wooden railway ties to prevent rot. If burned in an enclosed, poorly ventilated space, the fumes could kill. They had. Twice this month, not counting Mr Fry. As a result, articles had been run in the newspaper, stuck to the windows of every shop, and broadcast on the radio, reminding people to be careful about what they burned.

Ruth took her new-to-her phone from her pocket, set it to record, and held it in front as she went back inside. During the long years with barely any electricity, phones had been forgotten. Now, like most pre-Blackout technology, they were still viewed with suspicion. Many people believed an evil AI still lurked beneath the glass screen, eagerly waiting to use its digital virus to turn a human user into a self-absorbed slave. Ruth was ninety percent sure that that was just a myth, and one hundred percent certain that the phone was the greatest thing she'd ever owned.

The law had recently changed, allowing individual judges to decide whether technologically gathered evidence was admissible in court. Procedure had yet to catch up, and the official record still required a hand-drawn sketch of the crime scene rather than photographs. But the law didn't say the sketches had to be made *at* the scene.

The external metal staircase led to a perforated-metal landing. Beneath was a rainwater collection tray that led to a gutter, and ultimately to the water-barrel below. A pair of empty flowerpots guarded a post-Blackout doorway built around the frame of an old window. The door led into what, twenty years ago, had been a small bedroom, but that was in the era when families had a whole house to themselves. Now, it was a boot-room filled with coats, one pair of wellingtons, two snow-shovels, and a metal toolbox containing a plethora of screwdrivers, wrenches, and hammers. The room wasn't neat, but it wasn't messy. The tools weren't well kept, but they were usable. The coats weren't clean, but they weren't ragged. They were just old.

The door led into a hall. A new wall and door encased where the old staircase had led downstairs. The door was locked.

Another small bedroom had become a kitchenette with a sink and an electric hotplate, on which was a kettle. No fridge, but those were rare in Twynham, let alone Dover. No oven, but Mr Fry owned a restaurant. There wasn't much food in the cupboards, but again he'd find that at work. There was a tin of Satz powdered tea, another of coffee, and third containing biscuits.

When burned, arsenic gave off fumes that smelled like garlic. She'd noted that odour during her first, brief inspection of the scene. Here, in the kitchen, it was stronger than in the hall, and strongest of all close to the wrapped linen package on the counter. She sniffed. Yes, garlic. But also butter and bread. She unwrapped it and found a neat stack of garlic-bread squares.

The bathroom was functional, but without a water-heater. The bath had dust in the bottom, but the sink was stained with the ration-issue bright pink toothpaste. The seat of the rainwater flush toilet was up, and smelled of vomit. While vomiting was another symptom of arsenic inhalation, it was also a symptom of a glass too many.

Mr Fry didn't eat here. He didn't wash here. From the state of the bedroom, he didn't bring his girlfriend here, either. The linen was clean, but the bed was small.

The clothes inside the wardrobe were laundered and neatly pressed, neatly repaired. Mostly suits and shirts. Dirties were in the sack in the corner, which would probably be laundered by the same people who washed his restaurant's tablecloths. He must keep his chef-whites at work, probably in a locker close to a shower.

The room in which he'd died was the only one which showed some signs of actual living. There were two armchairs, facing the fire. On the walls were six pre-Blackout photographs. Three of an older woman, probably Mr Fry's mother. The other three pictures showed a younger woman Ruth guessed was Alicia Fry. Tommy Fry wasn't in any of the pictures.

The walls were lined with old paperbacks; thrillers whose old-world setting made little sense to those born after the Blackout, but which offered a comforting escape to those who mourned all they'd lost. In the corner, by the window, was a desk, and next to it a cabinet. The cabinet contained spirits: scotch, brandy, and absinthe. Eleven bottles, three unopened. A twelfth bottle lay on the floor. The label read scotch. The cap was off, the contents were half-spilled across the carpet. Next to the spilled bottle was broken glass from a smashed tumbler.

In the top drawer of the desk, she found a folded bundle of bank notes. In total, it came to fifty pounds. A fortune by her standards, but not for a successful restaurateur who, even in wartime, might take ten times that on a busy night. No, this wasn't the previous night's takings. But it was easy to find, so if robbery had been the motive for murder, that fifty pounds would have been stolen.

But was it murder?

Mr Fry had fallen between the two chairs, face down, left arm beneath him, right arm extended, his gloved hand close to the smashed glass. There was no vomit around his mouth, or on the floor. There was a smell which could be arsenic-induced diarrhoea, or just the inevitable outcome of death. She bent, holding the camera close to his face, using its zoom as a magnifying glass. Yes, there were some abrasions there, but if he'd fallen, that was to be expected.

She stood. He was wearing an outdoor coat and gloves, and his outdoor shoes, though not his hat and scarf which were on the chair. In the fire was ash, and a charred, circular log.

Feet clanked on the metal stairs. Ruth went outside, and met Sergeant Kettering and the two nurses on the steps.

"The waitresses have the all-clear," Kettering said. "I've told them to get dressed, and we're going to take a walk up to the restaurant. Did you see any keys inside?"

"No, but I bet they're in his pocket. He'd not taken off his coat."

"I'll take a look," Kettering said. "Did you sketch the scene?"

She held up the phone. "I took video. I'll use it to do the sketch later."

"People getting machines to do their work was how we ended up letting them do our thinking," Kettering said. "That's how the olden days became old, and we ended up living like this. Go downstairs, see if the girls are squaring their stories."

"Got it," Ruth said.

The women's half of the house was immaculately clean, with sprigs of holly on the doors, dried flowers on the hall-table, and framed charcoal sketches on the walls. The women were each in their own rooms. Neither was talking, though Ms Tembe appeared to be crying softly. Being deliberately noisy, Ruth clumped up the stairs to the internal door to Mr Fry's apartment. Not only was the key on this side of the door, there were bolts at top and bottom, both of which were stiff with lack of use.

Ruth went back to the front door, and flipped through the video until Kettering returned. She motioned Ruth out to the pavement. "I took samples of the ash, and I took the log. We'll send it all to the lab in Twynham."

"It's the same kind of log we found with the other two victims," Ruth said.

"Superficially," Kettering said. "We'll wait on the autopsy before we declare a cause. Berta has given the girls a clean bill of health."

"That's not like the last victim, the vicar," Ruth said. "The children upstairs from her all got sick."

"Yes, they got sick," Kettering said, "but maybe because they were upstairs, and these two lived downstairs. We'll ask the doc. Tell the soldiers to guard the house until we've figured out who next of kin are. Then send a telegram to the radio station and another to the newspaper, and get them to run another warning. I'll pop into the Chamber of Commerce on my way up to the restaurant and have them send runners to the shops. There's no harm in issuing another warning, but..." She didn't finish, but turned around, and headed back inside. "Ladies, if you're ready," she called.

Chapter 14 - Even Justice Sleeps
Dover Police Station

Though Dover now bustled with the influx of soldiers going east and refugees fleeing west, it had been an isolated and fortified encampment for most of the past twenty years. Seaborne raiders and pirates had encouraged refugees to head to the sooty metropolis of Twynham. But there were always a few people who wanted to return to France or beyond. There were European scavengers, and lately farmers, who wanted to trade. Dover survived. Dover thrived. Before the war.

The sign on the police station door read *always open*. It lied. The upstairs offices were now a set of apartments used by the never-there-long constables, and which Ruth currently shared with Eloise Kettering. Constables came, constables went, but Sergeant Kettering had remained a constant in Dover. Everyone in the city knew her, and knew if she wasn't in the police station, she could be found in the house three doors down and two over. When Sergeant Kettering, and now Ruth, weren't there, the station's door was kept firmly locked. Except now, the door was ajar.

Her hand dropped to her truncheon, undoing the clip as she cautiously eased the door open with her boot. She dashed in, nightstick raised, but she'd need a tree-trunk to subdue the man on the other side of the duty-desk. Six-six if he was an inch, and about the same wide, the old knife wounds around his mouth had left his lips ragged and his chin a map of white lines. His arms were like boulders squeezed into a sack. His gnarled, twisted hands were balanced on the desk, either side of a sawn-off shotgun.

"Gregory! Seriously not cool," Ruth said, lowering her truncheon. "I could have shot you."

"Not with a billy-club," another voice said. An American voice. A voice redolent of three-sided coins, four-dollar bills, and five aces in a deck. A voice which would ask for the time, then sell it back to you. A voice of charm sprinkled with deceit for whom law books were found in the fiction aisle of his personal library.

"Isaac," she said, turning around.

"What, no hug, no kiss?" he asked. He sat by the roaring fire in the marginally better-furnished corner of the lobby reserved for witnesses and victims.

"You should be sitting over there," she said pointing to the barred cell on the far side of the lobby in which, these days, they kept the drunken soldiers until they were collected by the military patrol.

"Ah, but I bring gifts," Isaac said. "It's the season, isn't it? Speaking of which, your decorations are a tad lacking."

"This *is* a police station," Ruth said, echoing the reply that Sergeant Kettering had given her when she'd asked if she could put up a tree by the duty desk. Seeing as the sergeant's own house dripped with baubles, Ruth thought the refusal unfair. "Where were you, anyway? You vanished without even a word. Not even a note."

"Do I detect a hint of worry?"

"Only for the paperwork you inevitably generate," Ruth said. "So, go on, where've you been?"

"The front," Isaac said.

"Behind the front lines," a woman said, walking through the doors, still drying her hair with Ruth's own towel. "I borrowed your shower. I hope you don't mind."

"No, it's fine," Ruth said, having fought, and lost, that particular battle before.

The slim woman with the tensed muscles and searching eyes was a killer, though Kelly preferred being called a sniper. She didn't have a surname, not that Ruth had yet learned, nor did Gregory. Gregory also had no tongue.

He'd been a baker, and married with children. They had been murdered in front of him, while he had been tortured, his hands broken, his tongue ripped out. He'd got his revenge though it had nearly killed him. He and Kelly were two of Isaac's followers, but Ruth still didn't know if that was meant in a literal or a religious sense.

Before the Blackout, Isaac had been a computer engineer, and a student of Ruth's adoptive mother, Maggie, who'd been a leading light at the very cutting edge of neuroscience and artificial intelligence. And due to that odd connection, Isaac treated Ruth as a younger sister, which was doubly infuriating since it was a connection Ruth had only learned of last month. He was a rogue, a bandit, a renegade, and a law unto himself. Which, as Ruth was fifty percent of the law in Dover, had been a growing problem until the war began.

"How far behind the lines did you get?" Ruth asked.

"Well, that is an *excellent* question," Isaac said, removing his hat, a grey beret which matched his overcoat, though not the urban camouflage and body-armour he wore beneath. "A very *good* question."

"You're going to give me a long preamble before answering, aren't you?" Ruth said. "It'll have to wait. I've got some notes to write up. There's been another poisoning."

"A murder?" Kelly asked, with obvious interest.

"Possibly," Ruth said. "But maybe just another accidental arsenic poisoning. It was Tommy Fry."

Gregory rapped his knuckles against the wooden counter twice.

"We liked him," Kelly said. "His baked apples were something special. You think he was murdered?"

"I dunno," Ruth said, walking over to the fire. "Okay, let's pretend you didn't just break into a police station, but actually had a right to come inside. You lit the fire. Now you want a drink."

"A capital idea!" Isaac said, and pulled a bottle from his coat. "We can share your gift. Now, who has a corkscrew?" He pulled off a glove.

"Ha! There! See!" Ruth said.

"See what?" Kelly said.

"When we found Mr Fry, he was still wearing his gloves," Ruth said. "But there was a broken glass, and a spilled bottle right next to him. If you came home and wanted a drink, you'd take your gloves off, yes?"

"Depends how cold it was," Kelly said.

"Depends how thirsty I was," Isaac said.

"Fair point," Ruth said, walking back to the counter. "Shoo, Gregory. If you continue standing there, I'll have to recruit you. And hide that gun. You know the rule: don't let me *see* you breaking the law. Is Mister Mitchell with you?"

"Sadly, he missed our rendezvous," Isaac said. "He must have been stuck in France."

"I've a letter for you from him," Ruth said, opening the small safe below the desk. "Here you go. I think it's a Christmas card."

"You do? Capital. Oh," Isaac said, his face dropped an inch as he opened the envelope. "It *is* a card. Not the festive kind, but a memory card." He took a tablet from his pocket, and inserted the card. "On which we have some videos and photographs. Last first, I would guess."

Mister Mitchell's face appeared on the screen, made square and bulbous by the proximity of the lens.

"Isaac, hi. I'm not going to make it to the rendezvous, but you'll have realised that by the time you watch this. The enemy have shoulder-mounted Igla missiles. They set up an ambush in Dunkirk for three freighters full of conscripts who were supposed to fortify the city. They've got radios, and AKMs. The radio antenna is extendable, and built on the roof of a truck. I've got footage of it, so you can figure out the range, but the people here estimate fifty kilometres, max. I've included the copies of the rest of the evidence, but I want you to bring details of what you learned at the rendezvous to me, here in France."

The video ended.

"Short and to the point," Isaac said, with a hint of bitterness. "That's Henry."

"What rendezvous?" Ruth asked.

"The navy wanted us to inspect the harbour for a spring invasion, but Henry and I were really there to meet a spy."

"We have spies? Wow," Ruth said. "Wait, does this mean you're working for the government now?"

"I'm building a future," Isaac said. "Just as I have always been."

"Fine, don't answer," Ruth said. "But if Mister Mitchell was in France, where were you?"

"Belgium," Kelly said.

"Where in Belgium?" Ruth asked, glancing at the map of Europe pinned to the wall. It was there to offer a modicum of reassurance to anxious parents asking for news of their conscripted children. The old France-Belgium border was strikingly close to Calais, Dunkirk, and the beleaguered enclave they called the front line.

"We visited a delightful marina-town called Nieuwpoort," Isaac said, switching the tablet off. "Are the gloves this man wore the only discrepancy in your case?"

"The downstairs neighbours weren't ill," Ruth said. "Mr Fry had come home with some garlic bread, which he left in the kitchen, and which makes it hard to tell if the garlic smell came from burning arsenic. He took off his hat and scarf, but not his gloves, lit the fire, poured a drink, and fell. The glass broke. I've got video."

"Then why aren't you sharing it?" Isaac asked, holding out his hand.

"Don't you want to watch the files Mister Mitchell sent?"

"I can review them on the train to Calais," Isaac said. "Despite the sound and fury, there is little mystery in war. Your case, however, is just the tonic to brighten a cold and dreary day."

"Tell that to Mister Fry," Ruth said, picking up a blank incident-form. "But I need the video to draw the official sketch."

"Capital, we can review it together," he said, bounding over to the duty-desk.

Ruth sighed. "Fine. Look, but don't touch. This is the third case in a month. Surely everyone knows to be a bit careful about what they burn."

"No one is careful when they're drunk," Isaac said.

"Right, but it was a big log in that fire," Ruth said, flipping back to the photo. "And he was an older man. Not old-old, but if he had garlic bread in one hand, would he have carried the biggest log upstairs? I suppose he could have made a separate trip, but if it was that cold, why not just go to bed? If he'd laid the fire before going to work, he'd have selected the logs while sober."

"Not necessarily," Isaac said.

"Well, fine. But the neighbours heard something at three," Ruth said. "If you came home that late, on a freezing cold night, why not go to sleep? Anyway, the body has gone for an autopsy so we'll have confirmation of cause of death in a few days."

"Then we have time to give you your gifts," Isaac said.

"It's *way* too early to be drinking," Ruth said.

"Ah, but I come with more than just the bottle," Isaac said.

"*We*," Kelly said. "Greg and me were there, too."

"Indeed, and instrumental to the venture," Isaac said. "Now—"

Before he could finish, the door opened. A soldier entered, then a second, carrying a large crate between them. They definitely *were* soldiers, but they wore brick-grey camouflage rather than the more common rural-green of the newly raised army. Though they had revolvers holstered at their belts, they carried giant longbows across their backs.

"Um, hello," Ruth said, as a third soldier entered, this a woman with a bow in her hand, a quiver at her hip. She held the door open for a fourth figure, who had a familiar face in an equally familiar blue police uniform, and rode in a jet-black wheelchair.

"Anna!" Ruth said, skipping around the desk as Sergeant Anna Riley, another member of the old Serious Crimes Unit, wheeled herself in.

"Hey, Ruth," Riley said nonchalantly, as if she always went around with a three-soldier escort. No, a *five*-soldier escort as another pair carried in another hamper. "Your letter said come for Christmas. You didn't say whether to bring a dish, so I brought them all."

"And some new friends," Isaac said, standing.

"This is Ruth Deering," Riley said, by way of introduction.

"Colonel Elizabeth Sherwood," the tall woman said. "Duchess of Albion and High Sheriff of Nottingham."

"You're from Leicester?" Ruth said.

"From the Last Kingdom, yes," the colonel said. "And we, *I*, am forever in your debt, Constable Deering. These small gifts can't settle such an account, but can be taken as a sign of friendship between my house and yours." She saluted. With a stamping of snow-flecked boots, her four soldiers did the same. The colonel turned to Riley. "Sergeant, until we meet again."

"Come home safe," Riley said.

The Leicester soldiers departed.

"Well, that was weird," Ruth said.

"It all seemed perfectly normal to me," Riley said, failing to hide her smirk.

"Oh, no, don't you dare! What's going on, Anna? Why is some colonel from Albion now in my debt? And how come you're here? It's great to see you, but I didn't think you'd be able to get any time off."

"The short answer?" Riley said. "Now the treaty has been signed, the separatist Kingdom of Albion is no more. The royal bodyguard has joined our army and volunteered for the front. Five hundred trained archers, who know how to track, hide, bushwhack and otherwise make a real nuisance of themselves. The colonel has arrived with the advance guard who were in Twynham for the signing ceremony. The rest will arrive here as soon as the trains can bring them south."

"They volunteered to go to the front?" Ruth asked. "That's awesome. And it wasn't in the papers."

"Military secrets usually aren't," Riley said.

"That explains why they're in Dover," Ruth said. "But not why you're here, and here with them. Or why they think they're in my debt."

"Commissioner Weaver gave me a few days off," Riley said. "I was hoping to speak with Dad, and with one of the soldiers he's got deployed with him. The food is a longer story."

"This is food?" Isaac asked, levering the crate open. "It is! Ham, canned rhubarb, pickled spinach. Mustard! Cheese! Beer!" he exclaimed plucking a black-glass bottle from the depths of the crate. "Nottingham True Ale. I'm not sure what the alcohol content is, but it's proof that God is a beer drinker."

The giant baker loomed forward, gently picking up a jar of rhubarb. He gave a deliberate nod of approval.

"Do you think Sergeant Kettering would let us borrow her kitchen, Ruth?" Kelly asked. "There's too much for that little stove upstairs."

"As long as there's enough for her and the kids," Ruth said.

"Greg, with me," Kelly said, plucking the beer bottle from Isaac's hand. "Sorry boss, equal shares, remember?"

"Ah, hoist by democracy once again," Isaac said.

"There's no rationing in Leicester," Riley said. "But because the ration is so paltry in Twynham, the king brought his own food down for the treaty-signing. That all came from his stores."

"How did you get the king's food?" Ruth asked.

"Ah, no," Isaac said. "I was here first, and so I should get to tell *my* story first. Trust me, Anna, you'll want to hear this, too. I have a gift for Ruth, you see."

"A bottle of wine, right?" Ruth said.

"The wine is to be shared," Isaac said. "No, the gift is this." He reached into his coat, and pulled out a small square of cloth tied with string. "Apologies for the packaging."

Ruth carefully undid the string. "It's a blackbird brooch," she said. "Very ornate. Growing up, I used to love watching them. How did you know? Did Mum tell you?"

"The gift isn't from me," Isaac said.

21st December

Chapter 15 - Spies and Fries
Nieuwpoort, Belgium

One mile off the Belgian coast, the sea roiled as the boat churned through the foam-topped waves. To a casual observer, it was a twin-masted wooden-hulled fishing boat. Someone who'd lived a life before the Blackout would note the diesel engine and ask where the fuel had come from. Someone with old-world naval experience might ask whether the wooden boxes mounted fore and aft concealed some form of weapons system. But there were no casual observers at sea, not according to the radar display mounted inside the cockpit where Isaac lurked, Mrs Zhang steered, and Kelly shook her head.

"I'm not wearing it," Kelly said.

"But you must wear a hat," Isaac said. "Everyone wears a hat at Christmas. Usually paper, but there is a war on, so compromises must be made."

"No," Kelly said.

"Mrs Zhang is wearing a hat," Isaac said.

"Hers is a captain's bicorn," Kelly said. "This is a beret."

"Ah, so your objection is to that specific hat, not all hats in general?" Isaac said. "A beret would be culturally appropriate."

"Cultural appropriation, you mean," Kelly said. "Anyway, aren't berets French?"

"Yes," Mrs Zhang said.

"Oh, surely it's close enough," Isaac said. "And we are close enough to the old border. And to the shore. Is that it?"

"Yes," Mrs Zhang said. "Wake Gregory."

"Kelly, wake Gregory," Isaac said.

"*You* wake Gregory, she'll watch for the lights," Mrs Zhang said. She raised a hand to her hat. "*I* am the captain."

"I knew I should have stuck with paper crowns," Isaac said.

"We're approaching the river," Mrs Zhang said. "Five minutes until we are within rifle range. There is no signal from Mister Mitchell."

"If he's here, he'll be waiting inside," Isaac said. "What of the— Oh, there it is."

From shore, a light flashed on-off, on-off, on-off.

"That's not Morse," Kelly said.

"Our spy is here, but Mister Mitchell is not," Mrs Zhang said.

"Time for the show to begin," Isaac said. He picked up his bag and left the cockpit with Kelly on his heels.

A large shadow loomed aft. Gregory was already awake, and had prepared the inflatable.

"Ah, you see, Kelly?" Isaac said. "Gregory is wearing *his* hat."

"A bright orange rain hat," Kelly said. "That's practical, and nautically appropriate."

"What if we say the beret is part of a disguise?" Isaac said. The diesel engine cut out. The world went silent.

"Bliss," Kelly said.

Gregory removed the battery from its on-deck recharging dock and slotted it into the modified outboard engine. He raised a thumb.

"Thank you, Mrs MacKay," Isaac said. "Now, there is just one last thing." He held out the spare beret.

By way of reply, Kelly donned her tactical helmet with the affixed night-vision rig. "There. Now I've got a hat, too," she said.

"Spoilsport," Isaac said.

Unlike the bustling freight ports and ferry harbours further north and south, Nieuwpoort had been a sedate marina town before the Blackout. The sandy beaches, seafront apartments, manicured gardens, multi-lingual shops, award-winning menus, historical trails, and affordable anchorage had been a lure to boat-owning tourists from up and down the coast. After the Blackout, it had become a hub for refugees. Those same pleasure boats had become rescue ships during the warlike chaos that followed the apocalypse. Inevitably, those rescue ships had then become plague carriers.

Built either side of the fresh-water Yser River, and lacking the heavy industry of the mega-ports further along the coast, Nieuwpoort had been an obvious hub for redevelopment and resettlement in the years since. First by farmers, and then by pirates from the north seeking a base from which to raid Kent and East Anglia. A naval bombardment had destroyed the pirates and devastated the city. More recently, settlers had returned: sailors, traders, ambitious farmers, retired adventurers, and the children of Belgian refugees who'd grown up on a diet of European myths. Nearly a thousand souls in total. Until the barbarians returned. Once again, the citizens had become refugees, taking to their boats and sailing west. It was a journey Isaac and Kelly travelled in reverse, sailing up the River Yser.

Travelling slow. Travelling quiet. In a boat with an electric engine he'd designed during his foolishly optimistic period when he'd assumed the silicon age would swiftly return. Like elsewhere, he'd established a small community to keep the technology safe, supporting them with guns, food, tools, training, and when taxes were reintroduced, with a very clever accountant. Kelly kept watch while Isaac steered, using a night-vision monocular to keep them in the middle of channel.

"This is us," he whispered when they'd travelled a hundred metres upriver, angling the near-silent boat towards the marina of an old sailing school which had become a fishing-fleet repair-yard before the most recent collapse.

As the ship bumped into the rotting tyres attached to the pier's side, Kelly jumped ashore. Isaac secured the rope.

"Clear," Kelly whispered.

Isaac took the radio from his bag, inserted an earpiece, and clicked a Morse *A-OK* back to their ship. "Shall we?"

Inland of the old sailing school was ornamental parkland which had been turned into fields. Over a decade ago, orchards had replaced the wild lawns. Two years ago, when the Belgian expedition had arrived, most of those trees had been felled, leaving only neat boundary-lines of apple and pear trees between the potato fields.

"Beer and fries," Isaac said as they picked their way between the trees. "Who needs more?"

"Apples make cider," Kelly said.

"Which will do in a pinch," Isaac said. "Far superior to wine, don't you think?"

"No comment," she said.

"Of course you agree," he said.

"Boss, I told you, I'm not taking sides," she said.

At the top of the parkland was a row of five old fuel-tankers, converted into low-rise water towers. From the front of each, and down a field-side drainage ditch, pipes ran to the river. A hand-pump allowed the tanks to be filled during a drought. On top of the tankers, industrial satellite-dishes had been converted into funnels to collect rainwater. Now, water dripped down the sides of four overfull tanks, leaving a trail of green moss edged with rust-red lichen. The fifth tank had split during the rapid freeze-thaw cycle at the beginning of the month, releasing an aquatic avalanche that had carved a gulley in the fields below.

By the rear of each tanker lay a jumble of broken pipes from the farm's irrigation system. On the roadside lay fire hoses used to top up the domestic water tanks of the local settlers who'd moved into the neighbouring block of single-storey holiday homes.

"Through there," Isaac whispered, gesturing to the cluster of semi-repaired cabins.

Kelly flipped down the monocular on the left side of her vision rig. "Nothing on thermal."

"We're too far from the trade routes for refugees," Isaac said.

"Hope that holds true for enemy soldiers," Kelly said.

"Murderers," Isaac said. "They can steal some lines from a book, but they're just another group of murderers. Henry is right on that score."

The pre-dawn quiet was broken by a warning yip from a distant dog.

"Half a klick south," Kelly said.

"No doubt woken by our spy," Isaac said.

"What do you want me to do if the dogs get close?" Kelly asked.

"Say meow," Isaac said, but he drew a pistol from his shoulder holster, and then the suppressor from its pouch.

The one-storey pre-fab terrace was littered with heart-breaking hints at the ambitions of the settlers who'd so precipitously fled. Where three of the red-roofed houses had burned down, the rubble had been removed and a trio of scaffold-frame windmills built in their place. Before the cloth sails had been ripped to rags by recent storms, the turbines would have been inefficient, and low power. But they would have kept a few lights on at night, and enough freezers to turn fishing from a daily chore into an optimistic excursion.

Opposite, three more cabins had been painted with a sun and stars motif, across which was a large sign reading *École*. The glass windows had been smashed, and the walls on either side were flecked with bullet holes. On the path outside were dropped suitcases, torn open. Their storm-drenched contents were mixed with the loot the terrorists had dumped after they'd searched the cabin.

"No bones," Kelly said.

To which another distant dog yipped a reply.

"We go south," Isaac said when they reached the main road beyond the fisherfolk's proto-settlement, *Albert I Laan*.

"We're following the train line?" Kelly asked.

"The tram line," Isaac said. "Belgium had a light-rail line running from the French border in the south all the way to the Dutch border in the north. Which sounds more impressive than saying it covered a distance of sixty-seven kilometres."

"Still sounds impressive to me," Kelly said. "The tram is why the navy want to set up a garrison here in the spring?"

"I doubt they truly intend to," Isaac said. "Their interest has always been in the Mediterranean, but Henry will write a report, which some parliamentary committee can cite as future proof that they considered all options before, reluctantly, focusing their efforts on reinforcing Montpellier."

"Except it doesn't look like Mister Mitchell is here."

"No, so *we* will write the report, and he can sign it. Or I could forge his signature for all that anyone would notice."

"He wouldn't like that," Kelly said.

"I suppose not. But we'll still write the report. Not for the navy, but for the European Union. They'll want to know how much repair work is required when they return. They *will* return, and *they* will build that train link."

"Was that why we went to Ostend?" she asked.

"To locate the tram-cars, yes," Isaac said. "Once they build an extension line from the border to Calais, they could link up with the heavy-rail line through the Channel Tunnel. Today's harvest could be sold in Twynham tomorrow."

"Construction brings permanence, and permanence brings progress," Kelly said, uttering their creed.

"If it brings a little profit, too, why not?" Isaac said. "This is our turning. The *Henri Cromberzlann* will take us to the N34. That will take us back to the sea, but behind the rendezvous at the seafront apartments."

A trio of dogs howled. This time, far closer.

Like the cabins, the buildings on either side of the road showed signs of successive waves of flight, fight, looting, and repair. Rubble had been removed from the road, while cars had been dragged aside.

Broken windows had been boarded. Broken doors had been barricaded shut, with a list of remaining loot daubed on the door in scavenger-script. Over that had been added the intolerant gospel of pain and destruction, scrawled in rote Latin by a hesitant hand who'd kicked over the paint-can when they'd finished. The colour was the same star-yellow they'd used at the school, and would have been a stark contrast to the red blood of the victim pinned to the door opposite. That corpse was now only a ribcage into which two knives had been hammered, pinning them in place as they'd died. A block to the south, a dog barked, confirming the fate of the other bones.

At the road's end lay a double row of apartment buildings. Isaac clicked a three-letter message in Morse, and got a four-letter reply.

"Our spy is still signalling," Isaac whispered. "It's that building there."

"Slow," Kelly whispered, tapping her goggles. "Person. Corner. Waiting."

They'd sent out one spy, alone. If someone was still signalling, and someone else was on the corner outside, there was a very good chance their spy had been caught, and the enemy had set a trap. But that was why they'd come ashore in the dinghy.

Kelly raised the carbine to her shoulder. "On three," she whispered. "Stay close."

Gun raised, he followed her across the road, to a rusting wreck of an old tram. She peered around it before ducking down, raising a hand. He held up a cautioning one of his own before tapping out a three-letter instruction. A long minute later, came the reply.

"At least one inside who is signalling to the ship," he whispered.

"One on that corner," she said. "Could be more in front of the building, or on the beach."

"Cover me," he said.

"Boss?"

Hands behind his back, he stepped out from beyond the wrecked tram, and began whistling Yankee Doodle.

Dawn was still an hour away, but the scudding cloud cover was already reflecting the light from beyond the horizon, adding shade to the shadows, out of which he saw the figure step. He switched key, and began whistling the Imperial March.

"Isaac?" the shadow asked. It was a man who sounded far wearier than his meagre twenty years. A man Isaac had sent into Europe as a spy to atone for his betrayal of Ruth, of his badge, and the people he'd sworn to protect: Simon Longfield.

"We had a deal, Simon," Isaac said. "You were to come here alone. There is someone atop the apartment block signalling." He took his hands from behind his back. In one hand, he held his sidearm which he aimed at Simon's head. In the other was the radio. "My ship is about to shell this building."

"No, don't!" Simon said. "It's kids! There are kids in there!"

"Children?" Isaac asked.

"Yes. Refugees," Simon said.

"Explain," Isaac said.

"I went looking for the people running things, like you said. The people behind the knights, and the coup, and everyone else."

"I know that. Explain the children."

"They were prisoners," Simon said. "We had to help them."

"Who is we?"

"Me and Matilda."

"Which still isn't an explanation," Isaac said.

"I found the knights and said who I was, and who my mum was, and about the coup, and how I needed to speak to their boss. They didn't care. They locked me up. Matilda helped me escape. So we tried again. I found a different group, and they'd have killed me if Matilda wasn't faster with her gun. But they had prisoners, too, and we couldn't leave them."

"So you've been wandering Belgium asking murderous brigands to take you to their leader?" Isaac asked.

"Of course. That's what you wanted, right?"

"Not exactly," Isaac said. He raised a hand, waving Kelly over, before tapping an all-clear on the radio. "Let's talk in the shadows. You were supposed to go to Switzerland."

"I tried," Simon said.

"How far did you get?"

"The other side of the German border," Simon said.

Isaac sighed. "And you brought the refugees back here?"

"So you could take them to safety," Simon said.

Isaac's earpiece squawked, not with Morse, but with Mrs Zhang's voice. "Lights on the beach. Half a klick south."

"Are all the refugees inside?" Isaac asked.

"Upstairs, yes."

"Then who's on the beach? You were followed, Simon."

"We were careful," Simon said. "I'm sure we were careful."

"Trouble, boss?" Kelly asked.

"We've got company," Isaac said, pushing Simon back through the battered apartment doors. "Lights on the beach to the south. Those dogs, they were in the south. Simon brought refugees with him, but the enemy has followed."

"How many refugees?" Kelly asked.

"Forty-two," Simon said.

"We can fit them aboard," Kelly said.

"Of course we can," Isaac said. "I do so hate being the good guy. Fine. We better go meet them."

"I can bring them down," Simon said.

"No, we're going up," Isaac said. "Kelly, numbers and time."

"On it," she said, and dashed up the stairs.

Isaac pushed the broken door as near to closed as the twisted hinges would allow, placing a three-legged chair in front of them. "Simon, Simon, Simon," he said. "You're not very good at following instructions, are you?"

"I tried," he said.

"Not very well," Isaac said, taking a cylindrical grenade from his bag. He wrapped string around the grenade and tied it to the chair, with more string around the pull-handle which he tied to the broken door. "I told you Switzerland. You decided to play the hero and got no further than Germany."

"You wanted me to leave them to die?" Simon asked. "They were chained up. That's what the knights do. They take prisoners, and chain them up, and torture them. It's a game. I saw it. They each take a turn to see who can get the loudest scream, the longest cry. One time, they wanted to see who could get the furthest spurt of arterial blood. They lined up this family. Eight of them and... and..." He trailed off.

Isaac carefully pulled the pin from the grenade. "Yes. I know. And other killers will have been doing the exact same thing to other civilians all over the continent. Switzerland was the answer."

"But you don't *know* that," Simon said. "You just said it was a hunch. But save one life, you save the world, that's what Matilda says."

"I get the impression she's the brains of your partnership," Isaac said, pushing Simon up the stairs. "Perhaps I should have this conversation with her."

The refugees were in apartment one, the pre-arranged rendezvous. The apartment occupied one half of the top floor of the five-storey building. A woman stood outside, a submachine gun gripped in her hands, but she visibly relaxed as she saw Simon.

"Matilda, this is Mr Isaac," Simon said.

"*Guten Tag*," she said.

"Not for another thirty minutes," Isaac said. "When day does arrive, we need to be gone. Simon saved you from the knights?"

"We saved each other," Matilda said.

From inside the room came muttered voices and muted crying. Isaac sighed. He raised his radio. "Kelly?"

"Three on the beach," she said. "Four behind the building. At least eight further south. What do you want me to do?"

"Come to the stairwell, and wait for the bang," he said.

Two years before, as the Belgians began cleaning up the riverside cabins, Isaac had spent a week selecting and decorating the apartment. New windows. New curtains. A new rainwater-flush toilet and a wood-burning stove. Though large, it had only two bedrooms, with most of the space being the open-plan living room. Floor-to-ceiling windows opened onto the wraparound balcony, in front of which he'd placed a telescope and a pair of chairs. Two more were set either side of the coffee table. Other than the stove, he hadn't installed a kitchen, but he had stocked the bar. The design was a deliberate blank slate. Not a home *for* the future, but a shape of *a* possible future. Not necessarily in Belgium. Not necessarily in Europe. But a future somewhere if it became impossible to remain in Britain.

In hindsight, his plans were a tad premature. At least the lack of furniture was a boon in that it left plenty of space for the refugees. Children. Women. A few older men. Their clothes were ragged, their shoes held together with cloth. The few recently scavenged coats, four of which Isaac recognised as having been in the master bedroom closet, only emphasised the rags worn beneath. Faces were lined with fear, dirt, and exhaustion. Some of the adults tightly clutched their children, others, just as tightly, clutched weapons. Knives and spears, and only a handful of handguns.

Isaac smiled. "In a few minutes, we'll leave here, and head to the river where we'll catch a ship back to Britain. Please follow the instructions when the time comes. Thank you."

"There is room for them all?" Matilda asked. "Forty, yes? You can fit forty on your boat."

"That's how many Simon told you could fit," Isaac said. "No," he added as Simon opened his mouth. "It wasn't a question. Yes, we will have room for everyone. You *appear* gormless, Simon. You *sound* gormless. But you're the kind of Englishman who accidentally ended up painting a quarter of the world pink. I am reminded of what General Washington said about your kind."

"What was that?" Simon asked.

"Fire," Isaac said. "You and I will have a reckoning when this is done, so let us get it done quickly. Get everyone up and ready to move. They need their hands free. Allocate one adult per child. This way." He led them into the smaller of the two bedrooms where a narrow window offered a view of nothing more glamorous than the neighbouring apartment block.

He opened the wardrobe. Inside, stacked nearly to the ceiling, were transparent, and clearly empty, plastic crates. He pulled them out, and drew his knife, with which he levered out the panel at the back. Behind, a hole had been cut in the wall, giving access to the elevator shaft. He sheathed his knife and took out a flashlight, shining it down inside the hole before leaning forward and unhooking a bag from inside the elevator shaft. He dropped the bag into the room before reaching back in and hanging his torch on that same interior hook.

"The harnesses are in the bag. Ropes, too. Four harnesses. The small loop is for a hand, the larger loop for a foot. Pull the hand forward, ninety degrees to the direction of descent, and it'll act as a brake. The shaft leads down to a basement parking structure. There is a service door linking it with the parking lots of the neighbouring apartments. We'll travel through those, then up, and overground to the river. Our ship will meet us there. For now, get everyone down to the basement. Kelly and I will delay our adversaries."

Isaac paused in the living room, near the main windows, to update Mrs Zhang over the radio, before returning outside, where he met Kelly by the door to the stairwell.

"The enemy must have followed them," Kelly said.

"I would imagine so," Isaac said. "They're half-starved, and won't be much use in a fight. We'll need to buy time, but the plan remains the same. Lure as many as we can inside." He opened the stairwell door, and began to descend.

"You trust Simon, then?" Kelly asked.

"Absolutely not," Isaac said. "But I do believe in judging people by the company they keep. It will take time to get the children to the parking structure. We need to slow the enemy down."

"How?"

"I shall talk softly," Isaac said. "When that fails, we'll skip the stick and go straight to the gun. Third floor."

"On it," she said, though he continued down to the second.

The gunfire hadn't begun. The grenade in the lobby hadn't exploded. The enemy was still getting into position. Presumably, they were aware of the number they were following, but not how poorly armed they were. Isaac made his way to an apartment with a view of the road, propping the cracked door open with a broken lamp before walking close to the window. He stopped a metre from it and fired, letting his suppressed shot shatter the glass.

"Hello down there," he called even as glass pattered to the sandy mud-drifts below. "Forgive me, my Latin is rusty. Should I say *Salve*, or *Ave*?"

By way of reply, bullets thudded into the cracked cladding surrounding the window.

He unscrewed the suppressor. "Can I interest you in a trade? A farm in Wales for anyone who joins our side?"

That produced a pair of single shots which thudded through the empty window frame and into the ceiling.

"Then this is your last chance," Isaac said. "Leave now, or die."

This time, he did hear voices. Too muted to discern the language, but the tone was one of orders being given. He sighed. It was always thus. He fired two random shots through the window, retreating back into the corridor even as a flurry of lead smashed into the room.

He raised the radio. "They're about to make entry," he said, and made his way back to the stairwell.

Damp plaster cascaded around the stairwell as the grenade in the lobby detonated, reverberating through the building.

Isaac jogged down the stairs to the fire door leading to the landing and wider stairwell above the atrium. The lobby had been repainted with soot and blood. Two shredded bodies lay by the door, motionless. A third screamed, outside in the street. On the third floor, from a road-facing window, Kelly fired. Their attackers returned fire, the anguished cries of pain lost beneath the barrage thudding into the building's wall.

Isaac leaned by the pillar, taking aim through the now ruined entrance.

The brigand curled around the corner of the shattered door. He'd been smart, using the cover of the building to avoid the rifle fire from upstairs. Smart, but predictable. Isaac's first shot smashed the knight's leg, causing him to fall to the floor where his assault rifle clattered out of reach. Isaac fired again, twice, into the brigand's back, before reaching for his radio again.

"Time to retreat," he said, pulling out a grenade and checking it had a red stripe before pitching it through the open doorway.

Counting, he ran back up the stairs, reaching them as the grenade detonated. Dust and spiders fell from the ceiling. He jogged up the stairs, and found Kelly by the door to the second floor.

"Three had assault rifles, the rest are using captured British semi-automatic rifles," she said.

"Indeed. But captured from where?" Isaac asked. "Go. Up. Oh, how I miss escalators."

At the top, leaving Kelly in the stairwell, he went back into the apartment. The remaining refugees were lined up in fours, with half already having descended. Simon remained in the bedroom, though it was an older woman who'd taken charge of fitting the harnesses.

"Where's Matilda?"

"Below," Simon said. "Are there going to be more explosions, because three people nearly fell."

"Nearly isn't did," Isaac said. "Go down with the next group. Make certain everyone knows to head to the river if they have to scatter." He took a step back, ignoring the confused and frightened looks on the faces of the refugees. They'd made better time than he'd hoped. But when he'd picked this apartment, he'd assumed there would be no more than four people forced to hastily flee. Of course, he'd also assumed it was the British authorities he would be running from. He smiled. He'd been wrong about that, and maybe it wasn't all he'd been wrong about.

He returned to the stairwell, where Kelly leaned against the wall.

"They're in the stairwell," she said.

"Good," he said, leaning forward to fire a shot down through the void between the bannisters. "Two minutes more, I think. How numerous are the enemy?"

"Two groups. Less than twenty in each."

"Interesting. That's a lot of people to send after some refugees." He checked his watch before firing a shot down the stairwell. A slug came in return, slamming into the wall only one flight below. "Fall back," he yelled. "Retreat! Run! Escape!"

"Enough, boss," Kelly hissed. "Don't oversell it."

"Did I tell you I once wanted to be an actor?" he asked, following her back into the apartment. Behind them, feet pounded up the stairs.

"Many times," she said.

They pushed the apartment door closed, and began dragging furniture in front of it.

"No," Isaac said, when two of the rear-most refugees attempted to assist. "We have a plan, and it requires you descending those ropes. Go."

Kelly pushed a last chair by the door, before taking up position in the living room, behind the central pillar.

Isaac raised his gun, and fired at the sea-facing windows, shattering the glass.

A shoulder thudded into the closed door.

"Time to depart," Isaac said, pulling one last grenade from his pocket. This had a green stripe. He pulled the pin, and followed Kelly to the bedroom as smoke began billowing from the broken window.

When they reached the basement car park, they found Simon there with a trio of armed refugees whose guns were pointing at the elevator shaft.

"You're looking the wrong way," Isaac said, detaching the harness, and pushing past them even as he turned on his flashlight.

"Are they ahead of us?" Simon asked, as Isaac headed towards the tunnel to the neighbouring building.

"Relax, Simon. All is going according to plan."

The first shake was soft, a rumble which began above, shuffling down the corridor's walls. The second felt like a wall of air trying to outrace the wind.

"Move!" Isaac yelled, bracing his hand on the wall. "*Vite. Allez.* Oh, what's hurry in German?"

The third earthquake was more sustained, a waterfall of sound, causing the ground to thump out of time with the roof. Behind them came a dust storm, sweeping forward faster than an avalanche.

Isaac ducked, turning his head and closing his eyes as grit swept over him.

"What is that?" Simon asked, coughing through the dust.

"The result of a missile fired from my ship," Isaac said. "Aimed at the smoke we left billowing from the apartment. What you hear now is the apartment falling down above our heads, so if you wouldn't mind running, that would be appreciated."

Three buildings along, the tremors continued while they were chased by a slow-moving river of smoke.

"Everyone still here?" Isaac asked. "Wonderful. Matilda, translate. We are going upstairs and outside. Matilda, you will follow Kelly. Everyone else will follow you. You will run to some old oil tankers which were being used as water storage, through a few garden-fields, and down to the river. Our ship will be there shortly."

"And should—" Simon began.

"No questions," Isaac cut in, and opened the door to the stairs. "No stopping. Wait for my word."

Above ground, the top floor of his apartment building was missing. The third and fourth floors were on fire. Glass, brick, and burning cloth cascaded from the candle-inferno. What was missing, for now, was the enemy, but not all would have been inside. Any who weren't would know exactly where to head. With dawn having arrived, there was nowhere to hide.

"Kelly, go," he said, stepping out into the street, making himself the easy target while he waited for the enemy to come.

After ten seconds, having seen no one, he began to feel foolish.

"What's the point of a grand gesture when there's no one to see?" he said. "But why *isn't* anyone chasing us?"

If the enemy weren't here, on the inland side of the block, they had to be on the seaward side. There could be only one reason for that.

He jogged around the building, following the side road until he could see the sea. And there, on the sand, he saw them. Two teams of five, sheltering among the wrecks. The most northerly group had a spotter who was now climbing back up a beached ship.

"Mrs Zhang," he said, tapping his radio. "They're on the beach. Two firing teams. Armed with mortars, I think."

"Where?" she asked.

"Sixty metres northwest of the apartment building. They want the ship."

He raised his carbine, emptying a magazine at the nearest team, hitting one, and causing the others to scatter. He was uncertain what weapons they had, but at least some had assault rifles, because those fired back.

Lead thumped into his chest, knocking the air from him. He rolled, coughed, wheezed, struggling to breathe while crawling back to cover. A hand grabbed his collar, half dragging, half carrying him back behind the corner of the building.

"Trouble, boss?" Kelly asked.

"Why are you here?" he asked, slipping his hand beneath his vest, searching for blood, but only found sweat.

"I heard what you said to Gregory," she said. "I gave Matilda a compass bearing to follow." She leaned around the side of the building, and fired a burst. A trio of explosions followed. Dull, but close by. "I think that was Greg. Can you run?"

"Let's find out."

They ran after the refugees, angling along the road. Every time Isaac tried to stop, Kelly ushered him on, until they'd caught up with Simon and the rear-most of the refugees.

"They're not following," Kelly said.

"They aren't following *us*," Isaac said.

Mrs Zhang reached the dock after the first set of refugees, but before Isaac and Kelly.

"Take us north!" Isaac bellowed, as he clambered aboard, increasingly furious as the pain from his chest made itself known. "Passengers below!"

He tore the plyboard cover off the heavy machine gun, swinging it around to face the shore, half hoping for a target.

A mortar shell hit the northern bank of the river. Another exploded in the water ahead. Isaac pivoted the machine gun left and right, but could see no target.

When Nieuwpoort was nothing but a smoke plume on the horizon, he let go of the machine gun, and entered the cockpit.

"They wanted my ship," Mrs Zhang said.

"I know," Isaac said. "Keep us heading north. And it's *my* ship," he added, halfway to the cabin door.

"My hat begs to differ," Mrs Zhang said.

Isaac went below. It was more crammed than the apartment. "We will soon be heading for Kent," he said, addressing the refugees. "By day's end, you will have a hot meal, a hot shower, and some clean clothes. The danger is over." He turned to Simon. "Not for you. On deck, please."

Matilda took his hand, stepping forward with him.

"Come if you want," Isaac said. "It'll change nothing."

Isaac climbed back on deck, leaning against the rail behind the cockpit.

"You knew how many refugees we could carry," Isaac said. "I take it there are more refugees in Europe whom you left behind?"

"And I'm going back for them," Simon said. "I know we had an agreement—"

"Yes, yes," Isaac said, cutting him off. "We'll get to that. You decided to set up a refugee-railroad, didn't you?"

"We kept clear of the train tracks *and* the roads," Simon said.

"Read a history book," Isaac said. "At some point, you told some refugees that they had to remain in Belgium or Germany because there wouldn't be room on this boat for them."

"We had to—"

"Just a yes or no, and that was a yes," Isaac said. "They knew we were bringing a boat here, Simon, and they wanted to destroy it. They had a mortar team on the beach."

"It wasn't just a mortar team, boss," Kelly said. "Mrs Zhang said they had a missile of their own."

"Wonderful," Isaac said. "Simon, the people you left behind were found, and tortured for information."

"*Mein Gott*," Matilda said. "Let me off, please. Here. I must go back."

"Very admirable," Isaac said. "But those people are already dead."

"*Meine schwester*," Matilda said, walking to the side of the boat.

Isaac sighed. "I'm sorry for your loss, but it is now too late to change the past."

"I tried to do what you said," Simon said. "I tried to get to Switzerland, and to find whoever is running this, but there isn't anyone."

"There is," Isaac said.

"What did you want me to do? Leave them?" Simon asked.

"Rule one in life is, if you're going to do a job, do it properly," Isaac said. "Whomever you left behind is dead, and we've lost Nieuwpoort as a rendezvous for future trips. From now on, you don't tell anyone where the coastal pick-up will be."

"From now on? You mean I can go back?" Simon asked.

"Since you're willing, it doesn't seem much of a punishment, but you still have your sentence to serve. Wherever we drop you off, you'll return, just you or Matilda, in exactly three weeks' time. But no more than the two of you. Under absolutely no circumstances, more than two. Leave the refugees inland. We'll arrange a way to bring them to the shore, and a better way of running this operation."

Chapter 16 - Three Victims
The Dover Police Station

"Wow," Anna Riley said.

"Thank you," Isaac said.

"I mean, wow, you really can spin a story," Riley said. "There's no way you abseiled down an elevator shaft."

"While I might have had to edit some points for brevity, it was only ever to aid clarity," Isaac said.

"You're expecting to meet Simon again in three weeks?" Ruth asked.

"Someone will," Isaac said. "Though I might leave the rendezvous to some of the European scavengers. I'll need to discuss it with Henry. Of larger concern is how we'll extricate any future refugees they send our way. The lion's share of those with Simon came from Germany. Establishing an enclave on the Baltic would give them a shorter distance to travel, while also drawing the knights away from Calais."

"You're going to the Baltic?" Ruth asked.

"Ideally, it would be a job for the navy, but Henry would have to put in the request." Isaac held up the tablet at which he'd been glancing while recounting his tale. "It appears he, in Dunkirk, faced a similar problem of a group of barbarians armed with far more than mortars."

"How can you, and the enemy, have super-weapons when our soldiers don't?" Ruth asked.

"These aren't super-weapons," Isaac said. "The opposite, in fact. Missiles and mortars were a common weapon of terrorists before the Blackout. I salvaged my equipment from a bunker while the army was busy pretending it was a navy. I imagine our enemy did the same. But honestly, Ruth, you surprise me. I assumed your questions would be centred around Simon."

"I don't know how I feel about that," Ruth said. She ran her fingers across the blackbird-shaped brooch. "I'm glad he's not dead, but I'm also glad he's not here. He's not, is he?"

"No. We dropped him on the coast before we crossed the sea."

"Good," Ruth said. She put the ornate brooch in a drawer of the duty desk. "How do *you* feel, Anna?"

"It wasn't Simon who shot me," Riley said. "He's making amends, and saving lives. That's good. What did you do with the refugees, Isaac?"

"Mrs Zhang is questioning them to see what they can tell us about their travels through enemy territory."

"Shouldn't military intelligence be doing that?" Ruth asked. "That's Anna's job, isn't it?"

"And it was Mrs Zhang's previous area of employment," Isaac said.

"Which is another of those non-answers that spawn a million more questions," Ruth said. "Fine. Why did you want Simon to go to Switzerland?"

"A hunch," Isaac said. "It's a country of bunkers and guns. An ideal spot for a crazed megalomaniac to plot war."

"That's not an answer, either," Ruth said.

"Don't bother," Riley said. "That's as near to the truth as we'll get from him. If Simon didn't make it to Switzerland, then what does this mean for the war plans?"

"Nothing," Isaac said. "They'd only have changed if I had some solid information to give to the medal-collectors. Instead, so far, it seems as if there is no real army facing us. No cohesion. No command structure. The killers came west under someone's orders, but there were no orders for what they should do next. Now, the majority have returned to the trade with which they are most familiar: banditry."

"Not all of them, not the people who followed Simon," Ruth said.

"Agreed," Isaac said. "There is a core group of properly trained, properly equipped fighters, who are recruiting rank-and-file crow-fodder from among the barbarian stragglers. In his video, Henry said they're using radio. I imagine after the stay-behind group of refugees were caught, a message was sent to this group on the coast. Perhaps, having been foiled by Henry, they decided a refugee ship would make for a valuable consolation prize."

"Why not attack the ships in Calais?" Riley asked.

"A very good question," Isaac said. "One we should ask again after we've viewed Henry's video."

"You can do that while I finish my incident report," Ruth said, picking up her pen.

Anna wheeled her chair over to Isaac who propped the tablet on one of the free benches.

Half listening to the audio of Mister Mitchell at war, Ruth distractedly sketched the morning's crime scene. "There. Finished," she finally said. "You know who the general is, don't you, Isaac?"

"I've met a few of them, yes," Isaac said.

"I mean the enemy general," Ruth said. "The leader. The person behind all this. Because you suspect there is one."

"I suspect there is a warlord. One individual giving orders to a core group via radio," Isaac said, pointing to the tablet. "This core group is able to travel with impunity, by truck, through the wasteland by buying safe passage with food and guns. The rest of the enemy are ill-trained fanatics who'd run if they weren't terrified of those to the east."

"You mean the leader, and you mean in Switzerland," Ruth said.

"I think Switzerland. Henry doesn't," Isaac said. "Perhaps he's correct. The evidence he collected suggests further east than that. The Black Sea, perhaps."

"Where they were, isn't where they are," Riley said. "The enemy has trucks, and oil. A refinery and a well. Find that, we find them."

"Indeed, but *how* do we find them?" Isaac asked. "There are thousands of hungry, cultish fanatics in France, Germany, and the Lowlands from whom the enemy can recruit a fresh army. Poorly trained. Ill-led. But so is our own."

"But we'll still win," Ruth said. "We have way more people in Britain to draw on. We can make new weapons. Better weapons. Any time it comes to a straight fight between us and the terrorists, we win."

"Which is what our enemy wants," Isaac said. "What does victory look like, do you think? Because right now, if we're victorious, so is our enemy."

"Now you've lost me," Riley said.

"Our enemy," Isaac said, "our *real* enemy, this warlord co-ordinating these assaults, first consolidated the terrorists and tribes, barbarians and war-bands into three groups. This took years. Nearly twenty of them, so it seems. He picked a group in the north, the south, and the east, and supplied them, ensuring their victory, and the defeat of all other rivals and all other threats. Then he pushed these three groups out of his own lands, towards us. His goal is to become a super-power. A nation-state. How is this achieved?"

"By building up the agricultural base," Ruth said.

"Yes, that's one way," Isaac said.

"Education," Riley said.

"Yes, that's another," Isaac said. "Rhetorical questions aren't so much fun when they get answers."

"Why perpetrate so much murder?" Ruth asked. "Why create so much chaos? Why not trade with the farmers in France? Why kill them?"

"The enemy wants a buffer zone," Isaac said. "They want Britain focused on rebuilding close to the Channel. The closer they keep us to the coast, the closer we'll always stay. People in Britain are tired of rationing. They'll endure privation for a few more months, but not a few more years. We *will* win this war. We'll kill the barbarians. We'll rebuild Calais. And in doing so, this warlord thinks *we* will have defeated the terrorist threat to his own borders. We'll become tied down in France and the lowlands. He'll be free to take over the lands to the east."

"Hard to do if he's butchered all the farmers," Riley said.

"Quite," Isaac said. "I said our enemy had a plan. I didn't say it was a good one. The Royal Navy's response is to push for control of the Mediterranean. Henry and I believe it will be much simpler just to kill this warlord. Of course, that does require finding him, and there we do keep striking out."

"Well, that's depressing," Ruth said. "Makes me almost glad I only have a murder to deal with."

"A murder?" Riley asked. "Who?"

"It might not be murder," Ruth said. "I'm not really sure yet. There was another arsenic poisoning last night."

"Same as the last two?" Riley asked. "Inhalation of chromated copper arsenate?"

"We've got to wait on the autopsy, and the lab report from Twynham, for confirmation," Ruth said. "But it does appear similar to the previous two. Did you read the reports?"

"Everyone in Twynham is talking about it," Riley said. "Not kindly, either. They've been mocking our Kent-cousins for kissing utility poles. Do you have notes?"

"Better. Video," Ruth said. She took her phone to the sergeant.

"Is no one using pen and paper anymore?" Riley asked. "The first two cases were confirmed as being arsenic poisoning, yes?"

"By the lab in Twynham, and by autopsy here," Ruth said. "The reports are on the phone too. There's a folder. I created it myself," she added with no small measure of pride.

"I think we need to upgrade you to a proper database," Isaac said. "I can install one before I head to the frontline."

"Yeah, like the sergeant would allow *that*," Ruth said. "She doesn't even like me having the phone."

Riley muted the volume from the phone, but kept watching. "Tell me about the first two victims," she said.

"The first death was on the night of the fourth," Ruth said. "Mr George Soakes, the publican who ran the Wire and Wrench on Cannon Street. Fifty-five years old. He'd had a row with his wife. She's been volunteering as a nurse since the war began, mostly because they'd agreed to sell the pub, but he'd changed his mind. If he'd not died, they might have ended up getting divorced. Family drama aside, they'd had a fight, so he was sleeping in the office at the back of the pub. But he was found dead in the lounge bar. A foot-long length of burned utility pole was in the grate."

"Just one log?" Riley asked.

"We sent ash, and the log, back to Twynham," Ruth said. "They confirmed arsenic in the ash. Tons of the stuff."

"Do you have the toxicology report?" Riley asked.

"In the filing cabinet," Ruth said. "But there's a photograph of it in the folder. Do you want me to show you?"

"Hang on. Found it," Riley said. "There's no mention of the alcohol content in his blood."

"Should there be?" Ruth asked.

"Yes," Riley said. "The doctor requested an expedited report, but just asked them to test the blood sample for arsenic. No other tests were performed. Was there a follow-up report?"

"Not that we got," Ruth said. "We asked for confirmation as quick as we could get it, because there was already quite a panic. Half the city brought their woodpile in here to have us tell them whether they could burn it. The doctor confirmed it was arsenic poisoning from the autopsy."

"How much suspect wood was turned in?" Riley asked.

"Over the next few days? A couple of trees-worth," Ruth said. "We ran a testing-station at the power plant. None of it contained arsenic."

"And how much was found at the pub?" Riley asked.

"Other than what was found in the grate, none," Ruth said.

"If I were an unscrupulous, or uninformed, wood-seller, and I'd chopped down a telephone pole, I would surely sell more than one log to each customer," Riley said.

"We assumed it was just one random log that had been at the bottom of the pile," Ruth said. "He'd been drowning his sorrows with his regulars before curfew. The military police closed him up for the night. We found an empty bottle of whisky on the counter. At first, we thought he might even have known the log was dangerous. He drank the whisky, chucked the log on, and breathed in deep."

"That'd be a very odd suicide," Riley said.

"Yes, and we threw out that theory with the second victim."

"When was that?"

"The fourteenth," Ruth said. "Mavis Dalrymple was the vicar at the Unified Congregation Church, but she also ran housing for the unaccompanied child-refugees. She lived in one of the downstairs flats. The kids are all billeted upstairs."

"Where's that?"

"Victoria Crescent," Ruth said. "That's about two hundred metres north of Canon Street, so definitely could have been serviced by the same wood-seller. Around four in the morning, some of the kids, who were sleeping in the rooms immediately upstairs, got super-ill. Lots of vomiting and diarrhoea. The sound of one of them falling out of her bed alerted the warden. The alarm was raised, everyone was evacuated, and that's when they found Reverend Dalrymple's body. She was in her sitting room, by the fire, lying on the floor. Again, the autopsy confirmed arsenic, and so did the tests on the kids upstairs. They survived, thankfully. But the diagnosis was inhalation of arsenic fumes rising from the floor below."

"But there was only one log in the fire?" Riley asked.

"Yep. I checked the woodpile. No other logs there."

"It's murder," Isaac said.

"That's what I was thinking," Riley said. "You ran a warning after the death of the publican?"

"In the paper, on the radio, and we put up notices in every shop," Ruth said. "We asked all the clerics to read a warning during their sermons, and the teachers to mention it in their assemblies. Everyone should have known."

"A vicar who takes in refugee kids certainly would have," Riley said. "Someone like that would have checked the woodpile herself.

Someone planted that log. Probably planted the first log, too. Who's the latest victim?"

"Tommy Fry. He was found dead this morning. He runs a restaurant on Biggin Street. His body was discovered by his downstairs neighbours who are both waitresses at his restaurant. They think he came home drunk."

"There's a broken glass and a spilled bottle," Riley said, swiping through the crime scene photographs. "What about the vicar, was she drinking?"

"A sherry bottle was on a stand near her chair, and an empty glass," Ruth said. "She'd been at the hospice, sitting with a dying kid. Leukaemia. His parents brought him to Dover for treatment, but the bandits... well, it was too far progressed by the time they got here. He died soon after midnight. She left a little after one."

"Reasonable that she might want a drink afterwards," Riley said. "Is there a connection between the victims?"

"Potentially," Ruth said. "All are just under sixty. They all went to school in Dover, and lived here before the Blackout. They attended the same school as Sergeant Kettering. But they weren't in the same class, or even the same year, as each other."

"How many people in Dover match that profile?" Riley asked.

"About forty, I think," Ruth said. "You could double it if you included other schools."

"Are you sure this was arsenic?" Isaac asked, leaning over Riley to look at the screen. "I saw a few cases of death through toxic suffocation in the months following the Blackout. Those bodies don't look right."

"There *was* an autopsy," Ruth said. "And you've got the lab result there on the phone."

"It's a serial killer," Isaac said, heading back to the fire. "Three odd deaths within a month? Targeting people who lived here prior to the Blackout? A vicar, a publican, and a restaurant owner, these are all people who serve others. I'd look for someone who was barred from the pub. Someone whose spouse was remarried in that church. Something like that. Poison is usually an indication of a female killer. Was the publican having an affair?"

"Probably not," Ruth said. "He had been, a couple of years ago. The wife didn't think there was anyone else now, but she could have been wrong."

"Or lying," Riley said. "This is Mr Soakes's autopsy report? It's not very detailed. Who's Dr Jenner?"

"She runs the mortuary up at the castle," Ruth said. "She was an oncologist, but they've moved cancer care to Hastings. Since Dr Long was sent to run the frontline hospital in Calais, Dr Jenner's been subbing in at the castle."

"But not just in the morgue?" Riley asked. "The doctors are overworked, aren't they?"

"So are the nurses," Ruth said. "The students are all on the wards now. Mum goes from one operation to the next. A couple of weeks ago, there was a mortar attack on Calais. They used the crematorium chimney as a target, but the med-centre was next door. A lot of the doctors and nurses were injured. Some were killed. They've been shuttling a lot more patients through the tunnel to Dover for treatment ever since. Why?"

"The reports on the first two victims are incomplete," Riley said. "There's no mention of an internal examination. No description of the lung tissue, or throat. No examination of the extremities or skin. It's a simple statement of cause, with the blood test as confirmation. The reports on the surviving children are far more detailed. There's even a follow-up on their recovery. You need to speak with this doctor before she performs Mr Fry's autopsy, and you should be in the room as it's carried out."

"Seriously?" Ruth asked. "I don't mind blood, but no one is supposed to know what a stomach looks like."

"I can go, if you like," Riley said. "Probably should do that before lunch, though."

"Ah, yes, indeed," Isaac said. "Speaking of which, how did you come to arrive bearing gifts and with an escort from Albion?"

"Ah. Interesting story. Actually, it's connected to Mister Mitchell. Can I have your tablet? Let me see… hang on… where is he? Here. This guy. Private Hamish MacKay." She held up the tablet for Isaac, and then for Ruth. "About a week ago, I got a letter from Dad. That must have been just after this incident in Dunkirk, because that's where it was sent from. It came with an urgent dispatch to Commissioner Weaver, so she must have had a copy of these videos. She didn't share them with me, though."

"Are you working for her?" Ruth asked.

"In military intelligence," Riley said. "Serious Crimes is now focusing on corruption and wastage in the military supply chain. I wasn't really looking for spies or subversives, just profiteers. That was until Dad sent me a letter with a lead about where Hamish MacKay used to work, and whom he worked with."

20th December

Chapter 17 - A Friend Called Flora
Police House, Twynham

From outside, the prefab cabin in the grounds of Police House had barely changed since it had belonged to the Serious Crime Unit. Only the ramp was new, though it had been installed with too steep an incline. Now that it was covered in ice, pushing her wheelchair up the slope was a full-body workout. Clamping her right hand on the chair's wheel-rim, Anna Riley edged the left wheel forward an inch before clamping that and moving the right. Left, right, left, right, she edged her way up the ramp. Her technique needed a lot of practice. According to her doctor, she'd have plenty of time for it.

By the time she'd reached the top of the ramp, she was sweating a river, but at this temperature that could quickly become a glacier, so she eschewed ceremony, and shunted herself inside.

"Morning, Flora," Riley said. "Did you know, in the olden-days people used to visit the gym *before* going to work. Madness."

Inside, there were two noticeable differences from when she'd worked in the cabin with her adoptive father and Ruth Deering. The first was the boxes. More had arrived since yesterday, stacked as near to the door as the navy couriers could reach, entirely sealing off the southern half of the cabin.

"Would you look at this? It'll take all morning just to organise," Riley said, as she eased her way past the potential avalanche, and towards the cupboard which concealed the electric kettle. It also concealed her stack of coffee. Real coffee. From actual beans, rather than a chemistry lab. A gift from the ambassador. But if getting into the cabin was an expedition, getting to the toilets over in Police House would require Sherpas, so she only made a small cup. She pulled the blinds, pulled off her hat and scarf, and hung them over the nearest box.

"Did they leave a note of what was in these boxes, Flora?" she asked.

Flora didn't reply. Flora couldn't. Flora was a pot plant. A rose. A get-well gift from the American ambassador before he sailed across the ocean to begin his campaign for the U.S. presidency during what was to be a reunification election.

Apparently, the rose was the national flower of both the old USA and old England, which struck Riley as cheating. Having thrown off the yoke of the mad king and his vulpine prime minister, didn't General Washington have an obligation to pick a more local flower? She'd written that question in her reply to the ambassador, a letter which she'd not yet sent. And because she'd not sent the reply, the question came to her every morning as a reminding alarm that the clock was ticking on the day she'd have to make a decision.

"So where shall we begin, Flora? Any suggestions? Nearest first?"

She opened the closest, and lowest, box, scanning the first few sheets before replacing the cardboard lid and trying the next.

The investigation had begun with a Christmas card from her father. The card itself was brief, but the accompanying letter was long. As usual, struggling with what to write, her father had resorted to what he knew and had written about a potential crime. A soldier he'd dragooned into his unit, Hamish MacKay, had been conscripted from the tank reclamation yard in Bear Cross.

The team reclaiming old main battle tanks was only one unit in a massive mining and recycling effort. The suburb, northwest of Bournemouth, had been devastated by the Blackout fires, then partially cleared before a new north-south railway line was hastily laid atop the neighbouring Ringwood Road. Afterwards, and due to that new rail link, the suburb had become a storage area for raw materials mined from the other coastal ruins and the derelict cities further north.

MacKay's civilian supervisor in the yard claimed to be a Mr Stevens, who also claimed to be a leader of the Loyal Brigade. She knew of the Loyal Brigade because Isaac had massacred them a decade ago somewhere on the outskirts of London. Yes, they were a group of separatist-nationalists who'd fled justice after a bout of pre-election violence and intimidation, but that warranted a jail term, not execution. Back then, her father still shared the cottage with her. Isaac had arrived, late, announcing the deaths as if it were good news. She'd never seen her father so furious before, and rarely since. Regardless, the group had been led by a man called Mark Stevens, and he was dead.

He *was* dead. The man at the reclamation yard claimed to be an *Andrew* Stevens, younger brother of the dead Mark Stevens. That had been easy to confirm. The rest, not so much. A wheelchair wasn't the best vehicle for undercover work, so, since the reclamation facility was now overseen by the Royal Navy, she'd requested the navy send their records. They had. All of them.

Two boxes later, she retreated to the kettle, and made another small cup of coffee.

"What do you think, Flora? Were the navy being helpful, or just trying to free up space in their records department? No, I don't know, either."

The coffee beans, and Flora, weren't the only gift from the ambassador. With them had come a pre-completed voter registration form that only required her signature. As Mister Mitchell had been born in America, and she was his daughter, she had U.S. citizenship. She'd not asked for it. She wasn't sure she wanted it. But America wanted her. They wanted everyone, just like Britain and the handful of other new-era proto-states whose populations had fallen to around eight percent of pre-Blackout levels. Beyond the borders, in the bandit-badlands where a census was as impossible as an education, no one knew how few had survived.

With the voter form had come the reason why she was having difficulty writing her reply. She had been invited to join the ambassador's administration after he'd won the election. *After*, not before. He didn't want her as a prop to be wheeled on stage during the campaign. *After*, with the arrogant assumption he *would* win. She had no idea what the job would entail, but it had been offered in full knowledge of her wheelchair. The election wasn't until November so she had time to decide, but less time with each passing day.

"I know, Flora, back to work."

Leaning forward, she flipped the lid off the next cardboard storage box, and picked up a handful of forms. A name caught her eye. Not of a person, but of a tank. Not really a name, but a designation number: BV214. She'd seen that number yesterday. Where?

She edged the chair backwards, scanning the boxes, and saw the one she wanted, but now at the bottom of a stack of six. Twenty minutes and one paper avalanche later, she had it free.

"Found it. BV214. Recovered from Hull. That's on the Humber, isn't it, Flora? Which means these records also link to… to…" She edged the chair back, looking for the box. "There."

Five minutes later, she had three sets of records for the same tank, and an understanding of how the records had been stored. An hour later, she had the story of the entire mobile unit.

"During the Blackout, thirteen Challenger tanks and a Jackal reconnaissance vehicle were sent to the Humber to protect food distribution. What do you think that means, Flora? Shoot hungry looters? Probably. But the vehicles were abandoned when the fuel ran out. A year later, the survey team arrived by sea to assess the damage. Here, it notes what was worth salvaging: nine 120mm cannons, nine 7.62mm machine guns, nine chain guns, and one .50-cal machine gun. Next form is from the reclamation team when they took a group of new recruits to collect the vehicles. They recorded nine cannons, nine chain guns, nine heavy machine guns, and one .50-cal. It says the vehicles were dragged to the train line. Next form is from the old Railway Company, stating the vehicles had been collected and brought south. Another form was filled in when they were booked into the reclamation yard. And here is the form which was sent to the navy six months ago. It only mentions the tanks, not the Jackal and its .50-cal machine gun. That form was signed by Andrew Stevens."

Her hackles were up, her suspicions rising. Between the digital virus and the EMPs, most old-world tech had been destroyed. Offshore oilrigs, navy warships, fuel refineries, air-traffic control; almost everything had stopped working. Among the few vessels to survive were the cruise ships which had sailed to England's southern coast. After the diesel ran out, some of the ships were converted to coal as a short-term expedient until overseas oil fields could be seized. Twenty years later, the navy still depended on coal.

Warships needed weapons. The dead tanks had them. The munitions factory making the 4.5-inch naval shells was a very deep crater, but the shell factory for the MBTs' 120mm cannons had survived the Blackout. Guns and turrets were claimed from tanks. It was a temporary expedient, since ships required a far more durable gun than a tank. Like the other expedients, this one had become standard practice.

Riley held up one of the more recently written forms. "The navy does like its paperwork, Flora. When they took a tank, they said so. Reclamation yard? It's a scrap yard. They took cannons and guns, turrets and armour. And here, where they didn't use it, they said it was being reclassified for target practice. But we need tanks now because you can't drive a warship to the Alps."

She had a hunch. Now she needed to confirm it. An hour later, she had. A minute after that, papers stacked on her lap, she pushed herself out the door, letting the steep ramp accelerate her a quarter way across the car park.

The door to the commissioner's office was closed, but the dragon of an assistant was absent from her desk, so Riley wheeled to the door, turned the handle, and pushed the door open.

Three figures occupied the comfortable armchairs in the corner of the room reserved for guests of nominally equal rank. Commissioner Weaver wore her uniform like a glove. An MI5 spy before the Blackout, she and Mister Mitchell had been locking horns for the twenty years since, though they had reached a detente during the current crisis. The other two were professional civilians. A man and a woman. She about fifty, he a decade younger. His head was shaved short at the sides, but left long on the crown. Hers was styled with a long-fringe centre parting. Both were popular fashions among those who had enough free time to care. They wore near identical high-and-tight-collar suits, but her scarf was a soot-stained grey, while his was a smoke-tinged green, marking them as politicians, but from rival parties.

As Riley wheeled herself in, the two figures pivoted around, but not nearly as fast as Commissioner Weaver stood.

"I'm *so* sorry," Weaver said. "This is the information on the solicitation sting at the sewage works. We'll have to continue this discussion another time." Using a handshake to get each of the politicians to their feet, the commissioner hurried them towards the door even as Riley pushed herself out of the way.

"What's happened at the sewage works?" Riley asked, when the door was closed.

"Oh, nothing," Weaver said. "But when I looked at those two, it was the first thing which came to mind. Why is it, as soon as someone is elected to parliament, they think that makes them an instant expert on everything? What is your view on putting convicts into uniform and sending them to the frontline?"

"Depends on what they've done," Riley said. "But I thought our shortage wasn't in recruits, but time to train them properly."

"Exactly. However, enlistment *would* reduce prison numbers, which is a manifesto pledge. It wouldn't do a damn thing to reduce crime or win the war. Regardless, I have to listen. You're wincing."

"I'm fine, ma'am. I'm just using different muscles to usual."

"If you over-exert yourself and end up back in hospital, your father will rush home from the front and Dr Deering will return from Dover. I've no idea how many people they'd drag back with them. Coffee?"

"No, thank you, ma'am."

"I shall. It's from the Americans, but I wasn't going to waste the real thing on those hyenas." She crossed to a walnut cabinet. Inside was an old percolator, ancient before the Blackout. "While it's gurgling, you can explain your haste."

"The Loyal Brigade is back, and they're stealing guns and ammo, ma'am," Riley said.

Weaver paused. "What? How? Where from?"

"The navy loves paperwork," Riley said. "They kept meticulous notes of what was found, what was salvaged, what came back to the reclamation yard for storage, and what they took to build their fleet. They demanded that the Railway Company and the reclamation yard keep just as detailed a record. It's the same now they want to repair tanks to send to the frontline. But unless you had all the forms next to each other, you'd never know things have disappeared."

"Where does the theft come in?"

"Tanks need guns," Riley said. "Guns need to be tested. Testing needs shells. They send in requests for three shells per cannon. If a gun works, they mark down three shells fired successfully. If the cannon explodes, they mark down how many shells it took."

"Explodes?"

"Apparently, yes," Riley said. "We have the documentation showing when that particular old tank was sent to be stripped for armour and treads. For the next tank, they only requested one shell, because they had two from the previous test-firing, unused."

"So they aren't stealing tank shells?" Weaver asked.

"I hope not," Riley said. "I'm positive they *are* stealing .50-cal ammunition. Here, this handwritten report lists ten rounds of .50-cal fired. But on this form, one hundred rounds were requested. In numerals."

Weaver crossed to her desk and picked up a magnifying glass. "Someone added a zero, changing ten to one hundred."

"Yes. Only on forms that were submitted on Tuesday through Saturday. Never on forms sent in on a Monday. The navy love their forms, and since they took over the reclamation yard, they write down everything. Guess who never works on Mondays?"

"Stevens. So he modifies the request form to steal ninety rounds of ammo each time. Ninety rounds of .50 calibre."

"He could have stolen the guns, too," Riley said. "The navy kept meticulous records, but only of things they were interested in. Specifically, the weapons systems from tanks. They weren't interested in the support vehicles that were abandoned with them. But the crews who were sent up to drag the tanks to the railway line often listed armoured cars or reconnaissance vehicles that were recovered. There is at least one which has lost its machine gun."

"At least?"

"I'm still making my way through the paperwork," Riley said.

"A fifty-calibre machine gun," Weaver said, "or a 12.7mm machine gun, is also known as a Browning M2, and is one of the most common heavy machine guns in service among pre-Blackout NATO nations. They had them on ships, on tanks, on trucks. Even planes and helicopters. And it was used by the infantry. It can fire eight hundred rounds a minute. You don't know how many are missing?"

"Not yet," Riley said. "Or how much ammunition."

"After you brought me that note from your father, I conducted a brief investigation," Weaver said. "Andrew Stevens used to be a tank driver in the pre-Blackout army. He served for three years. His brother, Mark, had served for seven, though in the infantry. It was Mark Stevens who was a founder member of the Loyal Brigade, and who died among the shattered concrete of London. About a year ago, when we put in the request for fuel with the Americans, when we began building the radio repeater stations, when we began looking to the future and saw it would be as troubled as the past, we sought old tank crews to work as mechanics. Some would then be promoted to driver-instructor, once we'd ascertained what vehicles we could put back into the field."

"You were planning for war back then?" Riley asked.

"We've been *at* war for twenty years," Weaver said. "It took the politicians this long to understand it. I wanted the caterpillar tracks, not the cannons. Even before the barbarians swept through Germany and France, a lot of the old trade routes were becoming impassable." She poured her coffee. "The Loyal Brigade were just another group of brigands using nationalistic imagery to mask fascistic daydreams. They seized control of the old royal estate of Sandringham, and were heading to Buckingham Palace when they were killed by persons officially unknown. I don't suppose he told you any of the details?"

"I don't know who you mean, ma'am."

"Of course not," Weaver said. "Before they were outlawed, these criminals caused endless trouble around the docks, fighting with sailors over which flag should be flown on which ship. They became the muscle for an extremist candidate during an election. Lost. Began a brawl at the vote-count, and fled before they could be charged with assault. They turned rustler, raiding farms and bushwhacking traders before they reached Sandringham. They were a nuisance. But they were wiped out, and more completely than most of the others, thanks to forces unknown. No? You won't tell me why Mr Isaac shot them all, or what he was doing in London?"

"I honestly don't know," Riley said.

"At present, it doesn't matter," Weaver said. "Mr Andrew Stevens runs a history lecture at a local pub every Sunday evening. I say history, but it is mostly contradictory mythology of his own invention. He wants Britain to become an empire again. Very anti-American. Extremely anti-French. Anti-war, unless it will result in the Union Jack flying atop the Eiffel Tower. Now he is stealing ammunition."

"There's only two possible reasons," Riley said. "Either he plans to use it, personally, or he's going to dismantle the rounds, and make ammunition for hunting rifles and old-world weapons. When we shut down the coup, we shut off the import of illegal ammo into the country."

"Interesting," Weaver said. "Is there a link between him and Longfield or any of the other plotters?"

"Not that I've found," Riley said. "But I've only just begun investigating."

"There is a vacancy among the criminal fraternity for an arms dealer," Weaver said. "However, this Loyal Brigade connection suggests he plans to use the ammunition himself. There is one obvious target."

"Do you mean the peace conference?" Riley asked.

"I do," Weaver said. "In two days, the treaty with Albion will be signed, and the last group of separatists will be welcomed back into the fold. We'll finally be able to remove our troops from the border towns and send them to the front. We had two thousand experienced Marines guarding the towns and rail links in the north, not to mention the logistics network supporting them. A thousand were redeployed yesterday. The rest must remain in place until the treaty is signed. We've emptied the training camps. Every conscript more likely to shoot the enemy than themselves has been sent to the front. They should arrive any day now, but they are civilians who've had a few weeks marching and shooting practice. The thousand we've already redeployed should reach the front within the next week, but this treaty frees up more than just the soldiers. Without being concerned about banditry in the Midlands, we can open up another half million acres come spring. The refugees in the south can be relocated. Rationing will end. The war will be won. But only if the damned treaty is signed!"

"Can't it be signed today?" Riley asked.

"You'd think so," Weaver said. "You'd think it could have been signed last week, but no. It has to be signed in person. In front of the press. Mr Das has insisted the newspaper be there, *with* a photographer. He wanted it to be carried live on the radio, though we managed to bargain him down to a recording which will be broadcast after the news."

"Why does he want the coverage? Doesn't he trust us?" Riley asked.

"Of course he doesn't. Though his public excuse is that this will be an example to our American cousins on how reunification can successfully be achieved. Cousins!" She spat the word. "As if he were the reincarnation of George VI. He's grandstanding, of course. What else could we expect from a man who calls himself King Alfred II?"

"If the treaty isn't signed, what would happen?"

"Nothing," Weaver said. "Literally. Our troops would stay in place, while Leicester will starve."

"And if Mr Das dies?" Riley asked.

"Albion would go into convulsions trying to decide who should take the throne. Parliament has now passed an act acknowledging Mr Das as the sole and rightful heir to the British crown. It's an absurdity since it was his wife who had the title. However, this was done so that when he signs the treaty, and he gives up all claims, we will delegitimise the claims of all the other pretenders. In return, Das gets five seats in parliament."

"There's only about ten thousand people in his fiefdom," Riley said.

"Yes. It is a chronically undemocratic degree of over-representation, but I will stomach it, if it brings peace. But now the act has been passed by parliament, if Mr Das dies, it is unclear who in Albion will take over. At the very least, we'll need a new treaty, and a new act of parliament, which will take weeks. Months. Time we just don't have."

"Would Andrew Stevens know this?" Riley asked.

"Very possibly," Weaver said. "Even if he doesn't, if he is looking for a target, he only has to open a newspaper. This morning's rag includes a list of which houses are renting out windows to people who feel compelled to wave. I have a warship in the harbour in case of trouble. The police-cadets are on crowd control. Far too much of our precious diesel has been allocated to a fleet of Bentleys because our prime minister doesn't want to ride a horse. The king will ride. In armour, you see." She clenched her fist, but relaxed it, and sighed. "Two days, Sergeant, and we can go back to winning this war. I will take no risks, and Stevens presents a very big risk indeed. What is your recommendation?"

"Go undercover," Riley said. "Not me, sadly. But I know some good officers."

"There's no time," Weaver said. "When you first brought me news of this letter, I put an agent of mine to work nearby. She now frequents the pub. But it's a family establishment which isn't hiring. Following the nationalisation of the Railway Company, it was easy to have an agent installed at the railway station, but he doesn't have access to the reclamation yard now it's under military control."

"Then let's arrest Stevens," Riley said. "We can hold him for seventy-two hours."

"For what?" Weaver asked. "It is notoriously difficult to prove ammunition which *isn't* there *hasn't* been fired. I might be able to get a warrant for his home, but it's unlikely he keeps anything incriminating there. Considering what befell his brother, he will have made preparations to flee. If he's not acting alone, detaining him will not eliminate the immediate threat."

"Then we should move the treaty signing," Riley said.

"Easier said than done," Weaver said. "Yes, we will detain him. We've no choice. But let's take a leaf out of *his* playbook. There were more than just guns reclaimed from the old world. I'll speak to the judge and see if we can finally be allowed to employ some modern surveillance equipment. I want you to find out how many guns and how much ammunition is missing, and report back here tomorrow at eight a.m."

21st December

Chapter 18 - A Woman's Cottage Is Her Castle
Priory Row, Christchurch

There's no place like home. There was certainly none like Anna's. The stone-walled, wood-beamed, lead-window cottage outside the ancient Christchurch priory had been claimed by her father back before the coastal sprawl around Bournemouth had been renamed Twynham.

The cottage was small, with two rooms upstairs, two down, and so old, it had been built before the invention of bathrooms. Thus hers, wonderfully, had been tacked onto the ground floor, where it occupied most of the space which should have been kitchen. That kitchen was still large enough to feed six, as long as two didn't mind sitting in the living room, which, currently, was home to her bed. To ensure there was wheelchair-room, everything else had been carried upstairs where it was out-of-sight if not out-of-mind, but utterly out of reach.

It was two months since she'd been shot. Two long, often lonely, months. She could stand. She could sit. She could push her chair faster than most people could walk. She couldn't run. She couldn't chase. There were lots of couldn'ts, but she tried not to think about them, or how there were noticeably fewer Christmas cards on her mantle than usual.

Her home was twee, with lead lattice windows, low beams, and an open fire in each room. Outside, as she was sure the American ambassador knew, were her decadently impractical ornamental rose bushes. But the real reason Henry Mitchell had picked this particular cottage was that it was on the route the power lines took from the new coal power station to the hospital. Isaac had tapped in, providing her father, and so her, with an unlimited electricity supply.

Her father loved electricity, and the gadgets which ate it. She was more sceptical, and so most had gone upstairs, but not the kettle. Not the electric heaters. Not the radio which currently played the national station while she slowly washed with soap and sponge from her seat in the bathroom.

The radio programme was light on news, heavy on Christmas songs. Most were ancient recordings from before the turn of the millennium, but there were ten new versions of those old hits, recorded in the station's own studio. Listeners were supposed to write in with their favourite, so as to pick a national number one. Despite there being no prize, either for artists or listeners, ten thousand people had already voted, if you were to believe the presenter. She didn't, but the radio helped pass the time as she laboriously prepared for work.

At the end of each day, she showered. While she'd still been in the hospital, her father had removed the bath, tiled the floors and walls, turning the whole space into a wet-room. According to Isaac, who'd helped, those were quite popular back in the old world. Riley liked baths. Showers were fine for getting clean, but not for washing away the worries of the day. Since the shower soaked everything, including toilet and sink, she didn't bother in the morning. Hot water and a sponge sufficed.

She didn't feel clean afterwards. That wasn't the point. She'd made the effort. Each day got easier, proving she was recovering. Getting better. Even if a little voice in her head said it only proved it was simply getting easier with practice.

Dressing was getting easier, too. Trousers were tricky, so she'd decided a long blue skirt was an acceptable uniform alternative. She'd cut hers from hem to waist, and sewn in a zip, so she could wrap it around. Socks were an impossibility, but she had a pair of long, fleece-lined boots, and another to change into at work. Not ideal. None of it was. But either she was a cop or she wasn't, and cops went to work.

To her hat she affixed a sprig of holly, because a smile stops more crimes than a bullet; it was a saying of her own that, by and large, had proven to be true. She'd hung some decorations around the mantle, and some more by the door. Not that she'd had many visitors. Most people who cared had gone to war.

She'd thought more people had cared, until she'd been shot. She'd enjoyed a hectic social life crammed into the hours she wasn't working a case. While stuck in hospital, and later in the cottage, she'd learned who her friends were. She'd learned who her ex wasn't, which was why he was now simply an ex.

It was a ten-minute walk from the cottage at the edge of the old Christchurch priory to Police House on Soper's Lane. By wheelchair, in the pre-dawn dark, down ice-strewn pavements, it took half an hour. She'd budgeted a whole hour so she could patrol the market, and claim her breakfast.

Just off Wick Lane, at the southern end of the old Christchurch high street, a plane had crashed during the Blackout. Whether by luck or skill, the pilot had brought the plane down in a car park. Mostly. As far as she knew, no one had survived the impact, but most of the plane had. Over the years, the rubble-remains of the nearby shops had been removed. The plane hadn't. The cabin had become a market, initially selling fish caught in the river, then fish cooked in a grill set up in one of the house-sized engines. Cooking implements, clothes, and books came next. Salvage, initially, and then newly made. Twenty years later, the market still thrived, especially at Christmas.

"Fancy a hat, dear? Welsh wool. Monmouthshire dye!" came the call from a hawker still setting out her wares.

"How about a new set of hammers, Sarge?" called a man from a stall beneath the old plane's wing. "Your old cottage will thank you come spring."

"Who needs an entire *set* of hammers?" Riley called back. "Isn't one enough?"

"That's it, Sergeant," the woman replied. "No one needs more than one hammer, but everyone needs a spare hat or three. I've a lovely one in blue. Just your size."

"Thanks, Alice, but I'm happy with the hat I've got," Riley said, tapping her police-issue cap, and wheeled herself on through the hawkers setting up their tables. Some sold hand-carved ornaments. Others were unloading pre-made gift-baskets. They were light on food this year, a consequence of the unexpected continuation of rationing. Next to that was the Yorkshire farmer selling hand-carved chess-sets with the well-worn sign: *custom orders taken for next year*. Next to her was the now empty table where her daughter had already sold every jar of Humber honey.

"One thief-taker special," an old man said, holding out a paper bag.

"Thanks, Luca," she said, taking the bag before handing over the banknote. "Extra mustard?"

"Nearly half a jar," he said. "And a biscotti for you to think on."

"You're a gem," she said, and wheeled herself on.

The hawkers weren't friends. Not exactly. Not like Ruth or Maggie, or even Isaac. They were neighbours. They were citizens. They were good people. Her people. She protected them. They paid their taxes. They kept the pavement clear for her wheelchair. The humans among them, anyway. Her wheelchair left her head at licking height for the draft-horses pulling the stock-carts.

"Leave her alone, Spot!" the drover said, tugging at the horse's bridle. "I'm so sorry, Sergeant."

"No bother," Riley said. "He must have mistaken the holly for mistletoe."

Yes, these were the good people. The people for whom she donned the uniform and slogged her way to work. So were the owners of the shops in the next block. Here, near Castle Lane, the buildings had survived the plane's impact and short-lived blaze. The more successful of the earliest group of plane-traders had swapped their stalls for the solid roofs of indoors. The candle-maker and neighbouring blacksmith had teamed up for a window display of menorahs and seven-branched Christmas trees made of salvaged steel. Opposite, the bicycle repair shop had strung reflector-lights like tinsel.

The bakery had little bread to sell, but it was doing a roaring trade in the un-rationed ersatz tea and coffee. Most of the customers, despite the notice in the bakery's window, were the drovers and hawkers making their way to the market. Each shop had the same notice: *Sign the Petition for the Wick Lane Redevelopment.* Now these merchants had reached an indoor-level of success, they wanted the plane and the market, and so their competition, removed. Despite the petition, these were her people, too.

The antique bookshop had a sign announcing a pre-Christmas paperback sale, and another sign advertising the Flower Festival up on Religion Row. That was tonight, but she doubted she'd be able to attend.

Religion Row was a nickname, but used so frequently it had stuck. Temples, synagogues, mosques, and churches of every flavour and hue had a home in that block. Every new religion aspired to have a branch there, and so acquire the legitimacy the address would bring, as well as the tax-breaks.

Each year, Religion Row put on a solstice display, which the synagogues always began over Hanukah, and the churches stretched to Little Christmas. This year's would have been a small event anyway, since Diwali had coincided with Eid, and had led to a duelling light show which she'd missed because of the cursed injury.

Up on the row, the trees were all decorated, with each church vying for the best crib-based diorama, though the convent's was always the most interesting. When she'd last visited Ned Ludd, they were still setting it up, and wouldn't even give her a clue what this year's twist would be. Poor Ned Ludd. At least he seemed to be happy living at the convent, where he kept himself busy sweeping and cleaning. He was a man who'd never be whole, but he seemed no worse for having been framed for murder.

Her favourite, though, was the Buddhist temple's display of dried petals that only lasted until the first strong wind carried the flowers across the city in a multi-coloured snowfall that briefly brightened the drab coal-dust grey.

Yes, these were her people. This was her city. Those were her traditions. But were they her future?

When she arrived at the commissioner's office, she found Weaver in company with a time traveller. Weaver's guest was dressed straight out of the 10th century. Or out of a picture-book version of that attire, modified with a few modern comforts. A gold tree had been embossed on the steel breastplate, with more golden trees on wrist and shin guards. Beneath was chainmail. Above was a steel helmet topped with a green brush of plumage. Between the gold-filigree cheek guards was the face of a woman of around thirty years old. At her belt, on the left, was a sheathed short sword. On the right was a revolver with as ornate a gold pattern as her helmet.

"Sergeant Riley, may I introduce Her Grace, the Duchess of Albion, Countess of Worksop, Marshall of Warsop, Warden of the Humber, Chief Magistrate of Leicester, and High Sheriff of Nottingham. Princess Elizabeth, Colonel Sherwood, daughter of King Alfred II. Did I miss any?"

"Except when on ceremonial duties, Colonel Sherwood will suffice," Sherwood said.

"Of course," Weaver said, "it is just that you *are* in your ceremonial uniform."

Riley said nothing. She thought a lot, but kept it to herself. One thing she'd learned young, mostly from her father's conversations with Isaac, was how to spot aggressive civility used strategically in a row one wrong word from erupting into a war.

Sherwood left the bait dangling, and turned to Riley. "I understand you have identified a potential threat to His Majesty?"

"I noticed a discrepancy in the paperwork," Riley said. "It's a threat. I don't know to who."

"Or, indeed, whether it is someone illustrious enough to be a *whom*," Weaver said.

"The ceremony is the obvious target," Sherwood said. "Both His Majesty and the prime minister will be in attendance."

"Agreed," Weaver said. "Last night, I conferred with my operatives. Stevens *is* a threat. He has claimed his brother's mantle as leader of the Loyal Brigade, and has been recruiting. Their belief structure is broadly incoherent, but it is based on a notion that there is some past golden age to which we could return if only we had the proper leadership. As such, I would doubt your father is a target. This group is many things, but monarchical is at the top of the list. If they attack the ceremony, it would be to kill the prime minister and declare your father ruler of a new empire."

"There have been no recent contacts with any subversive elements," Sherwood said. "We want this treaty as much as you."

"I do hope that's the case," Weaver said. "The alternative is bloodshed."

"You would threaten my people?" Sherwood asked.

"Bloodshed in *France*," Weaver said. "Yes, we could wipe out Albion. But we won't, because we are not barbarians. The barbarians are two hundred miles to the east, literally washing in the blood of children. Those troops in the north *must* be sent to the front. You can't disagree."

"I don't," Sherwood said.

"Then this is a threat to us all," Weaver said. "Can we sign the treaty today, somewhere further up the railway line?"

"You know that's impossible," Sherwood said.

"Then we have no choice but to launch a sting," Weaver said, and sounded enthused. "Sergeant, you're familiar with electronics?"

"Yes, ma'am," Riley said, thinking of her kettle, heater, and radio.

"Good. Did you identify how many heavy machine guns are missing?"

"At least six, ma'am."

"How much ammunition?" Weaver asked.

"Over three thousand rounds," Riley said. "But not much over. Most of the records before last month weren't tampered with. Since last month, every single one was amended. Ten rounds changed to a hundred, twenty to two hundred and so on."

"Assume two people per gun, and five hundred rounds with each," Weaver said. "Two guns would target the procession, the other four would cause chaos."

"With a Browning M2's rate of fire," Sherwood said, "and with that much lead in the air, whether your prime minister or my king is the primary target, they'll both die."

"And not just them," Weaver said. "Around twenty people regularly attend Mr Stevens's history talks. Not all of them work at the reclamation yard. Equally, we cannot expect all his followers to attend each of his lectures. Over a hundred people are employed at the yard in various capacities. The site manager, a former RAF captain named Thorpe, was a candidate in the last election. He didn't win a seat, but wasn't expected to. He's guaranteed a safe constituency in the next election. If he wanted to start a coup, he'd wait until he was in parliament."

"How can you be certain?" Sherwood asked.

"Because I have had far too much experience at quashing plots like these," Weaver said. "The more pertinent detail is that some, if not most, in the reclamation yard are innocent, but even if we were to detain all of them, we won't eliminate the threat. I'm going in undercover. I'll plant an electronic listening device. Stevens can't have stolen this ammunition alone, and so we'll identify at least one other suspect we can attempt to break."

"*You* will go in undercover?" Sherwood asked.

"*You* can't," Weaver said. "Do you have a few people you can trust?"

"Of course."

"Then find something less conspicuous to wear, and meet us at the train station's freight terminal in one hour."

Riley waited for Sherwood to leave before turning to the commissioner. "What's really going on, ma'am?"

"Sherwood is the king's daughter," Weaver said. "She is the eldest child. The heir. She runs their army and is the power beside the throne, except when she's measuring it for new cushions. She will certainly take one of the seats in parliament, and will lead their local delegation. This will be a valuable opportunity to test her mettle, and see whether it is all simply filigree."

"Do you think she's behind this threat?" Riley asked.

"I doubt it. She does seem loyal to her king. A bug is unlikely to reveal anything. Us demonstrating we've done everything possible will make her accept we have to abandon this foolish procession so we can sign the treaty tonight."

"So you're not planting a bug?" Riley asked.

"Oh, I am. And then I'm going to have my agent working at the station let slip that electronic listening devices have been left there. Stevens is the paranoid sort who'll want to check on his stash, and then make contact with his agents. We'll follow him, and arrest them all. The treaty can be signed. The soldiers can be redeployed, and we can end this damned war."

Chapter 19 - Boxed In
Bear Cross, Twynham

Soldiers from Leicester smelled like a forest after a summer shower, but not in a good way. Mulch. Decay. Sweat. They watched like hawks, ready to dive. Too often, she could feel them watching her wheelchair. After an hour in the boxcar with six of them, Anna's patience snapped.

"Do you guys not own normal clothes?" she asked.

"What's wrong with our clothes?" a corporal she'd been told was named Lancaster said.

"When Commissioner Weaver wanted you to change into something less conspicuous, she obviously meant civilian clothes, not urban camouflage."

"No one spots us when we wear this," Sherwood said. "Not even your Marines when they stumble through the ruins."

"Not until they feel our knife at their throat," Corporal Lancaster said.

"You mean to say felt," Riley said. "Past-tense, because in a few hours, that treaty will be signed, and you'll be law-abiding citizens like the rest of us."

With the exception of Sherwood, they were all twenty, give or take a year. Sergeant Lancelot York, Corporal Galahad Lancaster, and privates Boadicea Essex, Camelot Sheffield, and Guinevere Scunthorpe. Sherwood's name, and titles, had been assumed since the Blackout. What of the others? Were those the names they'd been given at birth, or had they chosen them when they'd joined Sherwood's murder-squad? The old-fashioned plate-and-chain armour worn by the occasional tourist and trader who made it to Twynham was their camouflage. This outfit of rubble grey, soot black, brick red, and weed green would make them nearly invisible in the ruins of the north. Each had stacked their longbow and quiver by the boxcar door. Other than Sherwood, none carried a firearm, and the colonel had exchanged her ostentatiously ornate revolver for an old-world Glock. The rest of her squad were armed with a hatchet and a long knife, both with a camouflaged handle. Somehow, that was worse than a gun.

"Just a few hours," she said, though to herself. She picked up the directional microphone, aiming it through the gap in the boxcar's wall.

Weaver had given her the surveillance kit just after she'd wheeled Anna up the ramp and into the boxcar. She'd never used the microphone before. Like most old-world technology, its use was banned in court. The individual components, however, were familiar enough from the gadgets her father collected. A long microphone, though this one had a gun-like handle, had wires linking it to the digital recorder. More wires led to headphones, one pair of which was currently around her neck.

The train had been waiting for them at the freight-yard. Eight empty flatbeds, one boxcar, one coal tender, and one locomotive. The old driver wore army green, though Anna was more used to seeing him in police blue, working the duty desk at Police House. Weaver, dressed in shabby overalls, had ridden up front. Everyone else was crammed into the boxcar.

After a brief and jolting ride, the train had stopped at a passenger platform just shy of the branch-line leading into the reclamation yard. The plan had been to drive the train into the yard itself, but a wooden barrier lay across the rails leading to the yard. When Weaver disembarked from the locomotive to open the barrier, a guard had approached. Before Riley could get the microphone into position, the guard had jogged back towards the main yard. More slowly, Weaver had followed, walking along the tracks until she'd stopped just before the gate. Now Weaver waited, and so did Anna with the microphone aimed at the undercover commissioner.

"Have you used one of those before?" Sherwood asked.

"Sure," Riley lied. "You?"

"Yes, up in the ruins," Sherwood said. "They can be very useful."

"You use electronics?"

"We use whatever keeps us alive," Sherwood said. "Anything we hear on this, or on the bug, won't be admissible in court."

"That's up to the judge," Riley said. "You're familiar with the laws?"

"Of course," Sherwood said. "As I say, we're familiar with whatever might keep us alive. And if the judge rules these electronics inadmissible, everything we find as a result of them could be thrown out, too. Including any arrests we make."

"We'll worry about that later," Riley said.

"Yes, that is the tradition here in the south, isn't it?" Sherwood said.

"Hostiles approaching," Sergeant York said. He was standing by a gap at the far end of the boxcar, holding an old-fashioned telescope to his eye. "Two. A greybeard and a lass. They'll intercept the commissioner at the gate."

Riley bent forward as much as her old wound would allow so she could better aim the microphone at Weaver. Sherwood picked up the other set of headphones. The rest of her team became as still as a mountain, as silent as the moon.

"Morning t'you," Weaver said, affecting a passable West Country burr, the words soft through the twenty-year-old headphones. *"Merry Christmas."*

"Is it?" a man's voice came in reply to Weaver. *"You don't look like you're delivering."*

"We've come to collect the finished tanks," Weaver said.

"What tanks?" the guard said.

"The finished tanks going to the front," Weaver said. *"Seven are due for collection, to be fast-tracked down to Dover, to reach Calais tonight."*

"You're in the wrong place," the guard said. *"Tanks get collected from the depot in Ferndown."*

"They said they'd be here," Weaver said.

"You've been sent on a merry dance," the gate-guard said. *"We just strip the machines for parts."*

"Are you saying you don't have any tanks here at all?" Weaver asked, her voice ringing with frustration.

"Not unless you can piece them together yourself."

"Typical of my boss, sending me on a goose-hunt up and down the country," Weaver said. *"That's a ton of coal wasted. Can I borrow your telegraph? Let me wire him a message. Assuming he replies. He was getting a new uniform today for the ceremony tomorrow with that pretender from up north."*

"He's a flag-waver, is he?" the second guard said. Her voice was only a few years past squeaky-young.

"He seems to have forgotten what we've all been through these last few years," Weaver said. *"I don't mind a proper king, but not that joker. You know he sold carpets?"*

From inside the boxcar came an uncomfortable shuffling. Riley waved her hand for silence.

"The telegraph is down," the older of the two guards said. "You better try the passenger station up the line, but we're expecting a delivery, so you'll have to move your train."

"Ah, what can you do," Weaver said. "Be seeing you." She turned back towards the boxcar.

"She didn't cast the magic spider," Corporal Lancaster said.

"It's not called a spider, it's a bug," Sergeant York said.

"Fine, she didn't cast the magic *bug*," the corporal said.

"Shh," Riley said, because, through the receiver, she'd caught a few more words. The two guards were still talking. Steadying her hand, she listened.

"Sounds like another recruit for you, Andy," the woman said.

"We don't need more recruits," Andy said. "We need more customers."

"Give her a gun and she might shoot at the king," the woman said. "That'd re-start the war with Albion."

"You're thinking too small," Andy said. "Albion's poor. The real money is in Europe. All those scavengers claiming farmland, they don't want hunting rifles. They'll want proper weapons. That's who'll make us rich. Not the crazies. They're useful as couriers, easy to keep loyal, but we don't need any more of them."

"You won't sell any more ammo to Leicester?" the woman asked. "That weird bloke yesterday said he wanted more."

"Nah, we'll fulfil the last order in a couple of days, but only once the treaty is signed," Andy said.

"Why do they want those machine guns?" the woman asked. "They could just ask the government. They'll be part of it."

"First rule of gunrunning," Andy said. "Don't ask what they—" But the rest of the words were lost as the two guards walked away.

"They're not a threat," Sherwood said.

"Pity," Corporal Lancaster said.

"Ma'am, do you want to arrest them?" Sergeant York asked, addressing Sherwood.

"We'll wait for the commissioner," Sherwood said.

Riley removed the headphones, mentally replaying what the man, Andy, had said.

From outside came a clunk of boots on the ladder. A moment later, the train shunted forward, while the door to the boxcar opened.

"Why are we leaving?" Sherwood asked as Weaver entered through the link-door.

"That was Stevens," Weaver said. "I don't know what he was doing on guard duty, but there was no point pushing things with the suspect. We'll go to the next siding, and I'll return alone, sneak in, and plant the bug."

"He kept talking after you walked away," Sherwood said. "You should listen." She pulled out both pairs of headphones and pressed play.

"See, he's no danger," Corporal Lancaster said, after they'd heard the brief exchange.

"He is," Weaver said.

"Not to us," Lancaster said.

"To all of us," Weaver said. "But he's not a separatist. He's a gunrunner, using the name of his brother's old gang to buy some loyal assistants."

"It isn't a threat to the treaty-signing," Sherwood said.

"It's a threat to the peace," Riley said. "He said he's been selling guns to Albion."

"We bought what we could, when we could, to defend ourselves," Sherwood said.

"He's going to continue selling guns after the treaty is signed," Weaver said.

"He'll find no more customers in the kingdom than he would in Bournemouth," Sherwood said.

"You're missing the broader point," Weaver said. "This isn't rifle ammunition. It's for a heavy machine gun. Why would anyone in Britain want that? It's not for hunting."

"Depends what you're hunting," Lancaster said.

"Quiet, Corporal," Sergeant York said.

"He's been selling heavy weapons to you," Weaver said.

"Not to me," Sherwood said.

"Then to whom?" Weaver asked. "Someone in your administration has been purchasing heavy machine gun ammunition from this man. Is it the same someone who was purchasing old-world assault rifles from the failed plotters?"

"We never bought those rifles. There were overtures, that was all," Sherwood said. "We opted for peace instead. It's the reason a treaty is being signed."

"Again, you're missing the broader picture," Weaver said. "The man is stealing munitions which should be sent to the front. He wants chaos, because that will facilitate on-going thefts. He thinks, after the peace, he'll still have a customer in your woods. Why? What possible reason could someone from Leicester have for purchasing army weapons? Only to make an attack appear to have been perpetrated by the army. An insurgency needs arms. An arms dealer needs customers. After the treaty is signed, your father will not be king. You will be a common citizen. Any other citizen could seize control of your power base. Who?"

"I see," Sherwood said. "There are… yes, there are people who might do that. I will investigate."

"I know how we could find out," Riley said. "It's going to be someone important, and someone who's here for the signing. He said someone came to see him yesterday. It should be easy to flush them out."

22nd September

Chapter 20 - Enter Stage Left
Die Englische Kniepe, Twynham

Another day, another dawn, another reason to question her vocation. Riley slowly pushed her wheelchair across the stage, taking in the auditorium. It had been a cinema twenty years ago, a theatre more recently. She'd seen *Hamlet* performed here, and *Pygmalion*, *First Contact*, and *Robinson Crusoe*, but *Remaining Days* had stuck with her most vividly.

The author had been the world's most famous before the Blackout. The ageing laureate had reworked his original novel into a new play, advancing the setting by a hundred years. The story had remained the same, a timeless tale of missed love, fading glory, and fleeting hope. Of course, what she remembered most was the man she'd been with. A man who'd not visited her once while she'd been in hospital, or since she'd returned home. That particular chronic misjudgement of character was surely reason to question her skills as a detective, as was her relegation to a supporting role in her own investigation.

She stopped her wheelchair next to the table, opened the box on her lap, took out the drum-magazine, and placed it on the table. Next to the magazine she placed the springs. Two of them, which she lined up with the inkwells.

Next to the inkwells were quills. Behind the table were two wooden chairs with high backs and carved armrests. Behind those was an alternating row of flags and armour. The suits of armour had come from a museum. She had no idea where the flags had come from. The props weren't for a play. This evening, the newspaper was putting on a reconstruction of the signing ceremony. Tickets had already sold out.

"Two springs," she called out, wheeling her chair back across the stage. "Magazine is gratis. An apology."

From the wings on the other side of the stage, a plank creaked. Riley slowly wheeled the chair around.

The figure who stepped out of the shadows was a man. He occupied, rather than wore, a green ankle-length robe which reminded her of the university wizards from the novels her father liked. The theatre's dim bulbs reflected off the gems in sleeves and hem. The red leather belt strained against his belly's bid for freedom. Every finger had a ring, while the gold chain around his neck had a gem in every link.

"Who are you?" he asked.

"The messenger," Riley said as she gestured towards the desk. "You know the journalists are going to sell all this," she added.

"All what?"

"The ink pots and chairs," Riley said. "They're being auctioned off in the paper. That's what I heard."

The man walked over to the table and picked up the springs. "I can't carry this ammunition. You should take it away."

She shrugged. "Yeah, they're auctioning it off to help the war effort, except they don't say *how* it'll help the war effort. I think they're doing it to help sell newspapers. Don't think they'll need the help tomorrow." She checked her watch. "My name is Sergeant Anna Riley. You're under arrest. Want to tell me your name?"

"You're a soldier?" he asked, looking around the stage.

"Police," she said.

"I see," he said, still calm, as he peered across the empty expanse of the auditorium.

"You were set up," she said. "The telegram was a fake. We arrested Stevens this morning."

"I don't know what you're talking about," he said.

"You do, because you just picked up those springs," she said. "We knew the suspect was someone from the Albion delegation already in Twynham. We sent telegrams to everyone who could, theoretically, be Stevens's customer from the north, saying Mr Browning's barrel was missing two springs. That'd be nonsense to anyone not in the know. But you took the bait. Kneel down, hands behind your head."

"Or what?" he asked, drawing a revolver from beneath his robe.

An arrow pierced his arm. He screamed, dropping the gun.

"Or that," Riley said.

Sherwood stepped out of the shadows.

"Elizabeth?" the suspect said. "What is this?"

"Treason," Sherwood said. "Or it was a few minutes ago. The treaty will have been signed by now, so I think we shall have to call it terrorism. The police can decide with what to charge you."

"It'll be a long list," Riley said. "Who is he?"

"John Boyle. *Former* Curia Regent," Sherwood said.

"Does that translate as court clown?" Riley asked. "Even I wouldn't wear a dress that long in this weather. Your hem's covered in slush."

"These are the robes of state," Boyle hissed through the pain.

"Not anymore," Sherwood said. "Sergeant York, the prisoner is incorrectly dressed."

Sergeant York stepped out of the shadows on the other side of the stage. He drew his long knife and sliced the blood-flecked robes from the prisoner, leaving him shivering in his underwear.

"Take him to the hospital," Riley said. "He's a prisoner."

"Make sure he lives, Sergeant," Sherwood said. "I will enjoy his trial."

"Yes, ma'am."

Riley wheeled her chair around, not bothering to watch the prisoner being escorted away. "Who is he?" she asked.

"My father's advisor," Sherwood said. "In the lost world, he managed a store for my parents while also being a local elected councillor."

"Was it his idea you should adopt the old names and styles?" Riley asked.

"My father says it was mine," Sherwood said. "I don't recall. But I don't remember much of those early years except the screams of pain and cries of hunger."

"The nightmares fade, but they never go away, do they?" Riley said. "So Boyle was the second-in-command? Then he could never attain the top spot while Albion was a monarchy. But in a democracy, he could become a political leader. Perhaps prime minister of Britain."

"Perhaps," Sherwood said. "What will happen to him?"

"He'll be offered a deal," Riley said. "He'll get life, instead of death, but it won't be comfortable."

"A deal? There's no need. I can find out who his accomplices are."

"It's not just about Leicester," Riley said. "Boyle wasn't Stevens's only customer. Why was Stevens using a defunct extremist group as a recruiting ground? No, the investigation has only just begun."

"But it's over for me," Sherwood said. "My father will want to thank you. I'm sure your prime minister will, too. *Our* prime minister," she added.

"You can't eat thanks," Riley said, "and I've a mountain of paperwork for my pen to climb, but we should report our success."

Outside was a cab, but not driven by a cabbie. Holding the reins was Ollie Hunter, the Canadian-born journalist who'd chased a headline across the Atlantic aboard one of the few steam trading ships.

"Why aren't you at the signing?" Riley asked.

"Because this is where the story is," Ollie said.

It was a struggle to get herself, and her chair, inside the cab, which left her too exhausted to talk. When they reached the hotel, she opted to stay inside, rather than spend the rest of the afternoon climbing in and out.

"I must change into formalwear," Sherwood said. She smiled. "And today will be the last day that has to be armour."

As the colonel trekked towards the hotel's entrance, the journalist climbed down from the cab, and jumped into the back. "So, Sergeant, mind answering a few questions?"

"Yes," she said. "But you'll ask them anyway, won't you?"

"Of course," Ollie said. "What do you make of the last-minute changes to the signing ceremony?"

"The location of the signing was changed to the train station's waiting room," Riley said. "That decision was made after it became clear there might be an attack on the convoy. With your newspaper having encouraged so many spectators to line the route, civilian casualties were a certainty."

"Ah, so it was the press's fault," Ollie said. "I bet we don't print that."

"I bet you don't," she said. "The ceremony was always planned to take place here."

"This hotel was called The King's Arms until yesterday," Ollie said. "Do you know why it changed its name to *Die Englische Kneipe?*"

"I don't think I can pronounce it, and certainly can't spell it," she said. "But I believe one of the owners is from Germany, the other is from the United States. As trade with the United States increases, and when peace returns to Europe, there will be tourists again. They'll ask for the hotel with the unpronounceable name. It's a good gimmick."

"You don't think the name, *Die Englische Kneipe,* sounds like a threat?" Ollie asked, his pen hovering hopefully over his notebook.

"I don't know what you mean," Riley said.

"Can't you give me one usable quote?" he asked.

"During a joint operation between military intelligence, the Serious Crimes Unit, and the royal bodyguard, a terrorist attack, which would have resulted in a great number of civilian casualties, was foiled."

Ollie scrawled that down. "Great. Perfect. And the quote?"

"That *was* the quote."

"No, that was an essay," he said.

"Co-operation always achieves more than conflict," she said.

"Perfect."

"I stole it from a play," she said.

"I know," Ollie said. "It's still perfect. Ah, there's the king."

"Where?" she asked, leaning forward to look through the window. Wincing at the sudden stab of pain, she leaned back.

"The guy in gold," Ollie said. "They say it's gold, but I'm sure it can't be. There'd be no way he could stand up."

"He's not as tall as I expected," Riley said.

"People always say that about royals," Ollie said. "Makes the prime minister look shabby in his suit. I suppose that's the point."

"No one looks happy," Riley said. "And that *isn't* a quote."

"They're having to restage the signing for the radio," Ollie said. "They forgot to actually speak while they were doing it the first time, so the official record is three minutes of pen scratching and paper shuffling."

"Ah." More carefully, she leaned forward again. The king's golden armour cast a glimmering glow on the ice around which he stood. But beneath it, he was a short man. Skinny, too. Worn. Tired. Squinting as if he'd rather be wearing glasses. He'd shaved his head in a failed attempt to hide that it was grey where it wasn't bald. A small mouth, a broad brow, a high forehead... She frowned. He looked almost familiar.

She pulled out her monocular, and more closely examined the king. "No," she said.

"No what?" Ollie asked.

"I could be wrong," Riley said. "But I don't think I am."

"Wrong about what?" Ollie asked.

"How would you like to gamble on getting the biggest story of the day?" she asked.

"Bigger than a gunrunner and the treaty signing?" Ollie asked.

"Much bigger," Riley said.

It took ten minutes to get there, and ten to get back, but forty, and the help of the nuns, to bundle their reluctant passenger into the carriage.

With it being an hour since they'd left, when they returned to *Die Englische Kneipe* the photographs had been taken. The car park was empty, except for Sherwood, who was still in armour, leaning against a pond-facing bench-seat until the carriage approached. As it stopped, she came over.

"We wanted a photograph!" Sherwood called as Ollie slowed the carriage. "My father—" She stopped speaking and moving as she saw the passenger. "Eddie?"

"He's been calling himself Ned Ludd," Riley began, but Sherwood had launched herself inside the cab, and grabbed the young man in the monk's habit, hugging him tight.

"Eddie!" Sherwood said.

"Gotta stay away from the light, Liz," Ned Ludd said. "Gotta stay away from the light."

"Eddie," Sherwood said. "It really is you! Come with me. Dad's inside. It's okay. There's no electricity."

"Gotta stay away from the lights," Ludd said.

Sherwood helped the man down.

"Go on, Ollie. You'll miss the story," Riley said. "I can manage getting down."

She didn't rush; there was no need. It took ten minutes, long enough for a short man, now wearing a suit, to come outside, alone. Among the trees, the branches shuffled as the shadows stood to attention.

"Your Majesty," Riley said.

"Not anymore," he said. "I'm just plain old Mr Das. I think I shall keep the Alfred. I've become rather fond of the name. You found my son."

"He's been calling himself Ned Ludd. He was set up as a murderer a few months back. He wouldn't tell us where he came from, so we've been boarding him at a convent where he'd been helping in the gardens. He really doesn't like electricity, does he?"

"When he was eight, he played around with the battery we'd scavenged from an old electric bus and had rigged to a wind turbine," Das said. "He received an electric shock. It caused some developmental issues. After his mother died, he ran away. Elizabeth found him in a ruin surrounded by trees. I wouldn't call it a forest, not then, but in the years since, he's been hacking away at the concrete, planting trees, building his own woodland. We rebuilt his ruin, made it into a cottage. He loved it. Until he disappeared. I assumed some accident had befallen him."

"I think he was being kept to be killed," Riley said. "If he died down here, by whoever's hand, we'd get the blame and there'd be no peace between us. This was the same group trying to sell you assault rifles. The same group linked to the horror show in France."

"And, one assumes, linked to today's little adventure," Das said. "I would like a word with Boyle."

"That's impossible," Riley said. "You're just Mr Das now. Boyle is in custody, and is thus due a fair legal process. But yes, I suspect Boyle has been working with our enemy for some time. He must have been involved in your son's kidnapping, and he'll be charged accordingly. And you know what that tells me? We could have signed this peace deal a long time ago."

"Perhaps so," Das said. "But I was never sure what variety of government would emerge here in the south. In the beginning, you were just the largest group of bandits. In that respect, it *is* ironic how events transpired. Now, please, tell me the rest of the story. How did you find my son?"

Chapter 21 - An Incomplete Autopsy
The Police Station, Dover

"You're seriously telling me that Ned Ludd is royalty?" Ruth said.

"He's a genuine prince," Riley said.

"But only of a carpet kingdom," Isaac said. "That's how King Alf met his wife, the duchess. Alf's parents had come to England to import Indian rugs, and to export English weaves back to India. Sandeep, as he was then, was in India learning about that side of the business. The duchess was eighteen and playing personal dresser to a major royal during one of their goodwill tours. The two met, fell in love, and eloped. It was a big scandal at the time. Depending on whose side you were on, she renounced her titles or was booted out of the family. But business boomed after she started doing the carpet fittings."

"So how'd he end up calling himself king?" Ruth asked.

"Her royal link was how everyone in the neighbourhood knew of them," Isaac said. "The charity work, and sponsorship of three local soccer teams, was why everyone listened to them when they began organising the local relief effort. They kept listening because the couple kept people alive. Robin Hood, Camelot, and other semi-mythical elements were adopted because they're good stories to believe in. Or so he told me."

"You've met him?" Riley asked.

"A few times, but long ago," Isaac said. "He's a smart man. The question now is whether he's smarter than the prime minister."

"What do you mean?" Ruth asked.

"Have you actually read the treaty?" Isaac asked.

"I read the summary printed in the paper," Ruth said.

"Exactly," Isaac said. "That's all anyone's read, if they've bothered to read any of it. The details are fascinating in how many there are. Pages upon pages, specifying the boundaries and borders of the new constituencies. So many pages a suspicious guy might suspect someone was trying to hide something in the small print."

"Like what?" Riley asked.

"Mr Das gave up all claims for himself," Isaac said. "But to do so, parliament first had to recognise him as the last and sole heir to the British throne."

"Because we're tired of pretenders, and a new one appears every week," Ruth said. "I saw that printed in the letters-to-the-editor page last week."

"No doubt written by Mr Das," Isaac said.

"No, it was from a retired coal miner in Llandudno," Ruth said.

"Was it?" Isaac asked. "Because it's only Mr Das who's renounced his claim. His kids haven't. They get to keep the titles, and use them if they want. This treaty means the only person alive who can stake a claim is Elizabeth Sherwood."

"The only title she wants is colonel," Riley said.

"For now, and she's volunteering for the front," Isaac said. "The newspapers will want to print her exploits. She'll be famous. You might not have a king today, but you could end up with a queen in a few years."

"We don't want one," Ruth said.

"Maybe not, but Das is playing a much longer game," Isaac said.

"Since I don't even know what the pieces look like, I'm not learning the rules," Ruth said. "Ned Ludd's gone home, so that's nice. And it was nice of the ambassador to give you a plant. Did you name it?"

"Name it?" Riley asked. "Who names their plants?"

"The ambassador gave you a plant," Isaac said. "He sent you coffee and a Christmas letter. Next thing, he'll be inviting you to America. Wait, did he?"

"Of course not," Riley said quickly. "I've barely met the man. I helped save his life and ended up in a wheelchair. He feels sorry for me, that's all. I bet he just wants a contact close to the centre of power."

"You're definitely that now King Alfred owes you the hugest favour," Ruth said. "Do you think Ned Ludd was being kept as a pawn?"

"To be used or sacrificed," Riley said. "Question is, why? This man, Boyle, isn't talking, but I think he was involved. If you look at the dates when the ammo went missing, it coincides with *after* Ned Ludd was in our custody. It seems that Boyle requested some heavy-duty firepower from Stevens. We don't know what he had planned next."

"He planned to kill the king," Ruth said. "That must be it. Sooner or later, someone would have figured out who Ned Ludd was. But if someone had gone after Ned in the convent, we'd have redoubled efforts to identify him. Especially if he'd been murdered with a heavy machine gun. Blimey, imagine the collateral damage! But the longer

Ned was there, the greater the chance he'd give a clue to his past we'd actually understand. Boyle had to kill the king."

"And kill Sherwood, too," Riley said. "I don't think he'd have got away with it."

"Doesn't mean he wouldn't try," Isaac said.

"He'll confess," Riley said. "He's going away for life, and he's got to realise, soon enough, there'll be some Albion-loyalists sharing his prison roof. If he wants protective custody, he'll talk. No, it's Stevens who's a bigger puzzle. As far as I can tell, before this month, there were only some very small thefts of ammunition, but he's clearly been selling weapons for a long time. How long? Was he small-scale, but looking to expand after we shut down the last group of smugglers? Or was he linked to the recent coups? How much of his stock came from Europe?"

"That's a lot of questions," Ruth said. "So how come you took a few days off to come down here?"

"Because we found a real treasure trove in his house," Riley said. "Nothing to do with gunrunning, but he had a lot of history books. He was putting some real effort into the Loyal Brigade persona. I'd like a few words with you about that, Isaac. Specifically, how they died."

"They were brigands, hiding out in the ruins of London, preying on runaways and scavengers," Isaac said.

"You killed them?" Ruth asked.

"I told them to leave," Isaac said. "They wouldn't. There was a fight. They died."

"I'll want more details than that," Riley said. "But I really wanted to speak to Dad, and with the private on his team. Hamish MacKay used to work in the reclamation yard, and since Dad trusts him, he's perfect to send back in, undercover."

"At the reclamation yard?" Ruth asked.

"No, to the prison where we're holding Stevens," Riley said. "Stevens will probably fall back onto his Loyal Brigade routine as a way of maintaining support from his followers, but why was he gathering them in the first place? I sent a telegram to the front, but if Dad can't get here in the next couple of days, I'll ask you to pass the message on, Ruth. In person. We want to keep this covert. But I've a couple of days holiday, so I can help you with your investigation."

"I think we can manage some brunch first," Isaac said. "It should be ready."

"Good idea," Riley said. "Go check on the kitchen. Ruth and I'll go through her case notes."

The door opened before Isaac reached it. Sergeant Kettering entered with Dr Maggie Deering behind.

"Anna! Kelly said you were here," Maggie said. "You're looking very well, dear."

"You look exhausted, Mum," Ruth said.

"It was long shift," Maggie said, taking the chair close to the fire. "There was a young man with piece of shrapnel lodged next to the femoral artery. He was supposed to be going to the specialist unit in Hastings. The jolting of the train carriage shifted the shrapnel."

"Which regiment was he with?" Ruth asked.

"None," Maggie said. "He's a schoolteacher, and a conscientious objector, who volunteered to help repair the railway south of Calais. The enemy left a shrapnel-bomb beneath a broken railway sleeper. He's fine, though. Or he should be. I hope." She rapped her knuckles on the leg of her chair and then smiled. "Never trust a superstitious doctor. I can't tell you how many times I used to say that when I was young. Ah, but it is good to see you, Anna. Did you get some time off for the holidays?"

"Not quite, but there's a message for Dad I have to deliver in person," Riley said.

"And how did you come to be in possession of all the food filling my house?" Kettering asked. "Or should I not ask?"

"It's a gift from the King of Albion," Riley said.

"Then tell me the story after I've eaten it," Kettering said. "Ruth, can you dig out the autopsy files on Mr Soakes and Reverend Dalrymple?"

"I've got them on my phone," Ruth said. "Anna was looking at them. Why?"

"I wanted Maggie to have a look," Kettering said, taking the phone from Anna and walking it over to Maggie.

"I'm not sure I can tell you much," Maggie said. "I've signed more than my share of death certificates, but I've not even witnessed an autopsy since medical school. My interest was always with the living, and there are plenty of those to keep me busy."

"You won't do the autopsy on Mr Fry?" Ruth asked.

"Dr Jenner will do that," Maggie said. "She was an oncologist until last month, but volunteered to stay when the rest of the team relocated west. She handles death certificates, autopsies, running the nursing-training programme, and overseeing paediatric care. She was running obstetrics, too, until Dr Fisher arrived from Scotland."

"Sounds like she's being kept busy," Riley said.

"She is," Maggie said. "We all are. Between the staff whom Dr Long took to Calais, and the specialists who were evacuated to Hastings, we're understaffed and overworked. We've had frostbite, dysentery, and gangrene. An appendix burst while the soldier was halfway through the Tunnel. There were three cases of botulinum poisoning we think is from a very, very old can of pork stew. We've had two crushed feet, not on the same person, two broken arms that were, and what I hope is only a bruised spine. Oh, and a very strange rash we thought was contagious was actually a reaction to the communal laundry detergent. That's *this* week, and *this* side of the French coast."

"It sounds terrible," Ruth said.

"Ah, it's not really," Maggie said. "We pulled together a front-line emergency hospital, a rear-lines operating theatre, and a behind-the-lines recovery centre without any help, or interference, from the navy. No, it was working perfectly until they shelled the Calais hospital. Do you have the rest of the autopsy report?"

"What do you mean?" Ruth asked, walking over to her mother, while Riley wheeled her chair closer.

"These are incomplete," Maggie said. "There's no mention of peri-mortem injuries on Mr Soakes's face. I know he had a fractured jaw, and a black eye, sustained two days before he died. A barrel slipped from the back of a dray. As he was trying to steady it, he slipped on the ice. His wife's working as a surgical orderly at the castle. They'd been fighting, and she was worried people would think she'd given him the black eye. There are no findings here on the state of his lungs or throat. That would be essential in determining the cause of death to be poisonous asphyxiation."

"Are you saying those deaths weren't arsenic poisoning?" Kettering asked.

"Oh, they were," Maggie said. "The report from the lab is incontrovertible, although they didn't perform a full tox-screen. There's no mention of blood alcohol, just the arsenic. It would be worth sending the lab a telegram, asking if they still have the samples."

"Here you go, Isaac," Kettering said as she scrawled a note. "Make yourself useful for a change."

"Your will is my demand," he said.

"Pretty sure that's not the saying," Kettering said. "What went wrong, Maggie?"

"With the autopsy? Nothing," Maggie said. "But we've been working double-shifts for a month. I imagine that, following a preliminary exam, Dr Jenner asked the lab to confirm the cause, and got busy with one of a million other urgent tasks. When Twynham confirmed arsenic, there wasn't much point spending a day to prove it. Here, it says they estimated the level of arsenic at 960mg."

"What's the lethal level?" Kettering asked.

"I believe it's somewhere around 0.6mg per kilogram," Maggie said. "This victim, the vicar, weighed 70kg. A lethal dose would be 42mg. She had about twenty times the lethal dose. Yes, I would say that's sufficient reason to declare a cause of death and return to the living."

"Could you ask Dr Jenner to prioritise the autopsy?" Kettering asked. "Two accidental asphyxiations is one thing. Three, and all of people I knew back in the gone-before? That's making my heart twitch."

"I could speak to Dr Jenner, and assist her," Maggie said. "But you tell Isaac that doesn't mean I don't want lunch."

"Oh, is it nearly ready?" Ruth asked.

"Not for us," Kettering said. "Sergeant, would you mind watching the office? The constable and I have an individual to interview."

"A suspect?" Ruth asked.

"I hope not," Kettering said. "It's Mr Fry's boss."

"I thought he owned the restaurant," Ruth said.

"Apparently not," Kettering said.

Chapter 22 - Scavengers
Petite France, Biggin Street

A freezing drizzle turned the gutter into a soot-grey river as they walked past the new homes on the old high street.

"I know Doc Jenner," Kettering said as she stepped over a semi-frozen pile it was best to think of as sludge rather than think of how many horse-carts still plied the streets. "She supervised my second bout of treatment."

"That was two years ago?" Ruth asked.

"Two and a half," Kettering said. "Worst way of spending a summer. But if you are going to have chemo, better to have it when the weather's warm."

"She wasn't your doctor the first time?"

"Five years ago? No, that was Dr Khan. He was a real gent. A Yankee from somewhere the corn stretched for days. During the Blackout, he was on a retirement holiday and stranded here. Do you remember when we sent the names of the American refugees across the Atlantic? His granddaughter saw the list. She was pregnant. Because of his service, and his age, Dr Khan was popped on the next ship. Got there just before the birth."

"Oh, that's nice," Ruth said. "There usually aren't happy endings to those types of stories. Dr Jenner hasn't been living in Dover for long, then?"

"She has, but she was away during my first bout of chemo, hunting for missing relatives of her own. She was a post-Blackout refugee from somewhere they spell doctor with a k. A cancer specialist before the crisis, she got drafted, working between here and Twynham. When I had my last bout of treatment, she was about to return to Europe again."

"To look for lost relatives?" Ruth asked.

"I think for a child. She's about fifty-five, so could easily have had a few pre-Blackout kids."

"But if she's gone looking for them, year after year, they won't be alive now," Ruth said.

"Doesn't mean you stop looking," Kettering said. "Hoy! Providence Smith, Fortitude Grodinski, Dependable Thatcher, I see you!" she yelled at three children, none more than twelve, and each younger than their over-sized clothes. Each held a shovel, with which they were emptying sand from a barrow onto the pavement. "What are you up to?"

"Spreading sand to melt the ice, Miss," the tallest of the three children said.

"It's sea-sand, so it's salty," the shortest said.

"Is it now?" Kettering said. "Sand will provide some grip, but it won't melt the ice. Providence, take that sand back to the building site where you found it. Fortitude and Dependable, use those shovels to pile up this snow. When Providence comes back, you can use the wheelbarrow to pick up some salt from the power station. Say I sent you. Do a good job, and you can swing by my house later tonight, and I'll give you something special for your tea."

Kettering and Ruth walked on.

"Kids should be in school," Kettering said.

"It's Christmas, Sarge," Ruth said.

"Their teacher, Mr Gwydolfin, was killed three days ago somewhere outside Calais. Sniper," Kettering said. "Kids should be in school. So should their teachers."

The restaurant was in *Très Petite France*, which was occasionally called *Rue Plus Grande*, and had been Biggin Street before the Blackout. The ground floor units were a mix of cafes, restaurants, and shops. Above were language schools, the French library, and law offices specialising in land claims and inheritances. The cobbles were painted red, white, and blue, with tricolour flags hanging between the Christmas decorations, except where it might obscure the posters. They were all the same, and all in French.

"What do they say?" Ruth asked.

"Reclaim, Rebuild," Kettering said. "Used to be those posters advertised for scavengers, now they want settlers."

"After the war, I hope," Ruth said.

But if the current bustle was any gauge, there would be plenty of volunteers. Dover had always hummed with refugees transiting to the mines in the north, or the factories of the big city. Now the city was bursting with those who'd fled the war, but unlike in previous migrations, hadn't continued their journey west. It was as if they knew this war wouldn't last. Ruth wished she shared their confidence.

Mr Fry's restaurant, The Revolving Wheel, was closed. When open, it sprawled along the street with tables outside a launderette, a seamstress, and an art-gallery. Outside, now, a large group, dressed nearly as loudly as they were talking, were in animated discussion until one spotted the two approaching police officers.

A small woman with questing eyes, a neat bowler hat, and a brown leather coat on which she wore a black armband, detached herself from the group. She was a hard-living fifty, with a weatherworn face and scars on her hands and neck. She leaned heavily on a cane as she limped toward them. The others made a pretence of moving a polite few steps away, while staying within eavesdropping distance.

"Hello, Madam Roseau. How's your boy?" Kettering asked.

"In France, where I should be," she said. "I am so sorry to hear of poor Monsieur Fry. Please, we should talk."

"We should," Kettering said.

Madam Roseau led them not to the restaurant, but to a small door next to it, painted with red, white, and blue stripes. The door led to a long corridor lined with old photographs, many from the era before the discovery of colour. Ruth recognised the Eiffel Tower, and guessed the rest must show vistas of very-old France, too.

The corridor took a ninety-degree turn into a glass-walled waiting area which overlooked a transparent-roofed garden where children in coats and hats sat in folding chairs, listening to a story in French. The teacher wore a black armband, too.

"We are short on classroom space," Roseau said. "But this doesn't mean that learning must cease." She led them along the glass wall, and behind a reception desk staffed by a young woman in a blue dress and shawl, who also wore a black armband.

"Everyone is in mourning," Kettering said, as Roseau ushered them into her office.

"For many people, and now for Mr Fry as well," Roseau said. "It is a great loss. He was an exceptional man. Can I offer you refreshments?"

"No, we're fine," Kettering said. "Did you know Tommy well?"

"Personally, no. Jean-Luc knew him. He helped with odd jobs. My father knew Monsieur Fry better still. Tommy accompanied him to Paris, on his first expedition."

"He did?" Kettering asked. "I didn't know that."

"When was this expedition?" Ruth asked.

"Three months after the Blackout," Roseau said. "They call us scavengers. I call us *récupérateurs*, which comes closer to the English word which best describes our mission. We will recuperate Europe. Restore her. But we began as scavengers. As refugees. My father was one of the first. After the Blackout, he returned to Paris to claim the old treasures, to preserve them. There were not many willing to risk the journey with him, but Mr Fry did. He saved my father's life."

"And you own Mr Fry's restaurant?" Kettering asked.

"We own the building," Roseau said. "But an artist cannot be owned, and Mr Fry was a magnificent artist."

"He was that good at cooking?" Ruth asked.

"He was a chef!" Roseau said. "But his artistry was with people. He always knew what to say, and how to say it so as to make them feel at ease. A meal was a moment of sanctuary, of peace, of escape from a troubled world. He will be missed."

"He was here last night?" Kettering asked.

"*Oui*. Working. Every night he worked."

"And afterward, he had a few drinks?"

"We were celebrating," Roseau said. "He was coming with us to Calais."

"To a war zone?" Ruth asked.

"We are going home," Roseau said. "If we don't return home, the terrorists have won. Yes, Calais is dangerous, but less so with each day. Refugees must have a reason to return. They need shops, cafes, farms, and schools. But it will begin with a reclamation crew, and they will require somewhere to eat." She reached down and opened a drawer, taking out a thin, hand-printed leaflet.

Ruth took it. "I don't speak French," she said, as she turned it over. "Or German. What does it say?"

"This is the request for funds," Roseau said. "We are opening ten businesses. Three farms, a fishing fleet, a hotel, one laundry, one blacksmith, one tailor, one medical clinic, and one restaurant. Supplies will come from Britain, as will the funding, initially. Future refugees will be resettled in Calais. And we will then resettle them further east as the army advances. We will rebuild roads and farms, and we will forge a new Europe, but it begins with this first small step."

"When was Tommy leaving?" Kettering asked.

"January," Roseau said. "Our initial customers would be the soldiers. In a few years, they would return as tourists."

"That's ambitious," Kettering said.

"Without ambition, what is life?" Roseau replied.

"I remember your father saying much the same thing to me eight years ago when he was putting together a similar expedition," Kettering said. "And that was his second. He wanted me to go with him."

"And you said no," Roseau said.

"Dover is my home," Kettering said. "And it's still your father's, and you're putting together the third expedition."

"The last expedition," Roseau said.

"I hope so," Kettering said. "But your father said the same thing to me eight years ago. Was Tommy contributing some money to this venture?"

"No. He promised to work for ten years. He would be paid, of course, with a dividend based on profits and a house which would be his in retirement."

"That's quite generous," Kettering said.

"No, because if he was in Calais, his customers from Dover would come to visit. Do you see?"

"Fair enough. What about his staff?"

"They would remain here," Roseau said. "His Dover establishment would remain open."

"What would happen to his house, because two of his staff live below?" Kettering said.

"We would continue to manage his house for him," Roseau said. "My son is a *réparateur*. He already looks after the downstairs of the house. He offered to renovate Monsieur Fry's rooms, *mais non*. Monsieur Fry was not ready to part with his memories. These are a lot of questions for an accident."

"It's just procedure," Kettering said. "What time did Tommy leave here?"

"A few minutes before midnight."

"After curfew," Kettering said.

"Curfew begins ten minutes after last orders," Roseau said. "It is impossible for the restaurants to be cleaned so swiftly."

"But you still had a few drinks afterwards?"

"Only one glass, maybe two," Roseau said.

"A glass of what?" Kettering asked. "Was he drunk?"

"We drank wine. When we locked the doors, he was happy, but not drunk. We have our own guards standing watch at night. They will confirm it."

"Did he leave here alone?" Kettering asked.

"He did."

"His downstairs neighbours said he had a girlfriend," Kettering said.

"Ah, Madam Sofia!" Roseau said. "While love is not bounded by age, she is a little too old for that description."

"Madam Sofia? She's French?" Kettering asked.

"German," Roseau said. "But I believe she has lived here in Dover for nearly twenty years. She would often travel with one of our summer caravans as far as they would go, and then continue alone."

"To where?"

"To search for her lost family," Roseau said.

"Do you have any contact information? A surname?"

"Jenner," Roseau said. "Sofia Jenner. She is a doctor from Germany, I believe. She ran clinics wherever the caravan stopped for the night."

"Doc *Jenner* was dating Tommy Fry?" Kettering asked. "That's a turn-up for the books, because it's a coincidence no newspaper would print."

"What coincidence?" Roseau asked.

"For one thing, responsibility for Tommy Fry's autopsy will fall to her," Kettering said. "I better get back up to the castle. How long were they dating?"

"A month, but they've known each other for a lifetime," Roseau said. "She often travelled to Germany to deliver medicines, but I had persuaded her to run a clinic in Calais. She would heal the soul, while Monsieur Fry fed it."

"Thank you," Kettering said.

"One last question," Ruth said. "Do you know Mr Soakes?"

"The owner of the Wire and Wrench? He died, too, recently, *n'est-ce pas*?"

"But did you *know* him?" Ruth asked. "Was he moving to Calais?"

"No, but he had agreed to hire us two of his drays, eight horses, and three stable-hands. In return, he would become the main… oh. You think there is a connection with his death. A connection means this wasn't an accident."

171

"What were you about to say about Mr Soakes?" Kettering asked.

"We were hiring his equipment, and he was to become our main reseller of wine from the Gravelines vineyard. Next year's harvest would barely qualify as vinegar, but there is a market even for that in a thirsty world."

"Thank you," Kettering said. "We'll have more questions later."

Ruth waited until they were outside before asking. "Do you think there are two Dr Jenners?"

"Absolutely not," Kettering said, picking up her pace.

Ruth skipped a step to catch up. "Mr Fry was employed by the French scavengers. Refugee children were sleeping above the vicar's cottage. The publican was backing this Calais project where Mr Fry was going to work. That's a link."

"A link isn't the same as a motive," Kettering said. "And we're still not certain on the cause of death. If Mr Fry left work at midnight, what was the sound his neighbours heard at three a.m.? This is looking less and less like an accident by the second, but there's one person who can certainly confirm it, so let's go to the castle and ask her."

Chapter 23 - Last Aid
Dover Castle

Dover's old hospital was one of the many buildings destroyed during the Blackout. The viral-AI had added a factor of ten to the thermostat, causing the fans to whir so fast the motors caught fire. With the fire suppression systems already disabled, and the local fire station already ablaze, there was no one to put out the inferno.

Dover's ancient castle, by contrast, had few circuits for the digital virus to infect. It had become an aid-station. Over the weeks that followed, it became the new hospital, and the centre of government for the rescue effort on both sides of the Channel.

As the weeks became months, the apocalyptic crisis became a new way of life. A new hospital was promised, and so was a new town hall, but priority went to the power station, then the water treatment plant, the schools, the walls, then dealing with the too-frequent pirate raids. Months became years. Twenty of them. The city was still governed from the castle, and still mostly governed by the Royal Navy. As need had grown, paediatrics, obstetrics, gynaecology, and oncology had been relocated to other buildings across Dover. The city's mortuary and morgue remained in the bunkers below the main castle. Now, it was full of old banquet tables on which lay bodies covered in moth-eaten tablecloths. At the far end, beneath a lamp and next to a fan, was a masked surgeon. But it wasn't Sofia Jenner.

"Hi, Mum. Who are all these bodies?" Ruth asked, picking her way between the sheet-covered tables.

"They're from Calais," Maggie said. "Graves can't be dug in this weather. After that mortar took out the crematorium a week or so ago, the bodies have been brought back here."

"There are so many," Ruth said.

"Sixty-three on the last train," Maggie said. "And these are only the people who are local to Dover, or whom we can't identify."

"How many remain unidentified?" Kettering asked.

"Thirteen," Maggie said. "They're at the back, over there. Everyone we've a name for is on this list. I've recommended to the council that civilians in the warzone start wearing dog-tags."

"I recommended we stick a trio of wind turbines on the cliffs," Kettering said. "That was ten years ago, and I'm still waiting for a reply." She picked up the clipboard, and began reading through the names as she walked over to the unnamed bodies.

"Did you take a look at Mr Fry?" Ruth asked.

"A look is about all I've managed so far, dear, but I promise I'm doing everything by the book." Maggie pointed to a textbook laying open on a small metal trolley, next to a row of as-yet unused instruments. "I've scraped beneath the fingernails, taken hair and blood samples to go to the lab. The next train is at two, and I've telegraphed them to wait for a package, but they'll keep to their schedule. Tissue samples will have to travel on the overnight mail-train."

"There's a couple of people I know here," Kettering said, having pulled the bloody sheets off the unidentified bodies. "This is Linda Chow, and that's Diane Ng. They were veterinarians from Northumberland. Came down to help with the horses. Volunteered to be nurses at the front. Said people had to be easier than animals since they could tell you what was wrong. Mario Veper is the guy without a face. He ran the crematorium here. I imagine he was working at the crem over in Calais."

"Are you sure that's him?" Maggie asked.

"From the tattoo on his arm," Kettering said, as she added their names to the clipboard list. "It's supposed to be an erupting volcano. His family used to live within the shadow of Vesuvius. I always thought the tattoo looked more like an ice cream cone. Never told him, of course."

"Do you want to claim the remains?" Maggie asked.

"It couldn't be an open casket funeral," Kettering said. "No, returning the ashes will be more comforting than bringing a ruined body back to his sister. Where's Doc Jenner?"

"I'd like to know that, too," Maggie said. "She didn't arrive for her shift. She was supposed to have signed off on the bodies we've identified so they can be cremated."

"Can you do that?" Kettering asked.

"I'll have to," Maggie said. "We can't keep them here. It's just not sanitary."

"We just heard that Dr Jenner was dating Mr Fry," Ruth said.

"She was?" Maggie asked. "Perhaps she saw the body and went home in shock."

"Is there anything you can tell us about Mr Fry?" Kettering asked.

"Not much, not yet," Maggie said. "The bruising on his face is interesting. He was found lying face down, yes? The abrasions on his temple and forehead could have been from a fall, but there's bruising around his cheek and mouth, too."

"Cheek and mouth?" Kettering asked, leaning forward. "It's on both sides of his face. Could that be from a hand clamped over his mouth?"

"That is one possibility," Maggie said. "Another is that there was a fight earlier in the evening. There are no defensive wounds, but he was wearing gloves."

"He'd been drinking," Kettering said. "At least a couple of glasses with the French scavengers."

"Madam Roseau didn't mention a fight," Ruth said.

"But Mr Fry left work at midnight," Kettering said. "The downstairs neighbours heard a thump around three a.m. There are three hours unaccounted for. That's plenty of time to throw a few punches." She held her hand above Fry's mouth. "That's a right hand, yes? So could it have been held over his face from behind as he was mugged?"

"Possibly," Maggie said. "But the bruising is very pronounced. There's also this, on his chest." She lifted the sheet, revealing where she'd cut away the clothes. "More bruising. It's hard to see in this light, but I think that could have been caused by a knee. I think someone knelt on his chest, pushing a hand down across his mouth."

"If that happened outside, there'd be mud on the back of his coat," Ruth said. "There wasn't."

"What's the cause of death?" Kettering asked.

"I would give a preliminary diagnosis of hypoxia," Maggie said. "It could be arsenic poisoning. But I would want a few more hours before I say any more than that."

"Could he have died from suffocation?" Kettering asked. "The killer clamped his hand over Tommy's mouth, preventing him from breathing?"

"I don't want to rush to judgement, because this isn't my area," Maggie said, "but if this bruising was caused by a hand, it didn't block the victim's nose."

"But this bruising happened soon before death?" Kettering asked.

"Absolutely. As did the abrasions on his face," Maggie said.

"So either he got into a fight at home, or somewhere indoors, sometime between midnight and three. The obvious place to look is his girlfriend's house. You saw Tommy's flat, Ruth. Would you bring a date home?"

"Um…" Ruth said, glancing at her mother. "I would say his was the home of a single man to whom love was a memory, recorded in a photograph."

"Good answer," Kettering said. "So maybe he got into a fight with the doc, went home, and killed himself. Do you know Dr Jenner well, Maggie?"

"Not at all," Maggie said. "I rarely leave the operating theatre except to go home. I've seen her around a few times, that's all."

"Sounds about the same as me for the last couple of years," Kettering said. "According to the leader of the French scavengers, she was going to run a clinic in Calais. Tommy Fry was going to run a restaurant there, just as soon as the frontline had moved beyond mortar range. They're opening up a string of businesses to encourage refugees to move home. Mr Soakes, the publican, was providing some support to this venture. The Reverend Dalrymple was running a refuge for unaccompanied children. Doc Jenner wrote up the autopsies for those two deaths. I *won't* say we've got a motive, but we've certainly got a link. Do you know where Dr Jenner lives?"

"There'll be an address with the nurse at the on-call desk," Maggie said.

"Would you mind coming with us?" Kettering asked. "I'll have to ask her about the autopsies, and I'll need someone to translate the medical talk into English."

Chapter 24 - A Car Park Cabin
80-B1 Folkestone Road, Dover

"This brings back memories," Kettering said as they neared their destination.

"Memories from your childhood?" Maggie asked.

"From my second bout of chemo," Kettering said. "I had my treatment at the White Cliffs Oncology Centre. So did all my friends."

It had taken them ten minutes to walk from the morgue to Dr Jenner's home, but it would have been seven if the castle-guard hadn't insisted on checking their I.D.s as they were leaving. The medical centre took up the southern side of the Folkestone Road. Before the Blackout, the centre had been a general practice clinic. Afterwards, as the long-term impact of radioactive fallout took grip on the local population, the clinic had morphed into a specialist cancer centre. As demand on both sides of the Channel had inevitably grown, the facility had expanded into the neighbouring shops. For the first time in a decade, it was now quiet, as cancer treatment had been relocated to the safer, and fresher, environs of the Hastings Hospital, further along the coast.

"Didn't you say Dr Jenner treated you, Sarge?" Ruth asked.

"She oversaw the treatment," Kettering said. "Only met her three times. Before the first session, halfway through to get a progress report, and a week after the last to get the all-clear. But all my friends who endured the same tribulation knew her name. She got good results."

The address they had was for 80-B1 Folkestone Road, which they found almost directly across the road from the oncology centre, and behind an ancient boarding house with a new sign declaring it to be student-nurses' accommodation.

Behind the crumbling brick mansion were three one-storey cabins, labelled A1, B1, and C1, erected in the old car park between the boarding house and a swathe of garden-farm allotments. Around each cabin was a high wooden fence.

"That's her name on this post-box," Kettering said, and pulled on the bell-rope. No sound came out.

"I bet she muffled the clapper," Maggie said. "When you work twenty-hour shifts, you don't want to be woken by the mail-carrier."

"We've got an audience," Ruth said, pointing up at the third-floor window where a pair of tired nurses watched them.

"What we need is a key," Kettering said. She knocked on the gate. "Constable, I think this is a job for you."

"I don't know how to pick that lock," Ruth said. "I've been practicing, but mostly with padlocks."

"I meant you should climb up and over," Kettering said. "There's no barbed wire, so you won't do yourself too much mischief. You can unlock it from the inside."

"Oh. Right. Sure," Ruth said.

A run, a jump, and kicking off on the door, she grabbed the top of the fence, almost fell, but managed to get her leg over.

"I also meant you should use that ladder over in those weeds," Kettering said. "Bit late now, so hurry it up."

"Yes, Sarge," Ruth said, but thought something worse. She dropped down, unlatched the gate, stepped back, and looked around. There were a few struggling firs, a few sticks in pots that might be dormant deciduous plants, two bicycles, one in better repair than the other, an empty cold frame, and a small tool shed with a snow-shovel leaning against it. At the side was a wooden bench, beneath a slanting wooden roof running from the cabin to the fence. The bench had a view of the allotment-fields behind the property where a few elderly garden-farmers guarded their plots from the uniformed conscripts crawling through the drainage ditches.

"No wood store," Kettering said. "And that's why." She pointed up at an overhead transmission cable running down into the cabin from a junction box attached to the nurses' boarding house. "And it's why she lived here. They're on the clinic's electrical grid."

"You're dead! Your unit's dead! The war's lost!" a sergeant bellowed from the allotments.

"No one could sleep through that," Kettering said, and pushed the front door. "Locked and no answer. Let's try the knocker."

From her belt, she unclipped the universal key: two foot-length levers, crossed over to form an X, with chisel points at one end, and a ratchet and screw at the other. By turning the screw, the chisel points were forced further apart, breaking the door's wooden frame, and releasing a very familiar smell from inside.

"Stay back, Doc," Kettering said, as she stepped inside.

The cabin, though built from materials salvaged from rural ruins, was well insulated. So well insulated, the foetid odour of death hadn't been able to escape. But beneath it was a smell Ruth had grown to know almost as well: the copper tang of blood.

"In here, Constable," Kettering said, from the end of the hall.

The front door was on one of the two wider walls of the oblong cabin. It led into a small boot-room filled with far more heavy-duty boots and coats than a doctor would need for crossing the road to her clinic. The partition walls on either side both had wool-lined concertina doors, both of which were open. To one side was the living room, and a broad window which would have offered a view over the allotment-farms if the curtains hadn't been closed. A bite had been taken out of the living room to make space for a small galley-kitchen. On the other side of the entrance-hall was the bedroom where a similar sized bite had become an equally small bathroom.

"Clear," Kettering said. "Come on in, Maggie. Gloves on, Constable."

"Is that Dr Jenner?" Ruth asked.

"It is," Kettering said.

The doctor lay on the bed, but her brains were spread across the pillow and the wall, where they ringed a small hole through which the bullet had exited the cabin. Her right arm was bent at the elbow, the hand close to her ear. A compact pistol lay on the pillow.

"It's supposed to be suicide," Maggie said.

"But is it?" Kettering asked.

"Do you have spare gloves?" Maggie asked.

Kettering pulled a pair of the thin leather gloves from a belt-pouch. "Constable, do you have that camera?"

"Do you mean my phone? Yes," Ruth said.

"Take a few pictures before we disturb the scene," Kettering said.

Ruth did, before stepping back so her mother could approach the body. Between the bed, the built-in wardrobe, and the small vanity-stand, the room was already crowded.

"Time of death was last night," Maggie said. "I can't be more precise without instruments, but I would say closer to midnight than sunset or dawn."

"Death by gunshot?" Kettering asked.

"She absolutely *was* shot," Maggie said.

"There's not much blood spatter on the pillow near the entry-wound," Kettering said.

"I wouldn't expect there to be," Maggie said. "But yes, I see what you mean. It's possible the heart had stopped pumping before she was shot. Can you open the curtain? I need some more light."

"I've a torch," Kettering said.

"Shine it over her face," Maggie said. "Yes. Here. There's bruising on her neck."

"She was strangled?"

"Possibly," Maggie said. "An autopsy will confirm it. We should send for a pathologist from Twynham."

"There's no blood back-spatter on the gun," Kettering said. "She's wearing a nightdress, thick woollen bed socks, and an almost matching woollen shawl. Sensible for the time of year, but not what you'd put on before committing suicide. Constable, check the kitchen for a wood-burning stove. I didn't see a chimney outside, but I want to be sure."

Ruth made her way to the living room. Two heavy-duty travelling cases were precariously balanced on the two-person sofa. Both were open, their contents disarrayed.

The kitchen had a sink on the wall adjoining the bathroom, a two-ring electric hotplate, and a small counter with cupboards above and below. Those above contained enough crockery for two, and enough tinned food for a late-night snack. But not for entertaining. Of course not. She was dating a chef, while the nurses would have a dining room in their boarding house.

Ruth stepped back into the living room. Yes, this cabin was a nice home. A single person's home, but still large enough to entertain a guest. It was technically smaller than the apartments on the upper floor of the police station, but Ruth shared those with Eloise Kettering, and with Isaac, Kelly, Gregory, and Mrs Zhang, whenever they were in the city. This was a nice place. Presumably owned by the health service, and included as part of the doctor's remuneration. But Dr Jenner was a senior physician. She could have afforded a place of her own. And if she wasn't spending money on rent, where *did* she spend it?

The travel cases were well used, heavy-duty, and very definitely post-Blackout in construction. The top and sides were coated in waxed wool that was worn at the sides and torn at an edge revealing the pine slats beneath. The corners were reinforced with steel. On one side was a pair of worn wood-and-leather wheels, with a tug-handle at the opposite side, but even empty they would be awkward to move. These were cases for carrying onto a train, or a cart, and which could double as a bench seat after arriving at a destination, but where was that?

The clothes Jenner had packed were hard-wearing, designed for life far beyond the comfort of electricity and running water. The boots were the same. On both pairs, the leather uppers were scuffed, but meticulously polished, while the soles were brand-new.

"Any chimney, Constable?" Kettering called.

"No, sarge," Ruth said. "She packed for a journey. She even got new soles for her boots. She packed, and before she packed, she visited the cobblers. She wasn't going to Calais until January, so it's a bit early for her to get ready."

"Not everyone leaves everything until the last minute, dear," Maggie said.

"I'm going to grab some of those soldiers training in the allotments," Kettering said. "We'll get them to stand guard. You keep looking. I'm certain this was murder, and I'm just as certain Tommy Fry didn't kill her." She shook her head and stepped outside.

Ruth returned to the cases, lifting up the remainder of the clothes. They'd already been rifled. Without knowing the victim better, it was impossible to know what was missing, but she found two books: an old-world walking guide, and a post-Blackout map, both of Ireland.

"Why Ireland?" Ruth said.

"What's that, dear?" Maggie called.

"She has a map of Ireland," Ruth called, as she took a step back, taking in the bookshelves. "A *new* map."

The books were an odd mix of genres. From the umlauts and eszetts, most were in German. The shelves were deep, and held a few knickknacks, ornaments, a box of sketching pencils, a book of matches, two candles, but no photographs.

Ruth walked back to the bedroom.

"How far ahead would you pack for a trip, Mum?" Ruth asked.

"These days, it doesn't take long," Maggie said.

"What about in the olden days?"

"If it was a long trip, seven days. For a short trip, it was three. I'd pack everything to see whether I needed to visit a store, or do laundry. When in January was she supposed to be going to Calais?"

"After the shooting stopped," Ruth said.

"Did you find a suicide note?" Maggie asked.

"No, but I'm pretty sure this was murder," Ruth said. "The suitcases were searched."

"It was murder badly staged to look like a suicide," Maggie said. "That's why I wondered if there might be a note. I don't think this gun matches the bullet. It's a purse-gun with a six-round magazine. I used to have something similar. The exit wound suggests a much larger calibre."

Ruth picked up the gun, and ejected the magazine. "It's empty. So we're supposed to think she only had one bullet for the gun? This was a hasty frame-job."

"You've been watching too many movies," Maggie said. "But, I'd say yes."

Ruth stepped into the bathroom. Technically, it was a shower room with a toilet and sink. One cupboard above the sink contained toothbrushes, two of them, and a neat collection of soaps. In the cupboard beneath the sink, between a stolen-from-work stack of toilet paper and a bottle of bleach were two jars which didn't belong. Ruth took a photograph, before removing a jar.

"Mum, what does arsenic look like, because I think I just found two jars."

Chapter 25 - A Burning Clue
80-B1 Folkestone Road, Dover

"Arsenic trioxide," Maggie said, examining the bottle. "This is a chemotherapy drug for leukaemia."

"So this type of arsenic isn't poisonous?" Ruth asked.

"Oh, it is," Maggie said. "This is incredibly toxic. It would be lethal if you administered too high a dose."

Ruth returned to the bathroom, and took out the other bottle. Behind was a box of re-usable syringes. "You said the lethal dose was in milligrams, didn't you, Mum?" she asked. "So one syringe-full would be more than enough for murder."

The door clicked open. "Find anything?" Kettering asked.

"Arsenic," Ruth said.

"Arsenic trioxide," Maggie said. "It's a chemotherapy drug."

"Really? They gave me carboplatin," Kettering said. "If you were using arsenic trioxide to murder someone, how would you do it?"

"An injection," Maggie said.

"I found some syringes, too," Ruth said.

"Interesting," Kettering said. "Mr Fry had some bruising around his mouth, as if someone had clamped a hand over it to stop him shouting. Someone could have injected him, pushed him down, and held their hand over his mouth until he'd died."

"They did something similar with Dr Jenner," Maggie said. "I think they held their hand over her throat until they had the gun in position."

"The soldiers have been practicing sentry duty in those allotments all night," Kettering said. "Some stand watch while others creep up on them. No one heard a gunshot. The killer must have used a suppressor, so we're looking for a different gun."

"What, and they just hoped we wouldn't notice?" Ruth asked. "I actually find that insulting."

"They were acting in haste," Kettering said. "Making it up as they went along, so there wasn't time to properly stage the scene. Officially, we still don't use cameras. Sketches and handwritten notes do miss so many of the details. The murderer must have hoped we wouldn't find Dr Jenner's body for a couple of days. By then, the time of death would be harder to pin down, so we'd assume Dr Jenner killed Tommy Fry, then killed herself."

"Well, now I *am* insulted," Ruth said. "But wouldn't they have struggled? If you stuck a needle in someone, they'd fight back. Mr Fry was still wearing his coat and gloves. The killer must have come inside with him. Reverend Dalrymple might have had one glass, but no way was she drunk. Could you use the syringe to fill the glass with a lethal dose of arsenic when the victim's back was turned?"

"An autopsy will tell us," Maggie said.

"This explains why there weren't proper autopsies before," Kettering said. "Injected or ingested, the arsenic certainly wasn't inhaled accidentally. Maggie, I'd like you to go back to the castle, take a look at Mr Fry, and see if you can find a needle-mark. Ruth, go with her and find a couple of older orderlies to collect Dr Jenner. Not students, please. I'll take the gun, and the photos, back to the police station and check the files for the deaths of Mr Soakes and the Reverend Dalrymple. No, not the deaths, the *murders*."

"You've seen a *lot* of murder in the last few months," Maggie said as they walked back to the castle.

"You wanted me to be a cop," Ruth said. "Wasn't that why I lied about my age to attend the police academy?"

"That was so you'd get a job with Henry," Maggie said. "I thought you'd be investigating counterfeiting and fraud."

"We did," Ruth said.

"I didn't think there'd be so much death to go with it," Maggie said.

"It's better than being at the front," Ruth said.

"I know," Maggie said. "Isn't that the sting in the tail? If you'd not joined the police, you'd have been conscripted instead. Ah, but what can we ever do but dream of brighter tomorrows?"

"It's not that bad, Mum," Ruth said. "And I like policing. And Dover. It's a bit too smoggy, but it's a nice place. Way nicer than Twynham. That city is just too big."

"You're a country mouse at heart, aren't you, dear?" she said. "Ah, but I can't believe, with the war so close, there were two murders here last night."

"But four murders in total, Mum," Ruth said. "There's the publican and the reverend as well. Doc Jenner signed off on those autopsies, didn't she? And you said she didn't do them properly."

"But the children living upstairs of the vicar *did* get sick," Maggie said.

"Could you toss some of that chemo drug on a fire?" Ruth asked. "Would the rising fumes make the children sick?"

"I suppose they would. But why go to all that trouble?"

"Dunno. Doc Jenner and Mr Fry were only dating for a month. Maybe she was faking the relationship. I saw his flat. I don't think she visited him there. If I were— I mean, not that I have. But—" She stammered into silence.

"Yes dear, I've lived a life, too. If he were bringing home a guest, he'd have kept his flat tidy."

"Right. Except he was leaving Dover. That was a flat in which he remembered the dead. I don't think he'd want to have a new girlfriend visit him there. He'd want to keep the memories separate. The scavenger woman, Roseau, said her son had offered to do some decorating and repair work, but Mr Fry refused. Plus, Doc Jenner wasn't with Mr Fry at the restaurant last night. If she wanted to kill him, she'd have done it on a night where they were out together. No, I think there's another killer. After they killed Tommy Fry, they had to kill Doc Jenner because she'd have realised who killed Tommy when she did the autopsy. The motive has to be something to do with those scavengers. Figure out the motive, and we'll find the killer."

"Let's confirm Mr Fry was given a lethal injection first," Maggie said.

But when they reached the morgue, they found it empty. All of the bodies were gone. Scrubbing the now empty tables was a soldier with a stripe on his arm and a patch over his eye.

"Almost done, Doc," he said.

"Where are the bodies, Jerome?" Maggie asked.

"Gone to be burned," he said.

"Where?" Ruth asked.

"It's not likely to be the power station, is it?" he said.

"Do you mean they were sent to the crem?" Maggie asked, and began running. Ruth quickly caught up.

Sparks flew as her boot's nails bit into the stone flags of the subterranean hallways. Chunks tore from the ancient rubber coating the ramp as they ran to the newest extension tacked onto and above the east of the castle. Splinters erupted when she staggered to a halt in the wooden corridor outside the crematorium, which was lined with bodies, piled two to a gurney, with one trolley almost blocking the swing-doors.

"Stop!" Ruth yelled as she squeezed herself through. "Police, stop! Stop burning the bodies!"

Two women in thick leather aprons were standing with heads respectfully bowed next to the furnace.

"What's wrong?" the elder of the two attendants asked.

"Just stop," Ruth said, looking around. "One of these bodies is a murder victim." There were too many bodies to count, but already far fewer than had been lined up in the morgue.

"Are you saying there's been a murder up at the front?" the attendant asked.

"No, here in Dover," Ruth said. "Can you turn the fire off?"

"It won't make a difference now," the attendant said. "We're ten seconds away from completion. But these bodies all came from the front. They're soldiers. We've got the paperwork."

"How many have you burned?" Ruth said.

"Tended," the attendant said. "Ten so far."

"I'll check the bodies in the corridor," Maggie said.

Ruth checked those lined up in the chamber, but none belonged to Mr Fry.

"He's not here," Ruth said.

"I've a list of every name," the attendant said, holding out the clipboard.

Ruth took it. Every number had a name next to it.

"Sergeant Kettering only identified another three, right, Mum?" Ruth asked.

"I think so, dear."

"Mario Veper," Ruth said, looking for the name. "Yes. Okay. That's the sergeant's handwriting. Someone filled in all the blanks, and then signed it at the bottom. They signed it Dr Jenner. Mum, how many bodies were brought back from Calais?"

"Sixty-three."

"There's sixty-four names," Ruth said. She turned to the attendant. "Who told you to burn the bodies?"

"Dr Jenner," the attendant said. "That's her name at the bottom."

"But not in person?" Ruth asked.

"Well, no. She had to go operate on someone."

"Who told you that?" Ruth asked. "Who gave you this form?"

"One of the orderlies. He brought in the first body, and told us to get the others."

"Disappeared, too," the young assistant said. "Left us lifting the bodies alone."

"Which orderly?" Ruth asked.

"Don't know his name," the older attendant said. "He was a short fella with grey hair except where he was bald. Had a ratty squint, like he was trying to see over his eyebrows, and spoke like he'd a pea stuck up is nose."

"I know him," Maggie said. "That's Peter Fishwyck."

"He actually works here?" Ruth asked. "Then we better get the admiral to shut down the castle."

"I'll find the admiral," Maggie said. "You better go fetch Sergeant Kettering."

"Hang on, what are we going to do with these bodies?" the attendant asked.

"For now, nothing," Ruth said.

Chapter 26 - The Stink of Guilt
Dover Police Station

Ruth was out of breath when she reached the police station.

"Constable, what is it?" Kettering asked.

"They burned the bodies!" Ruth said.

"Who burned which bodies?" Riley asked, wheeling her chair out from behind the duty-desk.

"Tommy Fry's body," Ruth said. "All the bodies that were in the morgue were sent for immediate cremation. The order was signed by Dr Jenner, but it can't have been her. The attendant identified a guy called... called..." She wracked her brains, and wished she'd written it down. "Peter Fishwyck!"

"You mean Stinky Fishwyck?" Kettering asked.

"The attendant said he was balding, with a squint," Ruth said. "Speaks as if he's got a pea stuck up his nose, though I don't know what that's supposed to sound like."

"I do," Kettering said. "He had his nose broken at the school prom. It wasn't properly reset."

"Did he live here before the Blackout, too?" Riley asked.

"He did," Kettering said. "Sounds like we've got ourselves a suspect."

"Maggie's getting the admiral to shut down the castle," Ruth said.

"He won't be there," Kettering said. "If he's our serial killer, he must have seen Maggie examining poor Tommy. While we headed to Doc Jenner's, he sent Mr Fry's body to be burned. He's covering his tracks, destroying the evidence, and any loose ends. But we weren't gone long. Stinky can't have gone far."

"Ireland," Ruth said. "That's where he wants to go."

"What makes you say that?" Riley asked.

"Because Doc Jenner had a couple of maps of Ireland in her bag," Ruth said. "He can't run away to Europe because of the war. He can't seek sanctuary in Leicestershire because of the treaty. That leaves Ireland. There's a ferry, isn't there?"

"Once a week to Dundalk," Riley said. "He'd have to get through Wales."

"He'd have to get out of Dover first," Kettering said. "The passenger train leaves at two. We've got half an hour to stop it. That's plenty of time. Sergeant Riley, can you go up to the station? Make sure the train doesn't leave until we've searched it, but I don't want any visible sign of trouble." She grabbed Eloise's worn crimson overcoat from the hook by the door. "Sling this over your jacket. Send a message to the city gates, and send Isaac to the harbour. No fishing boats are allowed to leave."

"Where are we going, Sarge?" Ruth asked.

"To make sure Stinky Fishwyck isn't actually the fifth victim," Kettering said.

Sergeant Kettering didn't run; she rarely did. Her view was if you had to run, you should have left ten minutes earlier. But they did walk at a clip faster than a jog.

"Do you know where he lives?" Ruth asked.

"Stinky Fishwyck? I do. Same house he's lived in for over forty years. He went to the same school as me. Same school as Tommy Fry, too. Stinky went to Europe when he was eighteen. Came back when he was twenty with enough cash to buy his house. I went on a couple of dates with him when I was young enough not to know better. I can tell you his nickname wasn't only because of his surname."

"He's a criminal?" Ruth asked.

"A campanologist," Kettering said.

"He sleeps in a tent?" Ruth said.

"He's a bell-ringer. You need to do more crosswords," Kettering said. "He used to travel across Europe ringing the bells in one church and then another. Or so he claimed. After I became a cop, he went onto my mental watch-list as a probable smuggler. But he never caused any trouble in Dover. Since the Blackout, he's been heading up the restoration fund at St Mary's. Put up a quarter of the money himself, so I heard. His income comes from renting property."

"He's a slumlord?" Ruth asked.

"No, just a landlord," Kettering said. "There's been no trouble from him in twenty years. I've given him a passing nod from time to time, but can't say I remember exchanging any words. He's an easy man to forget. An easy man to overlook."

Peter Fishwyck's house was on Bridge Street, north of the old supermarket that had become the site of the city's emergency, and still operational, coal power station. Until, or if, the hydroelectric dam on the River Stour was completed, the unfinished wind turbine was the only real evidence of the half-hearted effort to update the local power grid.

As they neared the old road on which the freight-rail tracks had been laid, linking the power station with the freight-rail Priory Station, the bell began to ring. The barriers at the new level crossing began to descend.

"Duck and run!" Kettering said, doing just that to dash beneath the descending wooden gate. "Once the freight-train's cleared, the passenger service leaves."

Ruth ducked beneath the first gate, but jumped the second, getting a cheer from a bicycling boy now waiting on the far side of the crossing.

"If that leads to a spate of kids playing hurdles on the crossing, I'll blame you," Kettering said, slowing again to a brisk walk.

"Sarge, couldn't Fishwyck jump on a freight train?" Ruth asked.

"He might if he's desperate, but the passenger service leaves first," Kettering said. "It's down here, the house right at the end."

"It's a nice street," Ruth said.

"He owns most of the houses on this row," Kettering said.

Either side, and dead ahead, were terraces of two-storey red-bricks. Few had more than two letterboxes by the gate, while many had pillar-balconies and rooftop gardens from which ivy trailed and coiled, offering a filter-screen against the belching power station. Metal Christmas trees were planted in every front garden, painted the same shade as the door, though decorated with varying degrees of enthusiasm. Outside every third house were on-road bicycle storage boxes. One of those was simultaneously being used both as a goal and a wicket. The children might have been playing two separate games, or possibly just another variation of the rule-free sludge-ball dominating the city's winter streets.

"Remember the kids are out here," Kettering said, as she tried the door. It was unlocked. The gate opened into a yard containing a suggestion box, a recessed tool-share cabinet, and a communal wood-store. Kettering headed straight for the green-painted door leading into the house. This door was locked. She took out the knocker, inserting it around the frame. With a crack, the lock broke. Kettering dropped the knocker, drew her gun, and nudged the door open.

From the double sink and broad window, this room had originally been a kitchen. Now it was an office-workshop dominated by a large bench on which was braced a ball-dented mailbox. On one wall were tools. On the other were filing cabinets, with one drawer for each property, and each drawer painted with that house's number.

Over their heads, they heard footsteps crossing the room above.

"Police!" Kettering called, as she pushed open the room's internal door. "Stop!"

The footsteps didn't.

The door led to a hall with stairs leading up. There were no carpets or rugs, but not much dirt, either.

Revolvers raised, moving quick rather than quiet, they climbed the stairs, angling for the room immediately above the kitchen. Kettering entered first, crouching the moment she was beyond the door. The room was empty.

It was an upstairs sitting room where a fire blazed, and papers burned. The windows were closed, but a bookcase had been pulled aside, revealing a ladder concealed in an alcove cut into the wall. At the top was a hatch through which the suspect had surely escaped.

Ruth bounded past the sergeant and was already climbing before Kettering could stop her.

"Careful, Ruth," she said.

Ruth didn't stop climbing. Smoke wisped around her, but from above descended a chilly downdraft.

At the top was a small hatch, propped open and built into the roof next to the chimney. Horizontal supports had been built out from the roof beams, propping up a flattened rooftop garden. Optimism must have fuelled the conversion because very little grew on this one. Perhaps not just optimism, because this platform garden linked to next-door's, and then to the flattened roofs of every house on the terrace, providing an escape route at least as far as the road.

"Stop, Fishwyck! Police!" Ruth yelled. "You're surrounded."

The suspect had just reached the scaffolding-pole barrier between his property and the neighbour's. He looked back at her before vaulting over the pole. But there was ice on the other side. He slipped, tumbling, falling to his back, sliding down towards the roof's edge. He grabbed a thin, vertical steel bracket. It bent sideways, but he twisted, turned so his feet were both braced on the icy tiles, his hands gripping the bracket. He pulled himself upwards, but the bracket snapped. He slid backwards, falling off the roof, and down into his own garden.

Ruth slipped and skidded her way to the roof's edge. The fall shouldn't have been lethal, especially since Fishwyck had landed on a tree. But that tree was made of metal, painted forest green, now decorated with blood from the corpse impaled on its star.

"Well, you don't see that every day," Kettering said, when she and Ruth both reached the front garden.

Blood dripped down the tree, mingling with the sooty ice on the frozen lawn. From the street came a victorious cheer as someone scored.

"The kids didn't notice," Kettering said. "Let's keep it that way. I'll go to the power station and send word for a couple of MPs, and for a stretcher. We better topple this over before he tears himself apart. I'll take his weight, you push at the bottom of the tree."

Trying to avoid the blood, steaming as it melted the frosty rime, she pushed until they had the body lying mostly on the ground.

"He ran," Ruth said.

"Yep. Which isn't always a crime, but it suggests he was guilty."

"And he was watching for us," Ruth said, looking up. "Watching and burning papers."

"I chucked a bucket of water on the fire, so maybe not everything burned," Kettering said. "I'll get us some help. Make sure those kids don't come in."

As the adrenaline wore off, the cold set in. Ruth shivered. It had been a quick death, if that counted for anything. Sure, it looked terrible, but it had all happened so swiftly, Fishwyck couldn't have known what was happening. He'd probably thought he'd escaped, along a rooftop route he'd obviously planned.

She looked up at the sky-terrace. Her half-formed thought, when she'd seen the flattened roofs, was that these were improvements made against the day the coal power station was shut down. Even then, even with clearer air, would people really want to climb up onto the roof? Probably not. And then there was that concealed ladder. No, the rooftop walkway had been built as a way out. So had the ladder. Had Fishwyck bought the neighbouring houses simply to build that walkway? That was a lot of effort. A lot of planning. A lot of time.

From the children came a shout of "Goal!"

"You're out!" came the reply, which then produced a shouted debate over the rules.

She bent down and checked Fishwyck's pockets. In his wallet were twenty pounds, a ration card, and a return ticket for Twynham for the two-p.m. train. Well, yes, that made sense. There were plenty of military and freight services, though not nearly enough, but currently only one civilian passenger service a day. She checked his other pocket and found a large old phone. The screen was cracked, and she couldn't get it to turn on. There was nothing else in any of his pockets. No old receipts, handkerchief, or any of the usual accumulated junk. That was suspicious in itself. So was the way the coat fell as she'd lifted it.

There was something in the lining. She drew her clasp knife and cut the fabric. Hidden inside, she found three sets of identification. A military I.D. for a Major John Trout, a Railway Company driver's card for John Dorey, and an I.D. card for a Reverend Jonathon Carp. For each, there was a ration card. But each I.D. was worn, each ration card had been clipped and stamped as if it had been half-used. With the cards was money: a thousand pounds, in the new notes. Why would a serial killer have fake I.D.s?

The gate opened. Kettering came in with Maggie and a naval officer with a captain's knot on his uniform.

"I say!" he exclaimed.

"Well, don't," Kettering said. "Just stand here by the door. Don't allow entry to anyone."

"Killed by a Christmas tree? That has to be a first," Maggie said. "But there truly isn't anything I can do here."

"Figure out a way of removing the body without traumatising the kids," Kettering said.

"I found some fake I.D.s," Ruth said. "And some money, all hidden in the lining of his coat. And a phone. But it's broken."

"Interesting. I'll take a look inside," Kettering said.

Ruth took out her own phone, and set the video to record.

"You give me that phone," Kettering said. "Then go to the railway station. Tell Sergeant Riley to let the train go."

"He had a ticket for the two o'clock train," Ruth said.

"Only one ticket?" Kettering asked.

"Yes."

"There you go. We've no reason to keep it here. But a telegram can outrace it if we find anything in the meantime. We'll get Mr Fishwyck taken to the morgue. Then we'll go back to the police station for lunch."

"Lunch?"

"Yep, it's been a long time since breakfast, and it'll be even longer before this investigation is over."

Chapter 27 - The Sound of a Motive
The Dover Police Station

"Where's Gregory?" Ruth asked as she brought down the last chair from upstairs. Because of Anna's difficulty with stairs, they were eating in the police station's lobby.

"The kids insisted he eat with them," Kelly said, placing another bowl on the table brought through from the evidence room.

"Oh, that's nice of them," Ruth said.

"Because they know the chef is their ticket from seconds to tenths," Kelly said approvingly. "Smart kids, that clan."

"I hope they leave some for Eloise," Ruth said. "Hmm, actually, I better put some aside."

Riley lifted the lid on a frog-eyed stoneware dish. "Are these dumplings?"

"Rhubarb and ginger," Kelly said. "Which are the secret ingredients to most of the dishes, except those with mustard."

"Flash," Riley said, snaffling one before replacing the lid. "Delish, too."

"Let me try one," Ruth said.

"Not before your mum gets here," Riley said.

"Seriously?"

"The privileges of rank," Riley said, taking another bite.

"It's a shame Mister Mitchell isn't here," Ruth said.

"Next year," Riley said. "And it's not long until that begins."

But when the door opened, all three women turned. It was Sergeant Kettering, Maggie, and Isaac.

"Why so glum?" Isaac asked. "You've solved a crime, stopped a spree-killer, and have a feast with which to celebrate."

"Are the bodies at the morgue?" Ruth asked.

"They are," Kettering said. "Both Jenner's and Fishwyck's remains are under guard. The admiral's having a fit, but it's a good lesson for her to remember the military answers to civilians. We've got a few hours before that train arrives in Twynham, so I'd say an hour before I send word to Commissioner Weaver. But is that word to search the train, or to search for someone waiting for it?"

"I doubt it," Ruth said.

"Well, let's eat while we discuss it," Kettering said. "Where are you going, Isaac?"

"You don't want this at the dinner table," Isaac said, lifting a battered plastic tub.

"What is it?" Ruth asked.

"Fishwyck's hand," Isaac said. "His phone is locked with a fingerprint."

"So you cut off his hand?" Ruth asked.

"It really was the easiest thing to do," Isaac said.

"Couldn't you have just logged in at the morgue?" Ruth asked.

"No, because the phone's screen and power-socket are broken. I'll have to dismantle it, wire this to my laptop, and set up an alternate power supply first."

"Just don't do it anywhere near the food," Kettering said. "And *you* don't come near before you've properly scrubbed. What have we got here? Looks not half bad."

"Greg says this is an appetizer," Kelly said. "He's got something bigger planned for dinner."

"The man's a genius," Kettering said. "Maggie, sit down. Ruth, help your mum. Anna, keep on helping yourself."

"Will do, Sarge," Anna said, taking another dumpling. "Do you think Fishwyck *is* a spree killer?"

"He's certainly a killer," Kettering said. "Those fake I.D.s, some running money, and a concealed escape route indicate he applied a good deal of thought and planning to his crimes."

"He was watching for us while he burned those papers, so he knew we'd come for him," Ruth said.

"He *suspected* we might," Kettering said. "He hoped he'd bought himself enough time to flee. It's pure luck we got that I.D. from the crem's attendants."

"What was on those papers he was burning?" Riley asked.

"Dates, times, and a shorthand code," Kettering said. "The paper was pretty thin, and most of it had burned, but I bagged a few of the larger fragments. We'll need a lot of context before we can crack it."

"It…" Ruth began, trying to speak around a mouthful of potatoes. She held up her hand as she swallowed. "Burning all the papers means he didn't plan to come back to Dover, but the timing doesn't add up."

"Try not to choke, dear," Maggie said. "This man's had enough victims."

"What doesn't add up?" Kettering asked.

"That ladder," Ruth said. "And the rooftop escape route, and those fake I.D.s, all required years of planning. But the first victim was only twenty days ago."

"The first victim we know of," Kettering said. "I think that's a condiment."

"This?" Riley asked, adding another spoonful of the crimson sauce to her plate. "I know it's delicious. What's the secret ingredient?"

"Gregory would say love," Kelly said. "But the real answer is honey."

"Goes well with everything," Riley said. "Especially an empty stomach."

"Do you think there were other victims before Mr Soakes, Elspeth?" Maggie asked.

"Soakes was the first killed with arsenic," Kettering said.

"Are we sure?" Riley asked.

"I think so," Kettering said. "When the war kicked off, they shut down the oncology clinic, and moved the patients to the residential centre in Hastings. They require a higher patient-to-carer ratio than can be provided on the front-line. Jenner would have had access to the meds, and could have stolen some when the clinic was packed up. In the haste of a move, it would have been easy to nab a few jars."

"That doesn't mean she didn't steal some before now," Riley said.

"True," Kettering said. "But I can't think of any unsolved cases which fit this M.O. No, I'd say Soakes was the first murdered with arsenic, but was it injected, or ingested? We might not have the bodies, but we can test the glass fragments found in Tommy's flat."

"I suppose we must also ask whether Mr Soakes and Reverend Dalrymple were murdered," Maggie said.

"I'm going to assume they were," Kettering said. "But was it Jenner or Fishwyck who did the deed? Jenner had access to the chemicals, and was able to alter the autopsy records. What was Fishwyck's role?"

"Sometimes serial killers work in pairs, don't they?" Ruth asked.

"Very rarely," Riley said.

"I don't think they were both present during the murder," Kettering said. "The victims were all killed inside their homes, or, in the case of Mr Soakes, his place of work. The killer was invited inside. Jenner's a respected figure, a doctor from the castle. I can see how she might talk her way into someone's home. Stinky knew all three since before the

Blackout, and knew the vicar from his fundraising at St Mary's. Yes, I can see how one or the other might talk their way inside, though I'd still like to know how. Both of them, at that time of night? It seems unlikely, particularly with Tommy. I think that had to be Stinky, acting alone."

"A spy called Stinky," Kelly said. "The headlines will write themselves."

"Can't be helped," Kettering said, "because we can't keep this from the press for long."

"More of the arsenic was chucked on the fire, wasn't it?" Ruth said. "The half-burned logs did *look* like utility poles. He must have kept a stash of logs somewhere. Mr Fry didn't have any in his woodpile."

"The waitress heard a sound at three a.m.," Kettering said. "That could have been Fishwyck returning to the flat to dump that log onto the fire. No fires in Doc Jenner's cabin, so he tried to stage that as suicide. If so, it confirms Jenner deliberately falsified the autopsy reports for Soakes and Dalrymple. Why? And why did Tommy Fry have to die? Why kill any of them? We're missing a motive."

"Could it have been revenge for something which happened before the Blackout?" Maggie asked. "Perhaps Fishwyck was diagnosed with an untreatable cancer, and he wanted revenge before he died."

"The dying don't need an escape route," Kettering said. "He built that ladder to the roof years ago. That level of planning doesn't really match with a spree-killer."

"When serial killers aren't caught, they grow bolder," Riley said. "They escalate. The murders can become more elaborate, more public, more daring. What if the use of arsenic *was* the escalation? Soakes wasn't the first victim, but he was the first victim since the gates were closed. That required Fishwyck to change his M.O."

"To injecting people with arsenic?" Kettering asked.

"No, to using an accomplice," Riley said. "He recruited Jenner to do the crime, so he could frame her for it. He got the joy of the kill, and knew he could vanish. Didn't you say you found maps of Ireland in the doctor's case?"

"One old, one new, yes," Ruth said. "I think she was planning to flee."

"And if she had disappeared, we'd have suspected her because of the paltry autopsy reports," Riley said. "Someone on the railway, or at the ferry, would identify her. The investigation would have stalled when it ran into the diplomatic wall that runs across the Irish Sea."

"Except from the moment he killed Tommy Fry, Fishwyck knew he'd have to kill Jenner," Kettering said. "So why pick him as his third victim?"

"For the challenge," Riley said.

"Revenge," Maggie said. "Because those are the three that betrayed him. It's why he had Jenner date Mr Fry."

"No," Kettering said. "Because the one part of this that wasn't well-planned was Jenner's murder. Ah, I was hoping for a simple answer, but we'll have to go back through every death in the last few years. Maybe longer. Maybe starting with the disappearance of Tommy's wife."

"Maybe not," Isaac said. "Because he wasn't a serial killer, or a spree-killer. Some of this data is corrupted, but these look like battle plans."

"Whose?" Riley asked.

"Ours," Isaac said. "There are other photographs of casualty lists, some letters. This one looks like a map-board, and from the stone-work, these pictures were taken in the castle."

"He was a spy?" Ruth asked.

"Looks that way," Isaac said. "Give me a few more minutes to confirm it."

"Is it possible, Sarge?" Riley asked. "Could Fishwyck really have been a spy?"

"Stinky became mysteriously rich in Europe when he was barely more than a kid," Kettering said. "And he crossed the Channel a lot before the Blackout. I always suspected he was up to something dodgy, but he never did anything to give me reason to investigate. Bell ringing is good cover for travelling. So maybe he was a spy before, or maybe just a smuggler, but he could have developed connections."

"Or he was a professional assassin," Kelly said. "Considering what he did this last month, that sounds plausible."

"Could be," Kettering said. "He worked as an orderly at the castle, so he'd have access to the gate, and to the hospital, and some of the stores. He shouldn't have had access to the wing used by the navy, and certainly not to their war-room."

"They might check the I.D.s at the gate," Maggie said, "but no one has ever asked to see mine when I'm inside. Nor have I asked to see anyone's."

"An old man with a broom doesn't raise suspicions," Kelly said.

"He was definitely a spy," Isaac said. "This is a photograph of the order given to the navy not to sink my boat when it was on its way to Belgium. This is how they knew we were meeting our contact."

"Simon and the refugees weren't followed?" Kelly asked.

"Seems not," Isaac said. "Which means we've got an even bigger rescue mission on our hands."

"You told the navy about your trip to Belgium?" Ruth asked.

"Of course," Isaac said. "I didn't want to be blown out of the water. There's a map of Calais which shows the location of the outlying guard-posts and bastions. Ideal if you wanted to get close enough to lob a mortar behind the lines. There's more, and even more that's been corrupted. But I'll untangle it."

"Fishwyck was a spy," Ruth said. "Huh. Okay, and Doc Jenner came from Germany. Didn't she travel to Europe with the scavengers?"

"And disappear for a few weeks at a time," Kettering said. "I thought she was looking for her lost family. We'll have to ask Roseau for more details. As a doctor, Jenner would be well placed to be a spy. Better placed than Fishwyck. So why have two spies in Dover? She could have gone with the rest of her clinic back west, or volunteered to work in Calais, and gathered information there."

"Because Jenner *wasn't* a spy," Riley said. "She was supposed to die, and be blamed for the other deaths. She must have been involved in trimming down the autopsy reports. Maybe because of blackmail. Maybe not. It is possible she didn't even know about the autopsies if the medical staff are that overworked. No, she was going to be framed as our serial killer. It's brilliant. Sick, but brilliant. If we'd discovered an oncologist had been murdering people with arsenic, we'd have looked back at every patient who'd ever died in her care, wondering if the cause on the death certificate was true. If, or when, we started wondering if there was a spy in Dover, we would have our suspect. Someone with access to the castle, and who'd travelled frequently in Europe. Fishwyck's cover would have been maintained."

"Except it went wrong," Kettering said. "It went wrong because Tommy Fry had to die. So why him?"

"Bring me some of those dumplings and I'll tell you," Isaac said.

"There aren't any left," Riley said.

"You ate them all?"

"There's potatoes and cabbage," Riley said.

"I'll take the spuds," Isaac said.

"And the answer?" Kettering asked as Ruth brought the almost empty serving bowl over to Isaac's bench.

"A fork would be nice," Isaac said. "And some of that sauce. The answer is timing," he added. "Every other night, there's a power-drain on this phone between one and one-twenty. He was doing something which took considerable power. Way more than just taking photos. At around two, most nights, the phone goes on to charge. Not the nights of the murders, though. The power drain is caused by an app called *Sounds*, which has a compression facility for transmitting data. That time is when he was sending data to his contact."

"By phone?" Ruth asked. "I thought those didn't work. I mean, I know you've got a network."

"You've got a what?" Kettering asked.

"I've been developing a mesh-net," Isaac said. "It's for when the law changes. Until then, it's an engineering project, and it doesn't link Twynham with Dover. It certainly doesn't cross the Channel. But I handed in our sailing plan on my way out the door. The time-stamp on that photo is four hours later. Even if Fishwyck handed the picture to a spy who jumped on a cross-Channel train, there's no way it could have reached the enemy in time for them to stage an ambush. He transmitted this data with technology."

"By cable? Telegram? How?" Kettering asked.

"Not cable," Isaac said. "The only undersea cables that weren't destroyed during the Blackout were those which ran through the Channel Tunnel. Those were severed at both ends, which is why we had to run the copper telegraph wire through. Trust me, if the undersea cables were usable, we'd be using them. The telegraph only gets you to Calais. These messages were sent too frequently for an enemy agent to dash back and forth across the lines. No, it's basically radio."

"But lots of people listen to the radio now," Ruth said.

"It's not words," Isaac said. "It's a compressed data transmission, which could be picked up a few hundred kilometres to the east."

"Dad said they had a radio-truck," Riley said. "So is that how they've been picking up the messages?"

"Yes and no, because the attack on us in Belgium took place *after* Henry captured that truck in Dunkirk," Isaac said. "From the images he sent, that truck was capable of receiving analogue radio signals up to about seventy kilometres away. Assuming advantageous weather conditions, it might manage twice that."

"Dunkirk's only seventy-five kilometres away," Kettering said.

"Yep, but there was no gear in the photos Henry sent which could decode this kind of data-burst. No, it wasn't that truck. We're looking for something with a much bigger antenna. Something which could, every other night, regardless of the weather, be listening for the message from a location way beyond the front line. Equally, there's nothing on this phone to suggest Fishwyck ever received a message from the other side. Someone, in France, was waiting and listening, knowing that was the time the message would be sent."

"In a truck?" Riley asked.

"Probably some vehicle, yes," Isaac said. "Maybe a military vehicle. Possibly a vehicle once used by a TV network for on-location live broadcasts. That receiving vehicle then decoded the message and came up with an attack plan. The attack plan was then sent, in code but over radio, to the truck Henry found, and to other similar trucks closer to the front."

"Fishwyck would need an antenna, wouldn't he?" Kettering asked. "I didn't notice one on his roof, and his neighbours would have. The murders all took place in the early hours of the morning. That must be when he was coming home after sending the message. The victims were all people who knew him by name. The vicar had been sitting up with the dying the night she died. Tommy was coming home late from his restaurant. Maybe Tommy told Fishwyck he and his girlfriend were moving to Calais. Having been seen, and seeing his plans falling apart, Fishwyck acted. He went back with Tommy, killed him, and then killed Jenner."

"What about the publican?" Ruth asked.

"St Mary's!" Kettering said. "The pub is opposite St Mary's church, and Fishwyck was organising the restoration work. Mr Soakes was sleeping in the pub. Soakes must have seen Fishwyck leaving the church in the middle of the night, and maybe the first time, Fishwyck talked himself out of trouble. But that's when he made his plan for killing off witnesses. The second time, he was prepared. He had the syringe. Reverend Dalrymple was the vicar for that church, and her place is on the way home for Fishwyck. More than that, the church would have been on the way home for *her*, after she'd been sitting with the dying. Maybe she saw him leaving, or saw a light inside. Would the tower be tall enough, Isaac?"

"It would, but he'd need a power source more powerful than a phone."

"How about a mains electricity supply?" Kettering asked. "Come on, Isaac. You can show me what we're looking for."

"I'm coming, too," Maggie said.

"Constable?"

"Um..." Ruth looked at the food still covering the table. "Someone should probably keep an eye on the police station."

"Agreed," Riley said.

Kelly picked up the bowl. "Unless you need back-up, Boss?"

Chapter 28 - A Serving of Suspicion
The Dover Police Station

"If there's a list of rules for policing," Riley said, "not letting a murder dent your appetite is up in the top ten." She speared a bread roll with her knife.

"Was the poison ingested or injected?" Ruth asked. "Either way, it does seem like Dr Jenner was being set up to take the fall. That's…"

"Evil?" Riley said.

"Yes, but complicated as well," Ruth said.

"Too complicated for these to be the first set of murders," Riley said. "We'll have to run two parallel investigations. One into Doctor Jenner and her work as an oncologist, and another into the espionage. We'll have to go through all of Jenner's patient records. Look at every death during treatment. The public will demand it as soon as this hits the newspapers."

"The trust in doctors will collapse," Kelly said. "Can't you keep it secret?"

"No, that would only make it worse when the truth got out," Riley said. "Openness and honesty, as frustrating as they can be, are the foundations of democracy."

"Do you think Jenner was a spy, too?" Ruth asked. "Or was she just another victim? The scavengers said she spent a lot of time travelling through Europe."

"Did they say where?" Kelly asked.

"Germany, I think," Ruth said. "I suppose that's something else we'll have to investigate."

"And where in Britain did they visit?" Riley asked. "Does this link back to Longfield, or the Railway Company? Does it link to Stevens and the Loyal Brigade, or to Boyle and his plans for Albion? One thing's for certain, this investigation is going to keep us beyond busy for the next few months."

"Yep," Kelly said, reaching for a bowl. "So we better eat now, while we can."

When Sergeant Kettering returned, it was with Isaac, but not Maggie.

"Your mum's gone to the operating theatre," Kettering said. "A train of injured came in."

"Oh. How many?" Ruth asked.

"That's unclear," Kettering said. "But it's all hands. The barbarians have launched an assault against Calais."

"They're trying to invade again?" Ruth asked.

"Not yet," Kettering said. "They're lobbing mortars. A *lot*. Must have crept in close during the night. If you go out into the street, and catch the right wind, you can hear our artillery replying."

"What did you find at the church?" Riley asked.

"A very interesting transmitter," Isaac said. "It's customised from commercial equipment with a warning label in German."

"It came from Germany?" Riley asked.

"Or Austria," Isaac said. "But if I were putting down a bet, I'd put my stake on Switzerland. While it seems increasingly unlikely that's where we'll find our warlord now, if only because it wasn't a nation known for its oil reserves, I bet that's where they've been until recently. The equipment was built overseas, and then brought in. It isn't complex, but like the phone, it required some degree of specialist knowledge."

"Old-world knowledge?" Riley asked.

"Yes, though not nearly as much as I have," Isaac said, walking back over to the laptop into which the broken smartphone was still plugged. "Despite the apparent complexity, it is a very simplistic system. The app does most of the work. Without the phone, it's barely more than a few long wires."

"Which are embedded in cement," Kettering said. "The power is diverted at the junction box. The church only has a couple of lights inside, but there are a few spotlights at the top of the tower which, before the current energy crisis, illuminated the streets below. The junction box, and the cement, are about a year old, installed when the restoration work began and the scaffolding went up."

"Could Fishwyck have installed it himself?" Riley asked.

"Could be," Kettering said. "Or he hired people. Could be the same people as built his walkway escape. That's where I'll begin my enquiries, find out how much of the maintenance work on his properties he did himself."

"What's the range of the radio signal?" Riley asked. "Isaac? Isaac!"

"Hmm? Oh, range? About two hundred and fifty kilometres. Could be more, but probably wasn't less. It tallies with the information Henry sent us on that memory card. The enemy has mobile units who drive mortar teams to an ambush close to the coast, after which they retreat to refuel and resupply. Now, if you ask me, that's the most fascinating aspect. Fishwyck wasn't in direct communication with the warlord, but this resupply team must be. However, considering the timeframe between Fishwyck transmitting the information, and the attacks taking place, someone in that supply unit is making the on-the-ground strategic decisions. Kill them, and we'll put a real crimp in these assaults. Capture them, and we'll learn in what sewer the warlord lurks."

"Two hundred and fifty kilometres?" Ruth asked, walking over to the wall-map of Europe. "And it was installed a year ago, long before the enemy began their attacks."

"Not that long before," Kettering said. "And not really *before*. They'd already caused havoc through Germany and Italy. Looking at the incursion with what we know now, the barbarians wintered outside of France, gathering their strength for a final push this past year. Consolidating, resupplying, enjoying their plunder."

"Waiting until this year's harvest," Riley said. "This final assault took place after the farmers had done the hard graft of stocking their grain silos and fruit barns. The enemy would surely need those supplies."

"Could be," Kettering said. "But I'll let the generals figure that out."

"Hang on," Ruth said. "If the antenna was installed a year ago, and only has a range of two hundred and fifty kilometres, then there must have already been an agent in France waiting to hear the message and then pass it on. An agent with electricity, and other supplies, too."

"Could be," Kettering said. "Isaac, when was the first message sent from that device?"

"Hang on," Isaac said.

Ruth turned away from the map. "Sarge, what kind of information would Fishwyck have had access to before the war began?"

"We'd have to ask the navy," Kettering said. "But this what I was warning you about. When you start to use machines to do your thinking, you stop doing it for yourself. Fishwyck was a landlord of a coastal city, a border city. A lot of people came through here on their way west, *and* east. He was perfectly placed to provide them with somewhere to stay. Somewhere to change their clothes, their identity. He had fake I.D.s on him, so he knows where to get false papers. He could have provided papers for other spies, provided them with a safe house, money, and whatever else they'd need before they continued their mission."

"I need to get back to Twynham," Riley said. "Commissioner Weaver needs to hear all of this herself. She'll probably want to see it, too. I'll inform the admiralty first, to make certain no one else can access the battle plans."

"Hang on," Ruth said. "A message was sent last night, and there's one sent every other evening, right, Isaac? Isaac?"

"Hmm? What?"

"Messages were sent every other evening, yes?" Ruth asked.

"Yes, for the most part. A few were sent out of sequence. But every other night, yes."

"So could we send one of our own?" Ruth asked. "Could we set an ambush for the enemy?"

"*We* can't, no," Kettering said. "Commissioner Weaver can't, either. It would have to be the Minister for War. It's probably a decision for the whole cabinet. Sergeant, there's a freight train in forty minutes. You take that, I'll inform the admiralty."

"Not so fast," Isaac said. "We've got a bigger problem."

"What do you mean?" Kettering asked.

"I just looked at the message sent last night," Isaac said. "First, let me say that I'm going to be having words with the admiral myself. No one gets away with treating me like I'm just another cog in the machine."

"What did the message say?" Kettering asked.

"One thousand Marines, who were garrisoned around Albion, are being sent to the front," Isaac said.

"Yes," Riley said. "Weaver told me that. There's a thousand more who'll be on the next train."

"Maybe that second group is travelling by train, but this first batch are on ships," Isaac said. "They were collected from the Humber, and will be making landfall in Nieuwpoort. Damned admiralty. They told me they didn't want to return to Belgium until spring. Well, they told Henry, but that's much the same thing. The ships will arrive tomorrow, and our enemy knows it."

"A thousand Marines?" Ruth asked.

"Aboard a small fleet. Two sloops, four steel-clad steam transport ships, and two gunboats. It's the naval force they used to remind Albion they were surrounded. They'll reach Nieuwpoort around midday tomorrow."

"Why there?" Ruth asked.

"It doesn't say," Isaac said. "But the attack Henry stopped in Dunkirk was targeting a conscript garrison arriving by ship. The information Fishwyck stole doesn't give the broader strategy, only the imminent troop movements. Nieuwpoort is the best harbour south of Denmark. There was a settlement there until a few months ago. Calais, Dunkirk, and Nieuwpoort are all within a few hours cycling of each other. There are good arguments for fortifying them all, but our strategy until now was to focus on the Mediterranean. None of which matters," he added. "We just sailed from there, and while we might have taken out some of the enemy, we didn't destroy any vehicles. Our enemy knows there is no garrison there. They've had time to dig in, and bring in another missile team. A mortar team would do the job just as well. The harbour is inland, the river would make a perfect kill-zone."

"Then I really better catch that train," Riley said. "Isaac, can you make copies?"

"Take the original," Isaac said. "I've disabled the biometrics, so you won't need the hand. Kelly, get Gregory, and tell Mrs Zhang to get our boat ready."

"Are you sailing to Calais?" Kettering asked.

"The military doesn't really use radio," Isaac said. "They have a few ship-to-shore sets to co-ordinate the artillery bombardment of enemy positions, but they don't use it more broadly, or widely, to communicate with ships outside the immediate theatre. The Humber fleet needs to be warned. It can't be by radio, so it has to be done in person. I docked in the harbour this morning. I saw the vessels at anchor. Mine is the fastest, and the only ship which can reach Nieuwpoort before the fleet arrives. So that's what I'll do. I'll redirect them to Dunkirk."

"But the enemy will still go to Nieuwpoort?" Ruth asked. "Can we send our army in to cut them off?"

"No," Isaac said. "Because the only available troops, the *real* troops who've learned more than the difference between a barrel and a bayonet, are in that fleet, sailing towards a trap."

"That's not entirely true," Riley said. "There is Colonel Sherwood."

Part 3
Ambush

France and Belgium

Henry Mitchell & Ruth Deering

23rd - 25th December

Chapter 29 - Back to War
The Channel Tunnel

The troop train had no connecting doors or seats. It was just one serpentine corridor festooned with straps, rails, and overhead grab-bars. Aboard were around two hundred passengers whose occupation was obvious by their clothing: squads of new conscripts in their ill-fitting green uniforms; soldiers returning from sick leave wearing new uniforms but old boots; the sailors in naval fatigues who'd been transferred from the less troubled Irish Sea; clusters of unarmed civilians, all older than the conscripts, going to assist in the enclave's administration; fifty-one Albion foresters in their urban-ambush camouflage. From the perspective of any observer, it was fifty-two foresters as Ruth wore the same uniform herself. It didn't fit.

People from Albion were tall, or maybe only the tallest were selected to join the royal bodyguard. Ruth had borrowed one of Sherwood's uniforms. Even with the trousers tucked into her boots, they overflowed nearly to the train carriage floor. The jacket had internal cloth ties which, after she'd tightened them, gave hers a blousy, rumpled appearance. She wished she was wearing her police uniform, but Riley had insisted. Not just because the camouflage pattern was less noticeable than police blue, but because of the old-world ballistic plates inserted beneath the fabric.

Those plates were apparently stronger than steel. It certainly felt like she was wearing a suit of heavy plate armour. But she didn't want to let her side down, so she kept her mouth shut and her eyes open. Corporal Lancaster appeared sick. Sergeant York appeared to be praying. Colonel Sherwood was watching those members of her company who were interacting with the other passengers. They were all clearly suspicious of this old enemy supposedly now on their side.

The foresters were attempting to allay those fears by handing out food. Small squares of pressed fruit that were somehow both sour and sweet at the same time. Each forester carried a waxed-paper block in their left breast pocket as part of a deliberate strategy for winning over stomachs and minds. It had worked with the civilians, who were raising their voices over the clatter of the wheels to question the Albion troops. It hadn't worked with the soldiers. That was understandable since the military had been running a siege around Albion for years.

Ruth had a million questions for the colonel, most of which were about Ned Ludd, but now wasn't the time, so she made another surreptitious attempt to adjust the uniform.

Each of the foresters carried a long knife and axe at their belt, a quiver strapped to their thigh, and a long bow as tall as they were. Ruth had an old-world M4-carbine, given her by Kelly. The foresters each had a government-issue revolver, too, looking out of place and strangely old-fashioned in a brown leather holster. Only Sherwood and Sergeant York had an old-world firearm, a polymer-grip semi-automatic pistol.

Oh, the foresters looked like soldiers. They looked dangerous. But so was their enemy, who had missiles and mortars, trucks and assault rifles, radios and grenades. Sherwood didn't look worried, though. Nor had she when Riley had explained the mission. Then, she'd looked interested, almost excited. Now, she was just watchful as her soldiers played diplomat among the civilians.

During the hasty briefing, Riley had linked the spy to the court-traitor, Boyle. Colonel Sherwood had quickly agreed to accompany Ruth to Calais to liaise with Mister Mitchell. He would decide what to do next. They had sent a telegram ahead of the train. If Mitchell wasn't waiting for them, Ruth didn't know what Sherwood would do, or what to do if the colonel decided to go north, hunting for revenge of her own.

Almost as troubling was how Colonel Sherwood's declaration of her rank had been enough to get them onto the platform. No one had questioned their right to board the train. A week ago, Ruth would have thought *of course not, who'd willingly want to go to a warzone?* Now she saw it as evidence of the same lax security which had allowed Fishwyck to gain such complete access to their war plans. Heads would roll over that, but hopefully not Ruth's.

The train shook as it bumped over an ill-placed rail. The brakes squealed.

"This is almost fun," Sherwood said. "Before the Blackout, we went to a theme park. I've a photograph of us on a rollercoaster. It came from a newspaper, taken by one of the parasitic reporters who followed us everywhere, but my mother kept it. I was too young to remember the trip, but this is what it must have been like."

"You should try riding up in the engine," Ruth said. "How good are you with that bow?"

"Not as good as Corporal Lancaster," Sherwood said. "He won the King Lear Cup, twice."

"Is that an archery contest?" Ruth asked.

"It is *the* archery contest," Sherwood said. "An archer must shoot an arrow across King Lear's Lake, and land it in a target floating on the Grand Union Canal. It's a three-hundred-yard distance."

"Very impressive," Ruth said, though she was little the wiser. "The enemy have trucks. Can arrows pierce metal?"

"It would depend upon the arrow," Sherwood said. "It would depend upon the metal. But that's not how we fight, and we always fight to win."

Ruth nodded, keeping her misgivings to herself.

The train had a locomotive at each end, powered by preciously scarce diesel, but this train was only used as a tunnel-shuttle. The lack of seats allowed more space for the stretchers waiting on the enclosed electric-lamp-lit platform.

"All out!" the train-guard yelled. His arm was strapped and bandaged across his chest, but he'd painted his corporal's stripes across the sling. "Make way for the stretchers!"

Ruth wasn't the only passenger who paused when she saw the injured. She'd seen the patients in the narrow castle chambers they called wards. But that was sanitised. Clean. These uniforms were stained black with blood and mud, except for the stark-white bandages wrapped around heads and chests, and encasing foreshortened limbs.

"Against the wall!" the corporal yelled.

"Stretchers in!" Sherwood called out.

Sergeant York echoed the order. "You heard the colonel. Double-quick."

The foresters moved like machines, and far quicker than the orderlies, almost leaving them behind as they carried the injured onto the train.

Ruth knew well enough not to get in the way, so watched and counted. Twenty-nine stretchers. Another fifteen walking wounded. Seventeen civilians. But no hale soldiers were returning to England.

With the last of the injured safely aboard, the foresters formed up on the dimly lit platform. The train-guard-corporal gave them an appreciative nod, before waving his flag. The doors closed. The train pulled off, and the guard walked back up the tunnel.

"Do you see your contact?" Sherwood asked.

"Mister Mitchell, no," Ruth said, looking around. She'd been to Calais before, but mostly she remembered the smoke and screams.

This new platform had been built inside the tunnel. Ahead was only darkness, starkly broken by flickering pools of harsh electric light. Behind were the receding lights of the train as it returned to Dover. The other passengers had already disappeared through a checkpoint near a dimly lit side-exit. From there, a woman in dark blue uniform strode towards them.

"Move it! Stop clogging my platform!" the woman yelled. She wore a naval uniform bearing the rank of petty officer. "Who are you?"

"Ruth Deering," she said. "Police."

"Dressed like that? Where are your rifles?"

"An arrow can kill as well as a bullet," a shadow said, detaching himself from the dark pool between two lights.

"Mister Mitchell!" Ruth said, unable to keep the sheer relief from her voice.

"Last time I checked," he said.

"And who the hell are you?" the sailor growled.

"Inspector-*General* Mitchell, military intelligence," he said. "They're with me. This way," he added.

The foresters fell into step, marching in unison without a command, leaving the sailor quietly fuming alone.

"This is Colonel Elizabeth Sherwood," Ruth said.

"From Albion?" Mitchell asked. "Good to have some reinforcements. I got Anna's telegram," he added, holding up a pair of yellow telegram slips. "Both of them. One to say she was in Dover, another to say you were coming here. She didn't say why."

"We should discuss it in private," Sherwood said.

"There's not much privacy on a battlefield," Mitchell said, "but I might know a quiet spot."

He led them after the now-disappeared passengers, and through a side tunnel. The walls quickly narrowed, forcing them to walk single file. Two metres tall, but only one wide, the tunnel had been an electrical conduit, though the wires had mostly been removed. Not enough lights had been added in their place. The shadows jumped and danced, but then vanished as lights ahead flickered on. Ten paces later, they stepped into an artificial cavern filled with wire cages, each three metres square, five rows deep, ten long. The lights went off before Ruth had time to properly inspect them though she'd seen each was empty.

"Not again," Mitchell said, pulling a truncheon-length torch from his belt. "The terrorists seem to know exactly where to hit to knock out the power. We keep having to switch to drawing it from Dover, but there's never enough, and always a few minutes when there's none at all."

"Are those cages for prisoners?" Ruth asked.

"Ammo," Mitchell said. "Back in the olden days, they stored emergency equipment here for a mid-tunnel accident. The scavengers used it more recently as a storage depot for non-perishables. Now it's used for ammunition."

"But they're all empty," Ruth said.

"Yep. Took everyone a while to catch on that this was the enemy's strategy," Mitchell said. "All that skirmishing, the midnight ambushes, it was designed to exhaust our reserves. Getting the injured back through the tunnel clogs the line, reducing our ability to bring up more. But you didn't come here for a tour of the front," he added. "So why are you here?"

"Because I can't write faster than the train can travel, and it's a really long story," Ruth said. With only a nod from Sherwood, the foresters formed a ring, facing outwards, at a rigid attention.

"Give me the brief version," Mitchell said.

"There was a spy in Dover, working as an orderly in the castle," Ruth said. "He sent all our battle plans to the enemy over radio. He's dead, only a few hours ago. Last night he sent a message about a reinforcement fleet heading to Nieuwpoort. A thousand soldiers, all from the garrisons around Albion. They're at sea. They'll arrive in Nieuwpoort tomorrow, at midday. We think they'll be ambushed with missiles like you found in Dunkirk and Isaac stumbled into in Nieuwpoort a few days ago."

"Isaac made it to the rendezvous?" Mitchell asked. "How is he?"

"As infuriating as ever," Ruth said. "There were about forty brigands there, with missiles, and they knew his ship was coming. The enemy spy knew about Isaac's mission. Isaac killed some of the enemy, but not all."

"And they're using radio, so they could have called in more reinforcements," Mitchell said.

"That's exactly it," Ruth said.

"What about *our* spy? Did Isaac make contact?"

"Yes, he's alive," Ruth said. "He only made it as far as the old German border, and came back to Belgium with some refugees, leaving more behind somewhere in the wild-lands."

"Okay, tell me about that later, but tell me more about this enemy spy."

"Every other night, he sent a radio burst to this side of the Channel, probably within two hundred and fifty kilometres of Dover. Maybe to an enemy radio-truck. That vehicle then transmits a battle-plan to the mobile attack teams, telling them where to strike. Isaac said that the message was encoded, and it probably wasn't being sent to that truck you found in Dunkirk. He thinks that's just one of the attack teams."

"He told you that? So he was in Dover? Why's he not here?"

"He's on his ship, and on his way to warn the fleet coming down from the Humber. He'll intercept them, and send them to Dunkirk."

"And why are you here?" Mitchell asked.

"To see if we can ambush the ambushers," Ruth said.

"It's not just conscript privates who need training for war," Mitchell said. "So do the generals and the politicians. They asked me to investigate whether Nieuwpoort would be a viable base for a spring offensive. It would have taken a couple of trips, and a survey by the Belgian settlers who were living there until a few months ago, but someone jumped the gun. They did the same with Dunkirk, and that was almost a tragedy. I think the navy's strategy is to reinforce the north so as to lure the enemy away from the south. The fighting there has been ferocious, but the enemy has a plan of their own, and it now involves dropping mortars on Calais. They want to sink our ships, deplete our reserves, force us to stay close to the Channel in the hope we abandon all dreams of repopulating the interior. That's good."

"Good? Why?"

"Our enemy is getting desperate," Mitchell said. "The brigands are getting hungry. We took five prisoners this week. Two were captured the usual way, but three actually handed themselves in. I was interrogating them when I got Anna's telegrams. I don't know how much to believe the prisoners, and I certainly don't believe they are as innocent as they claim, but this is the first time they've actually surrendered. They've been given Kalashnikovs, and sometimes ammo, sometimes grenades, and sometimes even a mortar, and sent here to attack. They say there's a prize for whoever can kill the most of us."

"What's the prize?" Ruth asked.

"To rule over the country of their choice," Mitchell said. "They've no idea how they're supposed to claim the reward, of course. Nor do they know how they're supposed to get more ammo or food, or when they're allowed to retreat. We can talk about that later, but we need to deal with this ambush in Belgium." He turned to Sherwood, who'd been listening as patiently as her soldiers stood guard. "Colonel Elizabeth Sherwood. Daughter of King Alfred, yes?"

"Yes, General," Sherwood said.

"Mister Mitchell is fine," he said.

"Do you remember Ned Ludd?" Ruth asked. "He's her brother."

"Really? Interesting. And what do you propose to do here at the front?"

"As Constable Deering says, we shall ambush the ambushers," Sherwood said.

Mitchell nodded. "You say they sent forty against Isaac?"

"That's what Isaac said. He was guessing."

"And what about the admiral in Dover, or the politicians back in Twynham?" Mitchell asked. "What do they think of this plan?"

"I guess they're finding out about it now," Ruth said. "Anna went to Twynham to tell Commissioner Weaver. I don't think Sergeant Kettering will tell anyone in Dover, not until she's sure there isn't another spy."

"So we're acting without orders?" Mitchell asked. "Did the spy receive confirmation that the intel would be acted on?"

"No. Never. Isaac said the messages were only one-way."

"The spy must have been receiving orders somehow," Mitchell said. "Okay, that's something else for us to discuss. Isaac's warning the fleet. We don't know if the terrorists will go to Nieuwpoort, or how many might be sent. If they send anyone, they'll have assault rifles and missiles, while you, Colonel, have your bows."

"With which we train every day," Sherwood said. "If Mister Isaac does not warn our ships, if the vessels enter the river, it will take only a dozen of those missiles to sink them and wipe out the soldiers. Those Marines were stationed outside our land. They terrorised our children, raided our farms, and attacked our kin. Believe me, there is no love lost between us and them, but they are needed to end this war. There is a risk in our band travelling north to intercept, yes, but there is an opportunity, too. We cannot afford to lose it."

"*We* can't, can *we*?" Mitchell said, with a slow nod of approval. "Calais is under attack. I can't draft any troops from the defences here. But if we go north, we can't support the defence of this city if here, rather than Nieuwpoort, is where they make their next push." He pointed at the empty cages. "Conscripts waste a lot of bullets. A concerted attack, supported by missiles, could break through to the tunnel. That's the risk." He raised his hand, lifting his cap. "But if Isaac can't find the troopships at sea, we risk losing an army and a good portion of our navy. Ah, I hate being a general. C'mon. We'll need some bicycles if we're to reach Nieuwpoort before dawn." He marched away from the cages, and towards a set of double doors.

"Isaac sent you this," Ruth said, holding out her bag. "It's some ammo and things. Maggie added some dinner. Gregory cooked it."

Mitchell took it. "Thanks. Are you sure you want to be here?"

"Nope. But no one else gets a choice," she said. "Do you really think we're winning?"

"I thought we were. Now, I see we're at a tipping point. This next battle, wherever it takes place, will determine the outcome."

Chapter 30 - Wooden Trenches
Calais, France

Beyond the empty ammunition cages, and a solitary and snoozing grey-bearded sentry, a metal staircase rose steeply to the surface. Above ground, the stairs led into a wood and sheet-metal corridor, reinforced with sandbags, but with an asphalt floor, making Ruth suspect they were in an old car park. A dozen yards from the stairs was a thick gate, currently open. The unfamiliar uniforms received a few glances from the walking wounded sentries, but the guards were more interested in rushing these last passengers through so the gate could be shut.

Beyond, more sheet metal and wood, and occasionally cement, created a maze of above-ground tunnels. Through the dripping cracks in the ceiling, the last of the day's light chased the first of the night's sharp winds.

"We put these barriers up to conceal the tunnel's entrance and exit," Mitchell said. "Follow the blue arrow."

"Why does the entrance need to be concealed?" Ruth asked.

"Mortars and snipers," Mitchell said. "Keep moving."

The blue arrow led them west. Every few yards, there was a break in the wall, revealing another set of corridors beyond, sometimes marked with a green, red, or yellow arrow, and even more occasionally with a name: Lancre, Vulcan, Caernarfon, or some other legendary place known only to fiction and myth. The blue arrow led them to a shipping container, where three soldiers and four bikes waited.

"Ruth Deering!" Sergeant Johannes said. "No offence, but I wish we were meeting again on the other side of the channel."

"Jo-Jo!" Ruth said. "Good to see you, Marine."

"It's soldier now," Jo-Jo said. "I'm a sergeant in military intelligence. Who's this lot?"

"They're our reinforcements," Mitchell said, turning to the tall young man whose drooping moustache would have been more impressive if he'd had a chance to shave the rest of his face in the last week. "Jean-Luc, I need bicycles for Colonel Sherwood's merry band. We're going to Belgium. We'll be cycling at night."

"*Pas de problème.* I will need two hours."

"And I need a dozen pairs of clean socks," Mitchell said. "Let's hope Santa brings us what we've asked for, but until then, you've got an hour to get the bikes up to the northern bastion."

The French scavenger gave a nod, and darted off, following a green arrow pointing towards Atlantis.

"Colonel, we'll be running from one piece of cover to the next," Mitchell said. "The bastion is two kilometres north-northwest of this position, on the old trade road."

"What's the terrain like, sir?" Sergeant York asked.

"Rubble, ruins, trenches, fires, mortar shells, and occasionally a sniper," Mitchell said. "Jo-Jo, Hamish, bring up the rear."

"Move! Move! Move!" came a yell from ahead, the word repeated with every other footstep as two dust-coated medics ran a stretcher towards them.

"Company, part!" Sergeant York bellowed, and the column of foresters flattened themselves into two lines, either side of the irregular corridor. Barely slowing, the orderlies ran past. The soldier on the stretcher had a bandage on her left leg, another entirely encasing her left hand, and blood coating her tunic.

"Bomb disposal," Mitchell muttered.

Before Ruth could ask a question, an explosion shook the walls. A second followed, louder, closer, but still a hundred metres away.

"Follow me!" Mitchell said, just as a third explosion landed close enough to patter shrapnel onto the roof. Somewhere among the maze of corridors behind them, someone began screaming.

Ruth skipped a pace, turning back to look.

"Forward, ma'am," Private Boadicea Essex said, gently pushing her on.

"Hey, careful."

"Yes, ma'am," Essex said. "Forward, please."

Wondering when she'd asked for a jailor-bodyguard, and whether she could be sent back without a receipt, Ruth jogged on.

Mitchell led them through the walled corridors, away from the rattling explosions, which sounded as if they were getting further away. Down the side-alleys, she saw clusters of soldiers running in every direction. When she tried to sneak a glance behind, she saw a few had tagged themselves onto the end of their column.

"Eyes front, ma'am," Essex said.

"Seriously?" Ruth muttered, but she obeyed, letting her mind be distracted by the puzzle of whether those tag-along soldiers thought the foresters were running towards danger or safety.

Behind came another pop-bang explosion, then a sharp scream instantly lost beneath a deafening roar. A tornado whirled along the corridor, shaking the ground, rattling the roof, and bringing down a wall to their left. Beyond was open ground.

Mitchell pointed into the open as a thunder-roar barrage tore through the sky. The column sprinted across a weather-cracked road and into a rubble-strewn street, while above the sky was ripped asunder by an explosive storm.

Mister Mitchell stopped outside a half-demolished house, propped up on all sides with cracked timbers. "In! In! In!" he yelled, motioning the foresters inside.

"What's—?" Ruth began, but was shoved into the ruin by Private Essex before she could finish her question. "Watch it!"

"Sorry, ma'am," Essex said.

The ruin had been a house, but now was the beginning of a trench system linking the cellars. From below rose the scent of smoke, the smell of cooking, and the stench of too many unwashed bodies, clustered too close together. The ground-floor ceiling had been reinforced with timber and rebar, while the cellar stairs had been widened, with more salvaged timbers laid across the floor as added protection for those dwelling below.

"We're not going down," Mitchell said, pointing through the wrecked house. "We'll stick to the surface, and travel between the barrages."

"Is Calais about to be assaulted?" Sherwood asked, as Jo-Jo and MacKay entered the building.

"Probably not," Mitchell said. "The brigands snuck mortars in at night, and lob their shells at any likely target. The navy returns ten shells for every one of theirs. There haven't been many mortars thrown at us since midday. I'd hoped we'd wiped out the enemy artillery, but it seems like some engaged their brain, and waited all day to fire. We've got to keep moving, reach the bastion before full dark. We can't use lights after nightfall until we're safely beyond the city."

Beyond the ruined terrace, Mitchell led them onto a road. The explosions had ceased, replaced now with the distant crack of rifle fire. Mitchell slowed their pace to a brisk walk while, now out in the open, the foresters changed formation into a loose four columns. Despite Private Essex's attempt to pull her to the centre of the pack, Ruth pushed her way to the front, and to where Mitchell led the way, and Sherwood led her troops.

The roadway was a river of churned slush, occasionally concealing a treacherously frozen ice-slick, or a partially melted ankle-deep pothole. Smoke billowed from broken windows, marking the campfires of those soldiers who thought frostbite a greater danger than the dice-roll odds of a mortar's direct hit. From inside, Ruth heard an occasional sob, an occasional song, and more than an occasional sigh of frustrated regret.

"If the enemy have mortars, why aren't there more trenches?" Ruth asked. Ahead, a trio of rats scampered behind a partially frozen trash heap.

"Because, until a week ago, there'd been three mortar attacks in a month," Mitchell said. "Meanwhile, to the south, there were a couple of thousand brigands. Some lone snipers, and some small bands who liked to set traps, then hide and wait. There was a large group from the emir's caliphate, and a regiment of knights, both about two hundred strong. Whether it was one sniper or a hundred terrorists, the enemy's tactics were the same, to bushwhack our people, and steal their supplies. That's where the navy expected the next set of attacks to be."

"You have civilians in Calais, too," Sherwood said.

"You're well informed," Mitchell said.

"Merely observant," Sherwood said, pointing at a nearly intact terrace where a woman in shirt and skirt took advantage of the brief respite in the shelling to check on the water barrel attached to the property's guttering.

"The civilians are volunteers," Mitchell said, "and mostly refugees from France and beyond."

"And you trust them?" Sherwood asked.

"As much as anyone in uniform," Mitchell said.

"How many attempts have there been to overthrow your government recently?" Sherwood asked.

"*Our* government," Mitchell said. "And it's one very long, interconnected attempt of which this terrorist assault is simply the last, and final, act."

"I admire your optimism."

"I'm usually a pessimist," Mitchell said. "But I'm certain the curtain's about to drop. Even more so now I know there was a spy in Dover. The reason for those corridors above the station was because the terrorists knew when the trains arrived. We had to vary which exits we used, and made sure the soldiers dispersed under cover. Now we know *how* the enemy knew our schedule. They knew, after the destruction of the clinic, our official strategy would be to return ten artillery shells for every one of theirs because of that spy. A spy who's dead."

"Is there only one spy?" Sherwood asked.

"Ruth?" Mitchell asked.

"I hope so," Ruth said.

A distance putt-bang explosion rocked the air, but nowhere close.

"The south," Mitchell said. "Yep, we're predictable, but so are they. A mortar team in the north chanced their luck, now a team in the south is trying for the prize. While our navy flattens another suburb, another team of terrorists up in the north will get into position. We've got about two minutes. That alley, then left, through the houses, and down the road beyond. We've got time, if we run."

"And time to spare," Mitchell said as he led them inside a row of once-identical dormer bungalows, converted, according to the bullet-flecked sign, into *L'Hôpital de Marck*.

"This is a hospital?" Sherwood asked, as she looked around the shell of a building.

"Before the war, this was going to be a new clinic," Mitchell said. "Jean-Luc's family were organising it."

Like elsewhere, the party-walls had been knocked through, and the internal walls had been pulled down. Here, though, this work had been done before the incursion, with the rubble long cleared. New rooms had been marked out, unpainted timber frames had been put up, giving a skeletal hint at where the wards and exam rooms would be. Some of those timbers had been torn down for firewood by green-clad soldiers. Eight of them now watched the newcomers with suspicion.

"Is Jean-Luc's surname Roseau?" Ruth asked. "I met his mum. One of the doctors who was going to work here was linked with the spy."

"Really? How's that?" Mitchell asked.

"Oh, it's quite a story," Ruth said. "Did you hear about the deaths from arsenic inhalation in—"

But before she could finish the air shook from a series of rapid explosions. The ground fell away, and she found herself on her hands and knees, an ocean filling her ears, and blood filling her mouth.

"Are you okay?" Private Essex asked as she helped Ruth back up. The soldier sounded far more concerned than any stranger should.

"Bit my tongue," Ruth hissed. "What was that?"

"Mortars," Mitchell said, brushing dust from his coat. "Very close. Just outside. We're safe for now."

Thunder rocked the sky as the naval battery returned fire.

"Six shells, yes, Colonel?" Mitchell asked.

"I thought it was seven," Sherwood said. She looked pale, though her voice remained steady.

"Seven? Well, soon they'll have none," Mitchell said. "Fifteen seconds after the navy ceases fire, we'll run."

One of the green-clad soldiers who'd been sheltering inside the clinic stood, and walked away from his fire. "Why have you got bows?" he asked.

"We're the Royal Bodyguard of King Alfred," Corporal Lancaster said.

"D'you mean you're traitors from Leicester?" the soldier asked.

"We're citizens, just like you," Sherwood said.

"Wotcha call us? We're soldiers," the man said.

"Oh, good grief, look east," Mitchell said. "Throw your anger in that direction, because we've got a war to win."

"You killed my uncle," the man said. "He was just a farmer. You lot killed him."

"Time to move on," Mitchell said, stepping in front of the angry soldier. "Back outside, Colonel, then due east to Avenue de Calais."

Outside, the naval guns had ceased fire. An expectant silence had settled over the city.

"Is that the end of it?" Ruth asked.

"I'll answer that in ten minutes," Mitchell said, waving the foresters on. "The enemy have changed their strategy. Around the time we found the missile team up in Dunkirk, they started focusing their mortars here. They send teams of two in at night, with ten rounds each. They fire from a couple of kilometres out. If we go hunting for them, they just run and hide, leaving the mortars behind. They didn't do this before. They're phasing out mortars from their attacks, hopefully because they're running out of mortar shells."

"Or they have a whole load of missiles," Ruth said.

"Or they're planning an assault," Sherwood said.

"Yep," Mitchell said. "Nice to have a bit of uncertainty in our lives, isn't it?"

A rifle cracked.

"Sniper!" Mitchell said. "Take cover!"

"Lancaster!" Sergeant York yelled.

Essex pushed Ruth behind a pile of rubble as a rifle cracked again. But where Ruth and Mitchell had taken cover, Private Lancaster had drawn his bow. The arrow flew faster than Ruth could follow.

"Easy," Lancaster said, as he lowered his bow.

"D'you get him?" Mitchell asked.

"I'm insulted you asked," Lancaster said.

"*Sir*," Sergeant York hissed.

"Sorry, sir. Yes, sir," Lancaster said. "He's dead, sir."

Ruth felt something damp against her side. She turned, reaching down, and found her hand came away red. But the blood wasn't hers.

"Medic!" Ruth called. "She's been hit!"

"Scunthorpe, front and centre!" York called. The other foresters formed a ring around their fallen comrade.

Private Scunthorpe unrolled a med-kit, cutting away Essex's jacket, peeling it back. "This is bad, ma'am."

"Can you stabilise her?"

Scunthorpe had already removed a pair of clamping scissors from her kit, and inserted them into the wound. "She'll need proper treatment."

"We're five minutes' walk from the bastion," Mitchell said. "Jean-Luc's people will be there. They'll have proper transport."

"Can we move her?" Sherwood asked.

"We have to," Scunthorpe said.

"Stretcher detail," York barked.

It took ten seconds for four of the foresters to make a stretcher from their long bows, their capped quivers, and a crisscross of webbing. It was clearly something they'd practiced, like the quick response to sniper fire, and so was the pace they set as they ran through the ruins.

Chapter 31 - The Cycle of War
Avenue de Calais, Marck, France

The bastion was less the fortress of Ruth's imagination, and more an overgrown roadblock. Beneath the highway overpass, the road was sealed with a thick metal gate. Above, on the road-bridge, was a jungle of barbed wire from which a sniper currently eyed them with dubious suspicion. A spotter sat next to her, watching the land to the north of Calais, ready to direct the currently silent artillery partially concealed among the roofless houses.

Waiting on the road, in front of the gate, were three carts, each drawn by two bicycles, with more bicycles loaded in the back.

As they slowed from an in-step sprint to a jog, Jean-Luc jumped from the back of a cart. "You have an injured soldier."

"Can you get her to the hospital?" Mitchell asked.

"My cousin can," Jean-Luc said. "As soon as you remove these bicycles."

"Sergeant, one bicycle per person," Sherwood said.

"You heard the princess!" York snapped, and began shouting the soldiers into action.

Mitchell took out pen and notepad. "I'm going to write a note to go with the soldier. She's to go back to Dover. Your cousin's to stay with her until she's handed over to the care of Dr Deering. There's still a lot of animosity towards Leicester."

Ruth looked towards the artillery pieces, aimed skyward.

"They're something, aren't they?" a man with a Scottish accent asked.

Ruth turned around, taking in the private still wearing army green trousers, though with a grey ski-coat instead of the standard-issue military tunic. "You're Hamish MacKay, aren't you?" she said.

"Depends who's asking," he said.

"Ruth Deering," she said.

"You're a copper, aren't you?" he said.

"From Dover, though I served with Mister Mitchell in the Serious Crimes Unit."

"Ah, got it," he said. "And you were with Sergeant Johannes when the bastards first attacked Calais. She mentioned you. But how do you know my name?"

"Mister Mitchell mentioned you in a letter to his daughter. Sergeant Riley came all the way from Twynham to Dover to see you."

"Why? What did I do?" MacKay asked, his face flushing nearly as red as his hair.

"Quite a lot to be proud of," Ruth said. "Sergeant Riley wants to recruit you into the Serious Crimes Unit."

"Oh?" MacKay relaxed. "Is that a promotion, or a punishment?"

"Probably a little of both," Ruth said. "But the work will be in Twynham."

"If it gets me out of this muck, I'm in," MacKay said. "Tell me more."

"I don't know much more," Ruth said. "You'll need to get the details from Sergeant Riley."

"Aye, nae bother. Will it involve these foresters? Did you see how that lad nailed the sniper? That was two hundred metres, if it was a yard."

"Two-fifty," Corporal Lancaster said, having wheeled two bicycles to within earshot. Both were the modern cross-country type, with thick tyres, thicker mudguards, heavy frames, sprung seats, seven gears, and a hook with which to tow a small cart.

"You're a bonny bowman," MacKay said. "How long does it take to learn?"

"All your life, mate," Lancaster said.

"Ah, same as engines, then," MacKay said. "I'm a driver and mechanic."

"Trains?" Lancaster asked.

"Trucks and ships," MacKay said.

"I'll swap you some lessons as soon as we find one of either," Lancaster said. "Here's your bike, ma'am," he added, holding one out to Ruth.

"Thank you," she said. "How's Private Essex?"

"She'll live," the corporal said, leaning against his bike.

"Good. Thank you," Ruth said. She smiled. Lancaster nodded. He didn't leave. "Is there something else? Private MacKay and I were discussing a police matter."

"Pretend I'm not here," Lancaster said. He grinned. "I'm on your protection detail. Orders from His Majesty. The King decreed you and Sergeant Riley are under his protection."

"You say that like I should know what it means," Ruth said. "Is this because of Ned Ludd?"

"Guess so," Lancaster said.

"That's what Private Essex was doing?" Ruth asked. "She was protecting me?"

"Yes," Lancaster said.

"She got shot," Ruth said.

"It happens," Lancaster said, with calm ambivalence.

"So you're willing to die for me?" Ruth asked.

"No, ma'am. But I *am* willing to die for my king."

"That's as daft as a river flowing backwards," MacKay said. "My nan says we should struggle to the end of days *living* for each other."

"My ma says something similar," Lancaster said. "And she was able to because the king saved her life, and her sheep. A bunch of Marines were chasing some runaways. We get a lot of those up in Albion. Crims seeking an escape from Twynham's jurisdiction. Didn't twig that we might not hand them over, but that didn't mean we'd let them live in a palace. This one barmpot was running away from murdering his ex-wife and her new lover. Hid out in my ma's sheep pen. The Marines thought she was helping the crims. The king was out riding, just him and the colonel, surveying the winter storm damage. He saw off your Marines without even raising his voice. Next day, he returned the murderer, and the rifle one of the Marines had dropped. Good man, the king. And that's why he *is* the king."

"Not any more, he's not," Ruth said.

"So some might say," Lancaster said.

With the help of the French scavengers, the bicycles were quickly unloaded, Private Essex was put aboard, and the cart was pedalled away, back towards the Tunnel. The rest of the scavengers remained behind. Nineteen of them, all dressed in an irregular uniform of mottled grey civilian clothes. The coats were waist-short, and ideal for cycling. Beneath the handful which were unzipped, she saw old-world body-armour. On their shoulders, each carried an almost-matching rifle. Old-world, with a longer magazine and shorter barrel than the British government-issue. At their waists were holsters, each containing what appeared to be a modern British service revolver. On their bicycles were saddlebags which were missing from the spare bikes the foresters were collecting.

"Hold this," she said, pushing the bike back at Lancaster, and made her way over to Mister Mitchell who was midway through an argument with Jean-Luc.

"It is our fight, too," Jean-Luc said. "Of course we are coming with you. Who else will show you the way?"

"Fine," Mitchell said. "Colonel, what's the size of your smallest unit?"

"One hand makes a band," Sherwood said. "Five people."

"Jean-Luc, I want a guide with each band. Someone who knows Nieuwpoort. Spread the others out. We'll get clear of the city, rest for a few hours, and approach Nieuwpoort before dawn. It's about seventy kilometres away, but we'll be travelling along the old trade road."

"When do we launch our attack?" Sherwood asked.

"We'll move in at first light," Mitchell said. "We'll attack when we encounter the enemy. We don't know where they are, or how many there are." He looked up at the gate, then at the small army of cycling soldiers. "This war's at a tipping point. We derailed the enemy's plans when we stopped them taking Calais. Now we have a chance of upending them again. Our goal is to alert the troopships to danger ashore, capture or destroy the enemy vehicles, and generally disrupt their attack. I won't say that this, alone, will end the war, but it'll buy us time."

Chapter 32 - Dug in
The Drummond-Dumond Farm, France

Ruth was used to cycling and had grown up pedalling the overgrown byways east of Twynham. These days, she preferred walking, though there wasn't always the time. But sprinting along an ill-repaired road, when the speed was being set by those in front, while she couldn't even see those far, far too close to her rear wheel, was exhausting. Making it terrifying were the occasional gunshots.

With over seventy in their cycling pack, they were an easy and obvious target. Though the evening resounded with an erratic crack of rifle fire, the bullets weren't aimed at them. The further north they cycled, the more distant the gunfire grew. At the next barricade, they got a breather while Mitchell reassured the sentries they weren't an enemy column launching a surprise attack from the south.

Beyond the barricade, their pace slowed. To escape the claustrophobia of being hemmed in by the giant foresters, Ruth nudged her way to the front.

"Where are we?" she asked.

"This is the Avenue de Calais," Mitchell said. "There was talk about renaming this whole trade road Avenue D'Angleterre, but most of our maps were printed in the old-world. Huh." He paused.

"What, sir?" she asked.

"Just an idea," he said. "Maybe a clue. That—"

Before he could finish, a gun cracked in the distance.

"Miles away," Mitchell said. "And we have a few miles more before we can rest, so we'll talk then."

As night settled, the road grew icy. With each wheel's turn taking them further from Calais, the asphalt was increasingly covered in mulch and storm-thrown branches. Their speed slowed, and while the gunshots became little more than a distant memory, so did warmth. A chill wind chased the moon, slicing deep between her clothes. Already regretting having moved to the front, when she saw a light ahead, she barely avoided reflexively braking and so causing a pile-up.

"Slow here, Colonel," Mitchell said. "I'll go on ahead."

While the others slowed, Ruth stuck by Mitchell's side as they cycled the last few hundred yards, and to a barricade built across a bridge.

"We're friendly!" Mitchell called. "Hold your fire."

He slowed to a halt just short of the bridge.

A sentry approached from deep among the shadows.

"Howdy," Mitchell said. "Henry Mitchell. Remember me?"

The soldier visibly relaxed. "A man hunting trouble is hard to forget," he said.

"Captain Ho? You're on sentry duty now?" Mitchell asked.

"What my troops do, so do I," Ho said.

"We're hunting another group of ambushers," Mitchell said.

"Do you think they'll attack here?" Ho asked.

"I doubt it," Mitchell said. "Dunkirk is more likely. Is your radio working?"

Ho shook his head. "They sent a new set, but they didn't send a transformer. We've no way to power it. We do have the telegraph now."

"Is it linked to Dunkirk?" Mitchell asked.

"And Calais," Ho said. "The line worked as of an hour ago. They didn't mention your arrival."

"Ah, you know what bureaucracy is like," Mitchell said. "The orders will probably arrive next week. We need a few hours rest, and I need to send a warning up to Dunkirk, and then we'll be out of here around midnight."

"Can I ask where to?" Ho asked.

"Better not," Mitchell said.

The presence of Sergeant Johannes and Private MacKay facilitated a curious, if cautious, welcome. The foresters offered squares of pressed fruit in exchange for hot water and warm stew, but the conscript soldiers were more interested in information. Ruth found a relatively quiet corner of an old barn in which to rest her legs. And promptly fell asleep.

A hand on her shoulder woke her.

"Let's take a walk," Mitchell whispered.

Outside, the bastion was quiet. Not asleep, but expectant. Filled with alert sentries frozen in place, anticipating an imminent attack.

Mitchell led Ruth through a curtained doorway, then another, and into a kitchen in which embers glowed in the grate.

"How's Anna?" he asked.

"Oh, um… fine," Ruth said. It wasn't the question she'd expected. "She arrived in Dover with Colonel Sherwood. She made sure the treaty was signed, and she reunited Ned Ludd with his family. She's as good as she can be and better than she might be. I don't think you have to worry."

Mitchell smiled. "Doesn't mean I won't," he said. "Thank you. And how are you?"

"I like Dover much more than Twynham," she said. "Mostly, it's been pretty quiet. Up until this business with the spy."

"So tell me about that," he said, as he unpacked the bag she'd brought from Isaac. "And I'll see what we have for supper."

She talked. He questioned. They ate, only occasionally pausing when, outside, there came a distant gunshot.

"It sounds like this spy is the missing link," Mitchell said when Ruth finished. "He kept the warlord, the master criminal, informed of the minor coups and petty insurrections, enabling him to put other pieces swiftly into play. With the spy dead, we've got the upper hand."

"If Fishwyck was the only spy," Ruth said.

"True," Mitchell said. "But you said the information was all taken from Dover Castle. The enemy only knew about the reinforcements going to Dunkirk, and Nieuwpoort, when news of it reached the war-room in Dover. I'd say that suggests there was one spy, albeit there has to be someone who was feeding this Fishwyck guy instructions."

"Do you think Dunkirk is safe?" Ruth asked.

"Tonight? Probably. The garrison is still building their defences. It's a slow business because they didn't inform the scavengers they needed civilian contractors for the construction. But they would be difficult to dig out, and our enemy prefers easier targets, like the ships which'll be sailing into Nieuwpoort."

"They were showing the Dunkirk film in the cinema in Dover," Ruth said. "Or they were trying to. The power cuts meant they kept having to shut. Once, they had to close halfway through the film."

"Did you get to see it?"

"No, because I made the mistake of reading one of Sergeant Kettering's history books," she said. "I know how the story ends even if the newspaper doesn't. They ran a headline saying *Victorious in Dunkirk Again*."

"That's the press for you," Mitchell said. "Even before the Blackout, the story of the Dunkirk evacuation had entered the realm of myth. That's half our problem. It's one hundred years since the last time a British force defended this coast, so people seek parallels. Do that, and you start to copy strategies, but those won't work for us in the here and now. Our enemy aren't soldiers. It's not an army. They're brigands. Thieves. Terrorists. The Hundred Years War would be a better comparison. Or the Mongol invasions. In fact, draw up a list of every conflict in history, ranked by similarity, and World War Two would be at the bottom."

"But we are going to win, aren't we?" she asked.

"I'm certain of it," he said. "There's still some work to be done on our part, and a lot of blood to be spilled, but we will. You said this spy has been feeding information to the brigands for a year?"

"Potentially," Ruth said.

"So he's got to be one of their last assets in Britain. I'll assume there are other spies, but his death will be a real blow. This week, during the recent spate of attacks on Calais, the enemy has been practically throwing their equipment away. No, we'll defeat them soon."

"You said that drawing parallels is only half the problem. What's the other?"

"It's the same as in every conflict, communications and logistics," Mitchell said. "We'll get better at those, but our enemy can't. Now, we better go wake everyone. The clouds are gone, so we'll have an easy time cycling the rest of the way. You can stay here if you want."

She smiled. "Thanks, but if this isn't a war, and if it is a crime, then where else should a police officer be?"

They left the farm-bastion as quietly as seventy people with bicycles could. The stars had come out to keep the moon company. But as much as Ruth welcomed the illumination, the infinite void between those celestial bodies sucked up every precious joule of body heat she'd stored during the brief respite.

At first, they cycled slowly, and in four packs, keeping a hundred metres between each group in case the enemy were close, preparing for another ambush of the bastion. But they reached Dunkirk without incident, and travelled through with barely a pause. The going was easy. The pace was slow. The roadway was frozen, but in no worse condition than the coastal paths on which she'd learned to ride.

Nieuwpoort was seventy kilometres from Calais, thirty from Dunkirk, and fifteen from the old border. But as they crossed that old demarcation line, the temperature plummeted, the wind rose, and the light fell as clouds scudded across the sky. Snow began to fall. Their pace slowed. Again.

She bowed her head, marshalling her thoughts, but they were already slipping into daydreams of blankets and roaring fires. As abruptly as it had begun, the snow ceased, and the clouds fled.

With no warning other than an indecipherable hand signal, the below-wheel slush became frigid water as the road became a ford between a flooded field and a burst canal.

The frozen tyre-spray and brisk wind brought an eye-stinging chill which crystallised her thoughts. She understood what Mister Mitchell had said. This truly wasn't a war. Not like the history books, *or* the history movies. They'd cycled over fifty kilometres without losing a soul. This really *wasn't* a war. Which didn't mean it was simply a crime. Whatever it was, she hoped it would end soon.

24th December

Chapter 33 - The Battle Ahead
Nieuwpoort

The worst part of cycling at night wasn't the darkness. At first it had been fun, but as the miles grew, more bicycles slipped, skidded, and fell. As one forester after another tumbled, jumped, and ran with their bike to catch up, Ruth couldn't help but dread she'd be next. No, the worst part wasn't the darkness.

It wasn't the cold wind in her face, the frozen spray drenching her legs, or the biting chill when they had to stop to replace a lost chain or punctured tyre. It wasn't the silence from her comrades, or the unusual and unidentifiable whispers from the surrounding woodland. It wasn't even fear of what awaited them at journey's end. Not as such. The worst part was not being able to judge distance, and so time, thus not knowing how soon the battle would begin, and thus how soon, one way or the other, it might be over.

When that moment came, it caught her unprepared. She was in the middle of the group, surrounded by foresters who raised a clenched fist even as they braked, one-handed, just short of an old road bridge cutting east-west above the trade road.

As Ruth dismounted, at the front Mister Mitchell led a five-forester squad up the on-ramp leading to the bridge above. They disappeared among the partial forest now growing from crevices in the concrete. Corporal Lancaster drew an arrow.

A whistle came from above. Then a word. "Loxley."

"That's the all-clear," Lancaster whispered, returning the arrow to its quiver.

Word came from the front to take shelter in the shadows beneath the bridge. As Ruth neared it, Mister Mitchell, alone, descended the wooded embankment.

"Jean-Luc, Colonel, here," Mitchell said, sheltering beneath a stubborn beech tree halfway up the slope. As he'd not explicitly told her not to, Ruth joined him.

"Trouble, sir?" Ruth whispered.

"Radio," he said. He held up a small handset, barely larger than her phone. "I grabbed this from the enemy in Dunkirk. Very short range, just a few kilometres, but they're unencrypted. I just heard a time-check. The enemy is here. Seven groups, plus a command unit. They're all to the north."

"This is Nieuwpoort?" she asked.

"It is," he said. "We're still a kilometre out. We made good time. Better than I hoped. I was expecting to be attacked at least once."

"Isn't it good that we weren't?" Ruth said.

"Good for us, yes, but not good for someone else," Mitchell said. "It means the brigands are elsewhere. Not our problem, of course, not immediately. I saw no tyre marks on the road we travelled, and none in the mud on that bridge." He took out a penlight, and a map. "We're south of Nieuwpoort. This is the N39, that's the bridge over the canal. Most of the other bridges are gone. About ten rivers and canals meet in Nieuwpoort, flowing through the city where they join the River Yser as it rushes to the sea. Just west of where these waterways connect, there's another bridge. If they didn't use that crossing, they'd have had to detour far inland. That's assuming they came from the south or the east." He tapped the captured radio. "But they are here. Colonel, we can't let those trucks escape."

"You said there are seven groups plus a command unit," Sherwood said. "How many in each group?"

"If it's one vehicle per group, up to ten," Mitchell said. "But it could be less. It could be a lot more. Assume each group is armed with assault rifles, mortars, and those nearest the river will be armed with missiles. They aren't expecting an attack from the south, that's our first advantage. The second is that our goal is simply to spring the attack before the ships arrive. We're going to assume that our fleet didn't get the warning, so a lot of smoke rising from the ruins should be enough to get them to avoid the shore. Jean-Luc, I'm going to give you a message to take to Dunkirk. At first light, they're to bring up reinforcements."

"Will you wait for them?" Jean-Luc asked.

"Nope, because I don't know if they'll come," Mitchell said. "We'll attack just before dawn. Colonel, this is more your kind of operation than mine. How do we do it?"

"Where would our ships make landfall?" she asked.

"On the southern bank of the river," Mitchell said. "That old marina was being used by some Belgian settlers prior to the brigands' arrival. It's the only dock in good repair."

Sherwood ran her finger over the map. "They'll wait until the ships have entered the river. They'll have at least one squad at the coast, ready to destroy any ships that attempt to flee, but most of their forces will be gathered along the shore. Their defences will have been built in expectation of an attack from the river, not the south. Seven teams plus a command unit? If this were me, I'd have two at the river mouth, and five along the bank, with the command team further back."

"Could be," Mitchell said. "The priority is making sure the ships don't enter the harbour. Colonel, can you disrupt the ambush while I go after the trucks? If I can find their command unit, I can try ordering a retreat over the radio."

"Of course," Sherwood said. "How will you find them?"

"That's the million-dollar question, isn't it?" Mitchell said, moving his light over the map. "Huh." He turned the map over, checking the front, before turning back to the map. "They're in Sint-Joris."

"How can you be certain?" Sherwood asked.

"Two reasons," Mitchell said. "The bridge to the east is down, but the road leads directly to the last bridge over the Yser. The second reason is that it's the only campsite in Nieuwpoort listed on my map. They used campsites in Ypres and in Dunkirk. And in Dunkirk, we found a map printed in Germany. My map came from Dover. Our enemy comes from a lot further east. They're using campsites for their rendezvouses. Campgrounds are listed on foreign maps. They have wide access roads, and few buildings tall enough to create much by the way of rubble. That's where I'll go. If they're not there, I'll continue west, and meet you at the bridge."

"Give me five minutes to instruct my bands," Sherwood said.

Mitchell took out a pen and notepad. "Jean-Luc, take this to Dunkirk," he said as he wrote. "All being well, the reinforcements you return with will be those who were on the fleet from the Humber. Ruth?"

There was barely enough light to see his face, but she knew what he was asking. "I'll stay, sir," she said. "If I go, I don't know how many of the foresters will go with me." That wasn't the real reason. Whenever she folded her arms, her hand touched the patch of blood left by Private Essex.

"Good luck, Jean-Luc," Mitchell said by way of dismissal.

"You think they're using campsites?" Ruth asked, as the Frenchman hurried back to his bike.

"That's what we'll find out," Mitchell said. "When we find the vehicles, I want Hamish to disable them. You and Jo-Jo back him up. Remember this is an investigation. We want evidence. Those trucks will be as good as a confession. Disable them, then take cover. It'll be dark and chaotic, and impossible to be certain who is friendly except that our guys have bows. I don't want you three to be shot by mistake. Go tell Hamish and Jo-Jo. I'll speak with the Belgians, and then we'll move out."

Corporal Lancaster fell in at her side as she jogged back to the rear. "Were you listening?" she asked.

"No one said I shouldn't," he said.

"Our job is to disable the trucks?" Jo-Jo asked, after Ruth had briefed her.

"Did he say he needs them to be driveable again?" MacKay asked.

"No. Why?" Ruth asked.

"Then it'll be nae bother," MacKay said.

Another hoot, another whistle, and the bands vanished into the shadows as the Belgian guides led the foresters down forgotten paths and lost tracks. Some headed towards the coast, some headed straight to the river. Within a minute, only their bicycles remained.

Chapter 34 - Sabotage
Nieuwpoort, Belgium

Mister Mitchell led from the front with a Belgian guide, Lily Wilwerth, at his side. She had a shotgun on her back, but a loaded crossbow in her right hand, which she used to show them the way. Her hand jerked left, then right, around bushes, between trees, and along almost invisible tracks. Sergeant York and his team followed behind, crouched low, bows ready, heads up. Then came Ruth, Jo-Jo, and MacKay, with Corporal Lancaster and his band bringing up the rear.

Grass rustled. Mud squelched. Ice cracked. Branches creaked, but between the trees, the starry sky made the going manageable. When they reached a road, Mitchell waved for them to wait as, doubled over, he peered at the ground. Whatever tracks he'd found, Ruth couldn't see them, but Mitchell seemed energised as he changed their course, and followed the road.

The steady advance became a series of short sprints, running from one piece of cover to the next. From a ruined house, whose fallen roof had slid, nearly intact, onto the front lawn, to a pair of old cars rusting one atop another, and into a ghost-burb of collapsed houses. Across the rubble, from one patch to the next, with Mister Mitchell no longer looking at the ground, but only at the horizon as he held the small radio close to his ear.

Beyond the houses was a half-cleared orchard with a yet-to-be-installed fence lying next to stacks of rotting branches, brush, and uprooted saplings. Mitchell waved everyone on, and into the cover of the trees.

"We're close," Mitchell whispered. "Silence from now on. Everyone wait here. Sergeant York, Madam Wilwerth, with me."

Mitchell crept away, leaving the others behind. Ruth sat on a damp stump, almost instantly regretting it. Almost. Between the carbine and ammo, the uniform and its reactive plates, and what had been, in retrospect, an absurdly long cycle ride, she was exhausted.

Corporal Lancaster abruptly stood, raising his bow just before a hoot came from the left. Mitchell, York, and Wilwerth reappeared through the undergrowth.

"There's a campfire," Mitchell whispered. "We found them. We'll wait another twenty minutes. Give the other bands time to near their targets."

Time stretched, allowing Ruth's mind to conjure all the possible deaths which were only minutes away.

Too soon, Mitchell stood. "It's time," he whispered, and held up his suppressed pistol. "Silence, remember. Password is Loxley, the counter is Camelot."

Jo-Jo and MacKay drew their bayonets. Ruth slung the carbine, and withdrew the collapsible truncheon Riley had given her back in Twynham what seemed like a lifetime ago.

Once again in a loose column, they moved away from the orchard, along the shadow of a bush-lined field, and to a scrub jungle at the edge of a two-lane road. Ruth could smell smoke with an oily, chemical edge to the fumes.

York and four of the archers dashed across the road, disappearing into the woodland-campsite beyond. Mitchell motioned the rest on, following the scrubby verge as it followed the road until it met the driveway leading into the old campground. On the road were the shadowy outlines of a vehicle, but beyond was a stark white light. There. Gone.

"There's the first truck," Mitchell whispered. "Give me five minutes to get in position."

With the Belgian guide and the four soldiers from Lancaster's band, Mitchell continued west. Ruth watched him dash across the road some fifty metres from the entrance.

"I'm on point," Jo-Jo whispered. "Lancaster, watch the flanks. Hamish, wreck the trucks. Ruth, watch our six. We stick together and tackle one vehicle at a time. Now, move."

New trees overhung the road. Shallow-rooted vines traced the cracks in the asphalt. Only a moonlit T where the road met the junction for the campsite was open to the sky. Reaching it, Lancaster paused, loosed, and nocked a new arrow, all in the time it took for Ruth to take two steps. The forester hurried on, following MacKay and the sergeant, before Ruth saw whom he'd fired at.

When she'd crossed the road, she almost stumbled over the body. The black-coated woman had an arrow through her chest and two rifles slung over her shoulder: an AKM, and a government-issue rifle.

"Ruth, remove the mags," Jo-Jo whispered. "Hamish, go."

Both magazines were heavy enough to be full. Ruth checked the dead woman's coat. There was another magazine in the pocket. Beneath was a belt festooned with knives. She left those, and stood. The truck had a boxy and windowless cabin with a door built into the back. In the shadows of the overhanging trees, she could barely make out the two-barred cross recently painted atop. She'd seen enough abandoned wrecks among the forgotten ruins of Kent and Dorset to recognise the vehicle as an armoured delivery van.

Ruth made her way to the cab just as MacKay eased the door closed. The Scotsman held up a bundle of wires. "Where's next?" he asked.

"Follow the road," Jo-Jo whispered.

"Car park," Ruth whispered, pointing to the bent and battered sign.

"Agreed. On me," Jo-Jo said.

Lancaster loosed again, this time twice. This time, Ruth heard the body hit the ground, and something metallic clatter across the asphalt.

Jo-Jo raised a warning hand, crouching. Ruth did the same, moving the truncheon to her left hand, and her right to the slung carbine.

"Clear," Lancaster whispered.

"Go!" Jo-Jo said.

They dashed across the road, and into a sliver of jungle. Stumbling through the thick ivy coiled around dying pines, Ruth nearly ran into the comparatively open expanse of a car park. Six vehicles: one bus, five trucks. No movement. Lancaster moved his nocked bow across the roofs. Ruth couldn't see the brigand the archer had shot.

"On me," Jo-Jo whispered.

Ruth heard the crunch of boot on frozen leaves. She spun, raising the truncheon even as she heard the word.

"Loxley!" came the call from behind.

"Camelot," Lancaster replied.

A forester stepped out of the trees, five metres away. Mitchell followed.

"The command unit isn't here," Mitchell whispered. "We found one guard, stoking the fire. Five chairs around it."

"We got two," Lancaster said.

"One vehicle's disabled," Jo-Jo whispered.

"Two enemy unaccounted for," Mitchell whispered.

A hoot came from the other side of the car park.

Lancaster replied with one of his own. A shorter owl-hoot came in reply.

"That's the tawny owl. It's Sergeant York," Lancaster said. "It's all clear."

"Go carefully," Mitchell said.

They reached the vehicles at the same time as Sergeant York.

"I got two, sir," York said. "On patrol. Just over there."

"Five dead, and five chairs at their campfire," Mitchell whispered. "I don't think there are any more brigands here. This isn't their command unit. That group must be up at the bridge, or maybe at the coast. Jo-Jo, I want you to complete the primary mission: disable the trucks. I'll take the rest west." He took in the vehicles. "Even if these were full, our numbers match so we've got the advantage. First light's less than half an hour away. You disable the trucks, we'll take care of the passengers. Move out." Within seconds, he, the guide, and the foresters had disappeared into the fading night.

"You heard him," Jo-Jo said. "Lancaster, on guard. Hamish, earn your keep."

They moved from one vehicle to the next: two armoured delivery vans, then the three boxy military vehicles whose forest camouflage was smeared with red and white paint. Ruth was more interested in the tyres, specifically the pair which didn't match the others, but which jutted beyond the raised wheel-arch.

They left the bus until last. It was a single decker with hinged metal panels hanging over half the windows. At the front, five mirrors had been bolted to the bodywork by the door. That door didn't match the rest of the bus, leaving a gap at bottom and top, but that made it easier to swing open.

When Ruth got inside, she saw most of the seats had been removed. In their place, on the driver's side of the bus, was a small bank of electronics and a generator. It was off. Closer to the back were weapons crates. It was too dark to read the writing, but when she tried lifting one, she found it empty. The box with food wasn't, nor were the three water jugs.

"Done," MacKay said.

"I want to check the roof," Ruth said.

"Why?" Jo-Jo asked.

"Because there's a wire leading up there. A thick wire. I bet there's an antenna."

"Where's the fuel?" Jo-Jo asked. "That's what we were looking for." She held up a red plastic fuel can. "This is empty. It's the only one here. Mister Mitchell was certain they were using a giant tanker to move their fuel."

"Like my nan says, what you see is what they had," MacKay said.

"Daylight's coming," Lancaster said. "We should get anywhere but here. This is where they'll come if any escape the net."

Ruth lingered a moment, looking at the equipment she was now thinking of as evidence, but there'd be time later to examine it all. She was the last off the bus. Above, the sky really was growing brighter. In turn, that only made the jungle forest darker, making the figure who stepped out of the trees a silhouette.

"Loxley!" Lancaster called.

The shadow vanished as the figure dropped to the ground. A second later, bullets spanged off the bus in a horizontal rain that began as a patter and grew into a storm.

A lead fist slapped into Ruth's thigh. She staggered sideways.

"Are you hit?" Lancaster asked, lowering his bow and grabbing her arm.

"Take cover!" Jo-Jo said as more bullets flew through the air. Lancaster shoved Ruth in front of the bus's cab where Hamish was now holding his rifle.

"Can we fire back?" he asked.

"If you can see a target," Jo-Jo said.

"Are you hit?" Lancaster asked Ruth again.

"No," Ruth said, feeling her thigh. "Just bruised. It was a ricochet. It hit the armour."

"Oy, Lancaster!" Jo-Jo snapped. "Get your head in the game. Take out that shooter!"

But from the jungle, the gunfire had ceased.

"I can't see anyone," Lancaster said, briefly easing around the cab before ducking back behind it. "What about you, Hamish?"

"I canna see nothing," MacKay said, now lying on the ground, peering beneath the bus, then around the tyres. "It's all shadows."

"A twenty-metre sprint gets us to the cover of the trees," Jo-Jo said, pointing ahead of the cab, and to where the campground jungle continued. "Get to the trees, go east, because they'll be coming from the west."

A bullet shattered one of the mirrors by the passenger door.

"Hamish, fire a shot!" Jo-Jo said.

The Scotsman's rifle roared, but a fully automatic burst came in reply, and from the jungle in front of the bus. The windscreen shattered. Glass rained down. MacKay screamed. The gunfire ceased.

"Got 'im," Lancaster said.

"But he got me!" MacKay hissed, rolling onto his side. "He shot my foot!"

The bullet had entered the boot's sole, close to the toecap, leaving a too-large exit wound in the leather.

"Good thing it wasn't your head," Jo-Jo said, before firing a burst into the jungle behind, and then another into the forest ahead. "Pick him up, Ruth. We're moving."

MacKay hissed again as Ruth hauled him to his one good leg. She looped his arm over her neck. "C'mon, then."

He wasn't a tall man. A front-line diet, following years of rationing, had left few with extra weight. But MacKay was still carrying his pack, while she was carrying the extra weight of all the old-world armour plates slotted into her uniform. They limped. He swore. Jo-Jo fired. So did their enemy, and there was far more than one foe. But the vehicles were between them and the enemy, and took the brunt of the gunfire.

"Keep moving," Jo-Jo said.

"Can't for long, Sarge," Ruth said, stumbling as she tried to push the branches aside with her carbine.

"Take the path," Lancaster said, darting in front, using his bow to point the way before vanishing back into the trees.

"Path? This isn't a path," Ruth said. "They were shooting their own vehicles."

"Numpties," MacKay said. "Bloody numpties. Just wish they were worse shots."

This part of the campsite had been filled with log cabins, where the roof had overhung the front porch on which had stood a bench seat. Ivy climbed the walls, while moss now overhung the roof, providing an external curtain to the shattered windows. But those log walls looked thick. Sturdy. Bulletproof.

"These'll do," Jo-Jo said. "Take him inside, Ruth. Lancaster... where's Lancaster?"

Ruth hauled MacKay up the steps. The cabin door was closed. The handle and lock were rusted shut. "Hold that pillar, Hamish," Ruth said, as she raised her boot and launched a kick. On impact, they were engulfed in a cloud of splinters as the worm-riddled door disintegrated.

Ruth waved her hand through the air, trying to clear it.

"Inside!" Jo-Jo hissed, backing up onto the porch.

"Loxley!" came a call from the jungle-forest. Lancaster dashed forward, running to a halt by the cabin. "Two down. Four of them still out there," he said. "More coming."

"So we'll hide and hope they miss us," Jo-Jo said.

As Ruth helped MacKay into the cabin, claws skittered across the floor, and a family of foot-long shadows disappeared through a large hole in the centre of the room. Steel brackets and a rusting sink were all that remained of the cupboards above the half of the room used as a kitchen, while a snakeskin of plastic was all that remained of the dining table.

"Lancaster!" Jo-Jo called, as she propped her rifle on the broken window-frame.

The archer ducked inside. "They're running from our people by the river," he said.

"Hold fire and wait," Jo-Jo said. "We'll let them flee. How's Hamish?"

"Barely conscious," Ruth said.

"Cut away the boot," Jo-Jo said. "You'll have to stem the bleeding."

Outside, dawn might be arriving, but inside, it was dark as a tomb and smelled twice as bad. Ruth took out a small reading light, a long-ago gift from her mother to use at the academy. By its glow, she saw the dark pool of blood around the private's foot, and the damp trail that led back to the door.

"Cut away the boot, got it," she muttered, drawing MacKay's bayonet. "This will hurt."

"It already does," MacKay whispered.

Light between her teeth, left hand bracing his ankle, she sliced the laces. MacKay twitched, but barely moaned, as she pulled the boot away. His foot was a lot smaller than it had any right to be, missing three toes and a chunk of flesh.

"Gauze," Lancaster said. "Fill the wound with gauze. Bandage it. Elevate it above his head."

"I don't have any gauze," Ruth said.

"Here," Jo-Jo said, throwing her a med-kit.

"Movement," Lancaster said.

A bullet thudded into the cabin outside, near the door.

"He shot my foot!" MacKay whispered.

"Yep," Ruth said, pushing the gauze into place. "But you'll dance again. Promise."

"Didn't do much dancing before," he hissed.

"Then you won't have much to relearn," she said as she grabbed a roll of bandage, wrapping it around his foot. The antiseptic powder quickly turned red. There were only two rolls in the kit, and she used both.

Another bullet slammed into the cabin.

Jo-Jo fired a three-shot burst through the door, then another. "I thought you were supposed to be some kind of sharpshooter, Lancaster."

"I'm supposed to be in the open, and they're supposed to be cowering inside," Lancaster said.

"What do we do?" Ruth asked.

"See if there's a backdoor," Jo-Jo said.

Ruth grabbed her carbine and made her way through the cabin. Behind the front room, a corridor led to a bedroom, a bathroom, and then another bedroom. There was no other door, but there was a window in the rear bedroom. Grime-smeared except the corner where it was smashed. In that hole, she saw a face. Ruth fired. The remaining glass shattered. The face vanished, but she didn't know if she'd hit her target.

"We're surrounded," Ruth said, returning to the front room.

"Watch the back," Jo-Jo said.

As she spoke, more bullets thudded into the damp timbers. Two made it inside, through the gaps where the windows should be.

"Mortars. Missiles. Grenades," Jo-Jo said. "This is a death trap. I've got a smoke grenade. I'll stand in the door and make myself a target. Lancaster, you take them out. I'll drop smoke. We'll run. Straight ahead. Into the trees. Ruth, get Hamish up. Lancaster, you stay with them. I'll draw their fire."

Ruth helped the Scotsman remove his pack, before lifting him into a half crouch. She took the revolver from his holster, putting it in his free hand.

"Ready," she said.

"Aye," MacKay said.

"On three, Lancaster," Jo-Jo said. "You better be a good shot."

The sergeant stood, flush against the door. "One, two, three." Jo-Jo leaned out wide, firing a burst into the trees before darting outside, and crouching down.

Instead of shots came a shout. "Loxley!"

Ruth slumped, nearly dropping MacKay as the adrenaline fled her body. They were safe.

Chapter 35 - Evidence of Victory
Nieuwpoort, Belgium

"Hamish did a thorough job, didn't he?" Mitchell said, as he bent over the severed wires beneath the truck's steering column. He looked across the car park to where two of the Belgian guides were re-bandaging MacKay's foot. "I can't fix this. I don't know if Hamish can fix anything until we've fixed him, so we can't drive the bus back to Calais."

"But we won, didn't we?" Ruth asked. It was an hour after dawn. Smoke rose from the centre of Nieuwpoort where Sherwood was hunting the ruins for any stay-behind brigands.

"We didn't lose," Mitchell said. "It's too soon to say more. We don't know how many fled, so we don't know how many are still hiding in the ruins. Sherwood captured a couple of the portable missiles and used them to blow up the mortar teams. The smoke over the harbour is a result of the shells detonating all in one go. There could be more brigands skulking in the ruins, but the foresters are hunting for them. No, we didn't lose, but it'll be days before we've got a real sense of how big, or small, this victory was."

"Is there any sign of the fleet?" Ruth asked.

"Not yet, but they weren't due for hours anyway," Mitchell said. "The missile and mortar teams were waiting inland, near the bridge. The rifle teams were waiting much closer to the marina. I guess their strategy was to wait until the troopships dropped anchor before using mortars to shell the ships. That would have encouraged the soldiers to disembark, where they'd have run straight into the assault rifle fire before the missile teams finished the ships."

"That sounds ambitious, if there were only fifty or so of them here," Ruth said.

"Oh, there were more than that," Mitchell said. "At least a hundred foot-soldiers. Could be twice that number. After the explosion it'll be impossible to tell how many were in the missile and mortar team, but I'd start my guessing at thirty, and wouldn't be surprised if it climbed higher."

"That's a small army," Ruth said. "Way too many to fit into these vehicles."

"Precisely," Mitchell said. "But that bus is their command vehicle. They sent that to war, but not the fuel tanker. So did the tanker leave with the other transport vehicles, or did the extra soldiers arrive on foot? In which case, since the spy only sent news of the flotilla's arrival a day ago, why were the enemy gathering near here?"

A distant rat-a-tat came from the direction of the harbour, causing two of the Belgian sentries to raise their rifles.

"Should we go help?" Ruth asked.

"Sherwood's people know each other, and know everyone not carrying a bow is an enemy. No, we'll give her space to work until she gives the all-clear, or the reinforcements arrive." He checked his watch before glancing up at the sky. "I'm going to take a look at the other vehicles. If I can get one working, I can get the injured back to the hospital in Calais."

"What shall I do, sir?" she asked.

"Be a copper," he said. "Start gathering evidence. Particularly fuel cans. Doesn't matter if they're empty. Put those on the bus."

"Empty fuel cans go on the bus, got it," she said.

There was one obvious reason the enemy might have gathered soldiers in this harbour town. Perhaps they'd not wanted to sink a ship, but capture one. Of course, that raised the question of why they wanted to send a raiding party to Britain. She began looking for the answer in the armoured delivery vans.

They were civilian, not military. Beneath the new red paint, all three were identical. They'd been found in the same place, then. Where? The maps found in a pouch by the steering column didn't help narrow it down. Aside from maps for France and Belgium, there were driving maps for Germany, Austria, Greece, Hungary, Ukraine, and Turkey. Her geography wasn't the best, but she knew wide swathes of Europe were missing.

Beneath the passenger seat, she found a paperback with the title *Der Herr Der Ringe*. Since it also had the author's name, she knew it was a story of hobbits and elves, and looked to have been printed, and translated, forty years ago in Germany.

She continued her search. A few brass cartridges, an old spoon, a few scraps of paper with doodles on them. A broken pencil, a mug, a tennis ball. None of it was very informative. She continued on to the next of the armoured cars, and found a similar assortment of junk, none of which she'd call a clue.

As she was sorting through the third, Mitchell came over. "Much luck?" he asked.

"I'm still eliminating impossibilities," she said. "In Dunkirk, and here in Nieuwpoort, do you think the enemy could have hoped to capture a ship?"

"Not with mortars and missiles," Mitchell said.

"No, I suppose not," she said. "Could they be waiting on a ship of their own?"

"To sail people to Britain? Possibly," he said. "We pushed the pirates back, but we didn't sink every boat."

"So could they sail a craft through our naval blockade, claiming to be refugees or traders from Africa?"

"Why?" he asked.

"To pick up the soldiers so they could take them to Britain," she said.

"Again, why?" he asked.

"Because our response to the attack on Calais was to raise a conscript army. The boss, the warlord, has to know we have the numbers to win in a straight fight. If we can't be defeated in France, why not attack Twynham? Blow up parliament. That would slow the war down, wouldn't it?"

"With a mind like that, I'm glad you're on our side," Mitchell said. "It's a possibility, and we can ask the navy to keep an eye out for ships. But if they had the capability to do that, why didn't they launch that attack three months ago?"

"Because they didn't think of it then, or they're desperate now," she said.

"Could be. Anything else?"

"I found some maps," Ruth said. "Turkey, Greece, Hungary, Austria, Germany, Belgium, France. Oh, and Ukraine. I'm trying to figure out where these vans came from, though. Wherever it was, all three of these armoured trucks came from the same place."

"The Humvees came from Hungary," Mitchell said.

"The who?"

"The military vehicles. It's an American design. They sold them to NATO nations. The AKMs aren't a NATO rifle, though. I think the guns came from a storehouse further east. The AKM is a reliable weapon, but it wasn't cutting edge. They were being phased out. There must have been a lot of rifles sitting in storehouses, half forgotten. At the beginning of the Blackout, our warlord knew where to find them."

"You mean the person behind the AI-virus," Ruth said.

"Isaac does. I'm not so sure. Whoever began this doesn't have to be the same person as whoever is running things now. None of which helps narrow down... huh."

"What?"

"Oil fields. The Knights of St Sebastian pushed from Poland to Ukraine. After the Free Peoples coalesced in Greece, they pushed north. The emir's caliphate roamed a lot, but often in lands famed for having oil. We know the warlord was equipping these terrorists. Why? Not just for *lebensraum*, but for oil. Historically, if you controlled the oil, you could get away with murder. Any luck with the fuel cans?"

"Not yet."

"They're the key. The fuel is, anyway. In the olden days, we could analyse the trace compounds, compare them to a geological report, and pinpoint exactly which oil field it came from. Now, I don't know how detailed an analysis we're capable of, but we'll try. Ah, the bikes are here."

Ruth turned. Entering the car park from the west were seven Belgians, Corporal Lancaster, and ten bicycles.

"We're leaving?" Ruth asked.

"The injured will be," Mitchell said. "The foresters are going to make a couple of carts which we'll use to transport the injured back to Dunkirk, just as soon as the reinforcements arrive."

"You couldn't get any of the vehicles to work?" she asked.

"I fixed the damage MacKay did, but I can't do much about the bullet holes from your gunfight. A bicycle cart will do the job. Five injured so far," he added, looking across the car park to a marginally intact cabin where the wounded were being gathered. "Not counting those who stuck on a bandage and returned to the fight. Five injured, and ten dead. So far." He shook his head. "But a thousand Marines saved. Back to it, Constable."

She headed to the nearest of the Humvees, but despite sating her curiosity, she couldn't see any immediate and obvious clues. It would take weeks to sort through the scraps of paper covered in half-played games and scrawled lines, which, going by the number of syllables, were poetry. Whether they were originals, or remembered, they didn't look like the Gospel of St Sebastian. No, the drivers weren't true believers, at least not believers in any of the three terrorist cults.

A shout from the Belgian sentries had her jump down from the cab, reaching for her carbine, but the cycling soldiers were led by Jean-Luc. The reinforcements from Dunkirk had arrived.

"Constable!" Mitchell called, already angling towards the injured, even as he waved Jean-Luc to follow.

Two foresters and a Belgian had cobbled three carts together using three bicycles apiece, with bow-staves, packs, and webbing for a truck-bed. It wouldn't be a comfortable ride, but it would be quicker than walking.

"Let's get the injured aboard," Mitchell said. "We'll take them to Dunkirk, and stick them on a ship."

"Sir!" Sergeant York sprinted into the campground. "Message from Colonel Sherwood. Ships approaching. Two gunboats, and a twin-mast sailing boat."

"Any troopships?" Mitchell asked.

"No, sir."

"How dangerous is the terrain between here and the river?" Mitchell asked.

"We've run the enemy to ground, sir," York said. "They're pinned down in an old bank, and in a below-ground car park."

"Good enough," Mitchell said. "We'll move the injured to the river, get them on a ship and back to Dover. Sergeant Johannes!"

"Sir?"

"Guard these trucks. No one touches them before I get back. Constable, grab a bike. Sergeant York, show us the way."

Finding herself one half of a two-driver ambulance-cart team, she kept her attention on the road. From her brief glances at the ruins, and despite the smoke rising ahead of them, this latest battle had done little damage to the time-weathered city. Broken glass and faded plastic already lay mixed with the mud, making a poor soil for the ivy coiling up, and inside, the shattered windows. Where the roads were flooded, they cycled straight through. Where they were blocked with rubble, they took a detour. When an occasional rifle shot echoed across the fractured ruins, they sped up, until they neared a row of leaking water tankers, now guarded by a squad of British sailors, and by a man in a long coat and beret.

"Henry, Ruth!" Isaac said.

"Your ship's here?" Mitchell asked.

"She is," Isaac said. "The troopships are on their way to Dunkirk. I brought the gunboats here to assist with the assault, though it appears we arrived too late to join the fun."

"We need to get the injured back to Dover," Mitchell said. "Can you manage it?"

"Indeed. I find the life of a boatman rather satisfying," Isaac said.

"I mean do you have the fuel?" Mitchell asked.

"Enough, twice over," Isaac said.

"And who is in charge here?" Mitchell asked, turning to the Royal Navy sailors, but Ruth was already driving the bicycle-cart down to the marina, so missed the rest of the conference.

Isaac's boat was as big as the two Union-Jacked gunboats with their cannons and heavy machine guns, but it wasn't designed for stretchers. Getting the injured aboard and below required forming a chain and passing the improvised stretchers from person to person, from shore to hold. When they were all aboard, Ruth made to follow the Belgians back ashore, until Isaac laid a hand on her shoulder.

"Yours is a return ticket," Isaac said. "Technically, one from Calais. You weren't supposed to join the assault."

"You're not letting me leave?" she asked.

"Absolutely not," he said. "There aren't many things in life I fear, but your mother's wrath is one of them."

As the ship pulled away from the shore, Ruth went below. With Kelly, Gregory, and Mrs Zhang assisting the medics, Ruth wasn't needed. She returned to the deck, managing nearly a minute in the freezing bluster before she retreated to the cockpit. There she found Isaac, standing by the wheel, quietly singing to himself.

"How was it?" he asked.

"You mean the battle?" she asked, collapsing onto the bench seat. "Dark. Cold. Confusing. We caught their radio truck."

"Henry said," Isaac said. "He gave me the hard drive."

"The what?"

"The part of the computer which stores all the information. He removed it from their comms set-up. It will be illuminating, I'm sure."

"Mister Mitchell thinks the answer is in the fuel," Ruth said. "Figure out where that comes from, and we work out where the enemy is. Where does yours come from? This ship burns it, right?"

"From the same source as the government," Isaac said.

"You steal it?"

"Since I put it to a use that is of international interest, can it really be called theft?" he asked.

"Yes," she said.

"Then perhaps you should ask no more questions," he said.

"Yeah, perhaps," she said. "Did we win?"

"That would depend on what you think a victory looks like," Isaac said. "To Henry, it was a quiet retirement where violence was but a bad dream. To me... well, perhaps it is not much different, though my dreams are decidedly less rustic. How does victory appear to you?"

But Ruth was already asleep.

The crossing took four hours, but when they arrived in the harbour, the sky above was already as dark as midnight. The dock was frenetic as ships were loaded with provisions and munitions, but that meant there were plenty of sailors to help take the injured up to the hospital. Ruth took a step after them, but paused when she heard artillery fire carried by the wind from across the sea. She wasn't a doctor; she couldn't help the injured. No, she was a copper, so she made her way to the police station.

25ᵗʰ December

Epilogue - Christmas Day
Dover

When Ruth woke, the wall clock said it was ten past seven. She was late for work! After the quickest shower, and still pulling on her cleanest uniform jacket, she jumped down the stairs to find the lights on, the door unlocked, and Anna Riley behind the duty desk.

"Didn't you go back to Twynham?" Ruth asked.

"I did, and I came back here with Commissioner Weaver," Riley said. "I said I'd keep an eye on things for Sergeant Kettering. Merry Christmas."

"Oh. Yes. Merry Christmas. It is, isn't it?"

"All day long," Riley said. "Christmas, anyway. I don't suppose it'll be merry for many people. How are you? Feeling okay?"

"I was at war yesterday, but got to sleep in a proper bed last night," Ruth said. "So compared to everyone still in France, yes. Where *is* Sergeant Kettering?"

"At the hospital," Riley said.

"Is she sick?" Ruth asked.

"That's where the casualty list is being posted. She's comforting the bereaved."

"There weren't that many dead," Ruth said. "And they were all Albion foresters."

Riley shook her head. "You didn't hear? Eloise said you were snoring loud enough to be heard in Llandudno, but I thought you'd have heard the commotion. Calais was attacked yesterday at dawn."

"While we were attacking Nieuwpoort? Oh. How bad was it?"

"We don't know yet," Riley said. "At least a hundred dead. Over three hundred wounded."

"On *our* side?" Ruth asked.

The door opened and a flurry of snow entered, bringing a harried woman with it. Mid-forties, wearing a scarf, mismatched boots, no hat, and a mis-buttoned coat. "Have you got list of the survivors?" she asked, her voice nearly a sob. "There's so many people at the hospital, and they're adding new names every minute."

"The hospital gets the list first," Riley said, lifting a clipboard from the desk. "What's the soldier's name?"

"Clifton. Private Maya Clifton, she's with the Dorset Rifles. She only joined up last month. Ran away to do it. I told her…" The words were lost in a sob.

"The Dorset Rifles?" Ruth asked. "They were the reinforcements Jean-Luc brought up."

"Brought to where?" the mother asked, looking from one police officer to another for a clue as to the fate of her daughter.

"We can't say, ma'am," Riley said. "But it wasn't Calais."

"Oh. So she's okay?"

"We can't say that, either," Riley said.

"No, of course not," the mother said, straightening her coat. "But she wasn't in Calais. No, of course she wasn't. She's fine. Of course she is. Thank you." She smoothed down her coat. "Thank you." She opened the door and hurried away, lest any additional information should rob her of this sliver of hope.

"They've been coming in since I got here," Riley said. "All night, all morning."

"What happened in Calais?" Ruth asked.

"At least three thousand enemy troops attacked Calais, armed with assault rifles and grenades," Riley said.

"Did they have trucks?" Ruth asked.

"Not that I know of," Riley said. "No mortars or missiles, either. They just charged. About a thousand reached the civilian quarter. It got real bloody. The sailors deployed from their ships. When word reached here, the European Quarter emptied. Every scavenger crammed themselves onto the shuttle."

"Three *thousand*?" Ruth asked. "We only faced a hundred or so in Belgium."

"At *least* three thousand," Riley said, holding up the clipboard. "Weaver's updating the figures on an hourly basis. We've got a few prisoners, but when the scavengers arrived, they massacred the enemy, taking revenge for their family and friends killed this last year."

"The enemy attacked Calais at dawn," Ruth said. "That's why the radio team had to send themselves to Nieuwpoort. The other troops were already in place. We lost a hundred?"

"A hundred have been identified so far," Riley said. "The final tally will be a lot higher. When the enemy broke through, they headed straight for the tunnel. That's where the civilians were, and the injured, and they were lightly armed."

"Oh. That's terrible."

"Horrific," Riley said. "But the attack failed. The enemy are broken. Some fled, but it's quiet up and down the front. Even south of Calais, all seems calm. This was their last chance to break through before the weather turned, and it failed. I won't say we've won, but we will."

"The weather's turned?"

"You outraced the storm by an hour," Riley said.

Ruth walked over to the door, peering outside. "Wow. Yes. Snow. *Real* snow. Is it like this in France?"

"Heavier, apparently," Riley said.

Ruth watched the flakes fall, and the drifts rise. "You can't drive a truck in this weather. The enemy troops are cut off. They won't get more supplies."

"Nope, they'll starve," Riley said. "While our conscripts will have time to train. I barely dare say it, but maybe future history books will say that this war really was over by Christmas. Speaking of history books, you should take a look at yesterday's paper."

"Why? Is there something good?"

"There's a letter from Mr Das. Pages two and three."

"They gave him two whole pages?" Ruth asked. "What did he say?"

"That it's time to put aside the fears of yesterday, and to embrace the promise of progress. He talks about his son, and the accident with electricity, but says accidents like that shouldn't stop us using technology to improve our lives. He says, when he takes his seat in parliament in January, he'll be putting forward a bill saying that technology should be allowed unless it is explicitly prohibited, rather than banned until allowed on a case-by-case basis."

"That's good," Ruth said, briefly scanning the paper, but she found her eyes were skipping from one paragraph to the next. "I'll read it later." She folded the paper and put it inside her coat. "What do you want me to do?"

"Isaac's gone to help Dad, and Mrs Zhang's gone to help Weaver interrogate the prisoners. Until they come back, or send a report, there's not much we can do except *be* here for our fellow citizens."

"What about Fishwyck and Jenner?" Ruth asked.

"Any investigation into Doc Jenner will require interviewing the hospital staff, and they're all worked off their feet. Sergeant Kettering's already made a start going through Fishwyck's house, so you should check with her before doing anything, but she said she'll be busy with the bereaved for most of the day."

"Oh. I could make breakfast," Ruth said.

"Gregory is doing that," Riley said. "And the Kettering twins are running the delivery service. I already paid them a pound each." She pulled a slip from the desk. "But I've got one job for you before the storm gets much worse. I need to know whether Hamish MacKay will join the Serious Crimes Unit before we send him west."

"Oh. You still want to recruit him?" Ruth asked.

Riley tapped her chair. "Ours is an equal opportunity bunch of misfits," she said. "An injury is a perfect reason for him to have been discharged, so will help when he goes undercover, but we'll need to alter his service record. Go see him. I'm sure he'll appreciate the visit."

Outside, the snow was belting down, while the wind whipped it into a flurry. Few people were out, and they were all on foot, heads bowed, struggling through the rising storm. Except at the castle. There, a small crowd had gathered by three chalkboards placed near the gate. An orderly was adding names to one, while two more were hammering a crude roof to the railings. A fourth was wheeling another chalkboard out from the hospital.

Two boards listed the dead. One, so far, listed the injured. The names were written small, forcing the civilians to gather close to read them. Some looked like they'd been standing there for hours. As she approached, a man howled with anguish as the latest addition confirmed his worst fears. A neighbour took his arm, helping him away.

Inside, the hospital was chaotic. Corridors were filled with patients on beds, and others in chairs. They truly were mostly civilians, with barely a uniform in sight. Ruth smiled, muttering a few quiet hellos as she picked her way between them, and around the occasional nurses who came to rush a patient into an operating theatre.

"Ruth?"

She turned, and saw Eloise, a clipboard in hand.

"Hey," Ruth said. "Is it bad?"

Eloise gave a shrug. "Oh, it's fine. Just busy," she said, in what had to be words to reassure the crowd of wounded. "Most people here are waiting for the storm to subside so we can discharge them. Why are you here?"

"I'm looking for a guy injured in Belgium yesterday."

"They're all in the Rochester Ward. That's the east wing."

Ruth made her way through the castle. Away from the entrance, the corridors grew quieter, though this only made it easier to hear the sobs and groans coming from the patients.

The Rochester Ward was quiet, though. Quiet, warm, and only a quarter full. Hamish MacKay was unconscious. Blankets covered most of his body, except for his leg which was raised in a sling. Even though his foot was completely bandaged, it looked considerably smaller than it should be.

"He just came back from the surgeon," a woman said.

Ruth turned. "Private Essex!"

"Glad to see you remembered," Essex said. She sat in a chair, next to one of the ward's electric heaters. She wore a patient's gown, but her own boots. There were six other patients in the ward. A woman sat on the other side of the heater from Essex; the others were in bed. Two men, two women, and one so covered in bandages it was impossible to tell.

"Is this the Albion ward?" Ruth asked.

"Seems to be," Essex said. "Did we win?"

"Yes," Ruth said with a certainty she didn't feel. "Yes we did. Very definitely. Thank you. Thank you all."

Essex shrugged. "Any news from Her Royal Highness?"

It took Ruth a second to realise Essex meant Colonel Sherwood. "Sorry, no," Ruth said, and felt suddenly guilty for having left the battle early, and spending most of the time since asleep. She folded her arms, and felt something crinkle beneath her coat: the newspaper. "But King Alfred wrote a letter to the newspaper. They printed it yesterday. Would you like to read it?"

"Maybe you could read it to Albert," Essex said, indicating the bandaged soldier. "I think he'd appreciate it."

"Of course," Ruth said. "But then you've got to tell me what Christmas is usually like up in Albion."

"If you tell us what it's usually like in Dover," Essex said.

"This is my first in Dover," Ruth said. "I grew up in a school at a refugee camp near Twynham. Now, those Christmases were fun."

The newspaper, and the war, were forgotten for a few glorious minutes as they talked about past joys, future happiness, and a time of peace which, despite the recent bloodshed, didn't seem so far away.

The end.

Printed in Great Britain
by Amazon